AUTHOR'S NOTE

THIS NOVEL DESCRIBES A JOURNEY, a return to oneself, after a time of trial – in this case, the difficult return of Bobby Russell to his family and community after the Second World War. Although the character of Russell was inspired by a real person, Russell's experiences are not his and the events of the novel are fictional. The setting is St. Thomas because it is dear to my heart, having spent many happy summer days in the 1940s visiting my grandparents there. I wanted to create as best I could the characters, the politics and the semi-rural society of the town, which I loved, and which no longer exists.

Cover illustration by Brian Metcalfe
Cover design by Roberto Rosenman
Back cover photograph by Robert McWhinney

ISBN 978-0-9949861-1-5

First printed, November 2016; minor corrections, December 2016.

INGLEWOOD PRESS
www.inglewoodpress.ca

Coming Home Alone

BRIAN METCALFE

For Clare, our fine friend

Warmest wishes

Brian

INGLEWOOD PRESS

Toronto

In fond memory of
Lt. Col. John Hodgetts O'Flynn

PRELUDE

EVERY MORNING AT ABOUT TEN, unless she had an errand in town, Margaret Ann Russell poured herself a cup of tea and read her paper. On this sunny April morning she took her cup into the sunroom and sat on the couch, staring across the fields to the elm trees by the creek. The fields were still unploughed and rough from the winter.

I'll have to get a man from somewhere to plough them if Archie won't do it, she thought.

"Canadians Advance Through Holland", read the headline of the St. Thomas Times Journal.

There was a blurred photograph of German officers standing in front of a heap of rubble that had once been a church. The telephone rang. She listened – three longs and a short – it was hers. Irritated, she laid down the paper and picked up the receiver.

"Don't call me this time of the morning, Marie," she snapped into the receiver. "You know I take my tea at ten."

But the crackling English voice was not Marie Barnes, the local operator.

"This is your long distance operator. I'm calling from Folkstone, England. I have a call here for Mrs. Margaret Ann Russell." The line crackled with static.

"I am Margaret Ann Russell." She set her bifocals on the table, her hands trembling.

"Will you accept the charges, Mrs. Russell. The call is from…."

The voice broke off. The line roared. It sounded like a storm at sea. "I'm here. Bobby. Bobby, It's me." She yelled into her receiver, but the line drowned in an ocean of static. She dialed Marie Barnes.

"I'm sorry, Margaret Ann, your call is gone. It must be the weather or the volume or something."

She rose to her feet, walked out of the house and stood on the front porch. Beyond the lane and the gravel road were the fields of the Summervilles' farm, the ploughing already begun, as hers should be. She stared at the road, wiping away a tear, wondering if she should go to town.

※

In front of the desk-sergeant in the Central Police Station in Folkstone, a red-faced, bleary-eyed young man in the uniform of a captain in the Canadian army hung up his phone.

"That was my mother," he shouted at the sergeant, who was watching him warily. "You heard her."

"I heard her, Captain, but you heard the line go wonders. You won't get another line out today." The sergeant glared. "So we know you have a mother back in Canada. But we still don't know what to do with you."

The captain's eyes were rimmed red; his face showed no emotion. The right sleeve of his jacket was torn and his trousers were spattered with mud.

"I don't care what you do," said the captain. "Put me somewhere I can sleep."

"I should charge you and lock you up. You blackened Constable Robbins' eye, and emptied the public bar of the Prince Regent Hotel with your antics. If it weren't for the circumstances…." He stared at Russell. "Been fighting for a couple o' years, have you?"

The captain nodded.

"You've got to stop fighting here, Captain. The war's in Germany now." The sergeant smiled briefly. "My inclination is to let you go, provided you give me your word that you will keep the peace and desist from assaulting my constables."

"You've got it, Sarge."

"Here are your papers, including your discharge papers."

"Discharge?"

"Yes, Captain, you've been given a medical discharge." The sergeant stared at him. "Don't you remember?"

"Look, I need to sleep. How do I get out of here?"

"You can't sleep here tonight. There's a cheap, clean hotel down by the docks, two blocks straight ahead, the Kent House. They'll give you a bed and breakfast."

The captain put on his great coat, nodded to the sergeant and left the station. A cold wind blew rain and mist from the Channel into his face as he walked unsteadily along the shiny paving stones towards the harbour, looking for the Kent House.

PART I

Lost and Wandering

1.

THE TRAINS WERE JAMMED WITH SOLDIERS in April of 1945 and the red-faced, disheveled captain wearing the shoulder patch of the St. Thomas and Elgin Highlanders drew no attention. Men in uniform were getting on and off all along the morning train from Montreal to Toronto, scarcely noticing one another. Russell was alone today; he was coming home.

He slouched in his seat, dreaming.

Marching into some Italian town. People standing beside the road, watching us. They're used to the Germans, don't know us. They watch from the ditches and gardens, suffering and fear in their eyes. Women, children and white-haired men with gaunt cheeks and dull eyes. Bodies frail, ranks of thin arms and legs and hollow chests. No confidence in them, the future is a threat, you can see it in their eyes. We are their future but they don't know what it is. For them the future comes from the barrel of a gun, from the sound of marching feet. The sound of our boots marching down your street, in your town, into your life, can't be stopped. We are men with no emotion left; we no longer think. We march, we kill; we can do anything. The women watching beside the road understand this intuitively. They watch from the shadow.

He woke with a jolt and tried to remember where he was. He often had trouble establishing a sense of his body, whether he was sitting or lying, and exactly where his limbs were. Sometimes, he

13

had the fear that he was disappearing completely. Only in his dream did he know where he was, always marching into the same town, looking at the same people. The dream, too, had been coming to him again and again, since his imprisonment in the German camp. He felt the muscles in his left arm and leg as he watched the farms through the window slipping by, the spring soil still dark. He looked at his watch; ten-thirty. Too early for a drink. He reached his hand in his bag and felt the reassuring shape of the bottle.

"Kingston, five minutes, rear door out."

He looked out the window and saw a mother standing at the door of a little wooden farmhouse, holding a child on one hip, watching the train go by. She shocked him. There were always women, standing in houses like that, children on their hips, in their arms, crying by their sides, houses gutted, lathing exposed, timbers burned. The troops would be heading north, through Sicily or Italy itself, or east through Holland towards the Rhine. These women made him furious. Just standing there watching, with their hollow eyes. He reached in his bag, took out the bottle, uncorked it and took a deep swallow. When he looked again the woman and her child were gone.

The brakes caught the big engine wheels and the train screeched to a halt. Passengers headed for the door. Maybe three hours more to Toronto. Get the next train to London, then get the London & Port Stanley. He should make St. Thomas by supper. His town was a blur to him. He could remember his mother, her face, could picture her sitting in the parlour reading, glasses on her nose. But that was all. His head ached. He thought that he was drinking too hard, but couldn't really tell. There were too many things to deal with. And his disappearing body, that was a real problem. And not remembering. Except for the women in his dreams, by the roadsides. So a little drink once in a while, shit.

At Bad Rudesheim, Russell had just walked out of the camp. It hadn't been bad, the camp. The commandant was a wounded infantry colonel who liked to joke around with his prisoners, all Canadians. They were allowed to play baseball, sing. During the last few weeks the guards had relaxed all discipline and had even begun to share their food. They knew what was coming.

None of the other men had wanted to leave with him, even the St. Thomas and Elgins. They did not want to fight, they wanted to be liberated. He was frightened. He imagined that if he escaped, he would regain his memory and get a sense of his body whole again. He would sit in the shade of the linden tree in the prison yard, looking at the brick wall and thinking that his memory was there, beyond the wall. He could remember a few things, his name, where he came from, and his family. But the name St. Thomas brought no images of houses or streets or people. He could remember the fighting, but further back, nothing. Except his mother.

One afternoon in March, when the men were walking back from the camp garden outside the town, he turned down a side street when they entered the town of Bad Rudesheim and began to walk west. He was free of the town in fifteen minutes and joined the streams of people, walking and cycling mostly, on the road. None of the German civilians paid him any attention, and the retreating columns of German troops, weary and beaten, barely looked at him despite his Canadian battle dress. He walked towards Holland, without money, eating only chunks of the black bread he had stolen from the camp kitchen before he left and drinking rain water. By the time he arrived at the combat zone there was very little fighting. Columns of Canadian troops were pouring out of Holland into Westphalia. He sought them out, and he had no trouble getting fed, finding a place to sleep. He even borrowed a little money. None of the officers in the battalions heading into Germany paid him much attention.

"Looking for my unit, the St. Thomas and Elgin," he would say, and be waved on, perhaps with vague directions to wherever the soldier thought the regiment might be.

He finally reached Canadian sector headquarters in a village beside a river. When he asked for his regiment he was told they were heading for the German border, fighting on the front. The colonel he was speaking to, a huge man well over six feet, took little interest in him until Russell, shivering, sat on the floor of the office, took a bottle from his kit, drank, and began to shake.

"Where are my hands?" he said, shaking his head. "Where the fuck are my hands?"

The colonel reached for his telephone. "Annie, send me two MPs. Got a captain here who needs medical care."

He remembered nothing of the hospital except a grey-haired medical officer. "War's just about over," said the officer. "So we're sending you home, Captain Russell." He wrote on a piece of paper. "Take this to the adjutant's office near the main gate. They'll fix you up with transport to England and then home. In the meantime, we'll notify your regiment."

He had gone to the adjutant's office, was given his transport, but then forgot about the arrangements. He hitched a ride across the Channel from Boulogne to Folkstone, in Kent, where there was a Canadian embarkation camp. At the dock an officious little man in some kind of uniform was checking the men who were leaving the ship against some kind of list.

"Russell, Captain Robert Russell, of the St. Thomas and Elgin Highlanders," he said.

The little man spent minutes poring over his list. He had a toothbrush moustache above yellow teeth that protruded.

"Can't find you here, Captain, nor any of your regiment. Can I see your papers please?"

Russell had been drinking on the Channel ferry. He looked down at the man.

"I'm going home. Get out of my way."

He brushed past the man, who yelled angrily. Russell kept walking. He looked back once and saw the man, quiet, looking forlorn with his list clutched to his chest. Sometime after that came the fight in the public bar of the Prince Regent Hotel. Someone there had wanted to keep him from going home, he thought. A cop arrived. The fight happened and more cops arrived. They took him to jail. Good sergeant there. Let him phone his mother. Heard her voice. He had to get there. The sarge let him go, free to go home.

He watched the platform as the train pulled out of Kingston.

Fewer uniforms. In England there were uniforms on every street corner, filling every train. And then the green fields, sloping down to Lake Ontario. And the towns, Belleville, Cobourg, Port Hope, Oshawa, quiet and orderly, built of red brick and limestone, with main streets and churches and court houses. There was no bomb damage; there were no sandbags.

Nobody knew he was coming, not the army, not his mother, not anyone. He liked that. He liked being alone and invisible. As long as he could find himself. His arms and legs. And his memory.

"May I take this seat?"

A man in a blue suit carrying an attaché case was smiling and looking at the seat where Russell was resting his feet. He removed his feet and the man sat down.

"Back from overseas?"

He nodded.

"Welcome home, Captain. I'm Jim Williams."

"Russell. Where you going?"

"Toronto. I teach history at Kingston Collegiate. I'm going down for a meeting this afternoon of history teachers studying the new high school curriculum."

Russell looked at him, intrigued. An ordinary man, a teacher, going about his ordinary teacher's business. Going to a meeting of history teachers. Could you beat that?

"Want a drink?"

The man across held up his hands.

"I'm not a drinker." The tone was fastidious. "Big changes have been happening here since you left. The CCF is going to do very well in the next provincial election. You know about the CCF?"

Russell shook his head.

"It's Canada's first socialist political party. A party dedicated to undoing the evils that capitalism has brought to the common man. Fair wages. Equal access to health care. Better schools. I'm running for the CCF in Kingston."

"We're Liberals in Elgin County."

"Liberals offer nothing to the working class."

17

"Nobody does, Jim. If you're ordinary, nobody gives you a goddamn thing. You have to take it. Like this bottle, Jim. I didn't have any cash, so I stole it. How's that for socialism?"

Williams fell silent and turned his face away. Russell stared out the window. More farms, the lake sparkling blue in the distance. He laid his head back on the cushion and took another swig, gazed at the fields and fell asleep.

He was wakened by the conductor shaking him by the shoulder; they had arrived in Toronto and the history teacher was gone. He gathered his bottle and put it in the bag; he felt for his arms and legs. Uncertain of his limbs, he left the train and looked for the departures board in the station. The next train for London left at five o'clock. Time to kill. He remembered Toronto from before the war; he had studied law at the University of Toronto. He left the station and walked out to Front Street across from the Royal York Hotel.

There were crowds of people in the street, ordinary people going about their business. Have to get used to that, he thought. No war here, situation normal. There was red, white and blue bunting hanging from the hotel windows. He read an advertisement in a bank window, a happy family – mom, dad and the kids – urging other happy citizens to buy victory bonds.

He walked over to Bay Street and turned north through the financial district. His head throbbed. He could not understand the flow of orderly traffic, the shops open for business and the solid, undamaged streets. He looked at the people passing by, carrying brief-cases or shopping bags, *but he heard the tramp of marching feet, the menace of armed men moving down a road, through a village. Don't you understand? What we could do to you? We could march into your streets and your houses, and level them, and you.*

As he stood at the corner of Queen and Bay, a girl with good legs, red-headed, wearing a summer dress, approached him.

"I'm off today,"she said to him. "What's your name?"

He looked at her. He couldn't see her face. He wanted to flee.

"Robert," he said. "They call me Bobby."

He turned and walked quickly away. As he walked further north the crowds got thinner. He crossed over to Yonge Street.

"Shine your boots, mister?"

A skinny boy about ten, in a striped tee shirt and shorts, was standing beside a shoe shine kit. Russell looked at his boots; they were covered with mud. Maybe from Folkstone, with the rain. Or maybe he had crossed the Channel with this mud on his boots. He raised one to the pedestal, and the boy went to work. The boy looked frail, like part of the war. Russell raised his other foot. He could see the Silver Rail, a tavern he had known before the war, a block up the street.

"That's fifty cents, mister. An extra two bits for the mud."

The boy saluted. Russell fished in his pocket and flipped him the coins, then walked to the Silver Rail. He took a seat at the bar, and the noise of the streets faded and he found himself again, knew where he was in the cool and quiet. He ordered a whiskey and started to think about going home. The London train left at five. He looked at his watch and it was two o'clock. Before he went to bed tonight he would see his mother. After three years. And what else? He couldn't remember and suddenly panicked. *There is more, I know there is more. People. What will happen when I get there?*

He sensed someone watching him and glanced at the long mirror behind the bar. He saw the reflection of a girl in a Women's Army Corps uniform, her hair braided, sipping a beer. She smiled, he looked away. *Where were his legs? He could not feel his legs.*

He became angry. He couldn't remember exactly when women had begun to seem alien to him. It had to do with them sitting in their bombed out houses and villages, surrounded by their children. It had to do with their passivity, their powerlessness, being somehow behind the war. *They had done nothing, they had accepted all the unspeakable, stupid....* He drank a large gulp of his whiskey, enjoying the burn in his throat and the blurring of his images. He wondered how his mother would look. He could imagine the hook of her nose, the sparkle in her eyes, the smell of peppermint that had always been part of her.

Men were always there. They were the matter of events, the

19

bricks and mortar, the structure. But women? The women had gone missing and so there was no meaning in them. We marched here, we marched there. We killed them and they killed us, bam, bam, bam, lose a few guys, and march some more. I got used to the senselessness, but the women bailed out. They encountered the madness, acquiesced, put up no resistance.

Someone slipped onto the next stool. He looked in the mirror. It was the WAC from down the bar. He was going to ask her to leave, but he looked into a face that silenced him. A slender nose with flared nostrils, full lips painted scarlet and violet eyes. She filled the bar with her presence and she required his complete attention.

"I'm lonely," she said. "I've no one to talk to."

She smiled when she spoke, and her words were staccato, like machine gun fire.

"I'm not the one," he said. "I'm catching a train."

"What time?"

"Five o'clock."

"Lots of time. Who knows what happens before five o'clock."

Hers was the rapid pitch and friendly smile of meeting in wartime, everyone moving through, moving on, so that if you met someone, and were hungry for love, you had to move fast.

"Look, Miss, I'm going home at five o'clock, and until that train pulls out, I'm just going to wander around on my own."

"You've been overseas?"

He nodded.

"You look so sad." He looked into the remarkable eyes, as she smiled a woman's smile of sympathy. "My name is Eleanor," she said softly. "Eleanor Archer. You're going home on the train to…?"

"London. Five o'clock. Then on to St. Thomas. I'm from there."

"Back to your parents? Your girl?"

"My mother. My father's dead." At the thought of a girl, he froze.

"She'll be waiting at the station?"

"Nobody knows I'm coming. The regiment is still in Germany. I just came home."

"What's your name?"

"Russell. Robert Russell."

"Bobby. Listen to me Bobby Russell. You're going to spend the day with me. You'll come to my house and get a bath. You smell and your uniform needs cleaning and pressing. You'll have dinner with my family, an experience that will make the war seem like child's play. And then, who knows? You can sleep at our house and tomorrow you can take the train to St. Thomas."

"No," he said desperately. "I'm going home tonight. I have to get there." But even as he spoke he knew that he would go with her, wherever she went.

"You can't go home tonight; you look like hell, and I suspect you're all messed up in some frightfully complicated way. You look like you're about to burst into tears and you're drinking as if there were no tomorrow. Come home with me. Get clean, sober up, and go home a functioning human being."

"I have to go home," he said faintly. "I have to see my mother."

"Of course. But right now you're coming with me."

She paid for the drinks and led him by the hand out of the bar.

"Why are you doing this?" he asked, as she waved down a taxi on the street.

"You need it. And I need it. You've been fighting for too long, and it shows. Think of me as your way back."

"And what do you need?"

"We'll talk later. It's fairly simple."

The cab took them north on Yonge Street and turned east into Rosedale. They drove down streets of stone and brick houses, their lawns green and hedges neatly clipped. The cab turned into a circular drive through a stone gate in a wrought iron fence. The tires crunched on gravel as the driver pulled up in front of a stone, Georgian house with Palladian trim and a grey slate roof. Eleanor paid the driver and led Russell, kit bag in hand, up the stone steps and inside the massive door. They stood in a hall tiled with alternating black and white marble squares. In front of them were two circular staircases which curved left and right and met at the second story. There were portraits on the walls of men in uniform, in lawyer's robes, and one of a clergyman. From somewhere in the house came the sound of a piano playing one of J.S. Bach's *English Suites*.

"It's so quiet."

"Nobody's here except Owen, my brother. He's the musician. Daddy's at work and Mother is somewhere doing something both useful in the war effort and respectable. And the others, who knows? Come with me."

She led him up the stairs and down the left wing of the second floor. She opened a door at the end of the wing. The room contained a large double bed covered in an olive green satin bedspread and an oak dresser and writing desk. There was a red and blue Turkish carpet on the floor. Another door led into a connected bathroom. He set down his bag, took off his boots and lay on the bed. Where were his feet? He wiggled his toes and watched them move.

"You're very kind," he said. "But I don't know you."

She didn't answer but went into the bathroom. He heard her turn the faucets and heard the water run into a bathtub. She stood in the doorway, smiling; she had taken her jacket off and rolled up her khaki sleeves.

"Take your clothes off and come in here."

He wanted to get under the bedspread and hide. He opened his mouth, but she shook her head and put her finger to her lips. He removed his clothes. She watched him as he walked past her into the bathroom and lowered himself into the tub. The hot water washed over him, his body felt whole, and he felt covered and protected by the heat of the bath. She knelt down beside the tub, a large sponge in her hand, soap in the other, and began to scrub his back.

"This is marvelous," he said. "But we've only just met. Do you think...?"

"Thinking has nothing to do with it," she said laughing. "I'm a doing sort of girl. And if you're worried about propriety, you can leave right now. No? You're going to stay? Then enjoy yourself."

He lay back in the tub and shut his eyes. She moved to the foot of the tub and washed between his toes. She went to a closet, got a manicure set and began to cut his toenails. Then she did his hands.

She went back to the cupboard, got a bottle of shampoo and began to rub it into his scalp. He shut his eyes. She poured pitchers of cold water over his head, jolting him. He opened his eyes, smiling.

"So you can still smile," she said. "I'm not too late."

She went back to the cupboard, produced a fleecy white robe, and laid it on a chair beside the tub.

"I'll wait in the bedroom," she said. "Soak as long as you want."

He stretched out his legs, so that his feet rested on the rim at the end of the tub. He felt clean. And suddenly there was nowhere to go and nothing to do, no deadlines, no timetables, no schedules, no plans, for the first time in as long as he could remember. Except he had to get home. And he would. But the water was warm and his body was relaxing. He could easily shut his eyes and fall asleep, but no, not in the tub. He pulled himself out and put on the white robe. In the bedroom she was standing at the window, looking down into the garden. She turned and smiled at him, but in a different way. The sympathy was gone. Her violet eyes were full of intent.

"Lie down," she said, and he lay down on the bed. "Here comes the hard part. I don't want you to talk. Just lie there. I'm going to make love to you." She took off her shirt and her army brassiere. Her breasts were full, the long nipples black as mulberries. He sat up quickly but she pushed him back on the bed.

"Don't worry, sweetheart, this is for me."

She took off her skirt and underwear and stood in front of the window. He watched her silhouette, heard birds outside the window. From below came the sound of the piano. She sat beside him on the bed and opened his robe. He had no desire for her, but could not move, transfixed by her hunter's eyes and her shining red lips. She bent over and kissed his cock. He lay back and shut his eyes. Her lips played over his belly, his chest, his lips. He felt himself harden, but it was an event far away, back in the ruins, back in the rubble, surrounded by what was unknown, like falling into a dark ditch with no bottom. She mounted him, and began to move up and down on him, her head back, her hard nipples swaying in front of his mouth, his eyes. Uninvolved, he watched her, feeling the fire far away. Sweat poured down her face, between her breasts, and her mouth gaped open in a hungry smile. She panted and heaved, and exploded, gripping him tightly, gasping. Then she was still, impaled on him, who had not moved, who was still hard in her. She let him go and laid her head on the pillow.

"I've never been raped before," he said finally.

"Oh God, I feel good," she said. "Are you all right?"

"As long as I'm not pregnant."

She slapped his shoulder and laughed.

"So you have a sense of humour." She looked fondly at him. "I had to have you. And no, you are not the first, nor the second. But don't be upset, it's not your fault. It's not anybody's fault, it's how I'm made. I only really feel whole when I'm loving someone. How wonderful that it's you, and you're so sweet."

"So that's why you brought me here?"

"I wanted you as soon as I saw you in the bar. You looked so lost. But don't do the sums, the little pluses and minuses. It was just good, it is good. I think, sometimes, that making love is all that matters. It's the only thing a person can do that doesn't hurt anybody, provided that it's done right."

He started to laugh, a desperate laugh, a defense against his passivity and confusion. She started to laugh too, but hers was rich and joyful with the pleasure of sex. He heard the difference, and fell silent. She tickled his ribs and they began to laugh together in the afternoon bedroom with the sunlight coming in beams through the curtains from the garden. There was still music from the floor below.

"Sleep now," she said finally. "There's a clock beside your bed. I'll set the alarm for six-thirty. Drinks at seven, dinner at eight. You'll meet my family."

"Won't they wonder what I'm doing here?"

"They'll know what you're doing here. There are clothes in the closet that belong to my uncle Hugh. They might fit you." She smiled fondly at him from the doorway. "Sleep well."

When she had closed the door, he got up and undid the grip. He felt the smooth glass of his bottle, and smiled. He went back to the bed, lay down and looked at the green linen blinds with silk tassels half-way down the window, burnished by the sun. Beneath the blind he could see trees, elms, an oak and an ash, newly green. On the wall was a print, a sketch of Notre Dame Cathedral, the one in Paris, not Montreal. There were also framed photographs of children; one six-year-old with pigtails, looking out with a mischievous smile. She could have been this woman, Eleanor.

What was he doing? He had missed the five o'clock train. He shook his head once, then fell asleep.

2.

He followed the music to the drawing room, walking unsteadily along the hallway, placing one foot after the other. From the doorway he saw Eleanor sitting on a sofa, reading a magazine. Beyond her, two young men were sitting on the carpet beside the phonograph, listening intently to the music. There was a vase of lilacs on a grand piano in the far corner of the room. Through the French doors he could see a brick patio enclosed by a stone balustrade, with a garden beyond. Eleanor put down her magazine. The two young men glanced at him and then went back to listening to their music.

"I shall fix you a drink. Father won't be home until later and Mother will appear at dinner. Over here we have my brother, Owen, and his friend, Peter." The two kept listening to the phonograph, smoking black cigarettes with gold tips. Eleanor went to a sideboard and poured him a double whiskey. Then she led him to the sofa.

"I seem to have missed the five o'clock train," he said, looking out at the garden. They both started to laugh. The two young men looked up, then returned to the music. "How did I get here?"

"I picked you up in the bar and brought you here."

"It's beautiful, this room. And the music."

Her eyes narrowed and he forgot about home. Her image overwhelmed him, her breasts with the black nipples covered with sweat, laughing, her eyes dazzling. The music ended and the needle clicked at the centre of the disk. "That was heaven," said Owen. "I didn't know he could play Rachmaninoff; I think of him as a Bach man. He's coming to Toronto, you know, next week."

"Do let's go, Owen."

"I'm out of cash. I've spent my allowance until June. Eleanor?"

Owen Archer was tall and slim, dark hair, dark eyes, and graceful movements. He turned to his sister and then noticed Russell.

"Hello," he said, extending his hand. "I'm Owen Archer, brother of Eleanor and this is my friend, the Reverend Peter Vincent." He turned quickly back to his sister. "Dearest one, I am short of cash and we absolutely must go to hear Schnabel next week. Do help me out."

"You haven't paid me back from last month."

Owen winced. "I know Els, I'm hopeless, but I just need money more than you do. Men don't pay my way." He stared at Russell. "Did you like the Rachmaninoff, Captain Russell?"

"If that's what was playing, well enough."

"Eleanor never brings cultured men home, do you, Els? But sometimes they're nice. Are you nice?"

Russell paused. "I used to be," he said. There was silence in the room.

"Leave the man alone, Owen," said Peter Vincent, a short, slender man with thick glasses and pinkish eyes. "He's on leave from something frightfully important, and shouldn't be harassed."

"He's been shot at by Germans, and hasn't had time to listen to Rachmaninoff," said Eleanor.

"Quite right. So how about it, Els? Thirty dollars until payday, the first of June."

"Oh, all right, bring me my purse; it's on the sideboard. And you won't get anything in June or anytime after if you don't tell Father your plans for next year. He's getting fed up, Owen."

Owen groaned. "I know, but if you could just let me have … ah, my dear Els, you are divine." She handed him the money. "I think what I will actually do next year is go back to London. It was all such fun, such lovely fun, before the war."

"Father won't pay for you in London."

"I'll go to Uncle Hugh and see if I can swindle some money out of the trust. And if not, I have friends in London."

Eleanor shook her head and turned to Russell.

"Owen's the nicest of my family. He goes to plays and concerts and discusses them with his little friends. You see, he doesn't actually hurt anybody."

"He seems nice."

She began to talk about her mother, but he couldn't follow. He was remembering the yellow brick wall around the yard in the prison camp. In good weather the men would sit leaning against the wall, smoking and talking. One of the guards, a fat old man who spoke English, liked to sit with them. Funny, he had good memories of that brick wall, the sun beating down on them, the smell of the cigarettes, the idle drone of voices.

"You're miles away."

"I was remembering something."

She held up her hand. There was a gleam in her eye.

"Oh, I adored the war. I was in London, driving for General McNaughton. Parties almost every night, and fabulous people, all my friends. I have never been so happy in my life, not a second of boredom. Of course the fighting and the killing should be shocking, but it isn't, for me. Keep me behind the lines with some champagne and music and I'm a happy girl."

"So simple for you," murmured Russell. "Sometimes I wonder what on earth I was doing there."

A plummy voice interrupted. "Dinner is served." Russell looked and saw a stooped man with sleek white hair and a dark suit, bowing from the doorway.

"Thank you, Wilkins."

He followed Eleanor into the dining room. Two women were already seated at a table set for ten. One was fat with untidy grey hair and inquisitive eyes, wearing a shapeless green dress. The other was thin with white hair, dressed in black, an ornate gold cross at her

27

neck. She barely glanced at them as they entered the dining room..

"This is Aunt Rosemary, my father's sister," said Eleanor. The fat woman nodded and gave Russell a brief and curious smile. "And this is mother's sister, Aunt Hilda." Hilda sighed but kept her gaze on her plate.

Russell took in the silver on the mahogany sideboard; plates, candlesticks and a tea service glistening in the light. Then, from the hallway, came the sound of a tenor voice singing: "My love is like a red, red rose…".

A peppy, completely bald man entered the room and sat beside Owen. He wore a checked sports jacket, a blue shirt and a yellow polka-dotted bow tie. His cheeks were brick red and his upper lip was covered with a silky grey moustache.

"My God, what have we here? The fair Eleanor with yet another young man. A soldier at that. Won't do you any good, Eleanor. Ask me. Ask Rosemary."

"If I ever need your advice, Uncle, I won't forget this generous offer." She turned to Russell. "This is my father's brother, Uncle Hugh Archer." The red-faced man reached across the table to shake Russell's hand and gave him a broad wink. Russell noticed that as he relinquished the handshake he tried to look down the front of Eleanor's dress.

"We thought you were in Boston, Uncle, so I put Captain Russell in your room."

"Quite right, my dear. Train leaves at ten this evening. Room is free." He stroked his moustache.

"I don't understand why it is that you need Hugh's room," said Aunt Hilda, fingering her cross. "Why not put Captain Russell in the east room, Eleanor, where most of our guests stay?"

"Strategic reasons, Hilda," said Rosemary slyly. "New friends like to be close to one another."

Rosemary smiled with merry malice. Hilda looked away.

"We should leave the captain alone," said Owen. "This is his first exposure to this menagerie. We'll put him off his dinner."

"Nonsense," boomed Rosemary. "Who is he and what is he doing here." She glanced at Eleanor. "Explain yourself, Captain."

"I just arrived from England," he began. "I'm going home to St. Thomas. I happened to meet Eleanor...."

"I picked him up in a bar," interrupted Eleanor and laughter broke out, from Hugh and from Rosemary. Owen smiled, Peter Vincent kept his eyes raised above the level of the conversation and Hilda looked worried.

"How vulgar," she said. "I can't imagine, Eleanor, that you would enter a public bar without an escort. Things are so changed. It's the war ... all this to-ing and fro-ing and disruption."

A young woman entered the room and took her seat beside Russell. "This is my sister, Janet," said Eleanor. Janet smiled and shook hands. She looked like Eleanor but was taller, with darker hair and sharper features.

"Any friend of Eleanor's is a friend of ours," she said quietly. "Although there have been so many lately...."

"Janet." Owen's voice was firm and annoyed.

"Isn't it wonderful that the war will soon be over," said Peter Vincent in his parson's voice. "We will all start our lives again."

They began to discuss the changes the end of the war would bring. Eleanor took Russell's arm and drew him closer.

"Everyone's here but Mother and Father," she whispered. "Can you bear it?"

Only Eleanor seemed real to him, her hand on his arm, the smell of her. He felt as if he were listening to the conversation of the others from some underwater cave.

"They're very different."

"Rosemary eloped with an American in nineteen twenty, to Chicago. She came back a year later alone, not saying anything. She was very beautiful, they say. Since then, all she's done is eat and watch Janet and me for signs of romantic involvement, which alarms her. And Hugh, of course. Hugh gives her fits."

"A ladies' man?"

"He's supposed to be a lawyer in Father's firm. What he really does is play golf and chase widows. He also controls the family trust, which means Father controls it. I can assure you, Hugh wouldn't do a thing without his approval."

"What about Hilda?"

"Mother's sister, her only close relative. Hilda says they come from an old English family, the Brunells. She can trace the Brunells back to some warlord of Richard the Lion Heart…."

Russell watched Hilda. She caught his eye, gave him a frosty smile and raised her eyes in renunciation to the window.

"And then there's my sister, Janet. She just got herself engaged to John Barnesworthy, the catch of the season, lots of money, also a lawyer in Father's firm. She disapproves of me."

"Why?"

She blushed, then started to laugh.

"She's afraid that I will do something so scandalous that it will end the engagement. The Barnesworthys are extremely stuffy." She looked at him with sparkling eyes. "Here's Mother."

A slender, grey-haired woman entered, moving slowly, her head erect, her eyes sad.

"You may serve, Wilkins," she said to the serving man. "Mr. Archer will be late." She looked around the table and smiled gently. "I hope you haven't all been waiting for me." They all shook their heads.

"Ah well," she sighed, and turned her melancholy eyes to Russell. "One never knows in this house. You, Sir. Are you a friend of Owen's?"

"He is Captain Robert Russell, Mother," said Eleanor. "He's a friend of mine. My mother, Mildred Archer."

She looked at Eleanor sharply then back at Russell, and gave the briefest nod of her head. The butler began to serve. Mrs. Archer delicately speared a piece of potato with her fork, lifted it gracefully to her mouth and began to chew with gentle, tight-lipped precision. Russell's head ached. Why was he not on the London train, heading home? Rosemary kept staring at him. The one time he caught her eye she ran her tongue over her gravy-covered lips, under the faint moustache below her nose, her eyes fixed on his face. He was relieved when Janet, sitting on his other side, began talking to him.

"You are returning with your regiment, Captain Russell?"

"Not with my regiment. They are still in Germany. I escaped from prison, made it to England, and now I'm going home."

"With a brief rest in Toronto, before returning to…?"

"St. Thomas," said Eleanor angrily. "Do be quiet, Janet. Captain Russell doesn't need a third degree from you."

Janet shrugged.

"We're going to the flicks," said Owen. "'Murder, My Sweet', with Dick Powell and Claire Trevor."

"'Murder, My Sweet'," said Mrs. Archer. "Sounds vulgar."

"It is vulgar, Mother, but it's fun. So much that's fun is vulgar."

The front door opened, and footsteps echoed across the entrance hall. A slender man, red in the face, with a clipped moustache and well-brushed grey hair, entered the room, wearing a three-piece striped blue suit, with a small carnation in his lapel. He took his seat at the head of the table and smiled at each in turn.

"I'm afraid I don't know you, Sir," he said when he came to Russell. "Edward Archer." Eleanor completed the introductions. Archer nodded briefly at Russell, mouthed the word welcome, and turned to his daughter.

"How fine you look today, Eleanor," he said, taking in her dress against the tanned skin.

"Mummy's looking lovely in her organza, don't you think?"

Archer smiled at his wife. His face was regular and gave the impression of an energetic and uncomplicated intelligence, an orderly and powerful man. The sensuality of the lips was balanced by severe blue eyes; this was a practical man who got what he wanted from what was possible.

"As always." He turned to Owen. "And what have you fellows been up to?"

Owen smirked. "I played the *English Suite* today superbly and smoked six Balkan Sobranies. Peter finished Madame Bovary and has solved a chess problem. Very productive day, I should say, all things considered."

His father frowned. "The war will soon be over, Owen, and with all these soldiers returning home, it's going to be a very competitive world. Men like Captain Russell here. You fellows are going to have to look sharp if you want to get ahead."

"We may never get ahead, Father." Owen's voice was passive and dreamy.

Edward Archer frowned again, then smiled absent mindedly. Russell saw that he was not really interested, as Archer began to concentrate on his dinner, motioning to Wilkins to fill his glass.

"Edward." His wife was glaring at him unhappily from the other end of the table. "I want to remind you about enlarging the sitting room window. The room is dark in the summer, gets no light at all. Surely you remember; I spoke to you about it on the weekend."

"Yes, my dear, I remember. Have you spoken to Mr. Miller about it? Getting a price and so on?"

"I haven't had time, I have been so busy at the committee. Surely this is not too much to ask of you?"

Archer sipped his wine, showing no emotion. "I'll talk to Miller on the weekend." He turned again to his daughter with a smile.

"And what have you been up to, my dear?"

"Captain Russell and I have been discussing the war, and enjoying each other's company."

"Splendid. Where are you from, Captain?"

"I'm from St. Thomas."

"Do we know anybody in St. Thomas?" asked Mrs. Archer.

"I know several people in St. Thomas," said Archer. "I went to law school with a fellow from St. Thomas named Allan Matthews, who's practicing there now, I believe."

"I know him. His firm is MacAllister and Matthews. They have done work for our family's company in the past."

Archer looked at him with interest. "What is your business?"

"A dairy. We are the only dairy in the county."

"Are you? Isn't that splendid. A dairy in St. Thomas. The good life, salt of the earth, eh? And I suppose you're going back now to help your father run things?"

Russell frowned. "My father's dead. I trained as a lawyer before the war. I'm not sure whether I want to practice law or...."

"A lawyer. With a good war record. Why don't you come and work with us? Archer, Campbell and Torrington. Good business, lots of variety, and some interesting clients who matter."

Russell looked at Eleanor, who shrugged. "That's kind of you. But I have to get home first, and see what's going on. I just arrived this week from...." Suddenly he felt extremely weary. "From overseas."

"Of course, of course. But don't forget us, Russell. We're always looking for bright young lawyers. By the way, d'you know Bill MacLean in St. Thomas? He publishes the newspaper, what's it called, the Times Journal."

Russell turned red. Bill MacLean. He could see a quiet, thoughtful man. His daughter Susan. The freckled face, the sound of her voice.

"Yes, I do."

"Paper's a Liberal rag, but Bill's all right. We represented his paper in a libel suit. The paper ran a story about communists in the farmers' co-operative movement. Completely factual piece. There are reds on all these co-op boards, so we had no trouble in court. I got to know Bill and his wife and daughter. Charming people."

Russell nodded but remained silent.

"Now, my dear." He turned to his wife. "I had lunch today with Colonel Drew." He looked briefly at Russell. "George Drew is Premier of Ontario, and will remain so after the election in June if I have anything to say about it." He turned again to his wife. "He is having a reception tomorrow at the King Edward to celebrate the coming end of the war. We are invited, and Captain, if you're still in town, you and Eleanor would be welcome."

"I'm going back tomorrow, Sir." Even as he spoke he sensed Eleanor beside him, her eyes on his face. "Although the reception … sounds very interesting. Perhaps I could...."

"Good, expect to see you there." He raised his eyes. "What is everyone doing tonight?"

"Captain Russell and I are going to see the city," said Eleanor.

"And Mildred?"

"I shall attend vespers at St. Mary Magdalene's, with Hilda," she said, looking around the table from face to face. She rose from the table, dabbing at her lips with her napkin.

"And I'm off to Boston, Eddie," said Hugh, "Train leaves at ten. You remember I told you I was going."

"Well, everyone out and about tonight." Archer rose. "I have some telephone calls to make. We have an election in June, Captain Russell, and I have to make sure that every Toronto riding has a good Conservative candidate."

Mildred and Hilda disappeared upstairs. Janet, after smiling ironically at Russell, followed them. Rosemary and Hugh walked away to the garden while Owen and Peter stayed at the table, talking quietly together. Russell walked back to the drawing room with Eleanor.

"And that is my family," she said. "Quite a zoo, wouldn't you say?"

"Your mother doesn't seem happy."

"She isn't. She is very bright, but she has absolutely nothing to do so she talks to Hilda about their bowel movements and the holy spirit, and tries to get Father to pay attention to her. But he doesn't. He has a girlfriend." Russell looked sharply at her. "Don't be so conventional, Bobby; you mustn't judge. Mother can be extremely difficult."

Russell smiled. "Life in St. Thomas has its advantages." He had to get home.

"I'm sure." She looked sharply at him. "You blushed when father mentioned the newspaper publisher and his family." She stared. "It must be the daughter."

"Susan."

"Susan. Is she your girl?"

"She used to be."

Russell got to his feet and walked to the doors overlooking the garden. He could see the outlines of the lilacs in the fading light. A swallow flitted from behind the coach house, over the lawn. The street lamps were lit. He stood there, with Eleanor behind him, watching twilight creep towards the house, wondering when he would leave.

3.

She entered his room in her night gown, shutting the door softly behind her. He had fallen asleep and was snoring lightly. She let her nightgown fall to the floor and crept under the sheet. He did not wake up. She put her hand between his legs and stroked, kissing his back. She felt him freeze.

"It's just me," she whispered into his ear, licking it. "I need you."

He looked at her. She was grinning from ear to ear.

"You mustn't think I'm a nymphomaniac or anything deranged. I can go long periods without sex. But you are delicious."

She lay back and drew his hand to her nearest breast.

"In the prison camp they used to wake us in the night like this, for punishment detail," he said, stroking her nipple.

"You will make love to me," she said, laughing. 'And you will do it now, or you will do one hundred pushups."

"*Jawohl*," he said without any pleasure, and came to her.

She guided him inside, kissing his lips, stroking his head, but there was no joy for him. Tonight he wanted to find his body and himself again, and he wanted to dominate her in the bed. But he could not intimidate her. She whooped with pleasure, wrapped her legs around him, and thrust back, biting his shoulder, kissing his lips. They finished together in a violent shudder, gasping for breath. She lay quietly under him, hugging him to her, kissing his chest.

"This is what we were made for, Bobby. Don't you know?"

He didn't answer. She got out from under him and propped herself up on one elbow. The moon shone on his face. There were tears in his eyes.

"What are you crying for?" she asked. "It's usually the girls that cry after sex, or so I'm told. It's never been my style."

He was silent.

"Can't we just be happy together?' She searched his face. "I'm not good at complexity, darling, truly I'm not. Can't we just be lovers?"

"I haven't known you, even for a day."

She laughed. "I come on strong, don't I?" He nodded. "D'you mind? Am I too aggressive?"

"Aggressive, you?" He started to laugh. "You're a one woman tank corps." She looked at him defiantly. "It's not you, Eleanor. I just need time."

"Are you going home tomorrow?"

He paused. "I thought I would stay and go to the Premier's reception."

"Good, I'm glad you're staying" She relaxed. We'll get to know each other, even like one another." She kissed him. "One more time, lover, before I leave you. I can't be here in the morning."

He was exhausted to the point of being numb, but could not sleep. He drank from his bottle, but his muscles stayed rigid. He left the bed and walked stiffly out into the hall. The house was silent, so he walked down to the entrance hall on main floor below. He stood still and heard, from behind the closed door of the drawing room, the sound of the piano played very softly. He went and opened the door quietly. Owen was at the piano, his black hair falling forward, playing 'Begin the Beguine'. On the sofa Peter Vincent and Mildred Archer were talking.

"First Paris, then south to Poitiers," Peter was saying. "Then we'll join the pilgrimage. It should take several weeks, ending in Santiago de Compostela."

"That sounds divine," Mildred whispered. "I need to get away from here."

"My darling Mildred, you mustn't be too pessimistic. Loveless marriages are common enough. You must find love elsewhere."

"I don't need him to love me. It's just that he is completely sordid.

All we live for is money and politics. It has ruined the children."

"Owen being homosexual is not ruin, my dear. And listen to him play, he is perfect."

"Yes, he is. If only he can make a life for himself, without his father's money. And Eleanor has the same problem. If she can only…."

"Find a man? She's too good at that, it seems to me. What about this soldier, Captain Russell?"

"She picked him up on the street. He looks too good for her." She dabbed at her eyes. "Eleanor has been cheated; we gave her nothing. She has only her looks, so what on earth will she be able to do? At least Owen can play the piano."

"A good-looking woman will always find a way. That is one of nature's laws."

"You're not serious. I don't want my child on the streets. Really, what kind of priest are you?"

At that moment, Russell shifted his weight in the doorway and the floorboard creaked. Owen stopped playing to look at him.

"Why, Captain Russell, whatever are you doing here?" he asked. "Listening to Cole Porter, or eavesdropping on family secrets?"

"I heard the music; gossip doesn't interest me."

"It doesn't matter," said Mildred Archer. "It's good for you to know how bizarre this household is. My advice to you, Captain, is to get out of here. You must have a family and a life back in St. Thomas. Go to it. Go before you fall in love with Eleanor, or before my husband gives you a job."

He stared at the floor. "I will go home, of course."

Owen began playing 'Smoke Gets in your Eyes'.

"Owen, must you play that music," said Mildred Archer. "Can't you play Chopin, or something?"

"It's too late for Chopin, Mother. At this time of night, only Tin Pan Alley will do. D'you want a drink, Captain? On the sideboard."

Russell poured himself a drink and the ache in his head disappeared. He could smell the perfume of the Turkish cigarettes. Mildred turned back to Peter. Owen began to play 'Deep Purple'.

Russell listened to the progression of chords and remembered the smell of a woman, sleeping upstairs.

4.

Russell paused, with Eleanor on his arm, before entering the ball-room which was decorated like a scene from an operetta. There were flags everywhere and a band in red tunics was playing a military march. Men in business suits and neat dress uniforms mingled with women in broad-brimmed hats. Along the wall a bar was doing a brisk business. The room was echoing with laughter, music and the buzz of conversation. He stood in his patched battle dress, with his tam under the shoulder strap, reluctant to enter the room.

"How gorgeous you are," she said, looking up and putting her hand on her breast. "My bonny Captain."

At the far end of the room there was a reception line, with an aide giving introductions. Russell noticed Edward Archer in the line near the end beside a handsome, florid-faced man, the Premier of Ontario, Colonel George Drew. When he turned to Eleanor, she was gone. This confused him; his leg muscles tensed and his head throbbed. He scanned the room and saw Eleanor talking to a tall, dark-haired young man. She was laughing and the young man looked down at her with an amused smile. Russell was alone and he wanted a drink. He would go back to Eleanor's house; then he would go to the station and get on the train to St. Thomas. But first he would have a drink.

"I knew you'd be here," said a voice at his shoulder. He turned and looked into the black eyes of Janet Archer. "You should go home, Captain Russell. This is no place for you."

"I am going home," he said, looking for the door. "Yes. I am."

"Good. You must be exhausted after fighting for so long." She saw him watching Eleanor across the room "She's talking to Geoffery Mainprize. Eleanor was engaged to him but it came to a disastrous end, no surprise there. Mother arranged it all, but El couldn't quite manage to give up her previous, a hockey player named Riordan. He was very good-looking. And Geoffery is narrow-chested and asthmatic, probably no good in bed, which Eleanor would need. He may even be homosexual. Mother never thinks of these things, of course."

Russell nodded and lurched off towards the bar, where a group of older women stood watching his approach with considerable interest. They all had their hair tinted in blue-grey permanent waves, were red in the face with smeared power and lipstick, and held their hand bags in one hand and an empty glass in the other.

"Perhaps this gorgeous young man would get us a top-up," said the first one he came to, her eyes out of focus.

"Sure."

The others flocked around with grateful murmurs.

"These old bats knock it back like there's no tomorrow," said the bartender. "Gin fizzes and Singapore slings. They don't order their own. Ain't lady-like."

Russell gave the drinks to the grateful women. "Don't go far, dear, we may need you again," said one, and they all smiled happily.

He got his whiskey and stood surveying the room. Although there were plenty of soldiers, he could see no fighters, just older men in neat, dressy uniforms.

There are no soldiers here. There is no fighting. This is peace, this is freedom. Why are these women laughing? Things don't add up here. Or it's me. Too much travel, from there to here, and too much booze. Susan. I have to get out of here. These pretty uniforms are false. No dirt, no wounds, no tears. My guys were real. And where is Ele ... Ele...? Whatever her name is.

He turned for the door and saw Eleanor walking towards him. She seemed to float, as if she were a figure in the simpler, more intense world of dreams.

"Where did you go? I didn't see you leave."

"I was talking to an old friend." She picked up the anxiety in his voice. "Don't worry, sweetheart, I won't run away."

"It's not that." He looked awkwardly around the room. "Your

mother doesn't seem to be here."

"She won't be. You see that woman in the yellow dress standing on the other side of the Premier's reception line? That's Helen Clarkson, Father's girlfriend. Her family owns a gold mine in Kirkland Lake. Clients of Father's firm. Isn't it romantic?"

Russell saw a handsome, tall woman of about forty, laughing and waving a bangled arm in the air beside two men, one in uniform, both looking at her with delight. Helen Clarkson was tall, with straight blond hair and an elegant figure.

"Does she bother you?"

"Of course not" Eleanor's lips were tight and her eyes hard. "Helen is intelligent and lots of fun. We get along." She took a deep breath. "Put down your drink and let's meet the Premier."

Oh man, this woman is holding my hand. I don't get it. I want to go home.

"Bobby, we're next."

They stood in front of the Premier as Eleanor whispered to the aide de camp.

"Mr. Premier, Captain Robert Russell, the St. Thomas and Elgin Highlanders, home from Europe, and Miss Eleanor Archer."

"Eleanor, how wonderful you look." The Premier beamed. "And who is this young soldier?"

"Thank you, Premier. Captain Russell is a friend of mine. He escaped from a German prison camp."

The politician's face beamed with delight. "By God, a fighting soldier. From St. Thomas?"

"Yes, Sir."

George Drew's face grew solemn and the blue eyes were calculating. "We're having trouble finding a candidate down there to go up against Grant MacKay, the Liberal Member. He's a drunk and a pervert, but they're Liberal down there, always have been. But a fine young man like yourself, Captain, with a war record. Why don't you run for us in St. Thomas? Come and talk to me about it."

Before Russell could answer they were passed down the line, shaking hands with an Anglican bishop, the Mayor of Toronto,

Robert Saunders, and finally, at the end, Edward Archer. He kissed his daughter on top of her head and shook Russell's hand.

"Daddy, George Drew wants Bobby to run in St. Thomas," she said.

Archer smiled. "First-rate idea. After fighting Germans, taking on the Liberals in Elgin County might be just the thing. Are you interested, Captain?"

"Our family has always been Liberal."

"No one holds that against you. You'd make a good Tory, coming from a business family. Think about it, Captain Russell. We don't care if you win; MacKay is probably unbeatable down there. But the Conservative Party of Ontario, of which I am chairman, would be very grateful if you carried the flag for us. And we do take care of our friends."

Before he could answer they were through the line. He found his drink again and stood with Eleanor at the edge of the ball room watching the reception line.

"Could you run as a Conservative?" She asked.

"If I did, I wouldn't have a friend left in St. Thomas, and that includes my mother. Anyway, I'm not a politician."

"Nobody's a politician, darling. Father isn't. Even George Drew is essentially a shy man. But it's business. It's how you get ahead."

Getting ahead. That's funny. I just want my legs back. But getting ahead. Ha, ha, ha. Just get through today, get some food. Although there's lots of food here, I think. Lots of women here. That's what makes it so complicated. And they want to make me a politician. Man, oh man, I gotta go home.

"I have to go home," he said.

"We'll go back to the house," she whispered.

"Okay."

Before they could reach the door the band stopped playing and the aide de camp called for silence.

"Ladies and gentlemen, attention please. I give you the Premier of Ontario, Colonel George Drew."

The heavy, handsome man waited for the cheering to stop, and

41

after surveying his audience, began to speak.

They stood by the door; it was too late to leave.

"Ladies and gentlemen, we're going to beat them. It's just a matter of time now." The room erupted in cheering which lasted for five minutes. Finally the band played 'God Save the King'; the crowd stood at attention and were silent.

The Premier continued, "No one can say enough about the sacrifice, toughness and good old Canadian guts of our boys overseas. We all know about it, we've read about it, and all I want to say is that their heroic deeds will enter the history of human valour unequaled." More cheering. "Now of course, we are working hard here at home to defeat the Nazis. The victory, when it comes, will belong to us as well as to our brave soldiers, sailors and airmen. We fought the good fight too, and with God's help, we will prevail." The cheering broke out again.

"Now as your Premier and as the leader of your Conservative government, it is my duty to look to the future, as well as to examine the past. When the war is over, exciting times will arrive for us. Our industries, held in check during the course of the war, are ready to roar ahead. We will have men returning from overseas wanting to put the war behind them and get on with things. And I suggest to you that here in Ontario we have good land, hardworking people and a government willing to lead. The future is ours, if we want to take it." More applause.

"Now I would not be doing my duty if I were to leave you with the impression that there were no problems." The smiles faded and serious glances were directed at the Premier. "There are among us, unfortunately, nay-sayers and doubters who reject our prospects for the future. I say to you, that having won the war, our next challenge is to win the peace. And that is exactly what we will do in the coming election. We will send the commies and their socialist friends packing." Loud cheers.

"I want to introduce to you tonight a young man, just back from overseas, who is an example to us of how we will win the peace, a young man who fought for us on the battlefields of Europe. A young man who suffered for us in a Nazi prison camp. A Canadian fighting soldier who is thinking of running for the Conservative Party in Elgin County. Ladies and gentlemen, I introduce to you Captain Robert Russell."

George Drew gestured to where Russell stood with Eleanor, and began to clap his hands. The whole room turned to look at Russell and began to cheer. Eleanor shoved him forward and he stood expressionless as the applause swept over him. The band began to play 'The Maple Leaf Forever'. He smiled briefly, waved his hand and stepped back beside her. The crowd roared.

"You're a hero, darling." She squeezed his hand. The Premier finished his speech. Russell was dazed. Men wanted to shake his hand and slap him on the back. There was lustre in the women's eyes.

"Eleanor," he whispered. "I have to get out of here."

Before she could answer her father stepped in front of them.

"Captain Russell, when you're through with your admirers, Premier Drew and some of the boys would like to meet you upstairs. Room number seven hundred and nine; take your time."

❀

The air in the suite was heavy with smoke, blended with the sounds of tinkling ice cubes and loud male laughter. Conversation stopped when the men noticed the young soldier with the weary face enter. George Drew had been talking intently with a huge fat man at the bar. At the hush he turned his head.

"The conquering hero," boomed the Premier. "The boys want to meet you, Captain, and you need to meet the boys. These are the fellahs that really run this province." The room filled with the rumble of self-satisfied laughter. "First of all, here's Tom Brennan, the Party vice-president responsible for Southern Ontario. He'll be helping you in St. Thomas." A tall, cadaverous man in a heavy blue suit and thick boots came forward and shook Russell's hand with a shy smile. The introductions went around the room, regional party leaders and fixers, financial supporters and hangers-on. They beamed at Russell; they asked him about the army and the war. And all the time, behind the back-slapping and the jokes, he could read the question in their eyes. Can he do it; is this the man for us? Like butchers sizing up a carcass.

Someone handed him a drink. He drained it, and the tension left his head. Men came up to him, giving him the pitch, telling him what a future he would have in the Conservative Party of Ontario. The room became warm and intimate.

He began to feel he belonged; everyone was so friendly. The Mayor of Toronto told him a joke that he couldn't follow, but he found himself laughing anyway, until the tears came. It had been years since he had laughed like that. He was beginning to think he could run as a Conservative in Elgin County.

"Bobby?" boomed one Party vice-president. "Are you with us?"

The room hushed. He looked around at the smiling faces.

"If you men think you can use me. I just have to go home and take care of some things before I commit."

The room burst into cheering, except Eleanor, who stiffened at the mention of his leaving. Edward Archer was beside him, drawing him over to a corner of the room. He saw through a haze Helen Clarkson, her direct, brown eyes and the full figure. She smiled at him.

"All this is very sudden for you, Captain Russell." Her voice was low. "Take care of yourself, and make sure this is what you want. These men will offer you the moon, but the moon is not necessarily what you get."

"Nonsense," said Archer. "The boys like him, and the Premier is impressed. You don't have to win in St. Thomas, Russell, just put up a good fight and then come to work with us. Interesting work, and connections for a political future. Next time round, you'll get a riding you can win."

"Right," said Russell. "The next time around. Just let me put my affairs in order. Have to go home. I have a mother there. And … and … things."

Suddenly he was sitting on the floor. His head was spinning.

"Take him home now, Eleanor," he heard a voice saying. "He's drunk."

5.

"Daddy says he wants you spiffed up." Eleanor watched him over her coffee cup, smiling tolerantly. "Your battle dress has got to go. You'll be politicking, meeting frightfully important people. So a tailor from Tewksbury's is coming here about ten."

They were alone in the dining room, finishing their breakfast. Russell looked down at the khaki legs of his battledress, annoyed.

"What I wear is my business."

"Your uniform made an impression at the reception. You were the only man there who really looked like a soldier, but from now on it won't do. Now I must go. Talk to Wilkins, you'll find him in his office off the kitchen."

She swept from the room. Russell sat fuming. He decided he would be difficult. He started towards the rear of the house, looking for Wilkins. He saw swinging doors and entered the kitchen, a bright room with a tiled floor, a huge gas range on one side, chopping tables, pots and implements hanging from hooks, bowls and bottles of cooking oil and bags of flour on shelves. He saw, behind a glass door to his right, a white head sitting behind a desk. He knocked. Wilkins looked up, sprang to his feet and opened the door.

"If you had only rung, Sir, I would have come to you."

Russell waved his hand dismissively. "Miss Archer tells me that a tailor is coming at ten?"

"That's right, from Tewksbury's. The very best available in this city, Captain Russell, I do assure you." Russell was annoyed by the confident, subservient smile.

"Well, you tell him to stay at home. I won't be needing him."

The butler paused, his face a mixture of embarrassment and patience.

"I wonder if that's wise, Sir."

"Wise? Wise has nothing to do with it. I won't be here and I don't want the damned tailor."

"Captain Russell, if I may say so, if you want to enter this world you will have to dress the part."

"What d'you mean?"

"You want to stand for the Conservative Party, and you will be associating with the Premier, Colonel Drew, the Mayor, and other people of standing. Your uniform will not take you past the first day in this milieu. If you want to be accepted and feel at ease, you will need some decent clothes."

The butler, a stocky man of about sixty, smiled with a glint of irony in his eyes. It occurred to Russell that this quiet man, who directed the operations of the household, would have a unique point of view on the Archer family.

"So, you're Wilkins, and you're the butler. Do you like being a servant here?"

"Mr. Archer is fair." The answer came without hesitation.

"No, no, man, that's not what I asked you. I asked if you liked being a servant here."

The man paused and smiled at Russell.

"That is a young man's question, if you don't mind my saying so. It's been a long time since I asked myself if I liked what I'm doing. Let's say it suits me." The man paused, then turned to Russell. "I have been observing you since your arrival here, Sir, and if you give me permission, I have some advice for you."

"All right, Wilkins, shoot."

"I don't know if you understand how different the world the Archers move in is from what you're used to."

"In what way?"

"You have spent years under arms, with the enemy trying to kill you. And you have survived it, so you probably think, if I survived that, I can do anything. This peacetime life has no terrors for me." Russell looked at him with interest. "Well, you would be wrong, Captain." Russell sat back down in the chair, keeping his eyes on the butler's face. "First of all, spending years in battle, worrying about being killed and killing others, changes you. You aren't the same man you were when you went in. Things that are grey to the rest of the world seem black and white to you now. You lose your patience and you lose your sympathy for people and their little problems. Ordinary life seems dull and meaningless."

Russell found himself nodding.

"Secondly, although it was a hard world you left on the battle-field, it is a hard world you are entering, but hard in a different way. The people who survive in it are not cruel or malicious, but they are very clear about what they want, and completely determined to get it. If you can help them, then you're tip-top in their books. But if you get in their way, watch out."

"You mean Edward Archer."

Wilkins paused. "Mr. Archer has always been very good to me. He needs me to keep this place going and I do it very well for him. But I know that if I became a problem for him in any way I'd be gone in two shakes of a dead lamb's tail. I've seen it happen."

"Why are you telling me these things?'"

"Because I hate to see a young soldier come home and make a mistake. If you're with Archer, you've got to be with him all the way. Now, you're right for the Tories. British. Protestant. Liberal Party is full of Irish and French. You vote Liberal and the next thing you know, the Pope will be running things in Ontario."

Russell bent his head, thinking of Edward Archer's hard eyes.

"Thank you, Wilkins. I will think about what you've said."

A rap came on the glass pane. Wilkins opened the door to a fair-haired maid who smiled at Russell.

"Excuse me, Mr. Wilkins, but the tailor is here. I put him in the sitting room."

Wilkins looked at Russell, who nodded and smiled briefly.

"If you don't mind, Sir, I'll stay with you during the measuring. I know what's needed and you have to watch these tailors, even the good ones."

6.

One week later, Russell, in his new dinner jacket, walked with Eleanor up the red carpet to the doors of the Albany Club. The Premier was holding a dinner for friends and associates in this club, the meeting place for Conservative politicians in Toronto. A white-haired doorman smiled and held the door. In the lobby they stared at dark mahogany paneling, crystal chandeliers, and oil portraits of Conservative stalwarts from times past. Edward Archer, prominent among the guests, had secured scarce invitations for Janet and her fiancé, John Barnesworthy, and for Eleanor and Bobby Russell.

During the week Eleanor had been introducing him as the Conservative Party's candidate in Elgin County. He went with her to the parties and dinners, thinking nothing, feeling nothing, saying little. It seemed that after the election, there would be a wedding and a job with Archer, Campbell and Torrington. Through the flattery and adulation, however, Russell dreamed of a train, leading him away to he didn't know where. One night, lying beside her on the bed in the green room, he told her that he wouldn't go to the Premier's dinner.

"Don't be difficult," Eleanor said, rolling over on top of him. "It'll be fun. Not like that reception today or the dinner at Nancy Sutcliffe's. There will be only top people there." She kissed him softly on the lips.

They were served drinks in a lounge with a thick carpet, comfortable leather chairs and sofas, a fire in the grate and wood-panelled walls. He noticed that every woman drank sherry and every man drank whiskey. Colonel Drew, wearing military decorations from the First World War, stood in front of the fire place with his wife, a handsome, heavy woman in a light blue evening dress. Beside him stood Edward Archer, accompanied by Helen Clarkson.

"Your father's here with...."

"With Helen. Mother will be having a headache tonight."

Helen Clarkson was laughing at a joke of the Premier's, laying her hand on his arm. He smiled at her. Then she turned to Archer and whispered something in his ear. Archer burst out laughing. She fascinated Russell. Statuesque, filled with humour, charm in her voice and in her eyes, graceful in her movements, she knew how to delight both the men and the women in the room without upstaging the Premier.

"Hello, you two."

Janet Archer entered the room on the arm of a heavy-set blond man, John Barnesworthy, her fiancé and a lawyer with Archer, Campbell and Torrington. Barnesworthy's grip was firm, his smile professional. He had the strong jaw and slack face of an athlete, and the thick middle of a prosperous lawyer.

"So I hear you're the sacrificial lamb for the Party in Elgin County," said Barnesworthy.

"I have to think it over."

"If Eddie's offered it to you, accept. He hates to be turned down, and you won't get a better chance."

"My family's Liberal. The whole of Elgin County's Liberal."

"That's got nothing to do with it. My family used to be Liberal too, but times change, and you go with the current if you have any brains. So just show the flag, and be a good party man."

Barnesworthy spoke with the weight of an experienced man of fifty, but when Russell looked at him he saw that he was in his twenties, his own age; so his harsh, aggressive tone and the lack of irony or humour in his eyes were a facade.

"Come on, children, join the old folks."

Helen Clarkson grabbed Russell by the arm and led him across to the group in front of the fire place; the others followed.

"We need some young blood in this group, George," she roared to the Premier. "So I went and got 'em."

"Helen always gets her man," said George Drew, to laughter.

A server announced dinner, and threw open the double doors. The dining room was lit with candles, shining on the silverware and crystal. Bowls of roses were set on the white table cloths.

"It's lovely, George," said Helen Clarkson.

The Premier waved his hand and a sommelier poured white wine into their glasses, while waiters set out silver salvers of lobster salad, resting on bowls of ice.

"To the Party, and to a glorious win on the fourth of June." Archer raised his glass to the Premier.

"And to George Drew." Helen Clarkson, sitting next to the Premier, raised her glass, then leaned across and kissed him on the cheek. "Our past and future leader and Premier."

The table rose, toasted Drew and applauded. He sat beaming, nodding, and patting Helen on the hand. When finally he rose he took the time to survey the room, trying to look at each person directly.

"It is my view, and the view of many in this room, that the years ahead are going to be years of unequaled opportunities and prosperity for Ontario. We are poised, in the heart of this continent, to leap forward after enduring the miseries of depression and war for the last fifteen years. We have a disciplined, well-educated work force. We have an abundance of natural resources, including the cheapest power on the continent from Niagara. Markets, both here and in the United States, will be wide open again when the troops come home and start to build lives and have children. People want automobiles, and new homes, and washing machines. And we here in Ontario are ready to make these things and sell them to the world. With all respect to our friend from Elgin County, things look so good not even a Liberal could botch it. The Liberals are no threat to anybody, my friends. We have other enemies we must face in this province. I mean socialism. I mean low tariffs. And I mean restrictions on immigration. These issues, these items, if not dealt with in a proper way, can threaten the prosperity and expansion that is our birthright."

"Hear, hear," was heard around the table.

The Premier took a sip of his wine. "I just want to remind you that in the weeks coming up to the election, I will be making three points to the Ontario voters. First, socialism must be defeated if we are to maintain the freedoms we have fought for; second, tariffs must remain high if our industry is to have a chance against the

American giant; and third, immigration must be open if we are to have enough skilled men at a reasonable cost to expand business in this province in the years to come. That is our platform. I am confident that you will join me in driving our message home to the people. Our future prosperity depends on it."

The executive and friends of the Party rose and toasted their leader again. A sense of self-congratulation and tribal solidarity spread over the dining room. They sat down and the waiters served the main course, roast venison in red wine sauce, duchess potatoes and glazed carrots. Red wine sparkled in their glasses. Eleanor turned to Russell.

"I don't understand this talk about socialism, do you? Why would anyone want to own everything in common?"

"If you already own things, bad idea; you lose. If you have nothing, good idea; you win."

"Well, I've got you, so why should I be socialist." She put her hand on his lap and rubbed the inside of his thigh. He smiled and turned to look at a short, angry man with a red face who was clearing his throat to speak.

"George," boomed the man, his caution drowned in alcohol. "Just one wee thing about this immigration business. Surely you don't mean totally open immigration? Without reference to where they come from, and what kind of people they are? "

"We favour immigrants from the British Isles, it goes without saying." said the Premier. "They speak the language, and they tend to be educated."

"And they aren't Catholic," said the man.

"Or Jews," said one of the lawyers.

"We have to be careful about this." The Premier was frowning at his plate. "Our Party favours freedom of religion. We cannot discriminate against other faiths."

"George, this province was built on the Protestant religion," said the man, weaving. "It is the foundation of our freedom and our system of government. We need to be careful when we let people in to Canada who are not from the mother country."

"This is not an issue that we control in the government of Ontario," said the Premier quietly. "It has always been my position that if we allow skilled, hard-working people into this province and keep out the socialists and idlers, then we won't have to worry about where they come from."

The little man staggered but continued to speak, his speech slurred but his conviction undiminished. Since Ontario was the industrial centre of Canada and the Conservative Party ran Ontario and they ran the Conservative Party, well, he believed that the country should pay attention to the voices in this room.

"Well, I don't know about that." All eyes turned to Helen Clarkson. "Some of us from elsewhere believe that there is life outside Toronto, and opinions worth listening to."

"Indeed, Ma'am, I am willing to believe you when you tell me there are people outside Toronto. One rarely sees them, is all. And their views on political questions are not significant. We are not running some vulgar American democracy here."

She turned to look at Russell. "Let's ask Captain Russell, who is not from Toronto. What about it, Captain? Should the people of St. Thomas let the people in this room think for them?"

Russell smiled. "People at home are independent. They will have their say. But they will listen, if the speaker makes sense."

"Independent!" Now Barnesworthy got to his feet, red from either drink or anger. "They vote Liberal even now. They vote for Grant MacKay for God's sake, a drunk. That's not independence, that's stupidity. Where's the common sense in that?"

Some of the men laughed and cheered. George Drew began watching Russell with interest. Eleanor looked worried.

"In my experience," said Russell calmly, "What is common sense changes from day to day, if not from minute to minute. And what looks brilliant from one hill looks absolutely foolish from another. I'm very sure, Mr. Barnseworthy, that if you were standing on Talbot Street in St. Thomas, rather than in this gorgeous room surrounded by your friends, you would have different thoughts about the intelligence of the citizens of Elgin County."

Barnesworthy hitched up his thumbs under his suspenders and cleared his throat.

"I have never stood on any street in St. Thomas, and I don't plan to in the near future." He looked coolly at Russell. "Possibly not ever. I agree with Robbie. We cannot worry about what every shopkeeper or farmer thinks about the important issues of the day. Leadership is what counts. And leadership starts right here, in this room. Our job is to lead the people where they need to go, not to worry about what every Jack and Jill in St. Thomas thinks or doesn't think. That is anarchy, not politics."

"We all have our views it seems." Russell stared directly at Barnesworthy. "And some are not shy about putting them forward. But where I come from, talk is given little value. Talk is cheap." He noticed Helen Clarkson smiling at him. "I would have thought that if the men of St. Thomas were good enough to fight for you, and in some cases die for you, then their voices should be respected in government."

"Bravo," said Helen Clarkson as others nodded.

"Don't pull that soldier-boy stuff on me. I was fighting just as hard here at home as any guy in a fox hole." Barnesworthy was redder than ever, leaning across the table and glaring at Russell. Janet tried to restrain him but he brushed her hand away. "The army did their job, but so did we. People don't understand that the real struggle was here, thinking our way through the crisis. Let the soldiers fight, and the leaders lead. Who do you want making political decisions, some guy who knows how to shoot Germans, or Premier George Drew?"

Barnesworthy looked around for the applause, but saw only people looking at him in embarrassed silence. Drew was whispering to his wife. Disgusted, Russell began to look around for an exit. Eleanor put her hand on his shoulder.

"Don't go," she whispered. "John's a loudmouth and a bully; even Janet says so. The Premier is annoyed; look at this face."

"Those are strong words, Mr. Barnesworthy," said George Drew, frowning.

Barnesworthy beamed. "Some things just have to be said, Mr. Premier. There is not enough respect out there for leaders such as yourself. The people in this room run the country, and a damned good thing it is, too."

"In politics, it's true, certain things do have to be said." The Premier began to talk quietly, as if he were in front of a class. "But it's also true that certain things have to be left unsaid. When I am on Talbot Street in St. Thomas, as I expect to be before the election arrives, especially if my friend Captain Russell agrees to stand for our Party, then I will phrase things differently from you. Captain Russell, or Grant MacKay for that matter, is elected precisely to express the views of the people of the area. That is how our system works."

Barnesworthy then sank back in his chair, drained his wine and motioned angrily to the waiter. He scowled as others at the table turned away from him. The Premier rose and, on his way to the lavatory, made a point of slapping Russell on the back as he passed his chair. Barnesworthy glared.

"Seems you've made quite an impression. It seems a uniform turns the heads of more than just the girls."

Janet grabbed him by the lapel and hissed angrily into his ear, then snatched away his wine glass and poured him some water. The big man sulked in his chair.

Dessert and coffee were served in the lounge, around a fire. Men were gathered around the Premier, discussing the outcome of the election riding by riding. Russell sat with Eleanor on a sofa away from the rest.

"Don't let John Barnesworthy bother you," she said. "He talks too much and can't hold his liquor."

"It's not just him. These Toronto people think they're living at the centre of the universe."

"I know what you mean." Helen Clarkson was standing in front of their sofa. "Toronto can be stuffy and self-righteous. Not for the likes of small towners like you and me, Captain."

He was warmed by her smile. "They seem isolated."

"Don't judge them all by John Barnesworthy. George Drew isn't like that, nor is your father, Eleanor." She gave Eleanor a dazzling smile. "Dear, I want you to leave us for a minute. I want to have a private word with your young man."

Alone with her, Russell tensed. This woman was different.

"I don't know how you do it, Captain, returning from the fighting and entering a world like this. Grey-haired old fogies just talking, talking, talking. It must drive you nuts."

He smiled. "They're so very confident. Over there we had no confidence."

"What do you mean?"

He shook his head. "Overseas, nobody was really sure of what they were doing, ever. And they all knew that whatever they were doing, there was always a chance that it wouldn't turn out well. So when the men talked, they were quieter and the tone of their voices was softer. They knew they could die. This room." He looked at the portraits on the paneled walls. "It's so solid, so comfortable. You'd never think, sitting here, what a howitzer shell would do to it."

She looked briefly alarmed. "Goodness, what a thought. Not going to happen tonight though; but I do understand. It's money, really. I often think that money is like sex, it can make you stupid if you don't use it properly. It's being isolated behind walls of money that makes them smug." She sat beside him on the sofa. "People come to Toronto to make money. They forget what life is like in Kirkland Lake, or St. Thomas."

"So what are you doing here?"

"Eddie." She smiled quietly. "He's good to me. My marriage is difficult, and so is his. Comrades in disaster, or something like that. I want to give you some advice."

"Everybody is giving me advice now."

"I don't just give advice, I give good advice." She patted his hand. "Go home. Don't stay here any longer. You can't possibly find out who you are and what you want in Toronto. Both Eleanor and her father are determined to sweep you off your feet. In different ways, of course, but you do understand what I mean." He nodded.

"Eleanor may be for you. Conservative politics and law at Archer, Campbell and Torrington may be for you. Or they may not. Go home and find out."

Before he could answer everyone rose as the Premier, his wife on his arm, left the room. He winked at Russell as he walked out the door. Edward Archer came and stood in front of their sofa.

"Don't listen to Helen, Russell," he said genially. "She's too frank. She'll tell all our secrets."

"You're too late, I already have. And here is the fair Eleanor. I simply told him not to let you two push him around."

"'Push him around'," said Eleanor. "Why would we want to do that?"

"Instinct."

The Archers looked at one another and smiled.

7.

Can't think of Susan. Nothing left for me. There is nothing she can do. *Women sit and watch. I hate it when they cry. Something is wrong. What happened? I remember killing, but no one killed me. Still, it went all wrong. Alec Symes, who used to work in the dairy, shot by a sniper ten feet from me. Ralph MacBain, from their farm in Sparta, burned to death when his ammo wagon caught a shell. So what? The problem wasn't the killing. It was the women standing by the roads. They watched, they cried, they begged. How could they stand there? That's what I hated more than anything. More than killing.*

Nothing worked. I couldn't get transport to the hospital for my wounded. I couldn't get food for them. We had to threaten a flour merchant in Livorgno with shooting to get bread for our wounded. And that asshole aide to the commander gives me shit, for threatening the fucking flour bandit. I felt like shooting him; no, it wasn't the killing. It was the random stupidity of men organizing themselves to kill or be killed. How could that be sane? What was the matter with them?

And here I am stuck in this house, screwing this woman. She's only happy on her back. Useless. It could be her by the road, staring at me marching past, crying. I see her up ahead, I see her falling behind. But no, there is only her and the bed. Sex makes you stupid. I have to go home.

"Bobby."

She was watching him. She was angry that he was not attentive. She assaulted him in her anger. She stayed until dawn, on fire for him, unable to be satisfied. She used her body as food, as a weapon and as the wall that kept him in the prison she had built. She entered his mouth, she bestrode him, she hit him, she cuddled him. There was no place in that bed where he could avoid her, wearied by the wetness of her lips, the sound of her whisper, his nerves drunk, his muscles sore. Three times he strove against her until he was exhausted and mindless, lying still on his back, staring at the ceiling, not thinking, not feeling, not caring. She would nestle in beside him, eyes shining.

❀

The next night Hugh returned early from Boston and arrived for dinner to find Russell alone, reading the newspaper. He sat down, winking and beaming.

"A little dickey bird tells me that you're going to stand for the Party in Elgin County."

Russell put down his paper.

"I'm thinking about it."

Hugh's red face grew solemn; he cleared his throat nervously.

"I asked Eddie for a good seat last time around, and this time. But he hasn't done anything for me." He looked nervously at the doorway, as if he were afraid his brother might return. "Can't see why, Russell. I'd be a good Party man, vote right, represent the riding and all that, fight the reds. After all, it's not as if you have to be Einstein to get elected to the Ontario Legislature. There's no

reason on God's green earth why they shouldn't give it to me."
Hugh's voice was indignant. "Now you seem to be the coming
thing. Maybe you'd put in a good word for me?"

Rosemary arrived in the doorway and the talk stopped.

"The next premier of Ontario, I hear," she said, sliding her huge
bulk onto her chair. "You don't waste any time, Robert Russell, with
your politics or with the ladies." She gave him a coy smirk.

"Shut up, Rosie," said Hugh. "We're talking politics here, man
to man."

Mildred Archer and Hilda entered, arm in arm, supporting one
another. They sat down quietly. Hilda looked devoutly at her plate
while Mildred looked at Russell, her eyes full of feeling.

"We prayed for you, Captain Russell, Hilda and I."

"That is very good, Mrs. Archer." He looked around the table,
wishing Eleanor were there. Owen and Peter entered. "Very fine."

"Yes," said Hilda, in a high, quiet voice. "The mystery of Christ
transcends individuals, and makes the impersonal, personal. You as
a person were in our prayers, even if we didn't yet know you. Isn't
that right, Peter?"

"Yes, indeed," said the priest pompously. "He transcends indi-
vidual differences with His complete and perfect love."

Eleanor sat beside him. She brushed against him as she took her
seat. "Let's go to bed right after dinner," she whispered in his ear.

"Oh, oh, oh," exclaimed Rosemary, leering across the table.
"What monkey business are you two up to?"

Edward Archer entered, surveyed the table with his cool smile,
and took his seat. Hilda immediately looked away from the table,
pain in her eyes. Mildred motioned to Wilkins, who began to serve
the dinner. Archer began to talk once again about the Conservative
Party's prospects in the election, now less than a month and a half
away. Owen and Peter whispered together. Only Hugh and Russell
pretended to be interested. When the dinner ended, Eleanor smiled
at him and left to walk upstairs to the second floor. In the act of
following her Russell stopped, looked up the staircase after her, and
turned away to the drawing room. Peter and Owen were putting a

record on the Victrola. The sound of a piano, from far away, entered the drawing room.

"No one plays Liszt like Paderewski," said Peter, his eyes full of emotion.

"Schnabel," said Owen

"Schnabel, my dear boy." Peter's eyes rolled to the heavens. "Schnabel is too regular, too German. He lacks the Slavic fire and passion."

Russell took his seat in a chair that looked through the French doors to the garden and tried to listen to the scratchy music.

"Have some brandy, Captain."

Owen was standing over him, looking at him in a kindly way, extending a snifter.

"You look down, Captain. You don't look like the handsome young soldier who's going to sweep through Ontario politics with my sister on his arm."

"He's still handsome," said Peter softly. "But he looks tired. Exhausted."

"It must be the war," said Owen coyly. "Or possibly Eleanor."

"Or both," said Peter.

Before he could answer he saw Eleanor frowning at the door.

"I was waiting for you."

"Soon," he said quietly. "Be up soon."

"I hate waiting," she said, and left quickly.

"When lovely woman stoops to conquer," said Peter Vincent.

"Not me, boys," muttered Russell. "I'm imprisoned, yes, but not conquered."

"The Captain may not be all the sleepwalker he appears," said Owen.

"Yes," said Peter. "Sleepwalker, that's exactly right. We wanted to rescue you, you know, but we didn't know how. It's a fact that interfering is not always the thing, you know."

The two looked at him with widened eyes, like a pair of sympathetic owls.

"I'm all right," said Russell. "How about another brandy?"

Owen rose and walked to the sideboard, suddenly throwing back his head and gesturing to the impassioned music that poured from the victrola. They continued to drink and talk, about the war, about London, and about Russell's returning home. He kept one eye on the garden, fading in the twilight. The music wove in and out of his mind; he was content.

"We have to leave," said Owen finally. "We're invited to a party. You'd be welcome to come with us, but I don't know if it's your thing. It's ... all men."

He smiled. "Thanks boys, but I better not. Eleanor and I...."

Russell sat for a few minutes and then walked unsteadily up the stairs and down the hall to the green room. Eleanor lay on his bed, smoking a cigarette, staring out the window.

"I got talking to the boys," he said, being careful not to slur his words.

"They're faggots," she snapped. "You knew I was waiting for you." She took a breath and her voice softened. "But here you are, finally."

She stubbed out the cigarette and put the ash tray on the floor. Then she drew back the sheet. Her long legs, broad, curved hips, the full breasts with the large black nipples lay spread out before him. He didn't move.

"Come here."

Her voice was low and hoarse. She pulled him down on the bed and began to undress him. She kissed his lips, his ears, his chest, and rubbed between his legs. He lay still and did not look at her. She took his cock in her mouth, grabbing his buttocks, but he remained soft. She sat on his chest, and began to hit him lightly in the face.

"There's no escaping me, you know," she whispered. "I will have you."

He didn't move.

"You're drunk. Or perhaps you're a faggot too, like Peter and Owen. Is that what you are, Bobby?"

She smacked him on the face but he didn't move. A light snore came from the bed. She dressed quickly and left the room.

Next morning he sat in the drawing room with his coffee, his head aching. Eleanor hadn't come down. The two brothers were talking in the dining room, preparing to go to work. Hilda and Mildred walked out the front door leaving for St. Mary Magdalene's. Rosemary came in from the dining room with her coffee.

"Nice day. What are you two up to?"

"Going to the station, Rosemary. Time to go home."

He left the house as soon as he could to avoid Eleanor. The London trains left at ten o'clock and four o'clock. He was too late for the morning train, but perhaps the four o'clock. He looked in the department stores and bought himself a pair of shoes. He ate in Diana Sweets on Yonge Street. After lunch he walked along Bloor Street to Christie Pits and found a softball game in progress. Two factory teams were playing. The men were either teenagers with crew cuts or older, some with grey hair. There were no players his age. He sat on the grass slope and watched the play. A boy sold him a bag of peanuts. Next to him on the slope two girls, teenagers, were sitting on a blanket. They kept watching him, whispering to each other, and giggling. He lay on the grass and soon he was asleep, dreaming of vacant-eyed women with gold earrings watching them from beside the road as they marched through the towns. When he awoke he looked at his watch. The time was four fifteen. He had missed the afternoon train.

Eleanor was not at dinner. Russell talked with Owen and Peter about London, but without any real interest. He was both hoping for and fearing Eleanor's appearance. And he was thinking of being on the train tomorrow.

"Has any one seen Eleanor?" asked Rosemary.

"Yes," said Janet, staring at Russell. "I saw her downtown this afternoon."

"When is she coming home?"

"She'll show up," said Janet. "She always does."

When he entered the drawing room after supper he felt himself a stranger in the room for the first time. Rosemary was the first to follow him and sat beside him on the sofa.

"I used to be beautiful, you know," she said suddenly.

Hugh walked in the door, whistling. Rosemary fell silent, looked away and sipped her coffee. Hugh looked at Rosemary, then back at Russell.

"I say, I hope I'm not interrupting anything, a little tete a tete after dinner?" He laughed. Rosemary glanced at him with open contempt. "Like to talk to you more about running in the election, Russell." Hugh's anxious gaze was fixed on him.

Rosemary snorted. "You don't have any money of your own and you don't know how to work at anything. What on earth do they need you for?"

"Rubbish." Hugh's face grew brick red. "I'm a trained lawyer. Work as hard as the next man. What the hell do you know about it anyway, is what I should like to know. Goddam cow."

Rosemary rose from her seat and walked to a chair in the corner. Hugh turned back to Russell.

"As I was saying, the Party needs experience. I've been around the block a few times, invaluable connections...." Hugh's voice began to trail off, as he kept glancing at Rosemary, who regarded him now with a cold sneer.

"Hopeless family," he said finally, as he lost his train of his thought. He went to the sideboard and poured himself a brandy as Mildred and Hilda entered the room.

"Hugh," said Mildred sharply. "You know you're not supposed to drink brandy if you've had wine with your meal." Sheepishly Hugh put his glass down on the sideboard.

Russell sipped his coffee and wondered how soon he could leave. Perhaps he would walk downtown and find a movie. He had noticed 'Meet Me in St. Louis' with Judy Garland advertised on a marquee. He looked up and saw Janet beckoning to him from the doorway.

"Father wants to see you now," she said in a low voice. "Tom Brennan's in there too, the party man from your part of the country. They want to sign you up for the election." The next train left at ten in the morning. He was determined to be on it.

"Don't do it." Her voice was almost a hiss.

"You don't think I could do it?"

"Of course you could, but why would you? Eleanor is no wife for you. She likes sex, but not children. But if she doesn't marry someone she'll drink and start to have affairs with golf pros, and failed lawyers. When she's sixty she'll be hanging around the bar at every party or wedding she can get to with all the other blue-permed sweethearts."

"But your father...."

She waved her hand. "Forget Father. You could fit in but it would ruin you. You'd be some minor appendage in the family or in the firm, like Hugh, only married to Eleanor. Now go in and talk to them, say goodbye, and get out of here."

Edward Archer was sitting behind a big oak desk in his study; in armchair to one side sat Tom Brennan. Archer was stroking his moustache, watching Russell like a hungry snake, his dark eyes unblinking.

"Here's the boy," said Brennan. "It will be a feather in our cap, to run Romaine Russell's son in Elgin County. You stand for the Party down there, and presumably you lose. Then you come down here and enter the firm, get you a start in life. The next time around you get a winnable seat and you're on your way. The only thing is, Russell, we need to hear from you. Are you with us?"

"No," said Russell.

The office went completely silent. Brennan's goofy smile faded; Archer's face tensed.

"Think what you are saying," he said quietly. "You will not be given this chance again."

"Thanks for the offer, but I have to go home."

"The Russells have always been Liberals," said Brennan. "Maybe you'll wait and stand as a Liberal after Grant MacKay ends up in the drunk tank."

"I'm not running for anybody," he said, getting to his feet. "I have to go home."

Archer began to leaf through a sheaf of papers on his desk, his face red and angry. "Tom, let's get another candidate, that high school teacher that wants to run for us. And Captain Russell, I presume you'll be leaving us soon?"

"Tomorrow," he said.

PART II

St. Thomas

8.

"I LOVE THE SPRING," said Susan MacLean, lying back on the picnic blanket and letting the sun warm her face.

"This was the worst winter ever." Her friend Jean raised a kohl-lined eyelid. "Cold, snow and no men. There were those pilots training west of town; cute, but gone in a month."

"Have you heard about Sally Graham's brother, Donny?" Jean tensed. "Killed in Holland. They heard yesterday."

"Donny? He used to babysit me." Tears glistened. "God, how I hate this war. Except there is no God. If there were, Donny would still be alive."

"It's horrible, but we can't just sit and blubber. We need to do something, and I have a plan." She glanced cautiously at Jean. "I want to raise money to help families who have lost a man."

Jean groaned. "But honey, the war is almost over. I want to live!"

"Forget living. I want a garden party, if your mom will let us use her garden. I need you to ask her."

"Oh, I guess," Jean nodded.

The girls had bicycled out to the meadow by Kettle Creek off the Lyndhurst Road just west of St. Thomas, the county town of Elgin County on the north shore of Lake Erie. It was the second week of April, the year was 1945, and the weather had turned warm and sunny right across southwestern Ontario from Niagara Falls to the Detroit River.

"But for now, forget the war and smell the grass." Susan stretched to the sun. "It's divine."

"Smell the food," said Jean, looking at the picnic hamper." God, I've put on five pounds since Christmas."

"You're looking great, Jeanie. Rubenesque."

"You mean fat." She stared at Susan. "But you are gorgeous. Auburn hair and blue eyes. And your figure…." She sighed. "God Susan, if I had your body I'd flaunt it."

"No men to flaunt for."

"Is that ever true. Sometimes I think we'd be better off without men. Just us."

She smiled sweetly at Susan.

"What would we do without men?"

"Oh, I don't know. The Sapphics seem to find a way."

The "Sapphics" were Rose MacIlwain, their English teacher at the Collegiate, and Helen Partridge, a librarian at the St. Thomas Public Library. The women shared an apartment on Ontario Street. They had developed a circle of girls who despised the culture of St. Thomas which they considered provincial and boorish. The young women learned to adore the poems of Tennyson and Swinburne and the music of Brahms, and they dreamed of trips to Paris and Greece.

"Rose is looking more distinguished than ever, with the grey in her hair," she said. "Quite handsome. The male of the couple."

"You shouldn't gossip. You have no proof."

"Of course I'll gossip." Jean tossed her head in the air. "Gossip is divine, and it doesn't need proof. And if they love each other it's better than what we've got. Which is nothing. Not a useful man in sight." She sighed. "I really want to get out of this town."

"Where would you go?"

"I want to study art in New York."

"Art? You've never painted in your life."

"So? I think Daddy would pay for an apartment in Manhattan. Greenwich Village. You could visit me in New York next fall.We'd see shows, go to parties and meet men."

"I'll hate it if you leave, Jeanie. You're my bad girl. My fun girl."

"I'm only bad in this town. I don't have your looks, so I have to be aggressive. I don't wait to be asked."

"So what am I waiting for?"

"Bobby."

Susan rolled off the blanket and began to inspect an orange and black lady bug crawling up a stalk of grass. "Bobby couldn't wait to get into his uniform and get overseas. Hopeless. The men were like boys with toy guns. They all wanted to go."

Robert Russell had been overseas for three years. He had been missing since November.

"You can't blame them for leaving this dump." Jean sat up. "No news of him?"

"None. I have to go over and see Mrs. Russell later today, but I don't think she's heard anything."

They fell silent. The meadow sloped down toward Kettle Creek, which was full from the spring run-off. It glistened in the sun as it ran through the fields and orchards to Port Stanley on Lake Erie, ten miles away. On the other side of the creek was a dirt road and beyond it an apple orchard, soon to be white with blossoms.

"Who's that?"

A figure trudged along the dirt road towards town. They saw a boy of about ten, with close-cropped hair, wearing a khaki shirt that was too big for him, torn shorts and on his feet a pair of huge army boots without laces, flopping as he walked.

"That's Calvin MacQuiggan," said Susan. "He's one of those MacQuiggans that live in that shack on the Russell farm."

"Whoever said there aren't any men left in St. Thomas?" They laughed sadly.

Calvin MacQuiggan glanced toward the laughter, lowered his head and kept walking towards St. Thomas, a solitary, ragged figure.

"What's he going to town for?" asked Susan.

"His father's that Archie MacQuiggan," said Jean. "As soon as his pension cheque arrives he heads for the Confederation House to drink with his friends. Calvin will be looking for him." She picked up a magazine, kicked off her shoes and wiggled her bare toes.

"Some little wifey asks Mrs. Eleanor Roosevelt in the Ladies Home Journal if she should tell hubby when he returns from the war that she's been having an affair, and if she does, would her husband be justified in leaving her. Eleanor says that honesty is best, and she should tell all. Then she says that a true relationship is based on love, and that hubby would probably take the affair as evidence that she no longer loved him. Eleanor could understand if the guy left." She threw the magazine on the blanket. "If that isn't the silliest, stupidest advice anyone ever gave anyone. And in the Ladies Home Journal."

"But Jean, surely she didn't love him, if she had the affair."

Jean scowled. "Love! Who knows about love? Sex is fine. Give me a guy with money and a car."

Susan turned away from her to watch the creek, gurgling across the meadow. She had trouble remembering Bobby's face.

"So are we going to watch the parade tomorrow?" she asked.

"What parade?"

"The politicians dreamed it up; they want you to know that St. Thomas is behind the war effort. Support the boys, knit sweaters and socks, buy bonds, that kind of thing. The Collegiate band will be marching and everyone will be there."

"Oh really," drawled Jean. "A band of little kids followed by boring speeches from old men. I think we should go and see 'Meet Me in St. Louis' at the Capitol. Judy Garland."

"We'll do both," Susan jumped in. "We can watch the parade from the Malt Shoppe, have our lunch and go to the Capitol for the two o'clock."

"Perfect. Then let's go down to Port Stanley for a swim. I haven't been for ages."

They both looked up at the distant sound of an automobile. A rolling cloud from the gravelly Lyndhurst Road across the valley came towards them as a dusty Ford rounded the bend, came down the hill, and stopped on their side of the Kettle Creek bridge.

"It's Will Matthews. And he's got his father's car." Jean's eyes narrowed with intention.

"You girls want to go for a ride?" said Will, hopefully. His dark hair was slicked down with brilliantine, and his face was pimply. He wore a straw boater with a blue and white ribbon, a blue blazer and white trousers.

"Will," said Susan, smiling at him. "We were thinking of going down to Port for a swim tomorrow at four. Maybe you'd come."

"Brilliant," whispered Jean. Will's face lit up.

"If I can have the car tomorrow. I'll have to ask Father."

"Tell him we'll pay for the gas," said Jean.

"You won't have to do that." Will spoke in his most mature, authoritative voice. "And I'm sure he'll let me have it." His smile broadened. "Anyone want a ride back to town?"

Jean got to her feet and gathered up her hamper. "I'll come. Will, can you bring my blanket?"

Susan lay back and stared at the sky. She smiled as she looked across the meadow. A breeze ruffled the grass and blew its sweetness to her nose. Birds skimmed over the meadow and grasshoppers jumped in the grass. She stretched her arms and legs and sighed. The ache was in her breast, in her blood.

There are two hundred and ten men from St. Thomas and around, all gone, she thought. No baseball team this summer, and Father can hardly publish the Times Journal for want of pressmen. Jean has it right. Maybe I should go to New York.

She stood up. "Damn Bobby, and damn this war." She walked across the meadow towards town.

Susan watched Margaret Ann Russell pour their tea. A slender, elegant woman, Mrs. Russell wore a pink and white striped dress, her hair coiffed blue-grey, gold bangles at her wrist, an aquiline nose and a fierce look in her eye.

"I may have some news," she was saying. "Last week at noon, Friday I think it was, I was sitting in this very seat when the phone rang. It was an overseas operator from Folkstone, in England, asking me if I would accept the charge. Before I could answer, the line broke up and I lost the connection. They didn't phone again."

Susan concentrated on her tea, then glanced around the room at the horsehair furniture, the upright piano, the Persian rug and the landscapes done by Margaret Ann herself. And there was the picture of Bobby in uniform taken just before he left, standing in front of the house, smiling, his bonnet cocked on his head.

"You think it was Bobby?'

"I know it was. I never believed he was dead."

"Be careful, Mrs. Russell. It might be something else…."

"I don't think so. I've never had a notice of any kind, missing in action, killed, not a word." She looked suddenly weary. "He'd better come back soon, the ploughing hasn't been started. I can't get Archie moving on it. And I've got Allan Matthews coming here every other day trying to get me to sell our piece of land on the Lyndhurst Road at the London Highway, where Archie lives. They claim they're moved by my predicament and want to help me. But I don't trust Allan. He thinks if he shows me his white teeth and strokes his perfect moustache I'll swoon and give him the land. Which I may do, but not because he's irresistible." They laughed. "But I can't run this farm much longer with only Archie MacQuiggan to help me. And I don't want to sell if Bobby is coming back."

She paused. "It's the not knowing. I can survive anything, as long as I know." Susan was silent. "My dear, you need to get out and enjoy yourself. Why don't you come with me to the Stork Club in Port Stanley Saturday night? There's a band from the States, Glen Miller style; we could have some fun. Allan Matthews wants me to go with him, the rascal. I need a chaperone."

"Mrs. Russell, I'd adore to," she said. "I'll bring Jean."

9.

"Look at them. They're pathetic," said Jean.

The two were watching the parade from the front window of the

70

Malt Shoppe. Jean rolled her eyes as the St. Thomas Collegiate band passed in front of them, rows of boys and girls more or less even, the trumpets and trombones ringing their celebration of the war effort off the red-brick facades of Talbot Street. Only the drum major, a skinny boy named Alf Bowser in grade eleven, had a complete uniform. The mothers' group, which had kept the band in slick satin uniforms in years past, had been occupied knitting wool items for the men on the battlefield. Most of the marchers had tunics, some had caps, none had proper trousers, so they marched and played in overalls, flowered skirts, flannel trousers and a variety of gym shoes, work boots, and saddle shoes. But the band blared 'The Maple Leaf Forever' with vigour as they passed the Malt Shoppe, marching east on Talbot Street to the City Hall.

"They're doing their best."

"Look, Edna Ferguson dropped her flute."

A carrot-headed girl with masses of freckles retrieved her flute from the road and struggled back into line. The band was followed by marchers from the service clubs and lodges, the Rotary Club, the Lions Club, the Orange Lodge, the Freemasons, the Knights of Columbus and the Legion of Mary. Tom Barnett, Master of the Orange Lodge, had objected to the inclusion of the Knights of Columbus and the Legion of Mary in the parade, on the grounds that Roman Catholics owed their ultimate allegiance to the Pope, not to the Empire, and were not free men and women. Mayor Al Parker had squelched the protest by observing in the Council debate that there were many Catholic soldiers under the ground in Europe, and some of them were our boys.

Behind the lodges marched the veterans from the Great War of 1914, grey-haired men in blue blazers and military caps, eyes front, striving to keep their stomachs flat and their feet with the beat. Behind them came the clergymen of the town: the Reverend Campbell Fitch of First United, the Reverend Allan MacBryde of Knox Presbyterian, Pastor Bill Jones of Calvary Baptist, the Reverend Timothy Willoughby, St. George's Anglican, and Father Peter O'Neil of Our Lady of Lourdes. Bringing up the rear were

Mayor Parker and his six aldermen, the provincial Member of the Ontario Legislature, Grant MacKay, and the federal Member of Parliament, Allan Sheppard.

"D'you know there's not a woman in that whole parade," said Susan. "It just hit me. Except for the band, not one female."

"Would you want to be marching with those old men?"

"I am definitely going to go with you to New York," said Susan, reaching for her purse. "But right now let's hear the speeches."

They followed the parade along Talbot Street to the City Hall, where the marchers had gathered around the War Memorial on the front lawn, under rows of flags, the Union Jack, the Canadian Red Ensign and the lodge flags. Father O'Neil invoked God's blessing on the Allied troops, who had were close to a glorious victory over the forces of evil. Pastor Jones and the Reverend Campbell Fitch, by agreement, had read Father O'Neil's prayer in advance, to ensure that there were no unacceptable Popish references in it that would outrage the town's Protestant majority. The band played 'God Save the King' and 'O Canada'. Then, one by one, Allan Sheppard, Grant MacKay and the Mayor addressed the crowd.

"Jean, there are your parents."

The Robsons stood with heads half bowed in the half circle of the town's prominent citizens.

"Where does she get hats like that," muttered Susan.

"Toronto. Milliners there make them for our store," said Jean. "They copy New York and Paris."

"There's Allan Matthews," said Susan. "The breeze tosses his grey hair just enough to make the ladies' hearts beat faster."

"Ugh," said Jean. "And there's his partner, MacAllister, bald as a coot and his neck stringy like a turkey's. How does Millie bear him?"

Beside the bald MacAllister stood his secretary and law clerk, Millie Hall, a stout woman in her forties with an enormous bosom, in a flowered dress. The rumour was that Millie was closer to her boss than a strict definition of her duties required. The town was of the opinion that MacAllister was too cheap to get married, and was content to find a sort of two-for-the-price-of-one deal in Millie. His partner, Allan Matthews, was a widower and the town Romeo.

"Who's Matthews after these days?"

"Mrs. Russell," said Susan. "He wants to take her to the Stork Club on Saturday night. I told her that we'd chaperone."

"My God, at their age? Count me in."

Jean was bored. There was little gossip about the procession of prosperous citizens. Their sins were committed behind the doors of their substantial houses, or occurred on vacation, far from the eyes of the curious citizens of St. Thomas. There had always been more interesting scandal among the lower orders who stood, on this day of civic rejoicing, in an undignified scrum down in front of the speakers, not a blue suit or a new spring outfit among them. There was Marnie MacBride, pregnant without a sign of a man. There was Jim Slouch, shacked up in his ramshackle place on the Union Road with some under-aged girl who, he claimed, was his niece from New Glasgow. And Elsie MacQuiggan, who bestowed her charms any Saturday night on the man who bought her beer in the Confederation House, with a little extra for her needs. Elsie was standing right under the platform, looking in a meaningful way at Jim Slouch.

"Look at Elsie MacQuiggan," said Jean. "Fooling around with Jim Slouch. She isn't wearing anything on her feet. She's barefoot."

"They say she wears no underpants." Susan's voice was hushed.

"Less to take off."

At the very edge of the crowd, sitting under a maple tree, was Archie MacQuiggan himself, a red-haired, freckle-faced man missing his front teeth, with a military tunic covering a huge beer belly. His two sons, Tom the postman and the lonely-looking Calvin, in his hand-me-down clothes and his father's army boots, were beside him.

"How did Archie get back from overseas so soon?"

"He got shot," said Jean. "Apparently in a place that makes the production of further MacQuiggans unlikely."

"Good for the Nazis," whispered Susan.

They fell silent as the Mayor finished his speech.

"And now, after years of suffering and sacrifice, our boys will soon be coming home. What a great day that will be, ladies and gentlemen. We'll go down to the station and there they will be, years older than when they left us. Not all of them will be there, for we are well aware that some of our boys have made the supreme sacrifice." Mayor Parker looked manfully at the horizon, then bowed his head.

"Let's get away from here," said Susan. "Where are Will and that car?"

❋

The beach at Port Stanley was deserted. The booths and shacks that lined the road behind the beach, selling cotton candy and hot souvenirs in summer, were closed so early in the year. Down to their left Kettle Creek, after miles of wandering through the fields and orchards of Elgin County, flowed through reeds and under a wooden bridge to empty into Lake Erie. At the mouth of the creek a pier jutted out into the lake, with fishing boats tied up alongside. They could see a fishermen working on his engine and hear the clank of his tools as he set them on the cement pier. The sky was cloudless, there was little wind; the lap of the waves on the shore was rhythmic, quiet.

"They say Cleveland is over there." Jean stared across the lake.

"I went there with my dad once,' said Will.

"There's nothing in Cleveland," said Susan. "Whatever would you want to go there for?"

"There are big companies and big money in Cleveland. Father has a client there who wants to do business in St. Thomas."

Will was lying back on the blanket eating a hot dog and drinking a Coca Cola.

"So your father has a real business client," said Jean. "I thought he made his money overcharging war widows to probate their husbands' estates. Good at holding their hands and such, is what I hear."

Will's face flushed. "Father does good work. You want a probate that stands up before a judge." He looked anxiously at the girls who were gazing out at the water. "Let's drive down to the Stork Club and see who's playing Saturday night."

Jean got to her feet, smiling sweetly. "Maybe we can get some fudge at the Sweet Pavilion."

"Why sure," said Will, pleased as they walked away.

The fisherman turned his engine over. The roar drove a flock of sea gulls cawing into the air.

"What about next year, Susie?" Will walked beside her, staring at the sand.

"Who knows? Maybe go to teachers' college. Daddy wants me to begin to work for the Times Journal." She felt distanced from the conversation, listening to the lapping of the waves.

"What about Bobby?"

"Mrs. Russell doesn't think he's dead. She thinks he tried to telephone her last week."

"I mean what about you and Bobby? He finished law school. Father says he'll have a good career in town if he wants it."

Susan's face turned red. "Lawyer, hah! The idiot couldn't wait to join the army, and it probably got him killed. He's not smart enough for me, even if he is alive. "

"Sorry. I didn't...."

"Shut up, Will." Jean walked between them. "Let's go see Judy Garland and have some fun."

Jean and Will began to hum, 'Meet Me in St. Louis, Louie'.

"The band this Saturday night at the Stork Club is from Detroit," said Will. "Gene Henderson and his Hepcats. Sounds like a live one."

"How would you know?" Jean smiled.

"Well, it sounds pretty good, like a real hep group." His face grew tense. "Are we all going Saturday?"

"I'll go," said Susan.

"She has to. She has to protect Mrs. Russell from your father."

"Like father, like son." Will smirked.

"You're a boy," Jean said. "And your father's ancient. We need some men in this town."

Will looked quickly away at the lake, now dark as the sun sank.

10.

Allan Matthews strode up and down the reception area of the offices of Matthews and MacAllister, Barristers and Solicitors. Millie was not at her desk, MacAllister's door was closed and Matthews was exasperated. He wanted to talk to his partner about what they referred to as the Russell deal. The man was just over six feet tall, with perfectly barbered silver-grey hair and a clipped moustache, sparkling blue eyes and handsome, regular features. His suits were made in Toronto, his oxblood English oxfords had a high sheen and his neckties were always silk, always striped and always impeccably knotted. This elegance, however, was a source of tension in the firm. MacAllister bought his shirts and suits in Reuben's Men's' Wear on Talbot Street, always at a sale price. He would wear plastic collars and clip-on plaid neck ties. If he took off his jacket on a hot day you could see yellow in the arm pits of his shirts. Matthews wondered how Millie could tolerate the man's smell. The door opened and Millie came out to her desk, carrying her stenographer's pad as she always did, adjusting her glasses and her blouse, her face flushed.

"We've finished our dictation, Mr. Matthews. You may go in now."

MacAllister was at his desk, reclining in his chair, a contented smile on his face.

"MacAllister, we've got to talk about the Russell deal. There are too many loose ends, too many unanswered questions."

MacAllister removed the pince-nez glasses from his skinny nose and rubbed them on his plaid necktie.

"What Russell deal, Matthews?" he asked in his clipped voice. "I know of no Russell deal. I know of a Mr. Tyler Van Kleef, of

Cleveland, Ohio, who would like to buy a piece of the Russell farm. I know a Mrs. Margaret Ann Russell, owner of said farm, who is reluctant to sell. And I know of a St. Thomas lawyer who boasted, in this very room, that he would have her signature on a sales agreement in a week, and that was six months ago. So in all honesty, Matthews, I cannot say I know what you mean by the Russell deal." The man began to clean his finger nails with the writing end of a lead pencil.

"I've explained to her that she'll get the very top dollar for the property, given the fact there's been a war on. But she's stubborn. She won't sell until she knows about Bobby, one way or another. Which brings me to one of the loose ends. Marie Barnes at the telephone exchange says that Margaret Ann had a telephone call from England last week. The connection was never made, but she thinks it was Bobby."

MacAllister cackled in a low, dry voice. "The letter said missing in action, so she could be right. But the odds are against it. Missing for this long, he's not a prisoner. I doubt we'll see our boy Bobby again."

Matthews paced up and down on the threadbare carpet. "Even if the phone call was not Bobby, I still don't like it. Which brings me to the other loose end, Tom MacQuiggan and those letters. I don't like him walking around town if Bobby Russell does show up here one day, knowing what he knows. If the story comes out that MacQuiggan was delivering Margaret Ann's overseas mail to you, we'll have some explaining to do."

"I'll have some explaining to do, Matthews. You stick to the widows. Which reminds me, when there are no more soldiers being killed and this probate work stops, what are you going to do for fees, eh? There'll be no more cuddling up to the war widows. You'll have to get real commercial work."

"Don't worry about my fees. I just want to be sure that this Russell business isn't going to explode in our faces."

MacAllister rose from his desk, scowling. "I do the thinking around here, my friend. Do your part and close the christly deal."

"I'm not sure I can. She won't sell until she knows about Bobby. If he comes back we'll have to deal with him. He's a lawyer now."

"Lawyer, bullshit. He's a boy dumb enough to volunteer to get hisself killed." He glared at Matthews. "And you're not sure you can sell Bobby Russell. If he comes back." MacAllister stood by his desk, cleaning his ears with his pencil. "But I have thought of that eventuality, Matthews; we'd expropriate. Even with a Tory government in Toronto, Grant MacKay can get it for us at very little cost. So you deliver Margaret Ann. and don't worry about Tom MacQuiggan. I've paid his father, who will have drunk the money away by now and won't remember a thing."

"I'm taking Margaret Ann to the Stork Club Saturday night. I'll go out and talk to her this afternoon."

"You do that. Earn your christly keep. In the meantime, I'll have to report to Mr. Tyler Van Kleef. He's impatient; push, push, push. I'm a real go-getter in St. Thomas, Matthews, but I don't even hold a candle to Mr. Tyler Van Kleef. The man wants it done yesterday. American, you know."

"Tell him I'm working on the sale."

"I'm going to tell him about expropriation. I'll talk to Grant today about it." MacAllister opened the door and walked out. Matthews, following him, saw Millie scurry away from the key hole.

Grant MacKay, the Member of the Provincial Legislature for Elgin County, farmed one hundred acres of corn and barley, with a herd of Holsteins, on the Union Road, five miles south of town. MacAllister drove fast, leaving a cloud of dust trailing behind him, until he turned off the gravel road and up the farm lane. MacKay was sitting on the porch, on a wooden swing. On the table was a pitcher of lemonade and two glasses. MacAllister chuckled; the lemonade was a ruse. MacKay was usually drunk before noon, and he liked to think that nobody knew. But George MacAllister knew. He knew everything there was to know about anyone who mattered in Elgin County. He knew that although there was lemonade on Grant's table, somewhere, within easy reach, would be a bottle of rye whiskey.

"Cousin George." MacKay was weaving on his feet, red-faced, flashing his country-boy grin. MacAllister frowned; he did not like Grant MacKay or his smile.

"Grant, good day to you." He sat in a wooden chair across from the swing, fanning himself with his straw fedora. "Kind'a hot for April."

"She's a scorcher. Have a glass of Marjory's lemonade."

MacAllister sipped at the lemonade and watched MacKay watching him. There was wariness and confusion in the man's eyes. It's the drink in him, thought the lawyer, who never touched alcohol. Teetotaling, in the beginning a family tradition, had become a business strategy for him, keeping him sharp, a step or two ahead of drunks like MacKay. Furthermore, he had a copy of a police report of MacKay's adventures in the Ford Hotel in Toronto, caught in a room with an under-aged girl one July night two years ago.

"It's about the Russell land on the Lyndhurst Road at the highway. Matthews and I have been trying to get Margaret Ann to sell it to us. She won't, or she may not."

"No law against it, Cousin George. Free buyer, free seller, it's the democratic way."

"We need it for the land assembly for the road extension. We got our Yankee business man with a piss pot full of dollars waiting to put up his auto parts plant as soon as we can guarantee him a road. The Russell land is the last piece we need and we're going to get it. But we need it now, before Van Kleef decides he needs another location for his plant. Another town, another county, where the politicians know how to get things done."

"Geez, George, I'll talk to Margaret Ann if you think it will help."

"We've had enough talking. I want to expropriate."

"Expropriate." MacKay scratched his head. "Jesus, you have to show it's in the public interest to expropriate."

"Do you think a plant hiring five hundred people is in the public interest? With all these soldiers coming home looking for work?"

"Yeah, sure." MacKay was beginning to sweat. "George, it's getting kinda' late in the day and I wouldn't mind a nip. I know you don't touch the stuff, but let's just go out to the barn for a wee one." There was pleading in his eyes. "Marjory doesn't like it, so I keep it out of sight."

They walked behind the house, past lilacs in bloom at the side door, to the wooden barn. Inside the main door there was a bale of hay to one side. Burrowing into the hay, MacKay pulled out a bottle of whiskey, uncorked it and took a gulp. He sighed with relief. MacAllister watched him, his nose wrinkling.

"There," said MacKay, wiping his mouth and looking red-faced and cheerful. "Now, let's discuss your problem."

"I need you to tell me how to get that land expropriated. That's what we pay you for."

"Right. So you got to do two things. First, you got to make it a public good. You got to give the government a position they can maintain. With all these jobs this plant will produce, it seems you'll be able to do that. The second thing is, you got to donate to the Party."

MacAllister spat on the ground.

"How much?"

"There's Party lawyers in Toronto. They get the money. About five thousand is what it would take."

"Shit. Five thousand dollars, for nothing. "

"Not for nothing, for the deal. And George, I'll have expenses of my own."

MacAllister's face hardened. "You're up for re-election this June. With the Party's support you should make it. However, if people understood everything you've been up to down there in Toronto with that little girl...." MacKay's eyes bulged. "Forget expenses. I want you to make this deal go through."

"Sure, George." MacKay was laughing nervously. "Listen, George, I appreciate your support all these years. Shit, it's the support of good men like you that make a career in politics the rewarding and enjoyable life that it is."

MacAllister sneered and began to walk away.

"Cousin George, why don't you cut Margaret Ann in on the deal? If there's money to be made, give her some of it. Avoid expropriation. Not so messy and maybe a lot cheaper."

"If we do that, and Bobby Russell comes home, then we would be dealing with him. We want it all tidied up before he comes back. If he comes back."

"No word from him, eh?"

MacAllister shook his head.

"That's a shame. He'll be missed around here." MacKay took another pull on his bottle; a far away look came into his eyes. "That boy was the best athlete this county ever produced. Do you remember that game against Strathroy, just before the war? Do you remember Bobby that night? He really won that game single-handed, batting four for four, with that big, red-headed, Scotch pitcher Strathroy had, throwing at his head. When he came to bat in the last inning, the score is tied and the bases are loaded, d'you remember?" MacAllister nodded, a genuine smile on his lips. "That pitcher has being trying to knock Bobby's brains out all night. Hit him with a pitch right on his shoulder the last time up. But Bobby comes to the plate and just stands there, not belligerent, that little smile he has on his face, looking the pitcher in the eye. Everybody knew what was going to happen. Even that dumb pitcher knew. He throws the first one at Bobby's head. Bobby ducks, and it's ball one. He throws the second one at his head and Bobby ducks again. Ball two. By that time everybody understands that the pitcher is afraid to pitch to Bobby. Sweat is pouring down his face. He turns to look at his coach but the coach just shrugs. He tries to throw Bobby a fast ball, but it's away outside. Ball three. Bobby stands up at the plate and smiles, knowing that the farmer can't defeat him. The pitcher gives it all he's got, gets a reasonable fast ball over the plate, and Bobby knocks it out of the park. And the thing was, everyone there that night knew it couldn't have ended any other way. That was Bobby Russell."

"He was quite a boy," said MacAllister grimly.

"Seems a pity, a boy with that kind of talent ending up as a lawyer." The man looked at MacAllister. "Sorry, George, no offence. But he was something. To see him playing the wing in hockey, swooping down the ice, with that graceful little hip swing he had, cutting towards the goal, with a shot like canon fire. It doesn't seem possible that some German soldier-boy could put an end to him just by squeezing his trigger."

MacKay took another swig. MacAllister turned away.

"I've got to go. Grant, figure out this expropriation. Get yourself down to Toronto next week, and come back with the who's and the why's and the wherefores by Friday."

"Cousin George, you can count on me."

Allan Matthews drove his blue Ford along the Lyndhurst Road, glancing frequently at Margaret Ann, who stared impassively out the window. "Turn here," she said when they reached the bridge just past the Russell farm house on the main Lyndhurst Road. The sun shone through the maple and elm branches that arched over the road, brushing the roof of the car. They passed the little school that Margaret Ann had attended as a girl, passed the shack where some of the poorer farmers were rumoured to distill corn whiskey in the winter, till they came to the Russell fields. They turned in the drive to the wooden house that the MacQuiggan family had rented from the Russells since the twenties. The grey clapboards showed only traces of white paint. There was a hole in the screen door, the porch was sagging, and the lawn, unmown, was littered with an old mattress, a bicycle without wheels and other discarded junk. Calvin MacQuiggan was sitting on the porch, staring at the car as it approached. Beside him a small girl, naked and smeared with dirt, played with her plastic rattle.

"What rent d'you charge them?"

"Usually nothing. But Archie's late with the ploughing."

They passed the house and pulled over a hundred yards further down the road. Out in the field the stout figure of Archie MacQuiggan sat on the plough seat, his broad buttocks spilling over its sides, flicking the reins over two big farm horses as they pulled the plough up and down the rows.

"Do you have a tractor?" asked Matthews.

"Archie won't use it. He says you can't really plough a field with a tractor. Horses have a feel for the land."

MacQuiggan stopped, got slowly down from his seat, spoke to the horses, and then walked to the fence.

"Good day, Missus Russell, Mr. Matthews." He wiped the sweat from his eyes. "Sure is a hot one."

"Archie, you're late with this ploughing. Everybody else has their land mostly done by now."

The big man looked away from Matthews' gaze and kicked at the soil.

"This here's a wet piece of land, Mr. Matthews. You can't rush the ploughin' on this here land. But I got a good team. We'll have her ploughed in, oh, a day or two more...."

"Just keep out of the beer parlour, Archie. Some of these rows aren't that straight. Mrs. Russell is counting on you."

"I don't have to be sober to plough straight." The big man laughed and his belly shook. "It's the wet soil. It's hard pullin' for the animals, so they tend to want to go sideways. It's a bugger keepin' 'em straight when it's this wet. An' I got Calvin to help me out, if I get pissed. Don't you worry none."

They drove in silence back to the Russell house for tea.

"Archie worries me." Matthews was sitting on the horsehair-covered chair. "He's drunk most of the time."

"But what am I to do?" She poured the tea. "I can't manage the farm on my own and Archie's the only available man now, with the war."

"No word from Bobby?" He sat straight in his chair, smoothing his hair unconsciously with his hand.

"He tried to call me last week. I know it."

"It may be so. But there are so many other things that call could have been." His face was tender, his silk tie straight. "The best thing for you is to sell. You won't have to worry about Archie being sober, or what you'll get for your crops. I can get a price for you that will leave you comfortable for as long as you live."

She set down her tea cup.

"I may sell," she said. Matthews' eyes grew narrow. "But I need more time. Give me a month. If nothing has happened by then…."

He struggled to keep his disappointment hidden.

"Take your time, my dear; this is a big decision. You know I'll do anything I can to help you. You're much more than a client to me."

He smiled; his blue eyes sparkled.

"Allan, you take good care of me."

"I'd do more if I could." She looked away. "You're a handsome woman, Margaret Ann. I wish you'd sell this farm and come with me on a little trip. Virginia or Palm Beach."

She smiled. "You are a rascal, but I am flattered. When this is all over, a little jaunt somewhere might be just what I need. But let's start with the Stork Club Saturday night."

"I'll pick you up at seven-thirty."

He embraced her lightly. She smiled as she showed him out the door. He cranked up the Ford and backed down the drive.

"I've got her," he said to his windscreen. "If we can wait a month, I've got her."

11.

"That man is divine. His voice makes me shiver."

"If only it were in English," said Jean. "I simply can't understand a word."

"Jean," hissed Susan.

The two were sitting in the flat of Rose MacIlwain and Helen Partridge, listening to Feodor Chaliapin sing the death scene from Moussorgsky's *Boris Goudonov*. The girls had kept in touch with Miss MacIlwain, who had taught them both English at the Collegiate. Helen was setting out plates of seed cake and biscuits. Rose sat with her eyes closed. At the climax of the opera Tsar Boris fell to the earth, the music softened and faded away.

"It's Shakespeare, you know," Rose said finally. "He based it on *Richard III*. Killing the prince, everything. But so gorgeous in Russian."

"It sure isn't Frank Sinatra," said Jean.

"Please, Jean." Rose's lipped were pursed. "In this room, with these dear girls, music must be sublime. God knows there's little enough good taste in this town. Tell them about your library board meeting, Helly."

"They won't let me buy poetry or fiction this year. They cut all the literature from my list. They may let me buy some fiction next year, but the Reverend Campbell Fitch would like to see me complete our Dickens holdings. He's very fond of Dickens, considers him a moral writer."

Rose threw up her arms. "Who's on the board, Helly? Besides Fitch."

"George MacAllister, the lawyer, Edward Kennedy, the Collegiate principal, and Somerville, who owns the feed store on Talbot Street. MacAllister's the worst. Every year he tries to cut my budget; he thinks books are an extravagance."

"Now, what are your plans for next year, girls?" Rose's voice was strict. "Nothing ordinary, I hope."

"If the war is over, Daddy is going to rent me an apartment in Manhattan so I can study painting at Parsons," said Jean.

"Gorgeous. The life of an artist requires passion and a sense of design and beauty. Passion you have, my dear, but a sense of beauty in this world would complete you. You must study to achieve it. Your problem will be men. They make girls stupid and distract them from the finer things."

Jean frowned. "What's wrong with men who like cars and sex?"

Susan giggled. Rose stood up from her chair, holding her glass in her hand. "Because such men are ordinary; you can find them on any street corner, should you be so inclined. Whatever you do, my dear Jean, don't be ordinary."

"Men make the money." said Jean. "And money will send me to New York. And it pays for your Russian music."

"Rose can forget that all of us don't inherit," said Helen.

"Don't be boring, Hellie." Rose's eyes were annoyed. "And now Susan, the quiet one. Have your marks come?"

"Yes. They are firsts and seconds. They would get me into the College of Education, but I'm not sure I want to be a teacher."

"Susan has to wait," said Jean. "To find out about Bobby."

"Bobby who?" said Rose tartly.

"Bobby Russell. He's missing in action; no one has heard of him. He and Susan were…." Jean shrugged. "She has to find out."

"I taught Robert Russell. A very bright boy, but insolent." Rose watched Susan's face. "So the handsome soldier leaves you waiting for his return." She shook her head. "Men have been doing that since time began. Don't sit, Susan, waiting for your life to begin again."

"Rose!" Helen Partridge's voice was stern. "Don't you pay attention, Susan. Rose forgets herself."

"I only mean," said Rose in a quieter tone, "that you should not take the conventional way."

"But who was it, Rose, who insisted that we tramp all over that Greek island, whatever its name was, looking for the exact place where Byron died fighting for Greek liberty? You like soldiers, if they have the right style."

"Bobby had style," said Jean. "No matter what he did, if you were around him you felt something good was happening."

Susan smiled. "I have to find out, one way or another. Bobby wanted to go to war. Bobby was not stupid. I don't know." She sighed. "In the meantime, I have to get home. Mother's fixing my dress for Saturday night at the Stork Club."

"The Stork Club?" Rose's sharp eyes fixed on Susan.

"Nice girls wouldn't be caught dead in the Stork Club, and Susie, at least, is a nice girl." Jean winked at Susan. "But Allan Matthews has asked Margaret Ann to go dancing Saturday night, and Susie and I have promised to chaperone."

"Insensitive men, sleazy music and bad liquor," said Rose. "That's your future if you stay in St. Thomas."

"Come with us on Saturday night, Miss MacIlwain. We'll get that bachelor farmer out at Sparta to dance with you. You'd love it."

"Don't be ridiculous." She moved to the Victrola and put on a record; Jussi Bjorling sang 'Nessun Dorma' from *Turandot*.

12.

The Stork Club was only half full. This early in the year the nights were cool and the crowd was sparse. Mayor Al Parker swung his wife, dancing cheek to cheek. Susan and Jean sat at the table next to their parents, the Robsons and the MacLeans. Beside Jean, Will Matthews slouched in his chair, his face red and his speech slurred. When the song ended Allan Matthews and Margaret Ann returned to their chairs.

"You two look good out there," said Jean.

Margaret Ann's laugh drew smiles from the surrounding tables. "I haven't had so much fun in ages. I don't know why all of St. Thomas isn't here dancing."

The Stork Club drew its clientele from the more sophisticated people in the towns within driving distance. London, Woodstock and Ingersoll were big enough to support lawyers and bank managers, men with summer suits, two-toned shoes and a taste for handsome wives and the light life.

"Here comes Vince Malone," muttered Allan Matthews.

Malone was a big man, well over six feet, wearing a white dinner jacket, black tie, black trousers and black patent leather shoes. His hair was slicked back and he grinned habitually from under a large nose, crooked from many breakings. His club had no liquor licence, but he looked the other way if patrons brought bottles and kept them out of sight. The rumour was that Vince had been a prizefighter in the thirties and had bought the Stork Club with his winnings. Others said that he had been a rum-runner during prohibition, organizing the Port Stanley fishermen to cross the lake at night to Cleveland with cargoes of forbidden booze.

"You folks enjoying yourselves?" He spoke in a gravelly baritone.

"Everything is dandy, Vince," said Allan. "Good band."

"Yeah, ain't they. Boys are from Detroit, here for two weeks. We got Benny Goodman comin' in late June, and Guy Lombardo in August. Tell your friends." A blond singer was now standing in front of the microphone singing 'I've Got You Under My Skin'. "Listen, Al, I got to see your partner, MacAllister. Tell him Vince'll be phonin' Monday. Some things we got to discuss."

"Anything I can help with?"

Vince smiled his lopsided smile. "I don't think so, Al. Now you folks enjoy yourselves."

Back at his table, Will reached under the table, brought out a paper bag and poured rum for himself and Jean. When her parents were looking the other way, Susan held out her glass.

"How many have you had, Will," asked his father.

"I'm fine." The boy was leering at Jean. He poured Coca Cola into his glass and took a quick swallow.

Allan and Margaret Ann went back to the dance floor. The band was playing 'Blue Moon'.

"Not a man under fifty," said Jean. "Except Will."

"Susan, that band leader has been watching you."

"Don't you dare say that." Susan turned her gaze to the band stand. Gene Henderson, a tall, dark-haired man in a white dinner jacket, smiled and waved his baton.

"There, you see. He smiled at you."

"He was just being a band leader. They have to smile."

"He's been watching you all night. We have to discuss this. Susan and I are going to the ladies', Will. Don't pass out."

"I won't." Will pounded the table.

The two crossed the dance floor, moving close to the bandstand. Henderson bowed as they passed.

"You see, I was right," whispered Jean.

They didn't go to the ladies' room. They went through the glass doors that led to a verandah that overlooked the beach and Lake Erie. The night was cool; the lake sparkled under the moon.

"It must be cool, but I don't feel anything," said Susan.

"It's the rum."

Down to their left the moon shone on the pier and on the fishing boats moored alongside. At the end of the pier a lighthouse sent its revolving beam now over the water, now over the land. They could see in the darkness red dots, the cigarettes of people strolling on the beach.

"Oh, Suse. I want a man tonight. But there's nobody here."

"Just any man?"

"Just about. I need some loving." Susan stared at her. "Don't look at me like that. It's normal. Didn't you and Bobby ever...?"

"Sort of."

"What do you mean sort of?"

"Well, you know. Don't you worry about getting pregnant?"

"I can't believe you. Don't you know about rubbers?"

Susan blushed. "Well yeah, I guess. So that's what you do?"

"Really, Susan. The guys have them. Will probably won't, so I have them with me." Susan looked shocked. "Yeah, I know. Well, I'm desperate. I'm going to give Will Matthews the night of his life."

Susan watched the lighthouse beam sweep the beach. The rum and the music were in her ears, in her legs and arms. She wanted to dance. She thought a man would be a good thing. The next time the beam lit her face she laughed out loud.

"But what about me?"

"You're on your own, Susie. Let's go back. Will's afraid to ask me to dance so he's getting drunk. Watch me stiffen him up."

As they crossed the dance floor, Susan caught Gene Henderson's eye and smiled. He smiled and nodded. Oh my, she thought, am I ready for this?

Will was alone when they reached their table. Jean pulled her chair closer to his. "Will." She laid her hand on his. "Susan and I were just complaining that no man seems to want to dance with us. Are we so unattractive?"

Will gulped. "Do you want to dance…?"

"I've been waiting for you to ask me all night. I'd adore to."

As they faced each other, Jean drifted into his arms. Will grabbed her, and started to circle the floor, holding her close. Jean winked at Susan, then put her hand behind Will's head and whispered into his ear.

"Excuse me, Miss." The waiter was looking down at her. "Mr. Gene Henderson sees that you are alone and wonders if you would like to join him." Susan looked over and saw Henderson sitting at the table by the bar with Vince Malone and the girl singer. He smiled at her. "Okay," she said. Without looking at her parents' table she followed the waiter across the floor. Henderson got to his feet.

"You looked all alone, so why not sit with us? This is our chanteuse, Shirley Damato, Vince Malone, owner of the club, and I'm Gene Henderson."

"I'm Susan MacLean." She said, and sat down.

"You from here, honey?" The singer had a pock-marked face, with scarlet lipstick and thick blue eye shadow.

"Yes. My father publishes the newspaper in St. Thomas."

"St. Thomas. That near here?"

"Just north of here."

"What's it like, living in St. Thomas?"

"Oh, it's all right. It's really quiet now, what with the war and all."

"Not enough guys, is that what you mean?" Shirley laughed."I dunno, honey, maybe you should count yourself lucky."

Henderson winked. "Shirley's been married so many times she's lost count. Even with a war on she turns them up. What's your secret, Shirl?"

"No taste whatsoever. Listen, I got to do a number."

She got up and went to the microphone, and joined the band. Vince Malone left to go behind the bar.

"Doesn't the band need you leading them?" she asked.

"No." He smiled. He was dark and slender. His hair curled over his ears and his dark eyes laughed at her. "They can play this stuff without me. I do my real work when we rehearse; give them the charts, do the arranging. You like our music?"

"I love it."

"We'll be here two weeks. Maybe you'll drop by again."

"Sure. You guys are great."

Henderson watched her, amused. She felt his eyes on her.

"Let's dance," he said.

On the dance floor she nestled into his arms. He felt good, his arms felt good. She pressed against him; there were tears in her eyes. This was life, finally. Jean passed her, with Will draped around her neck. The band paused. Henderson was looking at her, intrigued.

"How much have you had to drink?"

"Don't worry about it."

Shirley began 'The Boogie Woogie Bugle Boy of Company B' and they started to jitterbug. He swung her wide and she moved her feet and threw her arms up in the air. The drummer started a solo riff and she jived to his beat. Henderson stood and watched her. When the riff ended the floor applauded. The band started a slow, dreamy arrangement of 'Misty'. She moved back into his arms

"I love this," she said, her head on his shoulder.

"I'm only here for two weeks," he said, holding her tight. "We've got a gig in Toronto, the Royal York Hotel. Maybe you could come up there. I'd really like to see you again."

"I'd adore to," she said.

When the song ended, they went back to the table by the bar.

"You're quite a little dancer, honey," said Shirley.

The band leader was looking fondly at her.

"Susan." Her mother stood by the table. "We're leaving."

Susan heard the command in her mother's voice. She rose.

"Nice meeting you, Susan," said the band leader. "Hope to see you again."

The two women walked across the dance floor.

"Susan, what on earth were you doing, making a display of yourself like that? Really! Are you sure you're all right?" Susan nodded. "We're driving Allan and Margaret Ann home."

Susan nodded but said nothing. Outside the spring air was cool on her skin; she felt light and full of laughter. She got in the car with dance music in her ears.

"Your son and Jean certainly hit it off tonight," her mother said to Allan Matthews in her critical, I-know-what's-going-on voice.

"They'll never be young again." Allan's laughing eyes turned to his date. "Although, Margaret Ann, you're younger than these kids."

She giggled. They drove home slowly, watching the moon flicker through the elms along the highway, glistening off humps of cows sleeping in the pastures.

"Nothing from Bobby, Margaret Ann?"

"Nothing recent."

There was silence in the car.

PART III

Return

13.

HE TURNED BEFORE HE WAS AWAKE and saw the dark shadow of a woman sitting on the side of his bed, the woman of his dreams. He had seen her so many times, standing beside a road leering at him or rising from the waters of a lake fresh in the morning. There was no time when she was not near, hovering at the edge of his mind.

With a start he woke himself and turned on the bed lamp. Eleanor was sitting on the side of his bed; she had been watching him sleep. His watch read four o'clock. When he looked at her he could not see the features of her face, only the gleaming red of her lipstick and her hair shining in the lamp light. He lay still and watched.

"How are you, Bobby?" she asked, sweetness in her voice.

"I'm going home today," he said.

The room was silent. He tried to see her face, but there was only shadow.

"But I love you." He looked away. "You'd work in Father's firm, run for the Conservatives down in...."

"St. Thomas."

"St. Thomas. We were going to...."

Her voice was faded.

"I'm going home."

She shifted so the light fell on her face. Her eyes were empty and the elegant body seemed to shrink.

"I took you into this house, into my bed, there was nothing you

93

couldn't have. And now I'm just a body to you. No, not even that; a corpse, dead meat."

"When we met, I was going home." He hoped she couldn't see his smile. "And today I'll continue on my way."

She rose from the bed, fury in her eyes.

"You're a drunk. And maybe a queer."

He shrugged. "All the more reason for me to go."

She started to cry.

"You can't go now; there are no trains this late," she blubbered. Russell got out of bed and began to pull on his clothes. "For God's sake, take me with you. Don't you see, I've got to get out of here, this insane family … everything. I'll do anything, Bobby. Please take me."

"It's not late, it's early. I'm going to pack my bag, and then we'll go and get some breakfast."

They walked down Yonge Street. The stores were dark; there was still no hint of daybreak. From downtown they heard the clang of the first trolley of the new day. A milk wagon plodded down the street, the milkman half asleep on his seat. They walked slowly, the soldier carrying his bag with his right hand, the girl leaning on his left shoulder, her arm around his waist. In an all-night restaurant just off Yonge Street were cab drivers, two policeman, some nurses from the Hospital for Sick Children talking quietly, and the smell of coffee and bacon. They sat and faced each other; there were tears in her eyes.

"Perhaps you'll come back."

"I don't know what I'll do," he said. "There is the dairy."

"And your girl."

"That was a long time ago."

She couldn't eat her omelet. She pulled a tissue out of her purse, wiped her eyes and smiled at him, a sad little smile. He glanced at his watch; he wanted to leave on the train for London. Already her house and her family were memories. But he could not walk away from her. They talked and were silent, talked and were silent, not seeing the new day arrive until he looked out the window and saw people going about their business, and traffic in the street. It was too late to make the ten o'clock train; he would take the five o'clock. He paid the check and they walked out into the new day. For the next few hours they walked around the city, holding hands. They took the ferry to Centre Island and stood looking back at the city: the towers of the Imperial Bank Building and the Royal York Hotel. They returned to the city harbour by four.

"I'm going to the station," he said.

They were facing each other on the ferry dock. She put her hands on his cheeks and kissed him. He embraced her and she pressed against him; his desire for her returned. She leaped back and laughed.

"You want me," she said. "You still want me."

She turned and walked off the dock.

❁

When the train pulled out Russell slouched in his seat. He kept one hand around the bottle in his bag, staring out the window as they passed through Toronto's western suburbs: New Toronto, Mimico and Long Branch. He saw factories with dirty windows and rows of little houses. There were men in blue coveralls walking home from their shifts, carrying their lunch pails. Did they have a dining car on the night train to London? He couldn't remember. He wanted a drink.

At Port Credit, a stocky, well-built woman entered his coach with an infant and two older children, and took the seats just in front of him. The older two were under five, both blond, a girl in a flowered dress and canvas shoes and a boy in a tee shirt and shorts.

They annoyed him. He reached in the bag, got the bottle out and drank. It was something about the mother. After settling the two older ones she took a bottle from a thermos bag and started to feed the infant. Her breasts strained at her blouse; the baby was tiny, a new-born. The mother had blond curls down the side of her head, and a slash of red lipstick over thick lips. To him, she was one of those women who just ploughed ahead, had their babies and dealt with their kids unawares, as if that was all you had to do, as if the world would take care of everything else. He sucked on his bottle.

The world does not care. Having babies is not enough.

He fell asleep. When he awoke, the mother and her children were gone, and the train was rolling through farm country. The conductor passed by, told him that there was a dining car and that the next stop was Woodstock. He began to watch the towns and farms slip past. The sun was low and the shadows were long. He took another drink and began to feel good again. The train passed through a nameless town. The main street slipped by, with its three-story brick buildings and wooden telephone poles. There were side streets lined with solid brick houses with wooden porches under elms and maples. He glimpsed briefly a grey-haired couple sitting on a porch drinking tea. He could imagine the tone of their conversation and the flowers growing in their garden.

At Woodstock, a bearded Mennonite man in a black suit and his woman in her grey dress, apron and bonnet, entered the coach. Then came a farmer, thin reddish hair combed neatly over the skull, sunburned hands and red face covered in freckles, awkward in a blue suit. Two salesmen in better suits, carrying their cases, sat telling jokes. Russell gulped more whiskey and chuckled. He forgot about the dining car.

The train stopped a mile outside of Ingersoll and waited while a farmer drove his hay wagon over the tracks, sitting on the box and holding the reins, clucking to the horses. Russell stared; the scene reminded him of a day when he went out with Archie MacQuiggan and his brother on a hay wagon to harvest, when he was eight or nine. The men had forked the mown hay into the wagon for hours, sweating under the August sun. But that had been harvest-time and this was April. This farmer must be moving his hay from one place to another. He watched the wagon turn from the gravel road and head towards a wooden barn, surrounded by silhouettes of elms in the dusk. The engine started with a lurch and the barn and the farmer disappeared.

The train moved through the farm country, lush shadows falling over seed-laden fields and rail fences. As night fell, the straight gravel roads dimmed. He could smell the spring soil and he could hear the swallows, and the horses' hooves thudding on dirt lanes. Tears came to his eyes. The fields and the beeches and elms were fading into shadows. The houses were lit against the night and the dark silhouettes of the barns stood alone in the fields.

Oh my, oh my, where have I been?

He changed trains at London, boarding the London & Port Stanley which would take him to St. Thomas. He recognized the ticket-taker on the L & PS, Bill Shoeck, whose father used to farm near Talbotville. Shoeck nodded briefly at Russell as he punched his ticket and passed on without looking. Russell felt like a boy hiding from his parents, trembling to be found. Surely someone would recognize him. He took a seat in the front coach across from a couple he knew, Al MacEachern and his wife, who had sold their milk to the dairy before the war. They looked at him and looked away. Down the coach was a group of boy scouts with their leader, whom he recognized as Jim Gillroy, the youth coordinator at First United Church. Gillroy didn't recognize him. At the far end of the coach were three other men he knew, Albert Greaves, James MacTaggart and Wilfred Penhale, merchants in St. Thomas, talking in low, gravelly voices about commodity prices, which were too low, and local taxes, which were too high. They were heavier and greyer than he remembered. They didn't look at him. Now the world outside his window was dark and all he could see was the lights in the houses, surrounded by night. It was ten o'clock when they pulled into St. Thomas.

Russell was the last to leave the train. He stood on the sidewalk of Talbot Street, his bag in his hand. Across the street was the Grand Central Hotel. Down the street to the east there had been a taxi stand, Art's. He decided to take a taxi out to the farm. He walked past the familiar stores, Henry's Books and Stationery, Pincombes' Meats and Poultry and MacPhail's Quality Hardware. He passed the Times Journal offices. The front page from the day's edition was in the window. 'Drew Defies Liberals', read the headline. 'Our Boys Home by Fall', read a lesser line.

"Looking for somebody, soldier?"

The voice was challenging. He looked and recognized Gus Campbell, one of the town's constables, who had come up beside him. He didn't answer.

"We've had more than enough goddam broke soldiers passing through here on the make. You cause any trouble an' I'll be on your tail so fast...." The man saw Russell's face under the street light and froze. "Holy Geez, if it ain't Bobby Russell."

"Hello, Gus," he said.

The constable's face broadened to a happy grin.

"Lord, Bobby, you're home. Are the other boys with you?"

"No, they're still in Germany, sorting things out."

"What are you doin' here this late at night?"

"I just got off the train. Gonna head home."

"You hang on a minute and we'll have a police vehicle for you, drive you right to the farm."

"No thanks, Gus, I want to walk a while, maybe all the way."

"Okay, Bobby. Geez, it's good to see you." He paused. "Say, you gonna play hockey for us this year?"

"Don't know."

He shook the man's hand and walked on along the empty street. Soon the town would know he was home; Gus would spread the word. It was night and Talbot Street seemed small and quiet. He had imagined coming home in daylight, being met at the train. The buildings on the street annoyed him; they were so quiet, so ordinary. He tensed a little. He had watched through his binoculars as streets like this collapsed into dust. He heard the sound of guns, but there were no guns here, no one was running, no one was screaming. He had to get home. Taxi. Except there was no taxi. Before he came to Art's he came to the Confederation House. He had never entered the men's room of the Confederation House, nor had his father, but he wanted a drink. He walked through the door into the light and the smell and the roar of raucous male voices.

14.

The telephone rang in the parlour. Margaret Ann Russell lay down her Times Journal and picked up the receiver.

"Margaret Ann, it's Marie. Brace yourself." Margaret Ann froze, waiting for the words she had dreaded, but Marie said, "Bobby's home."

At first she stood without speaking, trying to make sense of the words she had heard. Then she became furious.

"That is nonsense. If he were here he would have phoned me."

"Margaret Ann, it's true." The indomitable voice crackled. "Gus Campbell saw him on Talbot Street not an hour ago."

"That's ridiculous." She slammed the receiver down, lowered her head, and let the tears come.

❈

Russell stood in the glare of the bare light bulbs in the men's room of the Confederation House. Straight ahead, Archie MacQuiggan was sitting at a table with three other men who had been wounded and sent home. Jim Gillespie was telling a joke and the other three were listening, red-faced and bleary, ready to pound the table and roar. The room was rocking with laughter and argument. It reeked of the urine in pools on the floor of the men's toilet.

"It's our Captain Russell." MacQuiggan recognized him. He was standing at his table. "Jesus, boys, it's Captain Russell."

As Russell walked to their table the men rose to their feet. Gillespie tried to salute but poked himself in the eye. Russell shook the hand of each man by turn. Alfie Becker came over with a tray of beer and put four glasses on the table in front of Russell.

"These beers is on the house, Bobby. Welcome home."

Instantly there was a circle of chairs around their table, men in work pants and heavy boots, thick necks and thick wrists, gawking at Russell, slender, neat, almost fragile in his battle dress.

Archie raised his glass. "You should have seen the Captain outside this two-bit little Eyetye town in Sicily, called Trefalu. Them Germans was a-pastin' us from the town, so the Captain, he takes a squad and goes around to the north of the town and walks right down the main street, like he was walkin' down Talbot Street on market day, and comes in behind the German command post without them seein' him. So he says to the German officer, 'Excuse me, Sir, we have you surrounded, hands high, *hander hoch*'. And they did put their hands up and surrendered then and there to the St.Thomas and Elgin Highlanders. Without us firin' a fuckin' shot."

The men roared. That was Bobby Russell. The cleverness of it, the elegance of it. Like him sweeping in from left wing on the ice in the arena, turning the defense and beating the goalie with a shift of his hips and a flick of his wrist, and there, look at that, the puck was in the net. They had all seen him do it.

In the midst of the cheers and congratulations he felt more and more perplexed. The rest of his men should all be here, drinking the beer and getting pounded on the back. But as the time passed he lingered. The town, the fields and back roads that he had dreamt of for the last three years were now all around him, and in the tavern, as the beer flowed, he felt safe.

The hotel closed at midnight. His mother would be asleep by now in their house just down the road. No point going home now. The men stumbled and weaved their ways out into the night. Archie picked up his bag. "Come on, Captain, we'll walk 'er." Outside, standing on the sidewalk waiting for his father, was Calvin MacQuiggan, forlorn in his father's boots and shirt.

"Mam told me to get you home," he said without expression.

"Shut up, I'm comin' home. This here's Captain Bobby Russell, home from the war."

Calvin stared silently. Russell remembered a tiny boy of three or four, one of many MacQuiggan children, often in their barn, playing in the hay loft. They walked west along Talbot Street until the pavement ended and they were on the Lyndhurst Road. The road sank down into the valley of Kettle Creek, the full moon was silver.

They crossed the creek at the bottom of the hill and came to Jim Robilliard's farm. A dog barked from the farm house porch. They kept walking, not saying a word, Calvin trudging along twenty feet behind.

"Have the fields been sown?"

There was a pause; he didn't think Archie had heard him.

"Yeah, Captain. She's almost done. Little wet this year, so we're a bit behind where I'd like us to be. Give me two days of dry weather, and we'll do 'er."

Even at night Russell could see the ploughed furrows in the fields of the other farms beside the road.

"How's business at the dairy?"

"I wouldn't know nothin' about that. Ask Mrs. Russell."

They passed several more farms – MacKenzies', Grahams' and Summervilles' and next was Russells'. He could see by the light of the moon that almost a third of the first field had not been ploughed. He saw the dark shape of the barn and beyond it, the house. They reached the lane. The mailbox still bore his father's name, Romaine J. Russell.

"Thanks, Arch. I'll probably see you in the morning."

"Good night, Captain. Calvin, get your ass in gear."

Russell walked slowly up the lane, staring at the house. The light was still on in his mother's room. His head was spinning and he did not want to bring her down. The swing seat, covered in orange and green striped canvas, was still on the porch. He put down his bag, took a cushion from the wicker arm chair and lay on the swing, rocking gently and staring up at the June moon. Soon he was asleep. Above him, in the front room on the second floor, the light went out.

15.

At four-thirty, the birds began to sing in the elm trees behind the house and the sky lightened in the east. The faint light crept over the fields, leaving the trees and buildings in shadow. At six-thirty the sun rose in full. Its rays brought out the green in the fields and caught the dew on the leaves of the apple tree in the front yard. An orange and white cat appeared from the side of the house and mounted the porch, mewing softly. Out on the road a truck appeared from the direction of Dorchester, heading for St. Thomas, leaving a plume of dust behind.

As the day began in Elgin County, the sleeper on the farm house porch was still. An hour later a door at the rear of the house opened and the cat sprinted around towards the sound, looking to be fed.

Eventually, the front door opened and Margaret Ann Russell came out to look at the morning sky. The first thing she saw was Calvin MacQuiggan, sitting on the lawn, his pants soaked with dew, staring at the porch. Then she looked down and saw the khaki-covered figure of her son sprawled on the swing seat, his mouth open, snoring lightly. She leapt back as if she had been hit, her hand on her heart. There he was, lying on the swing, sleeping, as if he had fallen from the sky. Her fine, handsome son, his black hair curly, the nice little pink lips, the straight nose, slightly flared at the nostrils. She looked closely and saw the patches at his elbows, the dirt on his boots and the lines at the corners of his eyes and mouth. Then she smelt the sour stink of yesterday's beer .

"Calvin," she called.

The boy rose from the lawn and approached several steps. She saw that he had a dark bruise on his left cheek.

"Do you know how he got here?"

"Me an' Pa brung 'im. From the Confederation House."

"Why aren't you at home?"

Calvin stared at the lawn. "Thought I'd watch 'im, just in case."

Russell shifted on the swing seat but did not wake. His mother stared at him and her relief turned to anger. She went into the kitchen, pumped a bucket full of water, brought it back and dumped it over him. He woke with a splutter and pulled himself up on the swing seat. Then he saw her.

"Hello, Mom," he said, without thinking.

She glared at him for half a minute, unable to speak.

"Where have you been?"

"In the war."

"I know that. Where were you last night?"

He shook his head and rose to his feet. The pain in his head was fierce. She stood beside him and grasped each shoulder, looking at his face. She saw the tired eyes; she hugged him close and began sobbing.

He put his arms around her."I was up town. It was late, I didn't want to wake you."

The first lie, she thought, smiling up at him. "You were drinking at the Confederation House," she said. "In all the years I knew your father, he never set foot in that place."

Bobby picked up his kit and walked into the house, his arm around his mother. Calvin watched them without expression. The man they called Bobby Russell had come home. Calvin didn't know what it meant, but he thought that it was good. He loved Bobby. When the door closed behind them, he turned and trudged down the lane.

Inside the house Russell stared at his father's black umbrella still leaning against the rim of the umbrella stand. She led the way to the kitchen and started preparing coffee. There was the familiar smell of gas from the kitchen oven.

"Are you hungry?"

"No. "

He sat at the table and watched her move from the stove to the sink, not speaking. She was angry that he hadn't phoned. But she wouldn't know about Toronto.

"It's good to be home," he said.

"Why didn't you phone me? How long have you been here?"

"I escaped about two months ago. Since then I've walked across Holland, talked my way onto transport home. It wasn't easy." He avoided her second question.

"Escaped from what?"

"From a prisoner of war camp. I told you in my letters."

"I haven't received any letters from you for almost a year."

"A year. That's about the time I was in the prison camp. I wondered why you never wrote me. Most of the men were getting letters from home."

"I wrote to the headquarters address in Holland. Nothing came back. I thought you were dead." A tear ran down her cheek.

"But the army knew. The Red Cross knew. The Ministry of Defense must have sent you a letter telling you I was a prisoner. They always do that."

"I never got it." She put the coffee on the table in front of him. "It doesn't matter now. You got through, you're alive. Have you phoned Susan?"

"No."

"You should. She may already have heard. Marie Barnes has been on the phone spreading the word. Jim Gillroy saw you on the L & P.S. last night and Gus Campbell saw you on Talbot Street."

"I'll walk up town. Go to her house."

"That reminds me, I have to be up at MacAllister and Matthews today at eleven to meet with Allan Matthews. He's got an offer for part of the farm, the fields where the MacQuiggans live. He thought I should sell it."

Russell turned to her.

"Where the MacQuiggans live? Why would we sell it?"

She looked uneasily at him.

"I didn't want to sell it. But they said I should. They said…."

"Do we need money?"

"No. We're fine."

He saw distress in her eyes.

"Why don't I go to the meeting at the lawyers?"

She smiled. "Do that, my dear. I've nothing more to say to them. Go and give them a surprise."

She began to clear the breakfast dishes away, humming. Her son finished his coffee and rose to his feet.

"Tom Allen has been very good at the dairy. He's run it more or less on his own, just checking with me when he had to spend some money. But with this business of selling the farm, I wasn't going to do anything until I heard about you. But if you weren't going to be here, I thought I would sell it."

And head off with Allan Matthews to Europe or Palm Springs, she thought. It wouldn't have been all bad.

"I'll go up to my room and find some other clothes."

"They're just as you left them. And have a bath."

He entered his room and saw, through the window, the apple tree, the barn and the fields that stretched back to Kettle Creek. In one corner of the room were a hockey stick and a pair of skates. Against a wall were bookshelves that held every book he had ever owned, from the boys' adventure books, *With Clive in India*, *With Wolfe at Quebec*, to his texts from law school.

He opened the closet to the smell of cedar wood and mothballs. His clothes hung neatly in a row, his shoes on the floor, and in a corner, two baseball bats. He lay on his bed. All around him was evidence of the person he had been, but it was as if the books, the clothes and the sports equipment belonged to someone else. He watched the sun streaming in the window and hitting the bedroom floor the way it had for every summer he could remember. His mother stood at the door.

"Give me those clothes you're wearing," she said. "And do get yourself dressed. You should leave soon."

He lay in the tub, pondering what she had told him. The land MacAllister and Matthews wanted had been in their family since the original settlement. His grandfather had built the house that Archie and his family were living in. He had helped Archie take the hay off those fields. In one corner there was a woods, with a creek running through it. He could see the creek in summer, with the water spiders and minnows skimming through sun and shadow, and the creek itself stretching back into the maple forest. Why did they want it? He lay back, let the water close over him and tried to imagine what it would be like to walk up town. They would come up to him in Talbot Street, slap him on the back and shake his hand. He didn't want their hands, their questions. He wanted the warmth of the bath and his bed.

Those are my hands, why do they look weird? Because I killed with them? No! They're weird because they're under the water. Mother doesn't know about my hands. She thinks I'm still her boy. And there's something about the sale of our land she's not telling me. That smile she has, when she doesn't want to be straight, wants to avoid you. I hate hiding, never facing what is. But then she smiles at me the way I remember, with her nose wrinkled and her eyes shining. Christ, I need a drink.

He strapped on his wrist watch; it was ten in the morning. He needed a clear head to talk to the lawyers. He'd take a nip after he got dressed, before he went up town, to take the edge off his nerves. As he shaved, the face in the mirror was flushed, with black circles under the eyes. His slacks and his jacket hung loose on him.

He opened his kit, took the bottle and drank.

In the kitchen Margaret Ann sat at the table waiting, playing with her hair. She wondered at the change in him. He obviously resented her interest, her questions, but she could remember him coming in after school and telling her about his day, sharing a joke, even in his last year of high school. She heard him thumping down the stairs.

"I'll get a haircut at Jack's, if he's still cutting hair, and then meet with the lawyers."

"Those clothes don't fit. We'll take them to Digby's in London and have them altered."

"They're all right." He was frowning.

"Aren't you rushing it? I could call the lawyers and reschedule the meeting."

"No." His voice was tense.

She saw that he couldn't wait to walk out the door.

"It's good to have you home," she blurted out.

"It's good to be home." He turned to her, uncertain, looking for words. "Mother, things have changed. A lot has happened. I hope…." He smiled. "I mean I think that, after a while…." He fell silent.

"I understand."

16.

Jean was waving from her booth when Susan entered the Malt Shoppe.

"Where have you been?" Susan said, as she slid into the booth. "I've been looking all over for you."

"Never mind that. I have the most amazing news." She stared out the window. "Look at that." She pointed to the street. "Who is that gorgeous-looking man walking up Talbot Street?"

Robert Russell in his white shirt, grey slacks and jacket, was walking down the middle of the street, followed at a space of twenty feet or so by Calvin MacQuiggan.

"It looks like Bobby," said Susan, her face white.

"It is Bobby," said Jean. "That's what I've been trying to tell you. He came home last night."

Russell passed by the window and continued down the street.

"He's alive," Susan murmured.

"He looks fabulous," said Jean.

Susan got up and ran to the street. She saw Bobby pass the old men sitting on the bench outside the feed store. They rose to their feet and began to follow him down the street. Susan also followed, her eyes riveted on his back. By the time he reached Jack Morris's Barber Shop there was a full procession, starting with Calvin, followed by the four old men from the feed store, and then Susan. Russell entered the shop. Jack Morris was standing by his chair, his white smock clean, his tiny mustache trim and his eyes twinkling behind his bifocals.

"Bobby," he said. "Long time no see. What'll it be?"

"A trim, Jack. Not too short on the sides and short at the back."

"I remember. Take a chair."

Russell chuckled, sat in the chair and stretched his legs. It had never been Jack Morris's way to approach a subject directly. He would stand by his chair, wielding his scissors, and let his patrons tell him what they knew, only occasionally asking a question. Russell looked around; the shop hadn't changed. Life Magazine and some baseball magazines lay on the table by the waiting chairs. Fly paper hung from the ceiling with two dead flies stuck to it. On the wall between the mirrors was a calendar from Liberty Farm Insurance Limited, showing a pretty blond girl on a swing under an apple tree. As the barber placed the towels around his neck, the old men from the feed store entered the room and took their places in the chairs along the sides, their eyes fixed on Russell.

"What are you fellahs doing in here," growled Jack. "You ain't due for a haircut, none of you."

"We came to see Bobby," said one.

"Hello, boys," said Russell. "It's been a while."

"Sure has," said another. "Guess you beat the hell out of them Germans, eh Bobby!"

"So they say, Fred," he said wearily. "So they say."

"Well look here," said the first. "We got some ladies callin'."

Susan and Jean were standing on the side walk looking in. The barber began to fidget. His shop was a centre of male society in St. Thomas, together with the Confederation House, the bench outside the feed store, and the hockey arena. The only women that entered his shop were mothers bringing their sons for a trim on Saturday mornings. The barber smiled as the women remained outside.

"Hello, Bobby," said Susan from the doorway.

"Hello, Susan."

The men swiveled their gazes from the barber's chair to the sidewalk.

"When did you get back?"

"Last night."

"Oh, I see." She looked at him without expression. "Well, are you all right?"

"I'm fine. I was going to phone you later on today…."

"Don't give it even one thought, it must be such a strain. I'll see you sometime. I won't be around for the rest of the day."

She turned quickly and strode back down Talbot Street to the Malt Shoppe. There was an air of relief in the barber shop.

"So tell us about it, Bobby," said one of the men. "What was it

108

like, fightin' them German fellahs."

Bobby shifted uneasily in his chair. The barber turned to the men, scissors raised.

"Leave him alone. The man's just got back home and he's all wore out. You want gossip, you head up to the beauty parlour and get your nails done."

The men watched as Jack lathered and shaved Bobby Russell. They saw the contours of his face emerge from the white foam, and the black shadows under his eyes.

"You gonna play baseball for the team this summer, Bobby?"

"I don't know what I'm going to do."

Bobby rose, paid the bill and walked out. On the sidewalk he found Calvin MacQuiggan, waiting for him.

"You'd better get back home, Calvin. Your mother will be wondering where you are."

Calvin did not answer, but followed him down Talbot to Erie Street. The offices of MacAllister and Matthews were in an old yellow brick house just around the corner from Talbot. He left Calvin sitting on the front steps and walked into the offices. Millie Hall's normally smug expression was rigid and grim-lipped. She looked angrily at one of the closed office doors before noticing him.

"Do you have an appointment?"

"I'm Robert Russell. My mother has an appointment and I'm taking it."

Her mouth fell in shock. "Mr. Russell! Good heavens, we had no idea. Back from the war."

She rose, knocked on MacAllister's door and entered the office. After several seconds George MacAllister emerged, his face flushed. He went to Matthews' office and entered without knocking, and without looking at Russell. Next, a statuesque blond woman came out of MacAllister's office, stenographic pad in hand, and followed MacAllister into Matthews' office. Millie was scowling and typing furiously.

Moments later, the blond secretary returned to the reception area and walked over to Russell.

"Captain Russell, Mr. MacAllister and Mr. Matthews will see you now."

As soon as Russell entered the office, Matthews rose to meet him, shaking his hand and clapping him on the back. "My boy, my boy, how wonderful to see you. Back safe and sound. Margaret Ann must be so relieved. How well you look."

There was a frantic note in the enthusiasm. Matthews kept making sidelong glances at MacAllister, who sat in his chair, watching Russell intently.

"So, Mr. Russell, welcome home," said MacAllister, rising briefly to shake his hand. "This is a surprise for us. How nice for your mother."

Russell looked at the tight smile on the lean, boney face and knew that MacAllister wasn't happy to see him. The lawyer's pale blue eyes blinked and flickered behind the pince-nez glasses.

"I understand you have been trying to get my mother to sell a piece of our land," Russell said finally.

There was silence in the room. Matthews looked at MacAllister, who kept his gaze fixed on Russell.

"We have an excellent offer for the land," MacAllister said. "We thought that it was in your mother's interest to sell."

"The land has been in our family since the beginning. Why would we sell it?"

"For money, Mr. Russell. Why does anyone sell anything?" His eyes remained fixed on Russell's face.

"The price is excellent, Bobby. Unheard of, in fact," Matthews added.

"We don't need the money."

"You don't need the land, either. You've got the dairy, and forty acres of good land on your main property." MacAllister's face was red, and his tone was flat and harsh.

"We'll decide whether we need that land. And I don't think much of you going after my mother while I'm away. The entire thing is fishy. Who wants this land?"

"The buyer prefers to remain anonymous," said MacAllister.

"I bet he does. Why does he want it?"

"That's no concern of ours, or yours. He wants the land for his own purposes."

"Bobby, we didn't put any pressure on your mother." Matthews' concern showed in his eyes. "We wanted the best for her."

"I see no reason to sell. We don't need the cash."

No one spoke. Matthews looked at MacAllister who, picking his teeth with the end of a paper clip, continued to stare at Russell.

"Captain Russell," he said finally, with a slight emphasis on the 'Captain.' "Where are your men?"

"In Germany."

"Yet you are here."

"I escaped from a German prison. I came home."

"Did you report to your regiment?"

Russell rose to his feet, struggling to remember.

"We're done here. Tell your buyer we're not interested."

He strode from the office. MacAllister scowled at his partner.

"Captain Russell doesn't look entirely well to me, Matthews, flushed about the face and wild in the eyes. I'd say he's into the sauce fairly well. Understandable. We put these boys under a lot of pressure. Nevertheless, Captain Russell doesn't look like he'd stand up to some real nut-cutting. For one thing, he may have deserted. What's he doing here? Does he have his discharge? I think we'll find out about that one."

"The boy's just back after three years fighting. Leave him alone."

"Tender sentiments. They give you credit with the ladies, no doubt, but they give you nothing with me. You've had your chance with the mother. Either there's something wrong with your approach, or she wants another stallion." MacAllister laughed and wheezed, took off his glasses and rubbed his eyes. "Tender sentiments were never my way. We're going to Grant MacKay to get expropriation started. I'm going to make sure the army knows where their captain is. We're going to get that land."

"This is going way beyond the practice of law, George."

"The law is a tool for those who know how to use it. But it's also a set of rules that favours some, not so much others. Let's make sure it's working for us. Furthermore, let's made sure that the environment outside the law is working for us. Captain Russell must not get in our way."

"We can't be too rough. The Russells are well-respected in St. Thomas."

MacAllister began to wipe his glasses on the sleeve of his jacket and chuckle. His eyes looked watery and his thin lips were purple.

"There's only one loose end, the mailman, Tom MacQuiggan, and those letters he swiped for us. We're exposed there, Matthews. I'll have to take care of that."

Matthews shook his head. "How much is this deal worth? How badly do we need it?"

"I need it. I want it. I'm going to get it." His laugh was bitter and cold. "You town boys don't know what it's like on a poor Scotch farm. I do. I've been there, and I'm never going back." He stopped talking until his anger cooled. "Now, Captain Russell interests me. On the surface, he's the handsome young officer, quite the spectacle to turn the ladies' hearts." There was venom in the flat voice. "But look beneath the surface and what do you see? He's shaky, not solid. Red in the face and blurred around the eyes, as if he's been boozing. A man like that shouldn't be in a position to decide about that property, with so many people affected, so many interests involved. He's weak, Matthews. He needs to be plucked."

MacAllister began scratching his ribs through his shirt.

"I want you to go out there one more time. Meet the two of them and this time quote them a figure. We've never done that before. Van Kleef will go ten thousand. Mention seven, maybe eight, to see what they do. Russell will turn it down, he won't sell. But keep the sales pitch going and be attentive to the mother, the way you have been. Business as usual. Now, on a different matter. How is Millie taking Grace?"

Matthews sat stroking his moustache. "She's sulking," he said. "She's not happy. She comes in, takes my dictation, and doesn't say a word."

"It's to be expected. Millie's run this office on her own for years. But we needed a real legal secretary. Grace can draft wills, commercial contracts, and can file at the court house for us."

"She's got quite a figure on her."

MacAllister patted his paunch. "Millie's not the woman she was and she's going to be riled at us bringing Grace in over her. Keep her happy, Matthews. Make sure … that she's attended to."

Matthews started to laugh. "I don't cuddle with the hired help, George, but I'll take her over to London for dinner. Help her get over you."

MacAllister ran his pink tongue over his purple lips and stared at his partner without any expression.

Russell walked back down Talbot Street with Calvin at his heels. The morning sunshine hurt his eyes. The men in front of the feed store waved and one called, "Welcome back, Bobby." He kept on walking. The town annoyed him. He thought of the malevolent expression on MacAllister's face as he asked about the other men of the regiment. Maybe he should have reported. He had reported to somebody, but not to the regiment. What had he been thinking? He couldn't remember. Right now, there was only his bottle.

"You goin' home?" asked Calvin.

"Yes, Calvin."

"What you doin' this afternoon?"

"Probably going to the dairy."

"Kin I come?"

He looked at the bruise still vivid on Calvin's head. There was no spirit in his face, just a fearfulness about the eyes.

"I guess. Doesn't Archie need you? Or your mom?"

"They don't need me."

"What do you do all day, Calvin?"

"Nothin' much. Sometimes I help Tommy with the mail, if he got a big load. Or I go fishin'. Or I walk up town and back."

"Where do you go fishing?"

"In the creek."

"What do you catch?"

"Nothin' much. Ain't fish in there. Only minnows."

Russell started to laugh. "Then why do you fish there?"

Calvin's face remained grave. "Because I like the minnows, the way they swim, like little arrows down there. And I like the way the sun shines on the water, if there ain't no clouds."

By the time they reached the farm, Russell was still smiling.

❀

He looked down at his bowl of tomato soup. His mother sat opposite him, sipping hers.

"So you don't want to sell?"

"No. Do you?"

"No." She shrugged. "They told me it was the best thing for me."

"There will be no more of that. I've told them the way it's going to be."

Margaret Ann was irritated by the pompous edge in his voice. The land didn't matter to her and she could see no reason not to sell it. The fields brought in little money and the MacQuiggans could be resettled. But she was annoyed by the way he had made up his mind as if she were barely present. She stroked her hair, wondering if Allan Matthews would still be coming around. Romaine had died in 1937; she had been a widow eight years.

"It's good to have a man around the house again."

Bobby grunted and kept sipping his soup.

17.

Valerie MacLean poured tea for Susan, for Jean and for Jean's mother, Ruth Robson. Ruth was a dark, sensuous woman, attractive despite the pounds that had given her a double chin and made her girdle bulge. It was four in the afternoon, and the women were sitting in the parlour of the MacLean house on Metcalfe Street. The ladies sat on green velvet chairs covered with lace antimacassars. There was a blue and orange machine-made Persian-style carpet, imported from Belgium; the walls were hung with wood-framed prints of the Eiffel tower, the Houses of Parliament at Westminster and various English and French cathedrals. Valerie was proud of the house she had decorated.

The Robson house on Margaret Street was acknowledged by everyone to be the first house in St. Thomas, however. Valerie struggled to keep envy from her thoughts, what with Ruth's unfair advantage, purchasing furnishings at cost through Robsons, their family department store. Life could be so unfair. On the table beside the teacups was a platter of cherry cake and butter tarts.

"So your man has come home, my dear," said Ruth Robson with the lift of an eyebrow.

"Robert Russell is not my man. Not anymore."

"Susan, he looks gorgeous." Jean rolled her eyes. "If you don't want him, give him to me. I have a position open."

"Jean." Her mother's tone was only mildly reproachful.

"I think you're being hard on him, Susan," said Valerie MacLean. "Those men have suffered for us."

"Not for me," Susan snapped. "They couldn't wait to get out of here."

"Now," said Ruth Robson, changing the subject, "I hear from Marie Barnes that Millie Hall is furious because MacAllister hired this legal secretary from London over her. Not only put her in charge, but wants her to take his dictation. And we all know what that means."

"I don't," said Susan. "Taking dictation is taking dictation."

"Not with MacAllister. Millie's been giving him what he wants for years." There was a scowl of either envy or disapproval on Ruth Robson's face.

No one spoke for several moments.

"Marie has more news." Ruth looked from face to face. "It seems that Bobby has told MacAllister and Matthews that he and his mother will not sell their land and the lawyers are very unhappy about it."

"Why would they care?" asked Valerie.

"Marie thinks they have some secret buyer. I think it must be someone from out of town. No one around here would buy it. It's poor land, only good for corn, according to Marie."

"And good for MacQuiggans," said Susan. "If it was sold, where would they go?"

"Enough of MacQuiggans, let's get back to men," said Jean. "What's Bobby going to do, now he's been dumped by Susan?"

Susan grimaced. "We're doing what women always do, talking about men."

Valerie smiled calmly. "Because men affect us, for better or for worse."

"Not me," said Susan. "I will not wait around for some man to give me a life."

Jean laughed. "I wouldn't mind getting out of town with a man by my side. Let's say to New York."

"Really, Jean." Her mother was affecting to be scandalized. "Valerie, we have to find husbands for these girls. Nothing else will answer."

"Well, we may not have long to wait," said Jean, looking out the window. "This looks like Bobby Russell coming up the walk." The women rushed to the window. Through the gauze they could see him mounting the steps to the front porch.

"Lord, Susan, he's coming here," screamed Jean, her hands to her face.

"Well, why shouldn't he come here?" Susan affected calm. "Our families have always been friends."

The doorbell rang. Valerie MacLean looked from face to face with a quiet smile, raised an eyebrow and went to the door.

"Why Bobby, how wonderful to see you looking so well. Susan told me you were back."

They walked to the living room. He stood in the doorway, smiling shyly.

"Come and sit beside me, Bobby, and have some tea," said Ruth Robson, raising the tea pot.

"Ruth and Jean, come out to the kitchen." Valerie turned. "I want to show you the recipe I'm planning for tomorrow."

Susan blushed. "Don't leave. Bobby must have lots of war stories to tell and he needs an audience. I'll go and help Mother."

"Susan, we're going." Ruth spoke in a firm voice. "Come on, Jean." She grabbed Jean by one arm and hauled her to her feet.

The women left and they were alone. Susan stared at the floor, her lips pursed.

"I wanted to say hello properly, Susan. It's been a long time."

"Well, hello to you."

He shifted uncomfortably in his seat.

"I wanted to tell you how I came home, and why I didn't phone."

"What makes you think I'm interested?"

"Well...." He stumbled for words. "We used to be friends."

"We did." She looked at him without smiling. "But that was then, a long time ago. And you left as soon as you could. With barely a good bye."

"There was a war on, Susan."

"'There was a war on'," she mimicked. "Is that why you didn't tell me what you were doing?" She looked at him angrily. "You couldn't wait to put on one of those ridiculous uniforms and join the parade. You have the nerve to come back and say you did it for us."

Russell was becoming annoyed. The teacup was shaking in his hands.

"It's easy to talk like that sitting here in St. Thomas, so far away from what was happening."

"I wasn't far away from anything. You were. You went away. I stayed in St. Thomas at the centre of things. It's you who doesn't know what was happening. This is where people were true to each other, where children were born, and crops were harvested."

His face hardened. "The world of women. So secluded, so hidden away, that smug and arrogant become normal."

"Smug. Arrogant." Her eyes flashed. "Now you walk back into this town as if you owned it, as if it was yours for the taking after years of neglect. You can't imagine what it was like here. All the young fools like you were gone. Only the crabby old men were left, ruling us and justifying everything by the war. Helen Partridge couldn't get money from the library board. Well, of course, you can't waste money buying books when we're fighting a war. Then the town council brought in a curfew for women and children, all of us off the streets by nine at night, as if the Germans were marching down the London Highway, heading our way."

She was on her feet, striding up and down the room.

"Nothing I could say right now will calm you. You're angry at me for some crime you think I've committed." He got to his feet. "I just came to say hello. I've done that, and I'll be on my way."

She stood in the centre of the room, forcing a smile.

"What are your plans?"

"I'm not sure. I'll look at the dairy and see how everything's going. Then think about practicing law. I had an offer from a Toronto firm."

She looked quickly at him.

"So you'll be working in Toronto?"

"I didn't accept it. It depended on me agreeing to run for the Conservatives here in the next provincial election."

"For the Conservatives? Here?"

"As I said, I didn't accept it. What are you doing next year?"

"Father wants me to work at the Times Journal. Or I might go to teacher's college in London. Or possibly New York."

She spoke with a toss of her head, as if he had no right to ask the question, and with that, the anger that had been brewing in him erupted. Her reddish brown hair and dark Celtic eyes, the slight freckles around the nose, the delicate red lips and full figure and her white summer dress annoyed him. Her beauty was wrong, standing there with her hands on her hips, looking angrily at him.

"Back to school. That sounds just right for you."

She caught the mocking tone in his voice.

"You'll have to wait a while to find what's right for you. This little town can't offer much to a man of your experience."

"I'm sorry. I'd better go."

The door opened and Bill MacLean, Susan's father and publisher of the St. Thomas Times Journal, entered. "Bobby Russell, by God." He strode into the room. "Wonderful to see you, my boy. We've all been so worried. But look at you, not a scratch. Doesn't he look great, Susan?"

Susan nodded. "Bobby was asked to stand for the Conservatives," she said.

"Bobby? Is this true?"

Russell explained the offer that Edward Archer had made in Toronto.

"Interesting you considered it. With you Russells it was always the old Liberal faith and the old Liberal Party. Times are changing." He looked at his wristwatch. "Got to eat and get back to the paper."

Russell looked at Susan with a brief smile, then walked to the front door. She said nothing. By the time he reached the street, he could feel the pain in his head.

She knows nothing. Her house could be rubble, there could be bodies lying in her street.

18.

That evening Russell ate supper with his mother. She had him kill a chicken which she boiled and served with dumplings and gravy, his favorite meal before the war. He sat in the dining room in his father's chair, desperately tired. It was as if the sleepless nights in the prison camp, the miles of walking across Holland and the gallons of whiskey had caught up with him all on this first night of peace in the house where he'd been born. His mother saw the slumped shoulders, the fragility.

"Did you go to Susan's today?" she asked casually.

"Yes."

"How is she?"

He shrugged. "She thinks I went overseas for the fun of it."

"She's been worrying for years. It's been hard."

"It wasn't fun!" he screamed.

Shocked, she stood still in the middle of the floor. "I know that," she said finally.

"I'm sorry. It's just that…."

When he didn't finish she looked back and saw him asleep in his chair. She went to him, shook him, and led him stumbling upstairs to bed. He collapsed and fell asleep, spending the first night in his bed with his clothes on. She turned out his light and closed the door.

Downstairs, unable to read her newspaper, she studied his picture on the wall. What had become of that innocent young man?

He slept until noon when he appeared in the kitchen, yawning and red in the face. As he poured himself a cup of coffee the front door bell rang. His mother returned from the hallway.

"The Thomsons are here. They farm between here and Dutton and they want to pay their respects."

He walked into the parlour. The farmer, in his overalls and grey shirt, sat stiff and awkward on the sofa, a sweat-stained straw hat on his knee. His tall, boney wife, uncomfortable in her white dress and Sunday shoes, sat beaming by his side.

"Mr. Russell," she began. "The Lord has preserved you, in answer to the prayers of those who love you. We are all so happy for you and for your mother, bless her soul, who has shown her courage during your absence. All's well that ends well, they do say." The lady continued with light in her eyes, her husband nodding and smiling automatically by her side. "Now, John didn't want to come here today, saying you would want your peace and privacy. But I said, nonsense, we've been bringing our milk to the Russells' dairy for thirty years, starting with your father, God rest his soul, and continuing to the present. It is our duty to drop by and welcome you home."

"Thank you. It's good to be back."

She turned and glared at her husband. He cleared his throat.

"Welcome back, Bobby. Glad you made it." Bobby nodded.

"Now we'll be on our way," Mrs. Thomson said. "We'll just leave you this token of our joy at your return, Mr. Russell. An apple pie." She handed it to him, beaming. "John says my apple pies are the best in the county."

When there was no response from the farmer she looked sharply at him. "Damn fine pie," he said.

"And you watch your language, mister. Well, Mrs. Russell, Mr. Russell, we'll be on our way. Let me say again how glad...."

It was five minutes before they left. Russell went to shut the door, but by that time there was another car in the lane. A stream of well-wishers was beginning: farmers from all around St. Thomas, including an old man with a few acres near Sparta driving a horse and wagon, people from the town, and the Mayor of St. Thomas, Al Parker himself.

"Let me say, Bobby, Margaret Ann, on behalf of the council and all the citizens of St. Thomas, how happy and grateful we are at your return. A people can ask for no greater sacrifice...."

The Mayor was in ceremonial style, his rhetoric rich, his pauses meaningful. Before he left he suggested that Russell come to a session of the council and talk to them about the war. Bobby nodded vaguely and said nothing. Parker left finally, shaking hands with Russell, his mother and others who had dropped in.

Among the visitors were wives of men in the regiment, looking for news of their husbands. Women in plain dresses with shy eyes, the mark of their deprivation in the firm set of the lips or in their nervous laughter, wanting to be told that their men were coming home. There were also widows. These women stood quietly, already alone, looking for an accounting, a description of what had happened. As he talked, Russell looked at them without smiling. He could recall the death of every man who was named to him, the bullet in the head, or the shell burst. After thinking about the soldier in question he would begin to speak, avoiding the spilling of blood, the destruction of the dead man's flesh, emphasizing bravery if it had existed, or comradeship. The women listened raptly, their eyes, brimming with tears, riveted on his face. When he finished each account, he would smile gently and shake her hand.

They left as quietly as they had come, stunned and wanting only to disappear without drawing attention. By early afternoon there were six cakes with brightly colored icing and eight fruit pies, sitting on the sideboard in the dining room. When everyone had finally gone he sat on the sofa, stretching his legs and rubbing his eyes.

"I've only been home a day. How did they know?"

"It's Marie Barnes and the party lines. She had the news all over the county the morning after you got here." She paused. "Now, I want us to go out to the dairy and talk to Tom Allen. He's been running everything with no help from anybody."

Tom Allen had been hired by his father as a worker in the dairy in the early thirties. Russell remembered a quiet, hardworking man, always in the plant, always reliable. As they walked out to the garage, they noticed Calvin standing quietly beside the lane, half way to the road.

"What's the news, Calvin?" yelled Bobby.

"It's Tom, my brother. He don't come home last night. My pa is mad."

"Was he drinking?"

"Tommy don't drink. He's a Christian youth."

"He'll turn up, Calvin." Russell grinned and turned to his mother. "You can't lose a MacQuiggan, even when you want to."

They drove in their Buick to the dairy, a low brick building with wooden outhouses between St. Thomas and Union. 'Union Dairy' said the black and white sign. There were several wagons loaded with milk tins lined up at the receiving door in the pasteurizing room. The smell of sour milk pervaded the entrance. They walked into the office where Tom Allen and a bookkeeper and a secretary, Vera and Shirley, ran the business. Again there were greetings for Russell. Tom Allen shook his hand and smiled, as usual saying nothing.

The manager closed the office door and took a seat behind his desk. The office was plain and functional, with a metal desk and file cabinet and a calendar on the wall from a farm equipment dealer. Bobby sat watching Tom, remembering the neatness of the man. He didn't appear to have aged. There were the same shy, respectful eyes, the same green plaid necktie and home-style haircut. Tom cleared his throat.

"Over all, we've done very well, Mr. Russell. We've been making good money all the way through. I have the financial statements for every year you've been away in this package, if you want to give them a look. We have five more dairy farmers selling to us than we had before the war. Sales are up, too. Local consumption has been rationed, of course, but we more than make it up selling to the military. Prices have been controlled, but our costs are controlled too, so that cuts both ways. If anything, they've declined. Labour has been the only real problem. You can't find an experienced dairyman now for love nor money. Fortunately, we still have Cliff MacIntyre as our chief dairyman. He's sixty-seven years old, but he can still work a ten-hour day when we need it. But beneath him, we've had to scramble. We got retired farm hands and women out in the plant. We're just getting by."

Russell looked at his manager, feigning interest, thinking of Susan. He tried to keep anger from his face, drumming his fingers on the desk. If he tried he could still bring to his mind a memory of her emerging from the blue summer lake, the water streaming from hips and shoulders, the sun glistening on her, tanned and laughing. Had she ever really been like that? His hands gripped the seat of his chair.

"There are opportunities for this dairy, especially now that the war is over. I've been explaining them to Margaret Ann for the last year, but she's not interested so she won't spend any money. And you gotta spend money now, even to stand still.

"They're making pasteurizers in the States now that can process four times the volume of milk we do, in the same space of time. One of these beauties would cost three thousand dollars, but it would replace those slow little machines we got now. We could also get better ice cream machines from a company in Cleveland. Freezes harder and faster, and lets you crush fruit and make flavours that we can't make. Chocolate, strawberry and vanilla, that's all we do, and we do it from syrups. I want to do peach, orange, blueberry and other fruits. We could be the first in this part of the world with these flavours. That would produce much larger profits for us, but we'd have to spend first."

Tom paused, his face lit with excitement.

"These are good ideas, Tom. Forward-looking." The manager's smile widened. "It's still early days for me, so you'll have to give me a chance to think things over." The smile lessened.

"Sure, Mr. Russell. Makes sense."

"Now I want you to tell me something else. MacAlister and Matthews up in town have been trying to get my mother to sell a piece of our land, out by the London Highway where the MacQuiggans live. D'you know anything about that?"

He saw the caution flicker in Tom Allen's eyes, the nervous motion of the tongue over the lips. The man knew something.

"That's news to me. What do they want it for?" He relaxed again.

"I don't know. Any ideas?"

"No. Margaret Ann didn't mention anything to me. That land is only good for corn, if I remember. Listen, why don't you come out and make an appearance in the plant?"

So the lawyers had been talking to Tom Allen and Tom was afraid to mention it. Russell knew that if Tom had discussed the land with his mother in any way, she would have told him yesterday.

As they walked into the plant they were hit by the smell of sour milk, stronger than outside, and the heat from the pasteurizers. Stooped, grey-haired men were taking milk cans from the delivery area, wheeling them over on dollies to a pasteurizer and dumping the milk in the top. Cliff MacIntyre was checking the thermometer on a machine that was heating its batch of milk. He saw Russell and walked over to the doorway. They shook hands.

"Welcome home, Mr. Russell. Everything ship-shape here, you can be sure. Come and meet the people."

Russell went to the men at the loading dock, to the women in the freezer-room making ice cream, to the women at the bottling machines, to the ice cream packers and to the men stacking the crates of milk and cream and the pounds of butter.

"They're a hard-working bunch, by and large," said MacIntyre.

"I won't have shirkers here. They work their day or they're out the door."

When they drove home the wind was picking up and the eastern sky was dark.

"It's going to rain," his mother said.

"Uh huh."

"What did you think?"

"About what?"

She looked annoyed. "About the dairy, and the job Tom has been doing."

"I was pleased. The two of you have kept things together."

He spoke with forced enthusiasm, but it satisfied her.

"I suppose he told you about the new machines he wanted to buy." He nodded. "He's probably right, but I didn't give him the money. We were growing as it was and making plenty of money. I didn't see why we needed more."

He turned the Buick into their lane. The rain had not yet started, but there were rumblings of thunder and lightning flashes. As they drove to the house he saw Calvin standing beside the porch, watching them.

"I got to find Tommy," he said as they left the car. "I got to find him fast or my pa is gonna lick me."

"He still hasn't turned up?"

"No he ain't, and they is all burned up at home. He never brought his pay home, so they ain't got no money. We eat beans an' turnips. He gonna lick me."

There was no fear in the dark eyes, just an intense stare. He looks too old, thought Russell.

"It's not your fault, Calvin. I'll speak to your father. Tommy will turn up."

"You better not. Then he be real mad." The boy shook his head.

"I got to find him. Maybe look by the creek. Tommy, he like to fish a lot, an' he like to fish by that creek."

"It's going to rain, Calvin," said Margaret Ann. "You come in and wait for the rain to pass. I'll fix you a sandwich."

Calvin turned away. "No. I got to find Tommy." He started to walk across the field, towards the creek that ran among the trees a quarter-mile away.

Margaret Ann shook her head. "Bad things are happening in that house. Beyond what I gave Archie for the ploughing he was supposed to be doing, the only money coming in for them was Archie's pension and Tommy's pay for delivering the mail. Then Archie drinks most of it away at the Confederation House. Times are tough, and I think he beats them."

"I better talk to him."

19.

They sat in the parlour drinking tea and watching the storm approach across the fields. He was trying not to think of the dairy, and the money for Tom Allen's machines. As the sky darkened he remembered his bottle. Not now, he told himself. When the knock came on the kitchen door, Margaret Ann rose, left the room and returned quickly.

"It's Archie. You'd better come."

Archie MacQuiggan stood in the kitchen, his face red, his beer-swollen belly straining against his belt, a sweat-stained straw hat in his hand. When Russell entered from the parlour, deference flashed in his eyes, modifying the anger.

"I hear you seen Calvin, Captain. I want that little bugger home. He has no business comin' over here and botherin' you. I told him time after time that if I caught him here, botherin' you, I'd give him what for."

Rage burned in the clear blue eyes.

"He's no bother, he's just a boy. He was here looking for Tommy."

"Tommy ain't been home, he's gone off somewhere. The whole goddamn house is fallin' apart. Well, you see Calvin, tell him I want him. He's gotta do the mail tomorrow. He ain't gonna find Tommy, Leona says. She says she got a bad feelin' about Tommy, and her feelin's is generally right. Well. I gotta get home. Good day, Captain Russell, Missus Russell."

The big man clumped out of the kitchen into the dark.

"I thought you were going to speak with him about hitting Calvin," she said.

"I was. I will. The time wasn't right."

"I don't see what time is righter than any other."

He stared at the carpet. "It's taking that rain a while to get here," he said finally.

They ate in the sunroom with a view across the fields so they could watch the storm. They had always done this; Bobby could remember sitting in that room as a child, drinking his milk and watching a hail storm flatten the field of corn. He could still hear his father, muttering about the damage and shaking his head, sitting in the rocker by the bookshelf. The storm was becoming fierce. The sky was black an hour too soon; they could barely see the trees at the end of the field and the wind was whistling under the eaves. The rain began, a few drops at first and then a downpour, driven by the wind, lashing the fields. Thunder broke with a crack and the flashes of lightning lit up the field.

"What are you going to do about that dairy machinery?" she asked.

"I don't know."

He let the annoyance sound in his voice. She kept silent, watching the rain splatter the mud of the fields. He thought he would go upstairs and have a drink. Before he could get to his feet, the thunder cracked, the lightning flashed, and in a moment of illumination an image flashed on his retina from the other side of the field among the tossing trees. Something, lighter than the dark trees, and small. He watched the spot, waiting for the next flash. It came, and there it was, the small figure, turning around and around in the rain.

"Look. Look there."

She looked, but the field was dark.

"What was it?"

"There's something out there. Wait for the next flash."

First there was a deafening crack of thunder and then several flashes of lightning that lit up the field. The figure kept turning and spinning against the dark of the woods. Then it disappeared in the dark.

"That's a person," she said. "It could only be Calvin."

He sat staring at the spot, but no lightning came.

"You'd better go and get him, Bobby. He'll catch his death out there."

He went down to the cellar and re-emerged wearing his father's slicker and rubber boots. He left without a word and began to trudge across the field against the wind, the rain lashing him. When he got to the woods he shone his flashlight around in an arc, and picked up Calvin, just at the edge of the trees, spinning in a circle, crying, his clothes plastered to his skinny little body, the water streaming down his face.

"Tommy's red," he cried. "Tommy's red as roses. I found 'im. Dead and red as roses."

He moved over and pulled the boy under the shelter of an elm tree.

"Where is he, Calvin? Where's Tommy?"

Without a word Calvin grabbed a corner of his slicker and pulled him back into the woods. They followed a path to the creek and turned right, walking along the bank. There was no sound but the wind and the rain, and the squishing their boots made in the mud. The creek curved around the corner of their farm and went to the road, where it passed under a bridge for the Lyndhurst Road. When they came to the bridge, Calvin stood and pointed under the bridge.

"There's Tommy," he said. "Dead an' red."

Bobby got into the water and walked under the bridge. The body of Tommy MacQuiggan lay on a gravel bank, against the bridge abutment. He was clothed, but his head lay on the ground almost detached from the neck; his blood stained the gravel.

"Jesus Christ," muttered Bobby.

Calvin had waded under the bridge and stood beside him.

"Poor Tommy," he said. "He liked to fish. He never hit me."

"Who would do a thing like that?"

The boy was crying and shivering. Bobby opened his slicker and drew Calvin under, putting an arm around him. The boy put his arms around Bobby's waist and began to howl, with a pure, animal-like sound of terror, hugging him as if he were the last rock, the last piece of firm land, before nothingness.

"Let's go back to the house, Calvin," he said finally. "There are things to be done."

"Can we leave Tommy?"

"There's nothing we can do for him now."

They climbed up the bank and walked back to the Russell farm. The fury of the storm had softened to a steady rain, with more distant thunder and flashes of lightning. Calvin kept his arm in Russell's, sobbing as they walked. When they entered the kitchen, Margaret Ann was washing the supper dishes.

"Lord, Calvin, look at you. You're drenched. You haven't got the sense God gave a fly."

Calvin stood still, shaking with cold, water dripping from his chin, his arms and legs.

"Tommy's dead," said Bobby. "We found his body under the bridge down the road. His throat was cut."

She raised a hand to her mouth, was about to speak, then didn't. She looked at the boy with moist eyes.

"Calvin, I'm going to put you in a warm bath and some dry clothes. Mr. Russell will take care of Tommy."

He went into the parlour and picked up the phone.

"Marie, get me Elmore Wayne at home."

He knew Marie Barnes would listen in on an after-hours call to the Chief of Police, and the murder would be common knowledge in town by morning. The deep, familiar voice of Elmore Wayne, scourge of moonlighters and drunken farm hands all over the county, came on the line. Russell told him quickly about Tommy MacQuiggan under the bridge.

"Damn, it's still raining." The Chief had been asleep. "Sit tight Bobby. I'll be there as soon as I can."

Russell shone his flashlight on Tommy MacQuiggan, who lay as before under the bridge, his head askew from his neck, his eyes sightless.

"Yep, he's dead." Elmore Wayne was crouching beside the body, whistling. "I guess you've seen a lot of this where you've been, eh Bobby?"

"This is worse."

"You don't expect this. Who in the name of thunder would do this to a dumb Scotch boy like Tommy MacQuiggan?"

Bobby shook his head. "At first I thought of Archie. He can be violent if he's drunk. But Archie was living on Tommy's pay check from the post office. He'd never kill his only source of income."

"This is no family killing, anyway. It's a neat, pro job, just a slice along the artery in the neck, bim, bam, thank you ma'am, no fooling around. Last murder I had was five years ago. Fellah in New Dundee, shot his wife and kids, shoots himself, blood all over the house, a slaughter. That's your typical family job. Messy. Whoever did this was cool. No emotion in it."

A car door slammed, voices were heard and the sound of feet sliding down the creek bank. Gus Campbell appeared, leading the coroner, Dr. Stuart, by the hand.

"Hello to the good doctor," growled the Chief of Police. "Tell us he's dead, Doc, so we can get him out of here."

"By God, I hate this horseshit late at night," grumbled the doctor, opening his bag. "Never find the stiffs in the daylight. Let's have a look." He moved the limbs back and forth, and looked in the mouth, depressing the tongue. He pressed the flesh on one arm and watched the mark he had made. "Been here at least a day. Real stiff. Obvious, the cause of death. Only question is when, and I guess who. Let's get him out of here. I can give you a better estimate on the time if I can look him over better."

"Gus, you wait for the ambulance and help the guy get the body out of here. Take him to the hospital for overnight. Then get Archie and bring him to the Russell place. Can we get a cup of coffee at your place?" Russell nodded.

"I thought the morgue was in London," said Russell as they climbed up the bank.

"It is, but we won't use the morgue on this one. We don't need an autopsy; the doc tells me he's dead and he tells me why. They charge us for the morgue and autopsies, and I don't want to spend any money on a case like this."

"Don't you have to have an autopsy if it's murder?"

The Chief smiled. "That's what they tell you in law school."

The rain had stopped, but the gravel road was wet, and the hollows and ruts full of water. Overhead the sky was clear and black, scattered with stars. The grass along the road was fragrant from the rain.

"Calvin found him?" asked the Chief.

"In the middle of the storm. Must have scared him."

"It's not good for children to experience that kind of thing," said the doctor. "It can disturb them permanently, affect their development."

"Calvin's already disturbed, and as for development...." Elmore Wayne snorted. "There wasn't going to be a whole lot of that anyway. Damn MacQuiggans. They're more trouble than they're worth."

On the porch they took off their muddy shoes and entered the kitchen. Margaret Ann set out a pot of coffee and cups.

"Keep your voices down. Calvin's asleep inside on the sofa."

Elmore Wayne questioned Russell about Calvin's movements, right up to the discovery of the dead man. He sighed.

"That damn council is going to expect me to find out who killed Tommy, when no one in his right mind would care a damn. No MacQuiggan is worth a pinch of coon shit. We'll have reporters down here from London, asking me their fool questions. And I'm going to have to cancel the fishing trip Parker and I were going to take on the French River."

"Into every life some rain must fall," said the coroner, a scholarly man with sad eyes. "You shouldn't go fishing with the Mayor anyway. Gives the wrong impression."

Before the Chief could answer, there was the clumping of feet on the porch, the door opened and Gus Campbell led Archie MacQuiggan into the kitchen. Archie's face was crimson.

"What's this about?" He looked uneasily at the range of authority scrutinizing him from the kitchen table. "You got no right to drag me here in the middle of the night, leavin' my wife and family alone. I'm a citizen and I've got rights, just like anybody else. I've a good mind to file a complaint with...."

Archie's blustering voice trailed off as he tried to think who he would complain to. Elmore Wayne sighed.

"Shut up, Archie. It's the first time in living memory you've been concerned about your wife being alone after dark, seeing as you're in the Confederation House most nights." Archie's mouth fell, and he began to sputter a defence. "Quiet." Archie closed his mouth and stood looking from face to face. "We called you here because your boy Tommy's been found under the Lyndhurst Road bridge with his throat slit. He's been murdered."

The fat, pink face went blank, and the red-rimmed blue eyes filled with calculation. As he absorbed what had been said to him, the calculation turned to fear.

"Dead? Murdered? An' you think I did it? You think I murdered my own flesh and blood? I never fucking did it. I never laid a hand on him for years. I got an alibi. I was in the Confederation House with Walt Scruggs and Earl Beaver. You can't frame me. I'll get a lawyer. I've got my rights, just like anyone else."

Elmore Wayne got to his feet.

"Archie, if I hear another word from you, other than yes sir, no sir, you're going to jail for a week, while I think of something to charge you with. Now I'm going to ask you some questions and I want you to answer them truthfully, because if you don't, I'll make your life miserable. Do you understand me?" Archie stared at the floor. "Do you understand me?" The Chief raised his voice. Archie nodded. "Good. Now I want you to tell me where you've been for every second of the last two days."

The big man tried to remember, striking his left palm with the forefinger of his right hand as he recited his whereabouts. The Chief scribbled notes in a spiral notebook. Russell was thinking of Calvin, asleep on the sofa. He could picture him sitting by the road, the bruise on his cheek, waiting to follow Bobby to town. He could see Calvin twirling in the rain at the foot of the field, dancing from horror. A boy alone, no flesh on his bones, no intelligence in his eyes, waiting for the end of the storm and whatever fate would do to him.

"Archie, you may go," said Elmore Wayne.

When Archie realized, that he was not suspected of the murder, cunning returned to the blue eyes.

"Now, Gentlemen," he began, in a respectful tone. "Mr. Wayne, Dr. Stuart, Captain Russell. This is the most by-the-Jesus, God-awful thing for a family man. You got to be a father to know what losin' a son does to you. He was my oldest boy. We'll never see him again. I don't know what we'll do." The three stared at him impassively, wondering where this obvious insincerity was leading. "He was a mailman. I got him that job. I worked for it and I earned it. I campaigned for Mr. Grant MacKay for the last two elections, all the farms on the ninth and tenth concessions. We got a right to that job, our family. We need that job." His voice was rising. "I want Calvin to get that job. It's my right. I've always voted Liberal. I voted for Mr. Parker in the last election. I want Calvin to get that job."

"You live outside the city, Archie," said Elmore Wayne. "You couldn't have voted for Al Parker." Archie stared sullenly at the floor. "Anyway, Calvin is too young to hold that job, and even if he were old enough, he hasn't got the brains for it."

Archie got angry.

"He'll do the job. I'll goddamn well make him do it. I'll teach hm." He looked around the room. "Where is he anyway? You say he found Tommy. Why didn't he come and tell me? I ain't seen 'im all night. Where's that little bugger got to?"

133

"He's asleep inside," said Margaret Ann. "And I don't want you to wake him."

"But he's got to come home and be with his family. He don't belong here, begging your pardon, Captain Russell."

Russell got to his feet.

"Let him sleep, Archie. In the morning we can talk about Calvin. I thought he might come and work for me for awhile. Light farm work, things I could teach him. Work out some wage for him, now that Tommy's gone."

Archie looked carefully at Russell.

"Well, Captain, I don't know." He shook his head as if thinking the idea over. "Calvin's only ten, so the work can't be too hard."

"No, Archie, light work."

"I trust you on that one. The other thing is, in our family, the way we work it … the pay, with Tommy, it came to us. So we could support the boy properly."

"Of course, Archie, we'd follow the same arrangement. The pay would go to you and your wife."

Archie smiled. "Geez, Captain, that's good of you. I better get back and tell Leona." He paused. "But this murder, Gentlemen, it don't make sense. Who in hell would want to kill Tommy?"

"That's the question, Archie," said the Chief.

The door slammed shut, and Archie's boots clumped down the porch stairs.

"Whoever did it got the wrong MacQuiggan, if you ask me," said Elmore Wayne. "To think I have to spend time on this when I could be fishing." He turned. "Thank you, Margaret Ann, for the coffee. Come on, Doc, and drive me back to town."

20.

Susan had not wanted to go to what she called "another old maids' soirée." but Jean accused her of being afraid of meeting Bobby Russell in the street.

"All right, I'm coming," she yelled over the telephone. "Bobby Russell is all you think of. It's not me who's obsessed with him." It seemed that everywhere she turned someone was asking her about Bobby.

Helen let her in with a quiet smile. Jean had already arrived; Rose was putting a record on the gramophone.

"Have you heard the latest?" said Jean. "A Marie Barnes special, hot off the wires. Tommy MacQuiggan's been murdered."

"And who is Tommy MacQuiggan?" asked Rose.

"The MacQuiggans live on the Russell farm. Tommy worked for the post office, delivering mail to the farmers on the concessions. Marie says Bobby found him under a bridge on the Lyndhurst Road with his throat slit."

"Who did it?" asked Susan.

"They don't know. Marie says Elmore Wayne is working on the case non-stop."

"Non-stop for Elmore Wayne means one step ahead of slow." Rose's mouth wrinkled. "I hope they catch him soon."

"How do we know it was a man?' asked Jean.

"Of course it was a man," said Rose MacIlwain. "No woman would dump someone under a bridge with his throat slit."

Jean continued. "Bobby Russell found the body, according to Marie. Together with Tommy's brother, Calvin. In that rainstorm last night. Bobby and Margaret Ann are keeping Calvin at their place until he recovers from the shock."

"That is such a generous, noble thing to do," said Helen. "So like Bobby Russell. I saw him on the street the other day. Quite a dashing figure, although careworn."

Susan rolled her eyes. Keep your mouth shut, she muttered to herself. I want to get out of here. I want to go dancing.

"Bobby looks adorable," said Jean.

"Can we change the subject?" Susan was irritated.

Rose stood by the window. "My dear, you should take your time. When you make your decision, make sure it is yours and yours alone. Don't let someone else decide that it's time for you to be

135

married, to Bobby Russell or anyone else."

❁

Susan and Jean left the apartment about eight-thirty and walked to Talbot Street. The town was dark except for the soft glow from the windows of the apartments over the stores.

"No street lights yet." Jean was looking in the store windows. "Typical. New York has street lights. Toronto has street lights. Look in the gutter there. They haven't even cleaned up the leaves from last fall. Horse droppings at every corner and nothing in the stores. We have to get out of here."

"I'll go to London. I'll go to teacher's college."

"Then you'll be back in some country school teaching farm boys to read and write. We'll go to New York and share an apartment. And share the men."

"Do we always have to talk about men?" shouted Susan. "It makes me sick."

"Hey, you girls!"

Gus Campbell, swinging his flashlight, was moving across the street towards them.

"Hi, Gus," said Susan. "How's Marion?"

"All right, I guess. Now you girls know you have to be off the streets by nine. That's this new curfew. It's the law."

"We've been on a mission of mercy, Gus," said Jean. "You'll have to make an exception for us."

"Mission of mercy." said Gus, scratching his head. "You'd have to tell it to the judge."

"What d'you mean, 'tell it to the judge'?" Susan was angry.

"Just jokin'. Hell, I know you girls since way back, and I ain't concerned. But there's a lot more people movin' through town than used to be. Soldiers and such. It pays to be careful."

"Yes, Constable Campbell," said Susan in a little-girl voice that made Gus smile.

"Do they know who did it?"

Gus drew himself up to full height and dignity.

"We've just opened the file in the MacQuiggan case. It's too early to jump to any conclusions."

"But do you know who did it?"

"Not yet." He started to walk away. "I've got to do my rounds. Don't be out too late."

"Yes, Constable Campbell," they chorused together.

He walked further down the street, shining his flashlight through the store windows.

"I've been walking down Talbot Street since I was old enough to go out by myself," said Susan, fuming. "Now it's Gus Campbell's business whether I'm in by nine o'clock or not."

"Never mind that," said Jean. "I have a very important question to ask. It's been bothering me for some time." Susan stopped to look at her. "Helen and Rose. When they make love, how do they do it?"

"Jean," groaned Susan, and walked on.

At home, Susan found her mother sitting in the parlour reading Life Magazine. On the cover was a large photo of American and Russian soldiers smiling eagerly and shaking hands across a ditch. Her mother removed her glasses.

"Susan, I'm going out to the MacQuiggan house tomorrow with some soup and preserves. I'd like it if you would come with me."

Soup and preserves, Susan thought. Florence bloody Nightingale.

"They're horrible. Archie MacQuiggan is just slightly more advanced than an ape. But I'll go. Where's Daddy?"

"At work, I guess."

21.

When the Oldsmobile reached the Russell farm, Valerie MacLean glanced at Susan, who, thin-lipped, was staring out the opposite window. She drove on until they came to an unpainted clapboard house.

"Gosh, it's sordid," exclaimed Susan. There was trash scattered on the lawn, the porch was sagging and the screen door, a hole in its centre, was swinging in the wind.

"Let's not judge, darling. They were not given our advantages."

They crossed the porch carefully, avoiding a loose plank in the floor. From inside the house came the wailing of a child.

"I told ya not to touch it. Touch it again, I'll give it ya again." The woman's voice was hoarse and loud.

They knocked on the door frame. The crying stopped.

"Who is it?' yelled the angry voice.

"Valerie MacLean and Susan."

Footsteps approached the doorway. Leona MacQuiggan stepped through the doorway. A short, stocky woman with reddish-blond hair stared at them, a too-often-pregnant stomach pushing out her belly and a red-eyed, dirty-faced girl of three on her hip. Tufts of red hair showed from the pits of her bare arms.

"What is it?" The blue eyes were dull with suspicion.

"We heard about your son, and have brought you some soup and things," said Valerie. "In my experience you can never have too much food at a time like this."

It took Leona several seconds to realize that the hamper was for her. A slow smile spread over her face. Susan noticed a bruise over her left eye.

"Very kind," she said. "Very Christian. I'd ask yuz in for tea, but the place is kinda messy. An' Archie don't like people comin in when he ain't here."

"You have a right to see anybody you want," exclaimed Susan.

"Archie ain't big on rights, Miss." The child on Leona's hip was beginning to whimper.

"Leona, I wanted you to know that we are thinking of you. Tommy's death must be a terrible shock."

"I'd say so, Missus. It cost us ten dollars a week in his pay. I don't know what we're going to do without that money."

"Archie will have to get a job," blurted Susan.

"And pigs is gonna fly, Miss." Leona broke into a husky, bitter laugh. "Archie'll plough in the spring, but much more than that he won't do. He says gettin' shot in the gut by the Germans has kept him from workin'. Although he weren't much fonder of workin' before the war, if the truth be told."

"All right, Leona," said Valerie softly. "We'll be on our way. Let me know if there's anything else you need."

She handed Leona the hamper. A flicker of emotion passed over the woman's face. The child started up to whimper again, and the woman shook it quiet. She stood on the porch watching them go, the hamper in one hand, the child held by the other.

"I couldn't live like that," said Susan, thinking of Leona's sagging body, the dank smell of sour milk, stale bread and bacon grease that clung to her and her whimpering child.

"I thought we could turn in at the Russells," said Valerie as they pulled out of the lane. "I haven't seen Margaret Ann since Bobby came back."

"No, Mother," Susan cried. "I won't. If you're going, let me out of this car right now."

Valerie pulled the car over to the edge of the road. Susan rolled down her window. Valerie opened her purse and took out a package of cigarettes.

"We've been friends with the Russells forever."

"I don't want to see him."

Valerie sighed. "Then you don't have to see him. We won't go today. But, darling, you can't pretend he doesn't exist."

"I don't want to see him."

"And you used to be inseparable."

"He was different then." She remembered the dark-haired young man she had loved. She could hear that bubbly, out-of-control laugh that meant he was bored and was going to stir things up, get something going. She could feel his arms around her and she remembered her desire. The lightness of him, the fun of him, the beauty of him came to her for a moment and then vanished.

"He's only been back a few days."

"I don't care, he's a mess. He walks stiffly, like an old man. His eyes are dead. He's all wrapped up in himself, as if the war is the only thing that matters, as if what we did here, living our lives, is insignificant. I think he's drinking too much. I don't remember him being red in the face the way he is. He's just...." She shook her head, looking for the words. "He's broken."

Valerie nodded. "Even so, don't you have any feeling for him?"

"Leave me alone!" Susan jumped out of the car. Valerie slowly got out on her side and leaned against the hood, watching her daughter sitting on a patch of grass along the ditch.

"My feelings are mine." Susan's voice was low and controlled. "Dad says we need to get to know each other again. Well, it isn't going to happen, so you all better get used to it."

"So what will you do? Go to teacher's college?"

"Jean and I are going to New York."

"New York." Valerie kept her face a mask. "And what will you do there? How will you live?"

"We'll get jobs writing for Life, or The New Yorker. There are hundreds of publications that hire writers in New York."

"But you have no experience and no contacts in New York."

"Jean has contacts, through her father."

"Bud Robson has no publishing contacts; the idea is completely absurd. You've been listening to Rose MacIlwain."

"It's not as absurd as staying here. And Miss MacIlwain has nothing to do with it. Why can't I have ideas of my own?"

"Of course you can. But I think you're affected by the problems you're having with Bobby. Even if it isn't Bobby, marriage is still the best thing for a girl like you."

Susan rose from the ditch.

"Whom would I marry? Some farmer, so I can raise a brood of little farmers and sell butter and eggs for my spending money? Maybe a shopkeeper? Harry Miller isn't married and could probably use help in the shoe store. I could manage the till and spell him off while he goes upstairs for lunch." There was anguish in her eyes. "I would rather be dead."

"If it hadn't been for this war, you and Bobby would probably be married now."

"And would that have been so wonderful? Would I have lived happily ever after?"

Susan was looking intently at her mother.

"Nothing is happy ever after. There are no fairy tales." She tried to keep the fatigue she felt from her tone. "I have been married for thirty years, and I have no regrets."

"Does he still love you?"

Valerie bristled at the question, but succumbed to its honesty. "It's different after this length of time. Whatever love is, it's not romance and kisses and dancing in the dark."

"He spends more time at that paper than he does with you. He hardly talks to you."

"Does he love me? You'd have to ask him."

"That's horrible. That you don't know. Do you love him?"

"I don't know about love. I don't want any other life, I know that. But you don't feel, after a while, the things you once felt. I guess I love him. I don't not love him. And without him, there would be no you. And he is kind; he respects our life."

"What does that mean, 'he respects your life'?"

"He loves his newspaper. He always goes to all press association meetings, in London or Toronto. Sometimes it seems as if we barely see each other from week to week. Once I thought he had a girl in Toronto."

Susan stopped pacing and stared.

"You look so shocked. Susan, my love, if we're going to talk about the way life is, then let's do it." Susan sat again, watching her mother's face. "One night last fall a woman phoned from Toronto when he was out and left a message and a number. When I gave it to him, he didn't say a word, who she was, anything."

"But how could you stand it? How could you let yourself be treated that way?"

"Because it was all right. The affair, if that's what it was, didn't last. He goes to Toronto on business from time to time. Whatever he does there he doesn't let intrude on our life in this house."

"Hear no evil, see no evil, speak no evil." Susan's voice was dripping with scorn. "I don't want that kind of relationship. I want someone who loves me. And I want to love him all my life."

Valerie felt old and exhausted.

"The reason my life is good is mostly you, my dear. The rest doesn't matter. I have everything I want. I wish the same for you." She stubbed her cigarette out on the car bumper. "Let's go."

Back at the house on Metcalfe Street, Susan poured herself a glass of lemonade and lay in the garden hammock. She began to swing gently. Her cat Cleopatra slept in the porch sunlight.

So Bobby had suffered. She didn't care; she wanted to go dancing. She lay in the hammock, shut her eyes and heard the sweet sound of saxophones, brassy trumpets and rich trombones, echoing over the lake. Then she was dancing. She felt herself leaning on Gene, hearing his soft, inflected voice in her ear. She jumped out of her hammock. Life was going to start for her on Saturday night.

Cleopatra got to her feet and strolled into the garden.

22.

Helen Partridge watched Russell wander down the central aisle of the St. Thomas Public Library reading the subject headings of the side aisles. He inspected the shelves from agriculture and animal husbandry down to zoology, shaking his head. She rose from her desk.

"May I help you?"

He turned; she could see him trying to place her.

"I was looking for a book on shell shock. You probably don't have such a thing. Just looking around, really. You're…?"

"Helen Partridge. I'm the librarian."

"Yes, of course. You were before…."

He shut his mouth quickly.

"Before the war. Yes, I was. Now, shell shock." Her smile was replaced by a frown of concentration. "I think I remember something. Come with me."

She led him to the Human Psychology sub-section and withdrew a book which she handed to him. *Battle Fatigue and Psychic Disorder*, by W.S. Rivers M.D.

"It's by an English doctor who treated men from the First World War. Someone gave it to us. It's the only thing we have."

"I'll have a look at it, thank you."

"Come and I'll make up a library card for you."

She sat on her stool, took out a blank card and began to fill it in. As she wrote she kept watching him. He was looking around the library as if he had never seen it before. His hands were clasped tightly behind his back; she could see the nail of one hand digging into the flesh of the other. Sweat was gleaming on his cheeks. His eyes were dead. She stamped his book.

"Due in three weeks," she said quietly. "If you haven't finished it, you can bring it in and get an extension. If you don't do that, and you're late, we have to fine you."

"Thank you."

"Captain Russell." He stopped as he was turning to leave. "Why do you want a book on shell shock?"

He hesitated. "The regiment will be back in a month or so. Some of them will be in bad shape. I thought I should know...."

"Of course." She was watching him carefully. "And how are you? I haven't seen you since you've come back."

"Thank you. I'm fine. Good to be back."

He said the words mechanically.

"Why did you come home early, before the rest of the men?"

She was beginning to irritate him.

"I don't remember ... maybe a medical discharge."

"Were you wounded?"

"Not exactly. A different problem."

"Captain Russell, do you want to read this book, really, to find out what's happened to you?"

"Ma'am, that's my business," he said quietly.

She sat back on her stool, suddenly aware of the chasm opening before her on the other side of the desk. He was frowning.

"I believe shell shock can be a serious condition. You need to talk to someone."

"Ma'am, talking is just talking. I don't need it."

He does need it, she thought. There was Dr. Stuart. The doctor was a man of the physical sciences, but he was taciturn, without warmth and sympathy. "Have tea with me," she said suddenly.

"Tea is the last thing I need." He thought of his bottle.

She looked away, embarrassed at the rejection.

"But talking about things can…. Oh, forget it. Silly idea."

He took his card, turned to leave, stopped and turned back.

"Thank you for the offer. It's just that I'm not sociable these days. You wouldn't enjoy it."

"Good to see you again."

He turned to go again, then stopped again. I do need something. She knows it.

"Look, I will have tea with you. Thank you. I don't talk to anyone and I should. Re-enter the human race."

She laughed. "Well, the St. Thomas variety anyway. Very well, Captain Russell, I would enjoy it."

It should be public, she thought, in the Malt Shoppe. Except he wouldn't be able to talk there.

"I'm off at three today. Come to my apartment at four. Second floor on the building next to Brown's Funeral Parlour on Ontario Street."

"All right."

She watched him walk away without a smile. Something about the way he moved was not quite right; the arms did not swing in time with his tread. Why was she moved by him?

As soon as he reached the street, Russell regretted accepting the librarian's invitation. Nevertheless, at four o'clock he found himself mounting the steps to the door of her apartment. Because I must talk to someone. Something is not right.

He knocked on the door. She opened it and smiled, as if his calling were an everyday occurrence. He sat on a brocaded sofa while she sat on a chair opposite, a low table and the tea service between them. He remembered that she shared her apartment with another woman, a school teacher.

"Rose MacIlwain and I share this place. You may remember her from the Collegiate."

"She taught me English. 'In Xanadu did Kublai Khan a stately pleasure dome decree'."

"Bravo, Captain Russell. Rose is visiting her family in London." He did not understand her embarrassed smile. "You look much older than I remember. Of course you are older."

"Yes."

He stared at the carpet.

"I can't imagine what you have been through, Captain, but I believe that it hurt you."

"Really?" He didn't trust the affectionate smile.

"Really. Human beings were not made for war. The mind, the soul itself, are not made to endure battle."

He laughed.

"The soul. What the hell is that?" He brushed his hair back from his eyes. "And human beings were not made for battle? What nonsense." She grimaced. "There were men over there, some of them from this town, who thought that the war was the best time of their lives. Cheap whiskey, cheap women, and a little action. Fun! What do you know about it?"

"Not much, I suppose, to someone with your experience. But war is unusual, Captain, a disease. Running a library is normal. The years you spent fighting were intense, but a life most people will never have."

The silence lasted several minutes. The tenderness she felt for his brittle anger and fatigue disturbed her; she did not want to think about what that might mean. She was too old for love, and in this town unorthodox ramblings of the heart were dangerous.

"It may be so. Most people here have no idea." He shook his head. "I didn't like it."

"And now we hear that you discovered the mailman who was murdered."

145

He remembered briefly standing in the creek under the bridge, with Calvin beside him.

"I'm used to the dead. But Tommy…."

He looked around the quiet room. There were photographs of Greek ruins, beside the impressionist prints. The Belvedere Apollo, the Parthenon, the site of the oracle at Delphi, with the sea beyond. No photographs of children, no family groups, no femininity in the furniture or the decor. The room had a calmness and clarity that relaxed him. More important, the woman did not intrude.

"I would like to know what you are experiencing, if you care to tell me."

"I have trouble remembering. Some of it is coming back, but whole patches of my time there are blacked out. For a while I couldn't remember this town or the people in it."

"But the fighting?"

He remembered describing to the widows the deaths of their husbands. "I can remember that if I have to."

"Perhaps you choose not to remember. Do you dream of it?"

He nodded and began to sweat.

"Why wouldn't you?" She poured him another cup of tea.

"The town seems different."

"How?"

"The streets seem small and mean. People seem complacent and ignorant. Even the fields seem lifeless and empty. This spring." He shook his head. "I can't stand it."

He spoke rapidly, as if anxious to get it all out.

"And Susan?"

He hesitated. "I don't like the company of women any more. Most women." He thought of Eleanor. "I didn't like the women over there. Hanging around the towns, getting in the way. Just standing there, doing nothing. Letting their homes be destroyed and their children. I can't stand passivity. Even my mother watching me and worrying. She's waiting for me to be the way I was. But everything's different." There was anger in his voice.

"Did you have girl friends over there?"

"In England. A few. But after a while I didn't want to."

"Are you homosexual?"

"No." He shook his head at her. "I don't want anything."

She rose and put a record on the turntable. The piano music was lyrical and passionate, but for him it seemed to come from miles away. She took her seat..

"You enlisted, didn't you?"

"Susan can't forgive me for that."

"You left her, that's all she knows. She's too inexperienced to have any understanding of what men do. The thing is, Robert Russell, you wanted to go."

He smiled coldly. "Big mistake. What does it matter, it's done with."

"You were passionate." He noticed she had abandoned 'Captain Russell' in addressing him. "You delighted us all with the way you threw yourself into everything you did. The men still talk about you playing hockey or baseball and as for the girls ... my dear." She rolled her eyes. He smiled. "If the war has killed that beauty in you, it is monstrous. Does nothing move you now? Does nothing excite you?"

He was about to shake his head when he thought of Calvin. Calvin MacQuiggan twirling in the storm against the dark of the woods, crying for his brother. Calvin at the mercy of his father.

"Calvin MacQuiggan moves me."

"Who's Calvin MacQuiggan? Wasn't the dead mailman named MacQuiggan?"

"Tommy MacQuiggan. Calvin is his little brother."

They heard the sound of a key in the lock of the apartment door. It opened and Rose MacIlwain entered, suitcase in hand. She saw Russell and froze.

"My, my, isn't this nice." She strode down the hall and closed the bedroom door with a slam.

Helen Partridge smiled evenly. "Don't worry, Robert Russell, she's been upset and it has nothing to do with you."

He rose to his feet. "Thanks for the tea. I'll be going."

"We will talk again, if you want to."

"I don't know. I'm not sure."

She walked to the door with him and took both his hands in hers. "I understand you're not sure, of women, of Susan, of me. So when we meet again we should talk about Calvin. There was too much in you, Robert Russell, for this war to kill. That's something that I know."

23.

As he walked down Ontario Street his muscles relaxed. She is intelligent. She doesn't ask stupid questions. But it's only talk.

On Pearl Street, past the beech trees in front of the Collegiate, he heard the familiar sound of bat on ball, around the corner of the school. On the baseball diamond, Fred Schumacher, his coach before the war, was hitting balls to a group of boys, some of them in the black shirt of the St. Thomas Black Hawks, his old team. He stood behind the screen, watching the boys scoop up the balls and throw them to their coach at the plate. Schumacher was a mechanic who worked at the Central Roundhouse, repairing the engines that hauled the freight trains across Southern Ontario from Buffalo to Detroit. He was greyer with a slight paunch, but his back was absolutely straight. As he watched, Bobby heard other voices, remembered other faces, other nights on the field. Spring practice; nothing had changed.

Schumacher put down the bat and began to clap his hands. "All right, two laps around the field, pull it out, let's go." Groaning, the boys threw down their gloves and began to jog. Schumacher turned, saw Russell, and looked away. Then he looked back.

"Bobby, is that you? Bobby Russell? Goddamn it if it isn't." His face broke into a broad grin. "Bobby, this is mighty fine. I heard you was in town again." He walked quickly around behind the screen and shook Bobby's hand. "When did you get back?"

"A week or so ago."

"Man alive!" Schumacher stopped, scratched his head, then began to smile. "Hey Bobby, maybe you can play centre field for us this year. We haven't got a real man on this team, they're all kids. Maybe some of the other fellahs will come back."

Bobby smiled. "I've been away too long, Fred; I'm an old man now."

"Shit," said the coach. "There ain't a ball player out there that could hit with you, when you were playin' in '37, '38. Look, here they come, runnin' like they got lead up their asses. Come on around, Bobby, I want to introduce you."

They walked onto the field as the boys trotted up, breathing mildly. "Boys, I want to introduce you to Bobby Russell, the greatest ball player to ever play for St. Thomas, our centre fielder from thirty-six to thirty-eight, championship teams, all three of them. Bobby hit over three hundred in each of them years and won the batting championship in the last year, thirty-eight, am I right, Bobby?" He nodded. "Now here he is, back from the war, and I want you to give him a real welcome home." The boys broke into a cheer. Bobby waved his hand and looked around the circle. Smiles, admiring gazes, some of which dropped shyly to the ground as they met his eye.

"Bobby, some of these boys think they can hit the ball. Why don't you take a couple of swings and show them how it's done?"

Bobby shook his head. "I've been out of it for too long."

"C'mon Bobby. You were the best natural hitter I've ever seen, and we got a pitcher here who thinks he's shit hot. Mackie, c'mere." A grinning boy with freckles and red hair stepped forward. "Bobby, this is Eddie Mackie. Go out and show him what you can do."

Russell shook his head, but the boys broke into a cheer. He took off his jacket and tie, walked to a bag of bats on the ground and selected one. Eddie Mackie strode out to the mound, another boy strapped on catcher's pads, and the others lined up on either side of the screen. Bobby stood at home plate, the bat feeling heavy in his hands. He swung the bat several times and the boys cheered. Then he stood up to the plate. Mackie wound up and threw. The first pitch

149

was high, and he let it go by, surprised by its speed. The second pitch came right down the middle, a fast ball that looked easy and he swung, only to hear the pop of the ball in the catcher's mitt. He had missed it by six inches. The boys groaned. The next pitch was a slow curve, and his swing was even further away. The boy threw six more pitches, and he hit only one, a weak ground ball on the third base side. The boys started to drift away and he saw, out of the corner of his eye, Fred Schumacher staring at the dirt. He returned the bat to the bag.

"I told you, Fred. It's been a long time."

"Hell, Bobby, it's natural. Fellah ain't held a bat for six years, with Germans shootin' at his ass, well, it's gonna affect his swing. I predict you take battin' practice for a week, you'll get your swing back. What you had, you don't ever lose."

Bobby put on his jacket and shook hands with Schumacher. He could see concern in the man's eyes. As he walked off the field he heard Eddie Mackie boasting, "That all-star didn't have a chance, couldn't touch me."

❀

It was five-thirty when he walked back to the City Hall. The police department was at the rear of the building. He found the door with 'Elmore Wayne, Chief of Police' stencilled on the glass. There was light behind it, so he entered. Elmore's secretary was a matronly woman who hadn't been around before the war and didn't know him.

"It's after hours, Mister, was he expecting you?"

"Russell," he said as he walked past her and pushed open the inner office door. The Chief was sitting behind his desk with his feet up, whipping a fly fishing rod back and forth. There was an open bottle of whiskey on the desk and a glass half full beside it. He looked at Bobby and a half-smile appeared on his face.

"You'd better knock before you barge in here like that, Russell. There's no telling what I might be up to."

The Chief winked, and tried a cast. The reel whirled and the line floated across the office.

"What can I do for you?"

Bobby settled in the chair. "What's the news regarding Tommy MacQuiggan?"

"He's dead." Wayne cast again, a smirk on his face. "As far as who did it, haven't a clue."

"There can't be many murders around here."

"One a year is an epidemic," said the Chief.

"So how do you go about solving one like this, with no motive, no suspect?"

"There's always a motive," drawled the Chief. "You find that, chances are you find your suspect. So you ask around, trying to find what happened. Anyone have a fight with Tommy recently? Did he have a girlfriend? Did he owe money? Any change in his behaviour, his habits? You ask around."

"And what have you found?"

"Are you asking as a concerned citizen, a friend of the family, or what, exactly?"

"The MacQuiggans have lived on our land for years."

Russell spoke with the assurance of someone who rarely has his motives questioned. The Chief, never one to go against the current, obliged.

"I guess that makes you the laird of the manor, Bobby." Wayne looked at him with an ironical smile. "Well, Tommy belonged to the youth group at First United and he had a job carrying mail. Those two facts make him unique in his family, who are known to have no fondness for gainful employment or for religion of any kind. If you could have taken Tommy away from his family, especially Archie, he might have turned out all right. The postmaster says he was a good employee, reliable and cheerful. Didn't have Archie's love of the drink. No one has any idea as to why he was killed. So there you have it, a totally inexplicable murder. Want a drink?"

Russell smiled. The Chief poured and continued. "Except we know that it isn't inexplicable. We just don't know enough. There's some little fact about Tommy, some incident, some something which, if we did know, would make us understand. We would understand why someone from out of town, experienced with a knife, would slit his throat and dump him under the bridge like that. Whoever did it knew that Tommy would be found, and didn't care. Usually when people in a community like this kill, they go to any lengths to hide what they've done. They bury the body at night. They burn it and scatter the ashes. They cut it up and plough it under; any manner of concealment. But not this fellah. He is saying, here's my work, neat and tidy, years of experience, I've done it before and I'll do it again, and don't worry yourself too much because you ain't never gonna' find me."

Russell nodded, savouring the whiskey. "So what do you do?"

"What would you do?" Wayne stared at Russell, who shrugged. "There's another thing. There has to be one person in this town, maybe several, who know what happened, and why. Whatever got Tommy killed, was local. Hell, as far as I can tell, the last time Tommy was away from St. Thomas was five years ago when he went up to London to sign on with the post office. It looks like he hasn't even been to Port Stanley since then. So whatever happened, happened here. And, when you think that the killer looks like a pro from the outside, you say to yourself, there must have been money involved to pay the man. So you're looking at a local person with some money who for some reason got angry enough with poor little Tommy MacQuigan to bring in some hood from Toronto or Detroit and have him killed. Hard to imagine."

He sighed and reeled in his line. "Other thing is, I can go snooping around this town for years without being the wiser. You know what these people are like; they don't even want to give you their name if you ask them a direct question. I tried asking Marie Barnes, the Bell operator, if she picked up anything unusual about Tommy in the last few months. She was insulted. She's not interested in low life like the MacQuiggans and wouldn't want you to think that she was up to date on Tommy's affairs. Although the murder caught her attention. She had it spread all over the county the morning after you found the body." He sipped his whiskey. "So that's where we are. An unsolved crime, and likely to remain so."

"You do the investigating yourself?"

"Naturally. We don't have detectives, we're too small in a town this size. Gus Campbell's the best of the constables, and he's too respectful to ask anybody a direct and personal question. So I do it. And this one, if I'm not careful, is going to cost me my fishing trip."

He cast again in a graceful arc. The door opened and Mayor Parker walked into the room.

"Private meeting? Just wanted to see if our fishing trip was still on, Elmore."

"Nothing private. Bobby wanted to know what was happening with the Tommy MacQuiggan case."

The Mayor waved his hand in dismissal. "Tommy MacQuiggan. Just a little fellah, not an enemy in the world. The town's upset; we don't have many murders here. On the other hand, not a case we'd want to spend a lot of money on. If Elmore can't figure it out, I'm damned if I'm spending tax money bringing the provincial police in."

"You bring them in," said Elmore Wayne, "and you lose control of your investigation. You get detectives and all of that nonsense. We want to keep it local."

Russell looked from one to the other. The Mayor and the Chief were both sons of railway workers, who had done well. Neither had any interest in the fate of Tommy MacQuiggan.

"Well, here's something else I need to know. Does either of you know why George MacAllister and Allan Matthews want us to sell our land to some unidentified buyer, enough to pester my mother for the last year or so to sell?"

Wayne looked quickly at the Mayor, who shook his head while clearing his throat.

"No idea, Bobby," said Parker. "You know lawyers. You never know what they might be up to."

Russell rose to his feet. The response had come too quickly, without reflection. Parker had been prepared for it.

"True. It just seems strange that anybody would want that land enough to put MacAllister and Matthews on the case. I thought you might have heard something." They shook their heads in unison. "All right, I'll be on my way." He walked out the door and shut it quietly. Wayne looked at Parker.

"Why didn't you tell him?"

"Why should I? He'll find out soon enough. Grant MacKay says they're going to expropriate."

Wayne whistled. "I didn't think MacAllister and Matthews had that kind of pull in Toronto, what with a Conservative government."

"They don't. But they got the money from this Yank from Ohio. That's where the pull comes from, no matter what the government. The other thing is, this boy looks like he's had the stuffing knocked out of him. Fighting Germans is one thing, but MacAllister's a mean, hungry son-of-a-bitch. I don't think Bobby Russell will have the stomach for the real nut-cutting."

The Chief shrugged, and cast another line across his office. "You're right, Al. I saw it in the last war. Some of those boys got burned out and weren't ever right again."

24.

All over the county during the next week, things paused and the days turned quiet. The crops were sown, and the farmers came into town earlier for a beer in the Confederation House. The conversation in Morris's Barber Shop quickly passed from Tommy's murder to the upcoming election, the weather forecasts for the next six weeks and the early season baseball results. In this summer lull it seemed to Bobby Russell that he was living in a slow-motion dream.

He set Calvin to work, hoeing the vegetable garden beside the house, carrying out trash and painting the tool shed behind the apple tree. The boy worked with meticulous care. It took him all day to paint the tool shed, a two-hour job, as he covered each square inch with the dark red paint, going back over each ripple in the old wood which had not been covered evenly. He started in the morning and finished when the smell of supper cooking was wafting out the kitchen door. Calvin stood beside the painted tool shed watching the house, waiting for him.

"Fine work, Calvin." he said. Something happened in Calvin's face, not a smile but a flicker in the eyes.

Russell would walk up town most mornings to buy a Toronto paper, read it in the Malt Shoppe, and do errands for his mother. He would go in and talk to Jack Morris if the barber chair was empty. Jack's topic these days was the upcoming election.

"If you look at it from the St. Thomas point of view, it's the Liberals all the way. Grant MacKay would have to rape the Mayor's wife in the middle of Talbot Street at high noon before these people would turn against him. Makes you wonder about democracy, don't it. Grant's so drunk these days I wonder he can hold his hand up in the Legislature to vote. He was in here having his hair cut last week and his neck set to shaking and twitching so that I was afraid I might cut it. Although, come to think of it, I might have done the electors of Elgin County a favour if I'd ended his political career right there. Not good for business, though, killing a customer."

Jack wheezed and his face turned red, the closest he ever came to laughter. When Russell asked Jack about the lawyers trying to buy part of his farm, the old barber shook his head.

"I heard nothing about it, Bobby. But one thing I do know, things is goin' to be happenin' around here. They all think that – Al Parker, Bill MacLean, George MacAllister and Grant MacKay. Parker was sittin' in that chair of mine just the other day saying that when the war-time controls come off, rationing and wage and price controls and that, there was going to be a boom. And it was going to hit here in Elgin County. Big things coming, according to the Mayor. Money to be made. Maybe they want your land for some scheme or other."

Twice he ran into Susan on the street. Both times she said, "Hi Bobby," and walked quickly by. He thought of Helen Partridge from time to time but did not go back to see her. His mother was delighted to have him home. He would catch her looking at him with a fond smile across the dinner table. But he knew she worried about him, and her constant watching annoyed him.

"Have you talked to Tom Allen about the new machines?" she asked him one night after supper, as he was settling in to read the evening paper.

"No," he snapped in a way that precluded further conversation; he went back to reading about the confusion over the death of Adolf Hitler, aware of the hurt in her eyes.

On a warm Thursday of the second week of his return, they went out on the back porch with their coffee. They faced east, watching the shadow from the house steal over the fields toward the woods, which were still sunlit. Down on the lawn by the sundial, Calvin was playing with a cardboard box, stuffing it with grass. The boy liked to stay with them after supper as late as he could, only going home when they went to bed. Margaret Ann was reading the Times Journal. Bobby had *Battle Fatigue and Psychic Disorders* on his lap, but he left it lying there as he stared at the fading light. He had started the book several times but had never read past the first page.

He had to do something. The thought tensed the muscles of his legs and brought an ache behind his forehead. He wanted a drink. The sequence was familiar. He would start by feeling a sense of urgency, the need to get on with things; suddenly he would be full of energy and enthusiasm. He was Bobby Russell, this was his town. It was time to get going, be up and doing. But the dreams of action inevitably faded, the demons would descend and he would think of whiskey.

On this night, lulled with the setting sun and the appearance of a crescent moon in the east, he considered going to Toronto. He had no obligations there, except possibly to Eleanor. He was free in Toronto of the stifling familiarity of St. Thomas, where everyone knew him. Furthermore, he had come to believe that St. Thomas was implicated in the war. The changing of the seasons in this little place, the crops of young men who almost seemed to rise from the corn fields, the triviality of daily life, all seemed part of a mindlessness that led every generation or so to war. War was the senseless pruning of a senseless herd.

He would put on a blue suit, grow a moustache and carry a polished leather brief case to Toronto and practice law. Not with Edward Archer, since that would mean Eleanor. She wouldn't take him now and even if she did, it wouldn't last.

Have to stop drinking. Have to....

The yard was now in shadow. Calvin walked towards the porch, holding a cardboard box. The boy stood and held out the box to Russell. Inside was a small robin with a broken wing, peeping softly.

"Where'd you get him, Calvin?"

"From the cat. The cat had him."

"He'll never fly. We'd better put him down."

"Put him down where?"

"Kill him. That's what put him down means."

Calvin moved away, withdrawing the box.

"Don't want to kill him. The cat was going to kill him."

"But he won't ever fly. He won't be able to catch his food. He'll die anyway."

"I'll get his food. Worms and bugs. They eat that."

"Okay then." He was looking at his mother, who was smiling thoughtfully at Calvin. "I'll go get an eyedropper and we'll give it some milk. See what that does."

The eyedropper was in a kitchen cabinet. He noticed an envelope on the kitchen table, addressed to him from the Attorney General of Ontario. He took it back to the porch, gave Calvin the eyedropper and a dish of milk, took his seat and opened the letter. As he read the blood flushed in his face.

"The government wants to expropriate our land!"

"Why? What does it mean?"

"It means that the government of Ontario, in co-operation with a company called Newcorp Investments, wants the land for the purpose of furthering a development at Lyndhurst Road and the London Highway, deemed to be in the public interest. It says I can get more information if I write to them, and there will be a hearing in Toronto on June 2." Russell rose to his feet, speaking very softly.

"MacAllister and Matthews are behind this."

He clenched his fists. Calvin stopped trying to feed the robin and stared at him.

"Do we get nothing for our land?" Margaret Ann asked.

"They'll pay us something."

He went to the living room, and picked up the telephone.

"Marie, get me Grant MacKay in Union."

He heard the phone ring, two long and two short, and then a woman's voice answered.

"Marjorie, this is Robert Russell. Is Grant there?"

"He's here, Mr. Russell, but he's not feeling well tonight. He went to bed early. Shall I tell him to call you in the morning if he's up and around?"

He's drunk, thought Russell. "No, I'll call him later if I need him. Good night."

He walked upstairs to his room and pulled the bottle from a shelf in the closet, hidden behind a pile of sweaters. He was relieved by the fire in his throat and took another swallow. Re-corking the bottle he put it carefully back behind the sweaters. He spent thirty seconds rearranging the sweaters so they looked exactly the way they had before.

He walked downstairs. He could win; he could deal with the land. He could handle MacAllister and Matthews, the government itself. He threw open the screen door to the back porch with tremendous power, so that it slammed against the door frame. His mother looked at him with a start. Bloody woman, he thought. Always watching me. And there was Archie, yelling at Calvin. Ordering him home.

"Archie. Leave him alone. He works here. You get on home."

"He's my boy, Captain Russell. I want him home."

Calvin edged towards the lane, leaving the box with the robin on the porch.

"Don't you move, Calvin." Russell heard his voice echo across the fields to the woods and back. "Archie, you leave now. He'll come when we're through here."

Archie glared briefly, then turned and trudged around the house, heading for the road. Margaret Ann went quickly into the house; Bobby stayed on the porch. The crescent moon was higher now. The fireflies had come out and were lighting the twilight with silver.

"Go home, Calvin," he said, "Your father wants you." He walked into the house, stumbled over a stair in the kitchen, and blundered his way upstairs. In his room he got the bottle, and took another swig. Then he lay on his bed in his clothes.

He saw the woman, rising out of the lake. He could not see her face. She was dark, blue maybe or black. The lake behind her was deepest, foaming red. She rose out of the lake of blood and stood, dark and unknowable, and above her shone a silver crescent moon. To one side on the dark shore a small figure knelt over a cardboard box and pulled out a bird with a broken wing. The bird cried and flew into the lake and was gone, and when he looked again, Calvin and the woman were gone, only an expanse of churning red remained. Beyond the red were white caps of waves, rolling in, rolling in. He saw seaweed, flotsam and other shapes and forms floating on the waves. They were bodies of dead men, limbs missing, heads missing, floating in to shore. What had he done? And where could he go? The questions came to him from a woman's voice, far out on the lake, beyond the bobbing bodies.

When he opened his eyes the sun was streaming in the window; he was in his bed. He was in his clothes, his head was splitting and his tongue tasted like paper. Fragments of his dreams lingered but the sun reassured him. He went to the bathroom and retched into the sink. He looked at his watch. It was ten o'clock, time to go. His mother was reading the paper in the kitchen.

"I'll pour you some coffee," she said.

"No coffee. I'm going up town."

"Where are you going?"

"To the lawyer's."

"You can't go like this. Your clothes are a mess and you smell of liquor."

He could barely see her, or hear her voice.

"I'm going," he said to the wall.

159

The new woman, Grace Connors, was not at her desk. Millie Hall looked at him and frowned when she saw him swaying in the middle of the room.

"Excuse me," she said, and rushed into MacAllister's office. Soon she re-emerged and went into Matthews' office. MacAllister came through his door and stood looking at Bobby, a smirk on his face.

"Come to do business, Captain Russell? Come into Matthews' office. You'll feel more at home there."

Allan Matthews rose from his desk, smiling, with his hand extended. Bobby didn't take the hand. The lawyer took in the angry scowl and the dishevelled clothes and his smile vanished.

"Good to see you again, Bobby. "

"Fuck you."

There was silence in the room. Matthews looked from Russell to his partner and back again to Russell. MacAllister continued to smile benevolently, as if things were happening as they should.

"What's on your mind, Captain?"

MacAllister's voice crackled like brittle paper. He drew a dirty yellow handkerchief from his pocket and blew his noise with a loud honk.

"You are trying to steal my land," said Bobby, waving the ex-propriation letter.

"Well, Sir," said MacAllister. "Land is not an easy thing to steal. You can't just pick it up and carry it away in the middle of the night. It pretty well stays were it is, and he whose name is on the deed owns it. It's a matter of law."

"Law." Russell spat the syllable "This goddamn letter...." He waved it again. "You're a pair of goddamn thieves, and I'm here to tell you that you won't get away with it, law or no law."

"Letter," said MacAllister. "What letter? May I see it?"

Bobby threw it at him. MacAllister picked the letter up and read it quickly.

"Captain Russell, your problem is not with us. The government of Ontario and Newcorp Investments, whoever they may be, want to take your land by legal expropriation. If you have a problem with what they're proposing, I suggest you hire a lawyer and fight it. But this has nothing to do with us."

"You lie," roared Bobby, spittle dripping down the corner of his mouth. "Give me back that letter." MacAllister placed the letter on top of Matthews' desk. Bobby snatched it. Matthews was looking increasingly uneasy, glancing at the door, glancing at his watch.

"You'll never win," Bobby yelled. "And I'll tell you why. Because I won't let you." He turned on his heel and walked unsteadily out of the office, slamming the door behind him. MacAllister snickered.

"The man's drunk. At ten-thirty in the morning he's drunk."

"It's sad," said Matthews. "I hate to see him like this."

MacAllister began cleaning his glasses with the end of his tie.

"Matthews, don't be a fool, it couldn't be better for us. The expropriation's going ahead. This drunken little prick sure hasn't got the backbone to stop it. He got a medical discharge from the army and he doesn't even know it. Don't worry. Everything's coming our way."

"Medical discharge?"

"I phoned Ottawa. Defence department. They sent him home when he got out of the German prison, he was so messed up. He doesn't remember that. He doesn't even know why he's here."

"I've known him since he was a boy and I've never seen him like this."

"That's good. How can he hurt us if he can't even think straight? Keep yourself together, Matthews. Be a man."

Allan Matthews looked at his partner with distaste. "This whole thing is getting out of hand. Tommy MacQuiggan was the last straw. You don't know what you're doing any more. We won't make enough money out of this to justify killing a man."

MacAllister paused and looked thoughtfully out the window.

"I never wanted him killed. And Malone says he didn't tell his boy to kill Tommy. He was supposed to scare him, make sure he kept his mouth shut about the letters he took for us. Well, he shut his mouth all right. Malone got himself a mad dog who went too far. But Tommy won't hurt us."

Matthews rose to his feet.

"I don't mind making money, and I'm not fussy about methods. I didn't mind sweet-talking Margaret Ann into selling the land. But stealing Margaret Ann's letters was stupid. He's come home, and the reason for stealing her letters is gone. Then Tommy MacQuiggan is killed, to keep him quiet about something that we never should have tried in the first place. And now we go to Toronto to arrange the expropriation for Van Kleef, who's nothing but an American with money. We side with him against our own people, against the Russells."

MacAllister rose to his feet, his face red.

"The Russells, the MacLeans. They're your people, but they're not mine. When my old man tried to get a mortgage in thirty-two to save that few acres of corn field he had south of West Lorne, they laughed at him. When my mother sold her eggs on Talbot Street to keep us fed during those years, they laughed at her. And when I showed up at the Collegiate, with patched britches and my father's shirt on my back, their kids laughed at me." His lips were tight and bloodless. "You're like them, Matthews. Exclusive. Look at this desk and this carpet. Look at your suit. You're soft like them. And like most soft people, you have no vision. This deal is going through, Tommy MacQuiggan or no Tommy MacQuiggan. There's nothing to stop it. Russell's nobody. So stiffen your backbone or get out."

On the other side of the door Millie Hall crept away from the key hole. She sat still at her desk and watched as MacAllister walked out of Matthews' office and into his own. Soon she followed him in and closed the door. The man stared at her, no expression on his face.

"What is it, Millie?"

"I thought ... I thought you might want me to ... I thought...."

She stared at him with pleading in her face. Then he swivelled his chair so his back was to her, and he stared out the window.

"I don't need you, Millie. Shut the door when you go out."

She walked from the room dabbing her eyes.

⚛

Russell walked down Talbot Street, his eyes blurred. He passed the Confederation House, the Grand Central Hotel and came to Art's Taxi where he hired Art to take him to the dairy. In the cab he sat fuming, thinking of MacAllister and his thin-lipped grin and his confident, high-pitched laugh. They would all be in it together, Al Parker, Grant MacKay, even Susan's father. At least they would know about it. When his father was alive, he was part of the collection of prosperous farmers and business men who ran the economy and the politics of St. Thomas and the County through the medium of the Liberal Party. That was what he was up against, decades of deals and the Liberal Party. They drove south on the Union road to the dairy and passed two wagons and one stake truck loaded with gleaming milk cans. Russell didn't even see them.

"I hear they want to take your land," said Art.

Russell looked at him, startled"Who told you that?"

"Tom Bell."

"Who?"

"Tom's one of the old guys who sits outside the feed store. He heard it in Jack Morris's while he was getting his hair cut. What do they want a piece of land like that for?"

"Don't know."

He paid Art and walked into the plant, nodded to Vera and Shirley and strode right into Tom Allen's office.

Tom, studying invoices, looked up startled. "Are you all right, Mr. Russell?" he asked, taking in the state of his clothes and the red of his eyes.

"Off course I'm all right. I want you to buy the new machines you were telling me about, the pasteurizer and the ice cream machines." He reached into his pocket and pulled out a check book. "How

163

much? I'll put the money into the account."

"Okay, fine." The manager paused. "This is good news, but I think we should go to Cleveland and look at the machines first. There are options, decisions I thought you would want to make."

Russell was tapping his check book on the desktop.

"You know more than I do about the machines. Tell me how much it will cost."

Tom Allen still looked uneasy.

"Does your mother know about this?"

Russell's voice rose. "Do you want to tell me how much the machines you want cost, or shall we get someone else to do it?"

"Now, Mr. Russell, I just wanted to make sure. Give me a minute while I put some figures together."

He reached into his desk and pulled out a file folder. He read carefully, then put some figures on a blank sheet of paper.

"The total for the pasteurizer and the ice cream machines is five thousand, four hundred and ninety-five dollars."

Bobby wrote the check, handed it over and walked out of the office, leaving Tom scratching his head. He felt good. Once he had decided to act, things fell into place. He would keep going, make the decisions and take actions. Clear the goddam terrain. By the time he reached the farm, he was smiling.

"They're crooks," he said to Margaret Ann in the kitchen. "Both MacAllister and Matthews. We'll have to fight. I'm going down to Toronto to find out who Newcorp Investments are, and why they want to take our land. In the meantime, I've given Tom the money to buy the equipment."

"This is very sudden," she said.

"We have to get moving again. We don't need any more talk."

25.

The rain began on Friday morning, so fine it was almost mist. When Russell looked out the sunroom window across the fields to the woods, he could only see a faint grey outline against a whiter sky. As the morning passed the rain grew steadier and the water ran down the roofs of the buildings, along the gutters and down the spouts.

"Good for the crops," said Margaret Ann, as she handed him his coffee

"Uh huh."

His head was sore but clear; he wanted to leave the house as soon as he could.

"Good porridge," he said cheerfully. "I think I'll go up town."

"That's nice, dear." She was careful not to look at him.

"Haven't seen Calvin since the other night. I might go over to MacQuiggan's first, and see how he's coming with that bird."

The rain had made him think of Calvin. It reminded him of the night he saw him dancing in the rain, the night they found Tommy. He went to the front hall, took an umbrella from the stand, and headed for the car.

The MacQuiggan house looked better in the rain than in sunlight. The cloud and mist hid the peeling paint and loose planks and rusty hinges. The house blended in with the land it was crumbling down to, the rain water singing to it, washing it, hiding it. He knocked on the door frame. After several seconds Leona came to the door.

"He ain't here," she said, looking at him apprehensively. "Archie went to town."

"It's not Archie I want. It's Calvin."

"Calvin's poorly. I can't let him out today."

He stared at her. She looked away and instinctively he knew.

"I'm coming in Leona. I want to see Calvin."

She drew herself up as if to oppose him, but he pushed past her into the house. He stood in the only main floor room, with an eating area beside the open kitchen, and several children's cots filling it. There was no sign of Calvin. He pushed past the stove and ice box to the summer kitchen, a lean-to structure attached to the rear of the house. At first the room seemed empty. But then he saw movement in a pile of rags in the corner furthest from him. He approached it softly and saw two thin legs sticking out one side of the pile, heels on the floor. No other part of the body was visible. He bent over and removed the rags. He gasped. Calvin lay on the floor naked, his body covered with red welts and scabs. His face was bruised and the lips covered with a kind of crust. The only sign of life was in the eyes that stared at Robert Russell without blinking. He turned to look at Leona who was standing in the doorway.

"Did Archie do this?"

She said nothing.

"Did Archie do this?' he yelled, and she nodded.

"Where is he?"

"Up town."

He formed the rags into a sling, and carried Calvin in it to the car. As he drove away he saw Leona in his mirror, standing in the doorway, staring through the rain.

❀

Calvin lay on the examining table without moving. Dr. Stuart was feeling the boy's limbs, pushing and prodding. Calvin lay limp. Outside the window, rain tattooed on a metal roof.

"Does that hurt, boy?' Stuart bent the boy's leg, scarred red with welts. Calvin said nothing. He twisted the other leg; there was no reaction. He went over the bones and muscles once more with his hands, then stood upright.

"Let's go outside and talk about this."

He covered Calvin with a sheet and blanket and followed Bobby from the surgery to his office. The doctor lowered himself into his chair and smiled with tired, mournful eyes.

"There are no broken bones. The beating appears to have been done with a belt buckle, which would not be heavy enough to fracture. There are a number of open cuts which may infect. We will put him in bed for a couple of days and cover him with cheese cloth soaked in brine. I hope that will keep the wounds from festering. That's one part of it."

166

He leaned forward and put his two thick arms, shirt sleeves rolled to the elbows, on the desk with a soft thump. "We'll take care of the cuts and bruises, but a beating like this can do more than physical damage. When I moved that boy's limbs in there, I hurt him but he made no sound. He hasn't uttered a sound since you brought him in. There is no life in his eyes. I don't know what we'll be left with, Mr. Russell, when the body is healed. It was such a frail, wee frame to start with."

"His father did it," said Russell.

The doctor grimaced.

"No doubt. You never see a child beaten like this by anyone outside the family. There wouldn't be the passion for it."

"Why doesn't someone stop it?"

"Why does the wind blow? Some things just are. These people are a very mixed lot, let me tell you." He gestured broadly to include the town and the county. "Look at that child, lying on my table. No animal would abuse his child in such a way. There are days, Sir, when I wish I had qualified as a veterinarian. A much cleaner and more salubrious business, I assure you."

"I'll have the father charged with assault."

"You'll be wasting your time. The law considers child-rearing a private matter. A charge of assault...." He shook his head. "It won't stick."

"We'll see about that." Russell rose from his chair. "One way or another, Archie MacQuiggan is going to be dealt with."

Outside the rain had become a steady downpour. He ran, but his hair was plastered flat by the time he reached City Hall. The Chief's secretary was away from her desk, so he brushed the water from his hair and barged through. Elmore Wayne was reclining in his easy chair, hands on his belly, lulled by the raindrops beating on his window. When Russell shut the door with a bang, the Chief opened his eyes.

"Goddamn it, Russell, you've got to stop sneaking up on me like this." He straightened his tie. "Man can't get some decent shut-eye without being side-swiped by a concerned citizen. Now, as I told you last time, we're trying, but I am not optimistic about finding Tommy's murderer."

"That's not why I'm here." He began to describe his finding Calvin. The Chief listened, his eyes narrowing.

"That sounds like Archie," he said when Russell had finished.

"I want him charged with assault."

The Chief's face tightened."I usually lay charges around here, Sir. People seem to like it that way." He paused for full effect. "There's no point in charging Archie with assault. A judge would say that a father disciplining his son is a private matter. Which is what Archie would claim he was doing." He scratched his chin. "But even if Archie has gone past the limits this time, what good would it do to charge him? How many kids live in that shack you rent them? Nine? Ten? Nobody knows for sure. What do you think happens to those kids and that pig of a woman if we lock Archie up? He ain't much, but he's all they've got."

"So we have to wait until he kills somebody."

"Sometimes it works out that way." He shook his head. "God, I hate these cases. Sometimes I think Archie should have been castrated, way back. Allowing that man to breed is a guarantee of misery for succeeding generations. I'm going around to the hospital to look at Calvin. And I may have a little heart to heart with Mr. MacQuiggan if I can find him sober. But I am not going to charge him."

Outside the rain was softer again. Russell walked out to Talbot Street and turned right towards the Confederation House. He stood in the doorway of the hotel's mens' room. It was three-thirty, and the only patrons were the old men, Tom Bell and Fred Chisholm, and a few farm labourers. This was Archie's crowd, but he wasn't among them. Alfie Becker, his gut hanging far over his belt, appeared from behind the bar and began to replace the empties on the table from his tray. As Russell watched this scene, Archie appeared from the toilets, struggling to button up his fly.

"Can't get 'er done up, boys," he roared to the table. "Even with half my balls shot off, she's still too goddamn large."

The laughter was raucous. Russell moved out of the doorway and stood by the table, staring at Archie. The table went quiet. Archie looked up; a grin spread over the fleshy red face.

"Captain Russell, by geez, sit and drink with us common men."

He didn't move and the faces at the table became curious, watching him.

"Calvin is in the hospital. I took him there this morning."

The smile faded from the big man's face.

"What's the matter with him?"

"He's been beaten to within an inch of his life."

Archie looked nervously around the table. The men were waiting in silence. He sipped his beer and then looked up defiantly, thumping the table so the glasses jumped.

"You got no call to mess with my business, Captain. He's a lazy, worthless little pup. I got to teach 'im, it's my duty as his father. How I do it is up to me, I guess."

"Many people seem to agree with you. However, the boy is in the hospital scarcely able to speak. You've gone too far." He looked directly at Archie. "So here's what we're going to do. When he gets out of hospital, he'll stay with us. We have a room he can use, and work he can do."

"You have no right to take him," roared Archie. "He's mine, not yours. I lost one boy already this spring, you ain't taking the other, by geez. I got my rights."

"You have your rights, Archie, and I have mine. I own the house you live in. If I hear one more complaint, you'll be moving on."

Archie, puffed up with fury, opened his mouth but closed it quickly. He glared at Russell, then looked at the ground. When he looked up, cunning had replaced anger in his eyes.

"Well, maybe the boy will be better off. Maybe you can learn him a few things I couldn't. Will you still be paying me his wage?" Bobby nodded. "Well hell, one less mouth to feed. Captain, you got a deal." He sat and drained a glass of beer.

Bobby walked down Talbot Street, heading for home. The rain had stopped and there was a band of light in the western sky.

Done. And now tomorrow. The tomorrows just keep coming. What to do? Calvin. I'll go see Calvin. Here's the feed store, where are they? There they are, in Jack's, yakking. I remember different old men hanging out on that bench before the war. Lined, rheumy-eyed faces. Must be dead, or lying in a bed somewhere. Like different kids playing ball. Things change, things are different. But not really. A field of corn is always a field of corn.

At the end of Talbot Street the pavement turned to gravel, the curbs became grassy ditches; the road dipped into the valley where Kettle Creek wandered among the farms. He could see the fields from the crest of the hill, squares of dark earth brushed with green. He barely knew where he was, walking down the road, putting one foot after the other.

Is this the Finlay farm? Maybe…. *It looks like I'm walking into that little village, what was it called, Villa…. Villa … something. East of Rome. Down in a valley. We had pounded it, the Germans had withdrawn. Almost nothing standing, rubble everywhere. That old priest trying to open the door of the church, which was jammed; half the church's roof gone. And the women … staring at us. We got a piper from somewhere. Marched in. Women everywhere and kids standing there. Hated that, the terrified eyes. And my men marching behind, the sound of their boots. Archie was still in the ranks; he hadn't yet been wounded out.*

A stake truck roared past and the driver honked and waved. The noise broke his reverie. He was walking along the Lyndhurst Road. His farm was just around the bend in the road, where his mother would be in the house, watching for him. Susan was waiting for him. *Beside the road, watching with dark, alien eyes.*

Without this war, we'd be married now, probably with kids. Didn't happen. Just a man, walking down the road.

When he was about five or six he remembered walking from the house and coming upon Archie beating a horse that wouldn't enter the barn, shouting at it, red-faced and whipping its back with a leather thong. Finally his father came out from the house and took the leather away. He remembered the look of incomprehension on

Archie's face, the shrug as he went along with what the boss wanted. The brutality was in the small blue eyes, the heavy set of his face, the weight of his haunches and the size of his fists. A perfect soldier, you would think.

There was now a band of blue sky in the west, and he could feel the onset of a breeze. Swallows were skimming over the wet fields. There might be a sunset tonight. He would sit in the sunroom with his mother and watch the sun go down. Maybe have a whiskey. By the time he reached their farm there was sun on the roof of the house. His mother was standing on the porch.

"How is Calvin?" she asked.

"In the hospital. How did you know?"

"Hettie James saw you taking him in to Stuart's surgery, and she told Marie Barnes. Marie heard from a nurse at the hospital. I heard if from Valerie MacLean." She paused. "You might have told me."

"There wasn't time, he was so badly beaten. I told Archie that Calvin will be living with us from now on."

"Oh, did you?"

"I guess I should have asked you, but no one else will take him. There's no place for him in that miserable little town."

"Miserable little town." Her eyes turned from him. "It wasn't the town. Had you not been drunk the other night and dismissed Archie the way you did, I doubt this would have happened."

"I don't remember any such thing." His voice was unsure.

"You're drinking too much. I'm surprised you can remember your name."

He turned and went inside, heading for the stairs and his bottle.

26.

"How are you, Calvin?"

The boy looked up, the eyes alive again, watching carefully. His head lay on the pillow, very still, and his lips were still crusted.

"Where is the bird?" he said in a hoarse whisper.

"What bird?"

"The bird in the box."

He remembered. The bird with the broken wing.

"It must be dead. No one has been feeding it."

The eyes on the pillow shut, and when they opened, the life was gone from them.

"Things die, Calvin. Don't be afraid." The boy stared at the ceiling. "You're going to come and live with us." The eyelids fluttered briefly. "You can live with us and help me out around the farm." The head turned and the eyes opened.

"He won't let me."

"Archie thinks it's a good idea."

"That's good."

❁

Russell walked down Talbot Street to Jack Morris's barber shop wishing that he'd remembered that bird. By the time he reached the shop he was muttering to himself. Mayor Parker was waiting, reading a magazine. As Russell sat down he noticed the old men crossing the street from the feed store, heading his way.

"I hear Archie MacQuiggan's got family problems," said the Mayor.

"Yes. Beating a ten-year-old boy almost to death is a problem."

"I don't like that." The Mayor was frowning. "There ought to be a law. As things stand now, there's nothing we can do."

At this point the group from across the street trouped into the shop. Jack rested his arms on the back of the barber chair, snipping his scissors in the air.

"You men get out of here unless you want a haircut. Best price in town." Jack was the only barber in town. "Otherwise, go back to your bench and get your sun tans."

The old men stood in the doorway, looking hurt.

"Geez, Jack, we just wanted to hear what happened with Archie," said Tom Bell.

"I ain't runnin' no pool hall," snapped Jack. "You bums already know Archie beat up his kid and put him in the hospital. So git. I won't have you pesterin' my customers."

"You gonna do something, Bobby?" asked Tom Bell, as they turned to leave.

"Maybe," said Russell.

The old men shuffled out.

"My, my, Jack, you run a tight ship," said Parker.

"Got to. Those bums are too tight to spend money for the movies or even some pool, so they think they can come in here and use my shop as a social club. They like the low membership fees." The old barber wheezed and cackled.

Parker took the chair. Jack covered him with a clean white cloth and began to examine the Mayor's hair.

"Look Al, it's thinner even than last time, you're really losing it. Why don't you let me sell you a bottle of the Gentleman's Hair Elixir?" Jack produced a bottle of a green, creamy looking substance from a shelf. "We recommend it in these circumstances. Look beautiful for the voters."

"To hell with the voters," said the Mayor, and then nervously looked around the shop to make sure no one had heard him. "I mean, I'll just let my hair go the way it's going. My old man was bald. Anyway, that slimy lookin' stuff probably won't grow mould on a stale piece of cheese." Jack chuckled as he put the bottle back on the shelf. He had yet to sell a bottle of the Gentleman's Hair Elixir.

"Say, Bobby." The Mayor was looking at him. "What's gonna happen to the kid? Archie might kill him next time."

"He'll stay with us," said Bobby. "We have a room for him."

"That's a wonderful thing." The Mayor's voice slipped into the deep baritone of an election speech. "What would we do without families like the Russells. Isn't that wonderful, Jack?"

"It is." The barber snipped around the Mayor's bald patch.

※

He picked up Helen Partridge just after three o'clock.

"You've had your hair cut," she said. "You look younger."

Women were always complimenting. "Nice dress," or "Nice haircut." He preferred the truths you got from men. "You fucked up, Russell, those Germans are still there," or "There is no hope this side of the grave."

"How have you been?" She looked tentatively at him.

"You've heard about Calvin MacQuiggan."

"Some of it."

Russell described what had happened to Calvin and mentioned his concern for the injured bird. When he finished they walked several steps in silence.

"That's sweet, about the bird," she said eventually. "It gives one hope for him. Are you involved with Calvin now?"

"We have to decide what to do about him. He can't live with his father anymore."

"Why would it be you that decides about him?"

"Because they live on our land. Because Calvin is alone, there's no one else."

"Then it's good that you're there, isn't it? Good that you can do something."

"It doesn't seem good. Just when I decide I want to leave this miserable place, I get sucked back in, because there is no way of preventing Archie from beating his son whenever he feels like it. There is no protection for Calvin. Not the police. Not the courts. Not the Mayor. Nobody."

"So why don't you leave and forget it?"

"I can't."

"Why not?"

He took a deep breath. "Because of the boy."

Is that true? Is there nothing but Calvin holding me here?

"How long have you been drinking hard?"

He stopped smiling, and glared.

"Am I drinking hard?"

"Susan says you are. Your face is red and your speech is sloppy.

174

And if you have been drinking today, it's still early in the afternoon."

"Well, at least Susan got one thing right." He looked defiantly at her. "I am drinking hard."

"Is it what you want?" He said nothing. "I suppose you'd be drinking a lot during the fighting. To blot it out."

"I didn't mind the fighting."

She turned to him. "That's hard to believe."

"You had no choice, everything was very clear. I liked that. You followed orders, and tried to keep alive. All the St. Thomas men were together. It was great when it worked; we were a good little unit." He smiled. "They depended on me. I had to keep them convinced that we knew what we were doing, even when we didn't. I had to make sure they got fed, their wounds tended, buried, whatever they needed. So I couldn't be drunk, though I drank. There was liquor everywhere, all the time."

"And seeing your friends blown to pieces?"

"You'd have to understand how very fast things happen. When someone goes, he goes, and you move on; there's no time to be sentimental. The next day, it's as if the dead man had never been there. You forget. The days and nights, the shelling, the moving forward, the moving back, it all keeps coming in a blur. It hits you after, when you have time to think."

"It hit you in the camp," she said. "You started to drink hard."

"Yes." His face was screwed up, twisted.

"Do you know why?"

"There was nothing else to do but think. And what was there to think about?" His face relaxed. "There was just this yellow brick wall, the dormitories, the cook house and the stupid guards, making you redo your bed, or sweep the floor. Old soldiers from the first war most of them. Not bad, but stupid. They would trade their home-made schnapps for the cigarettes we got from the Red Cross. Ha, ha, ha." Laughter lit up his face. "That's the Germans for you. They invade and conquer most of Europe, but they won't steal their prisoners' cigarettes." His laughter passed. "At first I thought of here, but then I didn't want to. So I tried to remember what happened to every man who was killed. But after a while, I couldn't sleep. So booze was the better option."

"An anaesthetic."

"Yeah."

"Have you been reading that book you took from the library?"

"I can't get past the first chapter."

"Why?"

"The man's a doctor. He wrote about the soldiers he treated as if they had a disease that he wanted to cure." He turned abruptly to her, shaking his head impatiently. "These men weren't sick. Whatever they did always made perfect sense to me. They were scared shitless, excuse me, and that made sense, they had reason to be scared. So they behaved rationally in the circumstances. They needed to survive and you can't survive if you're afraid all the time. So you do what you have to do for the fear. If booze it what it takes, then booze it will be. But I don't need some doctor telling me how he's going to cure me."

They walked in silence. She was concentrating on the mixture of bravado and uncertainty she heard in his voice, when she heard the quick intake of his breath. Susan MacLean was approaching them on the sidewalk across the street. She stared at them, caught herself and produced a dazzling smile.

"Lovely day for a walk," she called as she sailed past. Neither of them could think of anything to say.

"She missed you," said Helen after Susan was out of sight..

"She may have done. But it's over now."

"Perhaps."

They walked another block in silence. Then she turned to him. "I would never claim to understand what has happened to you. No one here can know that. But I can see a few things, and I want to say them." She looked at him and he nodded.

"When I think of you before the war, I remember a boy who was always up to something. You were playing games, going to dances, canoe trips, parties, fooling around on Talbot Street on Saturday night, driving Gus Campbell mad; there was always something. The kids worshiped you. They loved your daring, they loved your style and your humour. They were always talking about you. You were their leader. So when the war happened, it was probably inevitable that you'd be the Captain. You'd flash that smile, or give that crazy little laugh of yours, and the men would think, it's all right, the Captain's here, and he knows what to do. Is that the way it was?"

"I guess," he said. "Except the Captain didn't always know what he should do."

"Some were killed. You think you let them down."

"Not at all," he lied, but she held up her hand.

"I know you're a good, warm man, Robert Russell, and the killing disturbed you, no matter what you say now. You think that if you had done a better job you might have saved some of your men. But you had to keep fighting, so you repress the guilt." He said nothing. "As you say, drinking is a fairly sensible thing to do in the circumstances."

Still he said nothing, but she could see his face soften slightly. He smiled briefly at her. She smiled back.

"That smile brings back memories," she said. "What a rascal you were." They walked silently for several seconds. "I'm nearly finished; just one more thing."

"Say what you like," he said. "Words don't matter."

"Nonsense. Words do matter. What people think matters. Your problem now is what you think about the situation. You've been through a war, and it's been disastrous for you, as it would be for any complete, intelligent person. The trouble with you is, like many men and even a few women, you think that your experience is universal. If you had a hard time, the world must be a hard place. If the war was senseless, so the universe is senseless. If you come back and St. Thomas seems isolated and provincial to you, then human beings are boors and fools. And above all, because women played no role in this male orgy we call war, you dismiss us as irrelevant. It's arrogance, really. Which must be what angers Susan. Your sense that since you had such a terrible war, no one else can have a life worth living."

"Male orgy? It wasn't that much fun. And arrogant? You make me sound like a prima donna." He looked grim again.

"You're not a prima donna, but you are arrogant." She looked at him, perplexed, not sure how to reach him. "Look at Calvin, still caring for his little bird. What a spirit. If anyone has reason to give up hope, it's him. But he doesn't. He's facing his life with much more courage than you are, my dear."

He turned quickly. "Damn it, Helen. You've got me all summed up and analysed."

He began to walk away.

"Robert." She called softly to him and he stopped. "I wasn't there, and I don't want to judge." She smiled warmly at him. "But life does go on." She inhaled the May air and looked at the maple. "What a beautiful spring we are having. The summers have been gorgeous all through the war, which is odd. As if nature were compensating for the fighting. The rains this last week have made the soil smell so dank and rich. And I love those mild winds from the southwest, coming over the lake this time of year, and all around us the lush green growing. Is there anything on earth more gorgeous?" He shrugged. "This year will be important. To think that despite the years of war and killing, these summer months just kept coming back again and again, more powerful than guns and blood. Summer is inevitable, life is inevitable, they are the norm. Wars are freak events; they are nonsense."

"Words," he said gently. "Woman's words. What's in a word?"

"Everything. Behind the sound of the word 'summer' is our memory of each year, as it returns, pushing up from the earth, forgiving us our little sins. I remember the summer my husband died." Her eyes darkened. "The corn was knee high on the day he died. The robins and cardinals sang from the tops of the trees throughout that day."

"He used to beat you up, didn't he?"

"Yes." She thought for a moment. "Until the summer came and washed him away."

"Life goes on in Sicily now," he murmured. "Italy. Holland."

"So words are important. You lived before the war and here you are, thank God, living after it. What happened to you? What happened to Calvin? What happens to any of us? What words will you choose to describe your life? Will they come from the mad years you spent fighting, or from the rest of your life, including the beauty around you this very day, and the innocence and courage of Calvin MacQuiggan?"

"There is something in what you say," he said finally. "I will think about it."

"Do. And when you think of Susan, and the town, and everything here, choose your words carefully. Words matter." She began to giggle. "My heavens, don't I sound like a librarian!"

"I suppose," he said.

He stepped forward, the daring smile in his eyes that she remembered from years ago, and put his arms around her. She sighed and nestled against his chest, then quickly drew back.

"Be off with you," she said, her eyes gleaming. "I have to get back to the library.

⚛

He sat on the back porch, a whiskey in his hand. He had decided to drink in the open, not sneak it in his room.

She must be fifty but she felt good against me. Hair is grey, sagging tits, but she felt good. My God, what is the matter with me? It's the life in her eyes, the passion in her low voice. And more than anything she understands me and likes me. And she asks for nothing. And this stuff about words. Are my words really wrong?

He heard his mother enter the kitchen behind him and begin to rattle pots and pans.

"Mother." She came to the screen door. "Come and have a drink with me."

She opened the door and came out onto the porch, a merry smile on her face. "I haven't had an invitation like that for ever so long," she said, fixing her hair with one hand.

179

"Here's to you, my dear," she said, raising her glass. "So what have you been doing today?"

"I was up to see Calvin. He's mending somewhat. He asked about the bird with the broken wing he had here that night." He paused and sipped his drink. "Maybe we can get him a dog. He's going to be leaving the hospital day after tomorrow, they say."

"What a perfect idea. We haven't had a dog around here since Hector died. I'd like another springer spaniel."

"Calvin will be happy with any dog." He sipped his drink. "I was also talking with Helen Partridge."

"Helen Partridge? Were you looking for something to read?"

"Not really. She has interesting things to say about the war."

"I can't imagine what Helen could know about the war. She should never have moved in with Rose MacIlwain after her husband died. No man will approach her living the way she does. She needs to fix herself up, show an interest in life."

"Don't be so sure. She gave me a nice hug before she left."

Margaret Ann looked at him and raised an eyebrow.

"Whatever do you mean, she hugged you?".

"Any port in a storm, Mother. After all, who goes dancing with Allan Matthews?"

"Hush up, that's not the same at all. He's my age, and he likes women." She was trying to keep a straight face. "He wants to take me to the Stork Club Saturday night."

Russell noticed the satisfaction in her expression. "How can you go dancing with the man who's trying to steal our land?"

"I am going. Who cares about that old piece of land, anyway."

"Mother you can't. I don't like it."

She rose to her feet, her eyes flashing.

"You mind your place, young man. I'll go to the Stork Club or anywhere else whenever I want with whomever I want."

"Okay, okay. But come with me. Dance with whomever you like, but come with me."

"I'll consider it," she said.

27.

There was chaos in the kitchen of the Grand Central Hotel. The Grand Central was the only hotel in St. Thomas, if you ignored MacDermott's Railwaymen's Hotel, as most respectable people would. Today there was a special lunch order – Steak Delmonico for ten – but the recently hired cook had not shown up for work. The manager, Mr. Dooley, had tracked him to his boarding-house room and found him lying in his bed, drunk and snoring. The lesser members of the kitchen staff were able to produce the whipped potatoes, the string beans, the Waldorf salad and the apple pie with vanilla ice cream. But none of them knew how to produce Steak Delmonico.

"The Mayor will be here," said Dooley, wringing his hands. "And Mr. MacLean, the newspaper publisher, and Grant MacKay, and MacAllister and Matthews and their American guests. These are the leading men of the town. What will we do?"

The busboys, the waiters and the kitchen helpers stared at the floor, overwhelmed by the very mention of Steak Delmonico.

"Mr. Allan Matthews himself placed the order." Mr. Dooley flapped his hands and fluttered his eyes. "He is a man of travel and experience. He has been to New York and understands Steak Delmonico. Whatever will we do? We face total humiliation."

At first, the kitchen was silent, the staff paralyzed. Then Audrey MacLellan, the dining room manager, stepped forward.

"I don't see your problem, Mr. Dooley. The reputation of this dining room is strongest among salesmen and other such for our baked beans on toast, apple pie and mixed London grill. Steak Delmonico has never been a feature." Mr. Dooley stared at her with exasperation. "Now none of us here knows anything about this Steak Delmonico affair, but we must have the steaks." One of the assistant chefs pointed to a counter where ten slabs of bloody scarlet were arrayed. "And do we have onions?" There were murmurs of assent. "Good. Now my husband tells me he wouldn't ever leave me, for nowhere else in the world would he find steak and onions like mine. Now I propose to make it for this dinner, Mr. Dooley, and if these men are real men, with a taste for what's good, they'll walk away from our dining room satisfied as they have seldom been before."

The morale rose in the room. Smiles appeared on every face but Mr. Dooley's, who continued to be wracked by indecision. Eventually, however, he looked at Mrs. MacLellan in surrender.

"Alright, we'll go with it. God knows what they will say, but we've no choice. Now I want every other part of this meal to be perfect. Not a lump in the whipped potatoes, and perfect crust on the apple pie." He lowered his voice as he looked at each face in the room individually. "I know I can count on you."

In the hotel's private dining room, MacAllister and Matthews, Al Parker, Grant MacKay, Bill MacLean and three city councillors were sitting at one long table, underneath a portrait of King George VI and two flags, the Union Jack and the Canadian red ensign. A moose head was mounted on the wall opposite.

"How's the campaign, Grant? Any problems?"

"Nah." MacKay was sipping from a tea cup a liquid that was causing red spots to appear on his cheeks. "That socialist stuff may fool the railway workers, but respectable people and the Liberal Party will carry Elgin County."

There were confident smiles from everyone present.

"I don't know where our guest can be," said Matthews, looking at his watch. "He said he'd be here by twelve."

"He's driving from Detroit," said MacAllister, cleaning his teeth with a corner of his napkin. "Give him time."

The talk returned to politics and the chances of the Liberal Party across the province of Ontario. The leaders of Elgin County had been Liberal supporters since the nineteenth century. They were united against the Conservative Party, the party of big city privilege and Anglican, anglophile snobbery. The Conservatives' support of high tariffs was seen as keeping Toronto business interests rich and the Scotch farmers of Elgin County poor.

Mr. Dooley appeared at the door. "Excuse me, Gentlemen. Mr.

Tyler Van Kleef, and Mr. Tyler Van Kleef Junior."

A tall man, over six feet in height, wearing a tan suit, bald, with a fringe of grey hair, his blue eyes gleaming behind his spectacles, strode into the room, followed by his son, a younger version of himself. The young man's gaze sought out every man in the room aggressively. Tyler Van Kleef was introduced by George MacAllister, his lawyer. Van Kleef pumped every hand offered with a ferocity and vigour that made some wince, and said to each, "I'm real pleased to meet you, Sir," in a voice that could be heard in the lobby of the Grand Central. He then turned, with a fond smile, to the young man at his side. "My son, Ty Junior. Teaching him the business. You haven't done a real deal until you've done a deal with Ty Junior."

MacAllister ushered the two Americans to the table as two stout farm women carried trays of soup into the room.

"You were rather later than anticipated, Mr. Van Kleef," said MacAllister, in an unusually accommodating tone of voice. "Did you find our highway rougher than those super highways you're used to?"

"No, the road was fine. Got away later than I expected. Now tell me, how are you boys making out on the land assembly?"

The question brought an embarrassed silence.

"We're working on it," said George MacAllister.

"Sure are," said Grant MacKay. "We got the best Tory law firm in Toronto doing the expropriation."

"Expropriation," said Van Kleef. "What expropriation?"

"We ran into some resistance from the owner of the last piece of land, on the Lyndhurst road," said MacAllister finally. "He won't sell. We have to expropriate."

"What did you offer him?"

MacAllister looked at Matthews and coughed.

"Eight thousand," said Allan Matthews, tensely smoothing down his grey hair. "His mother, that is. We offered her eight thousand. But the son won't sell."

'Off course he'll sell; it's a question of price. I authorized ten

183

thousand. And you were to contact me if that was not satisfactory. We need that land, and we don't have to worry about a couple of thousand dollars here or there. I want to talk to this man. What's his name?"

"Robert Russell. He's just back from overseas and he's...."

"A soldier? Let me talk to him. I haven't yet met a man I couldn't sell to, provided he could think straight."

Alarm flashed on the faces of the two lawyers.

"Mr. Van Kleef," said MacAllister. "I must advise against a face-to-face meeting. Young Russell is an unusual case and requires careful handling. We have already put a lot of time and thought into him, and I would hate to see all our work ruined by a hasty...."

"But it's too goddamn slow." Van Kleef hit the table with a closed fist. "I need results, and if I can't get them here, there are other locations I'm prepared to consider."

"Mr. Van Kleef, as Mayor of St. Thomas, I assure you that there is no site in all of Southern Ontario as propitious for your project as this city." Conviction and sincerity throbbed in the Mayor's quivering voice. "Hard working, honest people. A location suitable to Buffalo, Detroit and Toronto. Cheap land. And, if I may say so, a forward-looking, business-minded local leadership. Everything you need is here."

"Except land. I can't build without the land. I'll talk to Russell."

Allan Matthews cleared his throat. "Russell appears to be in a very emotional state after his war experience, shell shock of some kind. We don't think he'll hold out for long. The expropriation is only a threat; we don't anticipate a serious problem. But the situation is delicate and requires careful handling. I urge you to let us finish the negotiation."

Van Kleef leaned back in his chair as the soup bowls were cleared away. "Boys, I'll give you another two weeks. But if you don't have the deal for me by then, all bets are off."

The lawyers looked at the politicians, who shrugged. MacAllister was red in the face.

"We'll get the deal," he said. "Count on it, Mr. Van Kleef."

The waiters came in the swinging doors with trays of steaming food. As they set the plates on the table, Allan Matthews motioned angrily to the head waiter.

"I ordered Steak Delmonico," he whispered angrily as the man stood at his elbow. "I told Dooley of the importance of this dinner. This is not Steak Delmonico."

"I'm sorry, Sir, but the cook is ill today. We had to make do with the staff we had."

Matthews' face was beet red. "Tell Mr. Dooley I wish to speak with him immediately after dinner."

The head waiter bowed and turned to leave.

"Best steak I've had in a coon's age," bellowed Van Kleef from the centre of the table. "Cooked with onions, just the way Mrs. Van Kleef does it. Isn't that a good feed, Junior?"

"Sure is, Pop," said young Van Kleef, his mouth full.

Matthews paused and stared, then sank back to his seat. There was silence in the room as the men ate their meal with gusto.

"There's something I want to say," said Van Kleef, as he pushed away from his empty plate.

"People attribute my business success to my ability to see what's coming and to be there first. Now I don't know how much truth there is to that. I owe my success as much to luck and the Good Lord. Still, so many people seem to think I know what's going on, there must be something to it. Right, Junior?"

"Sure thing, Pop."

"And I'll tell you boys, I have a feel about this town of yours, I have a vision. I see the auto parts plant standing four square on the highway, where there's only corn fields now. I see trucks speeding up and down the highway, bringing materials to the plant and hauling away the finished parts to Detroit, to become part of the automobiles and other vehicles that will be speeding over our highways in ever greater numbers. I see the citizens of this town prospering from wages, legal business, all manner of trade, commerce and other activity generated by the plant. They will wear better clothing. They will eat better food. The quality of the education in your schools will rise, and the religious faith of the people sitting in the pews of your God-fearing churches will deepen. You will walk forward into an era of prosperity and freedom. This is what my parts plant will do for you."

The St. Thomas men were delighted by this vision of their future. Each was translating the dollars that would flow from the auto parts plant to his corner of the town's economy. Van Kleef Junior, with the bored look of someone who had heard these words before, was picking his teeth with a gold tooth pick. The waitresses were setting out plates of apple pie and ice cream.

"But, boys," Van Kleef continued. "I have to have that land in two weeks."

"Goddamn it, Mr. Van Kleef," said Al Parker, rising to his feet. "You'll have it if I have to take care of Russell myself."

The men around the table nodded their assent. The apostle of prosperity through commercial development finished his pie and rose from his seat.

"Ty Junior and I will be driving out to the site, to conduct our own discussions. I had hoped to bring an architect up to survey it next week, but I see that will be premature. Get cracking, boys. Time and the tides wait for no man."

Tyler Van Kleef strode from the room, picking his teeth with his own gold tooth pick. His son followed. When they had gone, the men in the room looked at one another with purposeful stares.

"Boys," said George MacAllister in a whisper. "We've got to get that land." The assembly nodded as one.

"I agree with George," said Bill MacLean. "There appears to be an opportunity for our town here. But the Russell family has legal title to that land. More than that, the family have been respected members of this community for generations. He's served his country overseas. He's a fine young man, a friend of my daughter Susan's. We must treat him with respect."

MacAllister's face reddened. The Mayor looked doubtful. The councillors began looking uncertainly around the room.

"We all knew Romaine Russell," said Allan Matthews. "We've

sat with him in this very room so many times. He started the dairy, served on the council, a good party man. Margaret Ann is a fine woman, and a friend. I would not want to see their son sacrificed at the first mention of some American money."

"As your Mayor, I am in favour of anything that benefits our city." Parker looked uncertain. "On the other hand, I would not want to do wrong to one of our good old families. Perhaps we need to take another look at this."

The Mayor looked around the room, evaluating the impact of his words. For a full minute there was deep silence. Finally, George MacAllister, blue eyes flashing, rose to his feet.

"What kind of nonsense is this? No one is sacrificing Russell to anything, he's doing it to himself. He's had every opportunity to join this project, but he has refused us all. I've talked to him, Matthews has talked to him, but it does no good. He holds himself back, sulking and brooding like a girl without a beau to take her to the dance. Is he wounded? Not a scratch on him. Got a medical discharge, though; his nerves are bad. The pressure of war got to him, they say." Bill MacLean rose to his feet, but MacAllister hushed him with an angry wave of his fist. "This talk of the Russell family is all well and good, but this boy is no true son of Romaine Russell. He hasn't got the balls." MacLean sat down.

The men leaned forward as MacAllister continued. "And he's drunk most of the time. Now being drunk is not always an obstacle to effective service." There were chuckles as they glanced at Grant MacKay. "Leave Russell to me. We'll get our expropriation by the end of the month, before Van Kleef's deadline. But I plan to get our boy on side before then."

He looked around the table. There was silence until the Mayor cleared his throat.

"George has put things in perspective for us, in a way that I appreciate. No one wants to hurt Robert Russell, but he can't be allowed to stand in the way of progress. I'm sure we're all content to leave the issue in George's capable hands."

"Fair enough, Al," yelled Grant MacKay. "Now don't forget the election. I need every vote in this room." There was a rumble of easy laughter.

In the kitchen, Mr. Dooley was beginning to relax. "Well, Mrs. MacLellan, it seems the steak with onions was an acceptable substitute." His eyes fluttered with relief and gratitude.

"Of course it was, Mr. Dooley. Steak Delmonico indeed." Mrs. MacLellan tossed her head. "There isn't a man alive who wouldn't eat my steak and onions with the greatest pleasure."

28.

"Take it back, Eileen. It makes her look like a school teacher. That shipment that Father had in from Rothstein's in Montreal; there was the niftiest white dress that would be perfect for her."

"Yes, Miss Robson." Susan handed the dress from her dressing cubicle back to the saleslady. A number of rejected dresses lay on a chair in the aisle.

"I'm not sure I need a new dress," said Susan.

"Shut up. You're going to the Stork Club tonight and you're going in style. I hear Bobby will be there." Susan opened her mouth but Jean held up her hand. "Doesn't matter who's there, we're going to make things happen."

Eileen returned with a white dress on a hanger.

"Aren't you getting anything, Jean?"

"Darling, I have everything I need, believe me."

When Susan emerged from the change room she stood uncertain, avoiding their appraising stares. The white satin dress clung to her like a second skin from the high button collar to the flare at the knee.

"You look sensational," exclaimed Jean. "I love it. But if we're going to do it, let's go all the way." She walked over to Susan and undid three revealing buttons.

"Miss MacLean." The saleslady was alarmed. "This dress is stunning on you, but it is strictly a party dress. We could look at something more adaptable to different occasions."

Jean turned to her in exasperation. "She's going to the Stork Club tonight, Eileen. Doesn't she look divine?"

"Yes, she does," said Eileen, still nervous. "Should we wait until your mother sees it?"

"Don't worry, Eileen," said Jean. "Leave Mom to us."

Susan stood in front of the mirror, turning to see the dress from all sides.

"It makes you look like Jean Harlow," said Jean. "Except your hair isn't blond. But neither was hers."

"I'll take it, Eileen," said Susan. "Charge it to Mother." The two walked out onto Talbot Street, Susan with her box under her arm.

"If the men at the Stork Club have any blood left in them that dress will knock them cold."

"Do I want to knock them cold?"

"Of course you do. But what about me? I need a man. To squeeze me here." She put her hands on her breasts.

Susan's face fell. "Jean. How can you say that?"

"Because it's true. When they squeeze me, I feel like … I'll do anything. Oh, Susie. It's so nice."

She has made love, Susan thought. Was it beautiful? Did it hurt?

As they passed the hairdresser's, Margaret Ann Russell emerged.

"Why, Mrs. Russell, how nice you look," said Jean. "Connie's outdone herself."

Margaret Ann smiled. "Thank you, Jean. I'm going to the Stork Club tonight with Bobby." Susan concentrated on the sidewalk.

"Susie's got a new dress just for tonight."

"So we'll all be there, what fun!" said Margaret Ann, her eyes sparkling. Her laugh drew glances from the old men in front of the feed store, half way down the block

"Mrs. Russell, I hear that Calvin MacQuiggan is in the hospital," Jean continued.

"Yes, Archie beat him half to death. That man…." She shook her head angrily. "Bobby's arranging to have Calvin stay with us." Margaret Ann waved and walked away. "I'll see you tonight."

"Bobby this, Bobby that," said Susan as they walked to the Malt

Shoppe. "It's all she can talk about." Susan was thinking of Calvin, staying with Bobby and his mother. The arrangement disturbed her. He had a family. Damn him!

"There's a memorial for Tommy MacQuiggan tomorrow at First United. The Reverend Fitch will explain what happened to Tommy."

"Somebody cut his throat. That's what happened to Tommy."

"No, Jean, the theological explanation."

Jean groaned. "We don't need theology, honey, we need more dancing." Susan smiled . "Now, Suse, I forgot to tell you. Marie Barnes told my mother that the men had a meeting in the Grand Central yesterday. Bobby Russell's in trouble because he won't sell them that land on the Lyndhurst Road where the MacQuiggans live. They're going to take it away from him anyway. And they're not happy with him. They are calling him a drunk and a mama's boy."

"Who are?" Susan's voice and face were angry. "What men?"

"Grant MacKay, Al Parker, your father, and the lawyers MacAllister and Matthews."

"My father wouldn't say such a thing. Bobby has his problems, but he is no mama's boy. Who do they think they are?"

"They run St. Thomas," drawled Jean. "They can say what they like."

"I hate this town."

"So let's get out. New York City! For life and love!"

"Jeanie, I love you! Let's go!"

They laughed and walked down the street arm in arm.

At home, Susan went to her room, threw the box in the corner, and lay on her bed. The news of the meeting at the Grand Central had angered her. She imagined the men of St. Thomas in the Grand Central dining room interrogating him. He would be sitting in the middle of the room surrounded, a sparkle in his eye and a smile on his lips, listening. When he had heard them he would laugh and walk from the room. That's what Bobby would do.

"Hello, Susan."

Her father stood in the door way. She paused. "Hello." There was no missing the frost in her voice. "You were at the lunch in the Grand Central the other day. The one for the American."

"Tyler Van Kleef. He's going to do great things for this county."

"Does that mean you have to gang up on Bobby, take his land and force him out of town?"

"Force him out of town? Who told you this?"

"Jean heard it from her mother, who heard it from Marie Barnes."

"Marie Barnes!" He threw up his arms. "She's a menace! The lunch was arranged by MacAllister and Matthews, the lawyers for Van Kleef. They wanted to introduce him to the men of the town. Van Kleef wants to build his auto parts plant here, and it is going to bring St. Thomas into the modern world. There will be jobs for people and the whole place will prosper."

"And what about Bobby?"

"The Russell land is where the access road from the highway to the new plant will go. But he won't sell. He won't even talk about it, he just yells at MacAllister and Matthews. So they have no choice but to expropriate, in the interests of the wider community."

Susan looked perplexed.

"It's not the land. It's what you've been saying about him."

"What does Marie Barnes say we've been saying about him?"

"That he's a drunk and a sissy. That he can't stay sober enough to do the business of a man."

MacLean frowned and shook his head.

"I didn't say anything like that, nor would I. You know that. But MacAllister is a hard, mean man, and he did say things about Bobby that should not have been said." He patted her shoulder. "I regret that, but there is another side to this business. MacAllister is not completely wrong. Bobby has not been his old self since his return, and he has been drinking. It must be hard for you."

"I don't care, Daddy," she said. "Not anymore."

"Now, your mother tells me you've bought a new dress."

"Yes." She looked at the box in the corner. She had completely forgotten about the dress and the Stork Club.

29.

Russell picked up his father's gun, wrapped in oil skin, from the wooden cabinet in the corner of the barn. Rusty axes, scythes and adzes hung from nails on the plank walls. Old baby carriages and suitcases, piles of wood, cans of oil and paint, and a sofa with the stuffing coming out of the cushions, were all jammed together in a corner. He took the gun out of its wrapping. He felt the smooth wooden stock and sighted along the barrel. He stepped outside and aimed at a hawk circling in the sky but he could not pull the trigger. He put the gun back in the barn and thought of his bottle.

As he left the barn his mother drove the Buick up the driveway. She had had her hair done and walked towards him, confident in her stride. She had a quality he could only describe as gallant. She stood in front of him, smiling, with a twinkle in her eye.

"We're going dancing," she said with a laugh. "You'll have to dress up. Your father's clothes are in the closet in our room."

On the mahogany dresser in her bedroom was a photograph of his father at age thirty-five or so. He remembered the slightly-hooked nose, the good-humoured dark eyes, the cleft chin. His father had never wanted to play catch with him or watch him play hockey, but he had read to him at bedtime since Bobby was old enough to listen.

He could hear the calm, resonant voice even now, carefully pronouncing each word individually and correctly. He would lie still, dreading the time when the voice would stop. Finally he would feel a kiss on his forehead, the light would go out and his father's footsteps would retreat down the hall.

The dinner jacket was in the closet. He took off his slacks and slipped into the black-striped trousers. They were the right length but the waist was too big; Margaret Ann could fix it with a pin. The jacket fit him well. The double-breasted satin lapel crossed neatly and it buttoned flat on his stomach.

His father had never wanted to leave St. Thomas. Russell remembered him walking arm in arm with Margaret Ann around the back lawn and garden on a summer night among the fireflies, or coming down to the kitchen in the morning and nuzzling her from the rear as she stood at the stove in her kimono. He could hear the delight in her laughter. They had been content.

※

When they drove into the parking lot at the Stork Club Margaret Ann was smiling and humming. "Come on, Bobby, we're late." At the entrance they met MacAllister and Matthews coming out of the club.

"Margaret Ann, how wonderful you look." A beaming Matthews came forward. "Save a dance for me."

"We had some matters to discuss with the owner," said MacAllister who had never been known to indulge in any of the pleasures the Stork Club could provide. "Russell, I want to a word with you. Perhaps we could talk in town next week."

"We have nothing to talk about. I will not sell that land."

"You will sell that land." The voice softened. "The government has agreed that it is in the best interests of the entire community that the project go through. And it will go through. The only question is, how long will it take and what price will you get."

"What does that mean?"

"The faster you transfer the land, the more money you get."

"You don't control what I get. The expropriation commission decides that."

"True, but they traditionally pay at the bottom end. If you deal directly, you'll get top dollar for your land. I guarantee it."

"Your guarantee is worth nothing to me."

MacAllister stared at Russell with his cold eyes and snickered.

"Boy, you aren't whole enough or strong enough to win this one. Those butcher fields must be a terrible experience for a boy who's just left his mother. I can see you're wounded inside. You

193

drink yourself stupid. You seek the company of women. Drink your whiskey. Take tea with the ladies, but don't mess with the men." He walked away to the parking lot.

Russell stood in a daze. At some level the mean-mouthed man with the raspy voice and the cold eyes understood him. Taking tea with the ladies was fine for him. Or a whiskey.

His mother's laughter turned his head. Allan Matthews kissed her on the cheek and headed for the parking lot.

"What were they doing here?" Russell asked her.

"They have some business to do with the owner of the Club," she said. "Do you remember Vince Malone?"

"He's a crook. Why would they be dealing with him?"

"I don't know. Let's get inside. The band won't play forever, you know."

Heads turned in their direction as the head waiter led them to their table. He knew Susan was there but his eyes avoided the dance floor. Through the windows he watched a quarter-moon rise over the lake. He turned back and saw Jean and Susan sitting at a table across the room. He barely recognized Susan. She was wearing a white dress with a high collar and her hair was piled on top of her head in a way he had never seen before. "Everybody is here," said his mother. "And they're all looking at you, dear."

"Let them look," he said sullenly.

"And here's Allan."

Matthews had come back from the parking lot and was approaching their table. Vince Malone rose and crossed the dance floor to intercept him. They went to Malone's table. Malone was angry. He shoved his face right in front of the lawyer's and began to pound the table. Then he leaned back and with a wave of his hand dismissed Matthews, who rose and crossed back to their table.

"I hope we can put aside business for this evening, Bobby. I would like to dance with your mother." He smiled first at Russell, then at Margaret Ann.

"Your partner's deserted you," said Russell, ignoring the peace overture.

Matthews flashed him a wintry smile, and then looked back at his mother. "Shall we dance, Margaret Ann?"

Russell, left alone, watched the band leader, a tall man with a goatee wearing a white dinner jacket, leave the podium and walk over to the MacLeans' table. He leaned over Susan and she rose and moved to the dance floor, laughing too loudly, he thought. He noticed her white dress; he watched her nestle into the band leader's arms. He frowned and looked back at Jean, who caught his eye and smiled. He crossed to her table and asked her to dance.

She got to her feet and put her hand in his. The band began a slow, dreamy rendition of 'I Should Care'. The clarinet wove an obligato with the singer's husky voice. The drummer riffed softly, the base thudded, and outside the stars were shining. Jean folded into him. He could smell her hair and feel her hand on his shoulder, her breast against his.

"What's wrong with you and Susie?" she asked. "You'd better not hurt her again. She is my only friend. She is kind and she is beautiful. Her face and her body are divine."

He looked at her with a question in his eyes. "She's in another world from me. She doesn't understand…."

"Of course she understands. Look at her with the band leader. It's you who doesn't understand."

They looked. Susan was close to Henderson, looking up into his eyes.

"It means nothing to me."

"Is that really the way it is? Let's see."

She clung to him, hummed in his ear and moved her lips across his cheek. "We haven't danced since high school," she whispered. She pressed closer against him and brushed his cheek with hers. "You look so handsome tonight." Her husky voice seemed to whisper to him from miles away.

The band now started 'Anything Goes' in an up tempo.

She moved close to him. "Will you take me home?"

"Yes," he said.

"We'll talk later."

Across the floor, Susan kept glancing at Bobby dancing with her best friend. His face was flushed and the dinner jacket was too big for him.

"So, Sue, you think you might want to come down to Toronto." The band leader's voice broke into her thoughts. No one ever called her Sue.

"Yes," she said, her heart pounding.

Could she really be doing this? Bobby and Jean danced past. Jean had her left hand on the back of his neck. Susan shivered.

"Something on your mind, honey?"

"Just the music. It's so dreamy. Did you arrange this?"

"All the charts are mine. So when we leave here after next weekend, you want to come with us?"

"Yes." She was breathless.

She snuggled close to him; she wanted no discussion. If only she could just be whisked off to his hotel room in Toronto on a magic carpet. Out of the corner of her eye she saw Bobby leading Jean back to her table.

Russell walked to the men's room, relieved to be alone again. Was he going to take her home? He didn't know; he didn't care. Inside a boy with a pimply face in a rumpled grey suit leaned against the wall. Will Matthews glared at Russell.

"That's my girl you're dancing with." The tone was defiant.

"I was dancing with Jean. Is she your girl?"

"Damn right she is. Last week we did it."

"Does Jean think she's your girl?"

"That's between her and me. I'm telling you to butt out."

The boy attempted to be authoritative, but he was swaying. Russell was about to try and soothe him when Will shut his eyes, slid slowly down the wall and collapsed on the floor. He moaned, then began to snore gently.

Russell stepped over him and walked back to the dance floor.

"There's a patron in the washroom slightly under the weather," he said to a waiter. "He may be under age, too."

Matthews left as he approached his mother's table. "He thinks you don't want him around," said Margaret Ann.

"He's right."

She smiled. "Go easy, my son. There aren't many men in this town who will dance with me now."

"I'll dance with you."

"Not now. You should dance with Susan."

"She won't."

"She will. You're old friends."

He sat uncertain for a minute as the band started up, then rose to his feet and walked across the dance floor, putting one foot carefully after the other.

"Here he is," Jean whispered to Susan. "He wants to dance again. He said he'd take me home."

Susan looked at Bobby, swaying before them, unsmiling.

"Want to dance, Susie?"

Jean's face grew dark. Susan stood up.

They danced, without speaking. It unsettled her; she knew he was afraid to touch her. Her hand on his shoulder felt that he was skinnier than he used to be. Tears came to her eyes and she looked away. Damn, she thought. What's the matter with me? As soon as the dance was over she walked quickly back to her table. Russell followed and asked Jean to dance. The band leader approached the table; Susan smiled and rose.

"What's the matter, baby, you're all stiffened up." he said.

"I have a headache."

Margaret Ann and Allan Matthews were watching the dancing when the head waiter approached the table and whispered in Matthews' ear. "It seems Will has got himself under the weather," he said to Margaret Ann. "I'd better see what the problem is." He followed the waiter to the men's room.

Valerie MacLean wandered over with a bemused smile on her face. "I don't know what's happening tonight," she whispered to Margaret Ann. "Look at Susan with that American band leader. What can she be thinking?"

"Not much, if I remember." They laughed.

"And look at Jean vamping Bobby. She's not the girl for him."

"Why not?"

"She's too ... available. You know, sex and all that."

Margaret Ann smiled thoughtfully. "It wouldn't be the worst thing that could happen to him right now," she said.

"Margaret Ann, you're his mother." Valerie's tone affected outrage, but there was a smile on her lips.

Matthews came through the men's room door, holding his son under one arm, the waiter taking the other. The boy could barely move his feet. Will opened his eyes at the sound of the music, and saw Jean, her head on Russell's shoulder, dancing with her eyes closed.

"Jean," he blubbered. "I want to dance."

His father shook him and hustled him towards the exit. The patrons watched the boy's head loll back over his shoulder, looking for Jean, tears streaming down his cheeks, until the doors closed behind him.

"Jean again," said Valerie as she shook her head. "I don't know what's going on with the young people in this town. Nothing's been right since the war. Where will we get our grandchildren?"

"They'll find a way," said Margaret Ann. "They always do."

Russell drove the Buick in the drive at ten o'clock the next morning. He stood in the kitchen doorway, smiling sheepishly at his mother, who sat at the table with a pot of coffee and two cups. "Come and have some coffee. You can't have had much sleep." He took a seat without a word. He was still in his father's dinner jacket, but the black tie and cuff links had disappeared.

"I'm going to Toronto to fight this expropriation."

She scowled. "Bobby, it's Sunday. There's a memorial service for Tommy MacQuiggan in the Church and you're going, after you clean yourself up. And there's a letter for you. Hand delivered, no postage on it."

She took it out of her apron pocket and put it on the table. It was a legal-sized envelope addressed in blue typing.

"Robert Russell, Esquire," he read. "Rural route two, St. Thomas Ontario. Very official looking. I'm tired, I'll read it later."

He threw it on the table.

30.

The First United Church of St. Thomas, on Church Street, was a symbol for the parishioners of the prosperity that comes from virtue. Built of grey stone, its roof finished with copper and slate, its doors of stoutest oak, it stood among well-tended lawns and graceful trees. All the significant families of the town belonged. There were other churches in town, the more modest, red brick Salem United, near the east end of town, and of course the Roman Catholic, Anglican, Baptist and Presbyterian churches. But no other church embodied the hopes and fears of the citizens of the town or facilitated their political and business dealings as well as First United. George MacAllister had been an active elder for many years, watching the finances and overseeing repairs to the church building.

The regular Sunday service had been replaced by Tommy MacQuiggan's memorial. At a quarter to eleven the worshipers were gathering in knots outside the church, waiting for the Reverend Fitch to walk from his study in the manse across the carefully-mowed lawn to the church. Valerie MacLean and Ruth Robson stood among a group of wives, chatting amiably, when Rose MacIlwain and Helen Partridge approached from the direction of Ontario Street.

"Well, look who are coming to the service," said Ruth Robson. "Would you believe it?"

The ladies greeted the couple with the kind of polite warmth and obligatory good cheer appropriate at the temple of the Lord.

"Well, Helen, Rose, how lovely to see you."

Helen nodded and smiled at each woman in turn; Rose stood to the side, staring at a group of men across the lawn, distaste frozen on her face. Allan Matthews was telling a joke from his endless supply to Bill MacLean, Bud Robson, Al Parker, and George MacAllster. These men, with their dark suits and coarse laughter, represented everything she disliked about St. Thomas.

"Look at them," she muttered to Helen. "Just as smug and sancti-monious as any Pharisees." Helen pretended not to hear. "And now here's the Chief of Police. He has done nothing, I understand, to solve this murder and he has done nothing to deal with the father beating the boy, Calvin."

Across the lawn, Elmore Wayne joined the men.

"What's that English teacher staring at us for?" he said. The men turned to look and Rose lowered her eyes. "Unusual to see her and Helen at a service. It takes Tommy having his throat slit to get 'em into a pew."

"They're women, Elmore," said the Mayor. "Teaching English, running the library. Useful things. Necessary things."

"Women are the soft spot, the weak link," said MacAllister. "You can never trust them."

"Women vote, George," said Grant MacKay. "The Liberal Party is in favour of women."

"You're too harsh, MacAllister," said Allan Matthews. "Women are part of the sweetness of life."

"Speak for yourself," said his partner. "And for Russell too, I suppose. Look at him now, with his mother." Russell was still in his dinner jacket. He walked with his mother on his arm, staring straight ahead. "He's come direct from the Stork Club. He's still drunk. His mother's holding him up."

The Reverend Campbell Fitch, a tall man in his black robe and crossed white preaching tabs, strode manfully from the manse across the lawn. He exchanged hearty handshakes with several of the more prominent men and bowed to the ladies. The congregation followed their pastor through the oak doors. The Reverend Fitch took his place in front of the carved wooden chair and the people stood facing him. Behind the preacher stood the ladies and two men of the First United Church choir, in blue robes and white surplices.

Facing him on his right were the Canadian Girls in Training, in their blue and white middy uniforms, and to his left the Teen Youth Group. Sadie Murray, music teacher at the Collegiate, sat at the organ and began the hymn. Choir and congregation, hymn books open, sang:

"Holy, holy, holy; Lord God almighty,
"Early in the morning, our song shall rise to Thee.
"Holy, holy, holy; merciful and mighty,
"God in three persons, blessed Trinity."

"God in three persons," whispered Jean. "I never got that, Suse. A three-for-one sale."

"Be quiet, you're in church." Susan glanced at Bobby across the aisle; his head was bent and he was barely moving.

The prayers began. The people sat, apparently uniform with their bowed heads and quiet faces, thinking their thoughts as the voice of the Reverend Fitch, passionate but formal, proud and humble at the same time as only a shepherd of the elect can be, boomed through the church.

God, his voice makes me sick, thought MacAllister. The fool sits in his study writing his sermons or visiting the sick, no man's work. Then he dresses up on Sunday in his robes and there he is, standing there proud as a peacock and just as useless. He doesn't know how to read an invoice. They tried to cheat us with the bill for fixing the roof, and all the idiot can say is, "Render unto Caesar what is Caesar's." Man of God, my ass.

Jean was tired, but restless. Bobby had driven her home, then fallen asleep in the car; she hadn't been able to wake him. Look at Fitch, she thought, so sanctimonious, so pure. What I could do to him if I could get him alone. He'd love it. God I'm tired, it's making me crazy. I need to go home and sleep.

Allan Matthews scanned the pews until he located Margaret Ann, but her head was bowed slightly, turned towards her son. That boy, he thought, is going to cause more trouble than he's worth. He sighed, bowed his head and tried to listen to the words of the parson.

Bill MacLean usually ignored the words of the preacher, but he enjoyed Sunday service. For him, the rows of bowed heads listening to Fitch preach were symbols of social togetherness and community spirit. He believed that St. Thomas, with its democratic political system, its First United Church and its hardworking, plain speaking citizens, had reached a pinnacle of civilized development. As the parson droned on, Bill glanced around the church and smiled. The peaceful boredom, the sense of sobriety and submission, these were the things that mattered.

Margaret Ann tuned in and out of the Revered Fitch's prayers. She would say a prayer for Bobby, sitting restless beside her. Then she would daydream. She thought of dancing last night with Allan. She knew he was in the church somewhere but she would not look around. Bobby was leaning forward in the pew beside her, gazing at the floor, as he had been doing since they had taken their pew. She wasn't sure if he was awake.

Susan could not wait for the service to end. Fitch had nothing to say to her. There would be time for all this later on, when life settled down. But now she could only think of Toronto and Gene Henderson. Wow, she thought, even in church it's still a good idea. I'm going. She wondered how Bobby was this morning, but she would not turn and look for him.

Russell watched the sleekly-barbered ushers lead the citizens to their pews, the smiles of neighbourly sanctity, the kindly nods. He hated the pious expressions, the hushed voices, the Sunday assumptions of goodness. He disliked the mass ritual, the intoning of the prayers. He lowered his head to the floor and summoned up disturbing memories of destruction, shattered towns, dead soldiers, burning churches. Soon he was asleep, and the memories became dreams.

After the second hymn, the Reverend Fitch mounted his pulpit. He was a man in his forties, approaching six feet, powerfully built, the son of a farming family near Ingersoll. Fitch was aware of the figure he cut in his pulpit. He fought a life-long battle with pride; pride in his appearance and the sound of his voice.

"For my text on this sad morning I take the words of Paul the

Apostle in his epistle to Timothy, Chapter 1, Verse 9: 'The law is not made for a righteous man, but for the lawless and disobedient, for the ungodly and for sinners, for the unholy and profane, for murderers of fathers and murderers of mothers, for manslayers'.

"We know, as children of Christ, that there is a law that governs us all. And we know that he who breaks this law, the unholy and profane man of the scriptures, will be punished. In our community a great crime has been committed. One of God's faithful servants, Thomas MacQuiggan, has been murdered in a heinous, cowardly act. So we gather in this house of worship today to remember our brother, so cruelly dispatched from this earth, but we do not do so in despair for his fate because we know that Tommy goes to join the choir of just souls that abide with our Saviour. Justice is mine, saith the Lord. The perpetrator of this hideous crime will be brought to justice, oh Lord, for we know that in Thy way and in Thy time, Thy will shall be done."

He paused. The church was filled with coughs and the noise of people shifting in their pews.

"Someone in this community killed the innocent, the gentle, the harmless Tommy MacQuiggan. How can this be? We return, as we always must, to the words of the prophet, 'Let not the husband rest from vigilance, nor the bridegroom relax his care, for the viper has come in the night, to lay by the foot of Thy servants, oh Lord'."

"What the hell does that mean?" whispered Jean.

"Shut up." Susan's lips were pursed.

"We know," continued the Reverend Fitch, "that nothing happens in this world that has not been foreordained by God. 'God sees the little sparrow fall, it meets His tender view.' God knows about, and understands, the death of Tommy. We do not. He understands when and how justice will be meted out to the killer. We do not. But we trust in Him not to leave us alone in a meaningless world, where evil things occur without reason, and pass away without justice. We know there is a plan; we know we are loved. That is our faith.

"Without faith, we die. With faith, we live with Jesus forever. Tommy is dead, but he died in the faith. For that reason he lives with his Redeemer in eternal bliss. So on this Sunday morning we remember Tommy, but we do not despair for him. He knows joy that we cannot imagine. He has gone before, on the road we will surely follow. He has gone to that land where the lion lies down with the lamb, where the unjust man cannot enter, and where the just sing forever in the divine choir of Zion."

"Nonsense! A lion lying down with a lamb!" whispered Jean.

"Shhh."

"Therefore, when you pray for Tommy MacQuiggan, pray that his example, of goodness in the faith, will live with us here as we struggle to fulfil God's plan for us. Pray that Tommy will live in our hearts, and that we carry the reflection of his goodness forward in our lives. And pray for justice, for Tommy, for his killer, for all of us. Praised be the Lord."

The final words rang throughout the church. The blue eyes burned from the pulpit. Then Fitch threw his arms wide, and bowed his head, like a singer who had finished his aria.

"I ask you to bow your heads for a minute or two to pray, and think of Tommy MacQuiggan."

Jean had a joke ready, as to how she would prefer to think of any man but Tommy MacQuiggan, but kept quiet. Susan tried to think of Tommy, but found her mind wandering to thoughts of the Stork Club, moon on the water, the lush sound of the dance tunes. Her father was thinking of what a good effect the sermon would have on people who might suspect the efficiency of the town's police and Chief Elmore Wayne. MacAllister was fuming with disgust. The boy had his throat slit by a pro from Detroit who left no traces; this preacher is a fool; the killer will never be caught. Margaret Ann was thinking of her husband suddenly, wishing that he were still with her. Where was the justice this man preached, if she had to make do with Allan Matthews? Russell was relieved that the sermon was over; he had wakened just as it ended and had not heard a word.

"A beautiful sermon, Reverend Fitch," said MacAllister out on the lawn. "Your words were a comfort and an inspiration."

The other prominent parishioners, a platoon of flowered dresses and sober suits, lined up to compliment their pastor on his sermon. The lesser citizens, farmers and merchants and their wives, spilled out into the street. Susan and Jean stood with Allan and Will Matthews, Margaret Ann and her son off to one side. Russell looked at Jean but she avoided his gaze. He looked down and noticed that he was still in his father's dinner jacket; then he remembered the night before. Susan was staring at him with an unreadable expression. He looked away; he wanted to go home.

"Why don't we all go together to the Grand Central for lunch," said Matthews. "Sunday roast beef."

"I've got to get Mother home," said Russell forcefully. "She's been under the weather this morning."

"Me, too," said Jean. "I seem to be exhausted, although I can't imagine why." She gave Bobby a grimace and turned away. Susan followed her, leaving Allan Matthews and his son to make their way to the Grand Central Hotel's Sunday roast.

"That was some nonsense about me under the weather," said Margaret Ann to her son as they drove out of town in their Buick. "It's you who looks like you haven't slept for a week."

They drove home in silence. As they turned into their lane, Bobby gasped.

"Look, on the porch. It's Calvin."

Calvin was sitting quietly in his cotton hospital gown. The bruises on his arms, legs and face were still visible.

"Why aren't you in the hospital, Calvin?" asked Russell.

"Was time to leave, I guess. I know you got work for me."

"Boy, you'll have to go back." Margaret Ann's voice was soft with concern. "You haven't mended yet."

A tear rolled down his left cheek.

"You want to stay and help us out, Calvin?" Bobby sat down beside him on the porch. "Is that what you want?"

Calvin nodded. Bobby put his arm around him.

"We can fix that. Come inside and let's have some lunch."

The boy followed them into the kitchen. The envelope with the blue typescript was still lying on the table. He sat down, picked it up and opened it. He read it through once, looked at his mother, then looked at Calvin.

"Calvin, you better go out to the car and see if Mrs. Russell left her bag there." The boy rose and left the kitchen. "Listen to this," he said to his mother, and began to read.

"'If you want to know what happened to Tommy MacQuiggan, then find out what happened to all the letters he was supposed to deliver to Margaret Ann Russell over the past year, but didn't'. It's signed, 'a well wisher'."

They stared at one another.

"The letters I sent. Telling you I was a prisoner."

"Tommy delivered my mail. He wouldn't divert your letters."

Russell stared. "Someone wanted you to think that I wasn't coming back." They looked at one another simultaneously, with dawning suspicion.

She thought a moment. "Allan wouldn't do that."

"MacAllister would."

"Then who sent this letter?"

"An experienced typist. Looks like a lawyer's letter."

"Millie Hall."

Calvin re-entered the kitchen. "Weren't no bag in that car."

"That's all right, Calvin," she said. "I've found it."

31.

"It wasn't me that wrote your letter."

Millie sat rigid in her seat at the table in the corner of the Malt Shoppe, her cup of tea untouched. When he phoned her to ask for this meeting she agreed without discussion; he heard in the receiver her barely audible, "All right." She had been nervous when she first sat down and was watching him warily.

"I thought you wanted to discuss some legal matter before going to the lawyers. This letter has nothing to do with me."

Millie was in her forties. A round, full figure and a face that had been attractive. Russell could see intelligence in the grey eyes, but something else, a murky quality. She avoided his gaze.

"I didn't say it was you, Millie. But it was well typed on legal stationery, which narrows the field considerably."

"How dare you accuse me of this!" There was anger in her voice, but pleading in her eyes.

"I'm not accusing you. Look, now we've finished our teas, let's just go home and forget it." He rose from the table. "I'm sorry for wasting your time."

He reached in his pocket for his wallet. She was staring at the table again; suddenly she was breathing in gulps.

"Sit down," she said. "Please sit down."

He sat down. Tears were running down her cheeks.

"I wrote it," she said. "I wanted you to know."

"Know what?"

Suddenly Millie was breathing hard; Russell was afraid she was having a seizure. She wiped her eyes and sat up straight.

"MacAllister arranged for Tommy to show him all the mail for your mother, for a year or so before you came home. He looked at each letter that came for her, and some of them he kept."

"So they never reached my mother?"

"That's right."

"Do you know where those letters are?"

"He has them. They were in his office safe. Knowing him, he would have destroyed them as soon as you turned up. For which we all thank the Good Lord." She smiled weakly.

"Why did he do it?"

"He thought that if your mother believed that you might be dead, she would be more amenable to selling the land they need for this American."

"Does Matthews know about this?"

She nodded. "He knew about it, but it wasn't his idea. In fact I heard them arguing about it. He likes your mother. He kept telling MacAllister it wasn't honourable. MacAllister laughed at him."

Her words were bitter. Looking at her, he understood; an

207

aging beauty who had deceived herself that her relationship with MacAllister was more than a market transaction.

"Millie, does the name Newcorp Investments mean anything to you?"

She stared dully at him.

"No. Who are they?"

"It's the name of the company behind the expropriation order."

She was shaking her head. "Not one of our companies, I'm sure of that."

"Who killed Tommy?" He spoke quietly, watching her face. She winced.

"They hang killers." Her voice was husky. "He didn't do it. I know what people think of him. But he isn't always hard. He can be very soft, if he isn't worried about his business affairs. I made him forget business." The tears came again. "I have to go home."

"But Tommy's dead." He talked urgently, trying to hold her. "And MacAllister has a new girl, I hear."

She flinched as if he had hit her, but she did sit down.

"He didn't do it." Her face was hard now, and she spoke in a rapid staccato. "He just wanted to scare Tommy into keeping quiet about the letters. According to what I heard, they arranged with Vince Malone to have one of the men from Detroit come down to talk to Tommy and put the fear of God into him. Killing wasn't part of it, but the guy went too far. These guys are all on drugs, you never know what they'll do. Mr. MacAllister was upset when he found out Tommy was dead." She stopped to catch her breath.

"And Matthews knew?"

"They were partners." She picked up her purse, keeping her eyes from his. "That's it, Mr. Russell. I'm going home. God's will be done." She walked quickly to the door.

❀

Millie had not returned to her desk when Russell entered the offices of MacAllister and Matthews. Grace Connors told him that both partners had left for the day. He decided to walk the three blocks to Matthews' house on D'Arcy Street, a stone house with a wide front veranda under a maple tree. When the door opened Will Matthews stood staring at him.

"What do you want?" His voice quavered.

"I have to see your father on business."

"Any business you have here you can state to me."

Allan Matthews came up in the hall behind his son. When he saw Russell his face fell. "Come in."

Will tried to walk into the house with dignity. Matthews led Russell into a study off the hallway. It was finished like his office, with leather chairs, a kilim carpet on the floor, and framed reproductions of portraits by Gainsborough and Joshua Reynolds on the wall. A fire had been laid in the grate but not lit; the summer night was warm.

"That boy has some growing up to do," said Matthews as they sat in two armchairs. "Made a fool of himself at the Stork Club." He shook his head sadly, watching Russell at the same time. "I don't know when you were last in this house, Bobby. What can I do for you?" He smiled but there was no light in the famous blue eyes. "Why don't we start with a glass of whiskey?"

"Not for me."

"All right." His face was distorted with tension. "I've been expecting you."

"About Tommy?"

"Yes."

"I know who killed him. And why."

Matthews stared at the floor, then looked up with resignation in his eyes.

"He wasn't supposed to die. Malone's man was told to give him a talking-to. MacAllister...." He started to shake his head.

"I'm sure you wouldn't have wanted murder. But what about the letters? You knew that my letters weren't being delivered."

Matthews nodded, keeping his face down.

"But that was such a stupid thing to do. It was bound to come out

209

sooner or later. And to deceive her that way."

Matthews took out an embroidered pocket handkerchief and blew his nose.

"The scheme was MacAllister's. He didn't tell me about it until it was underway." The man looked away, hearing the weakness in his words. "He was furious when your mother wouldn't sell. He gets in a rage when anyone blocks his path. And he has a poor-boy complex, you know. He despises anyone born with property or wealth. When I found out, I told him exactly what you just said. It was stupid and it wouldn't work. But he blew sky high, told me not to meddle in his arrangements, and if I wanted to withdraw from the Van Kleef scheme he would buy me out. We both have interests in the new company. So I stayed in."

"You went along."

"I did." He shrugged. "I was determined that your mother would get a fair price. I would never have let her be cheated. I hope that both of you will believe that. I am very fond of her, as I was of your father. I stayed in partly to protect her interests." He sighed. "But really, I stayed in because ... because that's the sort of person I am." His face relaxed. "I like good clothes and good company, good food and good drink. I don't like causing pain, to anyone, but occasionally one has to make choices."

He spread his hands and smiled weakly. Russell could see, even in this confession, the compelling charm.

"I have to go to the police with this."

"I know. I may go to jail. I'll definitely be disbarred." He shook his head. "What bothers me about it is Will. He's not mature, not strong. I can't imagine what this will do to him."

"There's a lot to be sorted out," Russell said quietly.

"Do you want a drink?" Matthews rose and walked over to a liquor cabinet. Russell shook his head. "When Jane and I were first married we used to go around with your parents. We'd take the train to Toronto for a concert and stay overnight or drive to London for a dinner and movie. You remember Jane?" Bobby nodded. "I couldn't have married a woman who wasn't beautiful. The four of us were good-looking, we turned heads in restaurants. Those were the days." He sipped his whiskey and smiled. "Now it seems like a dream. Jane died just after Will was born. Then your father died. And now this mess."

Russell could see that the man was not looking for pity. He was reviewing his life, adding the years up.

"Your father had a sense of humour and he was tricky, an unbeatable combination. He started that dairy with nothing; people were saying he would never make it. But he knew more little tricks. God knows where he learned them. If he owed money and couldn't pay, which is the ultimate crime in this part of the world, he would put his arm around you, tell you how it was, and what he was going to do for you. It worked. People liked him and wanted him to succeed. I did the legal work for the dairy, acquiring the land, letters patent and all of that, and I didn't get paid for five years. But when he did pay me, he took the four of us to Toronto, presented the check over dinner at the King Edward, and then on to a concert. Nellie Melba, I think it was. That was your father." He smiled at Russell. "You look like him. A bit more on the serious side, but the war would account for that."

Russell wanted to end the interview.

"Look, Bobby, do what you have to do." The fine face was serious, the reminiscing over. "We did it, and we'll take the consequences. But before you leave, I want to give you a piece of advice." Russell's eyes narrowed; he was in no mood to be patronized by this aging gigolo. "Get out of this town. You've got your youth and you're an able and attractive young man. Go where there are other bright young people you can work with. And play with. Go to Toronto, London or New York, Montreal even. Don't stay in St. Thomas. I did, and it was my big mistake." He smiled fondly at Russell. "Have we said all we have to say?"

Bobby got to his feet. "Yes. You know, when I leave here, I'll be going to Elmore Wayne."

"Of course. Say hello to your mother for me." He winked, but it was a mockery of the wink he would have made the day before.

"He ain't here. He's at the political meeting at the Collegiate."
Elmore Wayne's wife stood in the doorway of the modest house on
Tecumseh Street, wiping her hands on her apron.

"I never knew Elmore to be a political man."

"He ain't, but he's there for the government in Toronto. There's
socialists and I don't know what all manner of wild people running
for the Legislature. Them in Toronto wants Elmore to keep an eye
on things."

Russell walked to the street and began the six blocks to the
Collegiate. Socialists in St. Thomas. He smiled to himself. It could
only be one of the railway workers running for the socialist party,
the Co-operative Commonwealth Federation, the CCF. Reuben
Denoff, who owned Reuben's Men's Clothing on Talbot Street,
was rumoured to be a communist. But Bobby had heard all kinds of
rumours before the war about Reuben, one of the few Jews in town,
and discounted them. Socialism had little chance in Elgin County.
Farmers, merchants and owners of modest property were agreed on
the value of the Liberal Party and the need for rain.

In the Collegiate auditorium a man he didn't know was speaking
at the podium. Grant MacKay and Porter, the history teacher and
Conservative candidate, were sitting in two chairs on the stage, the
speaker's chair empty beside them. The moderator was Kennedy,
the high school principal, who sat at a table with a clock, timing
the speeches. Behind them was a backdrop of wine-coloured stage
curtains, at the top of which was a portrait of King George in military
uniform, over the Union Jack and the Canadian Red Ensign crossed.
The speaker must be the CCF candidate, Bobby thought. He was
a man in his thirties, lean and red-faced with big hands, awkward-
looking in a brown tweed suit.

"We are all workers, whether we work in the plant, on the farm
or in our shops, that's the point. We are all labour, and unless we are
united, we will be exploited every time by the capitalists in Toronto
and New York. United we stand or divided we fall, brothers, there

is no other way for us. Labour must be represented in the political system. We are the majority. Now is our time, and we finally have a political party formed to represent our views, not the views of the fat cats in Toronto. The old parties will tell you they're on your side, but when it comes to the showdown, they turn their backs on you every time."

"But will Grant Mackay sober up if we vote for you and he has to look for a job?" came a voice from the crowd, and the auditorium filled with laughter. Grant MacKay smiled and tried to look dignified. Porter was laughing and the young railway worker at the microphone had a smile on his face. Russell looked around the room and spotted the Chief of Police sitting in the front row. He walked to the Chief's seat, bent over and whispered in his ear. Elmore Wayne rose and followed him out of the hall.

"Who is that speaking?" asked Russell in the lobby.

"Ray Murphy. He works in the roundhouse for the railway repairing engines, some kind of mechanic, steward in the Railway Workers Union."

"I hear you're keeping an eye on him."

Wayne stared at him. "Who told you that?" Russell shrugged. "Well, it's not a secret, I guess. Toronto wants us to report the names of any communists and radicals who might be a threat to freedom and democratic government. Shit, I can't send Ray Murphy's name down as a political radical. He's just a young fellah with a nice wife and two kids who wants higher pay and benefits. I got nothing to report." He shook his head and looked again at Russell, a hint of irritation in his eyes. "Sometimes this town gets under my skin. Nothing's ever quite what it seems. Do you realize that Bill MacLean is about to switch his paper's support to the Tories and the school teacher Porter?"

"But this town is Liberal. Why would he do that?"

"He says that Grant MacKay is a drunk, which is true, but it was true five years ago, so what's so special about it now. Then he says that the Liberals are against immigration and business development. There may be more truth to that. But I think the real reason is that he wants to sell his newspaper to some Toronto Tories." He scowled at Russell. "Now tell me what's on your mind. I can't be long out here."

"I know who killed Tommy MacQuiggan."

Wayne turned to him with a jerk. Russell told him about the letter, his interview with Millie Hall and his conversation with Allan Matthews. Wayne began pacing up and down the lobby, shaking his head and muttering.

"I don't need this. The Mayor and I are supposed to go fishing. MacAllister, Christ. And Vince Malone. And a goon from Detroit. How in the name of thunder did those two smart lawyers get into foolishness like this?"

"It's mostly MacAllister," said Russell. "On his own Matthews wouldn't do this sort of thing."

"No sane man would get up to this sort of thing. But MacAllister ain't sane. He's crazier than a loon in love. Lord, lord, lord. I got to talk to Parker."

"About what?"

"About how we're going to handle this."

"What do you mean, handle this? You just arrest him. The Mayor's got nothing to do with it; you need a Crown Attorney."

"Don't you go telling me my job." The Chief of Police paced a few more steps and came to a stop. "You go off to wherever you're going. I'll deal with MacAllister and whoever else needs to be dealt with. Come and see me in the morning. We'll have to take a statement from you. Then Millie Hall. Then Matthews. Damn. I won't ever get fishing."

He turned and walked back into the hall. Russell walked out to Talbot Street and west towards the Lyndhurst Road.

❀

As he walked up the drive towards the house, a figure stumbled out from the spruce trees that lined the driveway.

"Boss." The hoarse voice was familiar. "Boss, Boss." It was

Archie and he was drunk. Russell recoiled at the stink of his breath and his unwashed body.

"What is it, Archie?"

The man came up directly in front of him, put a huge hand on his shoulder and stared into his eyes from no more than six inches away. The smell was intolerable. He removed Archie's hand from his shoulder.

"They say you're gonna sell us out, Boss. They say you're gonna evict us, put us out on the highway, and sell the land and our house to some rich American."

"Who said that?"

"The women. Leona heard it from them at the market. Marie Barnes says it."

"There you go. Is everything Marie Barnes says true?"

Archie sank to the ground, not hearing.

"I never meant Calvin no harm. I walloped him for his own good, just the way my old man walloped me. You can't turn us out like that. We got nine kids, and we lost Tommy, and Jesus Christ, Boss, I got half my balls shot off, serving my country, yeah, serving my fucking country. You can't do this to a vet, it ain't legal. What would we do?"

Archie's mat of red hair fell over his eyes, his belly spilled out from his shirt and his feet were bare. Russell shook his head.

"I'm not going to sell you out. We may get expropriated, but that's not my doing. If it happens, we'll see what's to do."

Archie's sobbing increased; he fell to the ground and flung his arms around Bobby's legs, his cheek on the left shoe.

"You're my boss. We always been yours, Captain. Please, please, please."

Russell yanked his leg away. Archie groaned.

"Boss, I got an idea. There's Leona. She's been kinda lonely since I come back. I can't do much with her, cause of my wound. Maybe you could, you know, visit her some night."

It took several seconds for Bobby to understand the offer. Images of Leona came to him, her short muscular body with the red hair down her back and under her arms, the belly sagging from many childbirths. He turned on his heel and walked into his house, leaving Archie sobbing on the driveway. He found his mother in the living room, reading the paper. She put it down to look at him.

"What is it?"

"Archie has just offered me his wife for my bed, in return for not selling the land and driving them to live in the fields."

"That man," she said, smiling grimly. "There's part of me that would love to see the end of him. Leona MacQuiggan indeed."

"Don't worry, she's not my type." Her eyes sparkled. "Anyway, I don't think the problem will arise. After what I've discovered tonight, I doubt we'll be expropriated." She looked seriously at him. "But you're not going to like all of it."

He told her of the his conversation with Millie Hall, of the reason for the diversion of his letters, letters from the Red Cross, and from the army. Her face went blank. When he told of Tommy's killing she simply stared. Finally he began to describe his conversation with Allan Matthews. She sat rigid; her face grew angry, then relaxed in sadness.

"Poor Allan," she said.

"Poor Allan? Why not poor Tommy?"

"Of course." She sighed. "Allan is decent and kindly. Lots of fun, but nothing there in a pinch. MacAllister was too much for him. There is something feminine about Allan in that way. Perhaps that's why I like him."

"You'll have to stop seeing him."

She scowled.

"That's not for you to say, Robert Russell. You know how judgmental this town can be. I intend to stand by him, and I expect you to show him the same generosity and mercy."

He nodded. Her eyes focused on him and he understood once again how formidable she was.

32.

"They arrested the lawyer MacAllister this morning," said Jack Morris as his scissors began to snip around Robert Russell's ear. "They say he fought it. It took Gus Campbell and Charlie Beechum and two others to put him away. Gus has a black eye, they say. They're going to charge him with disrupting the mails. Can you believe that?' The scissors waved in front of Bobby's nose. "It don't make no sense. Except it's supposed to be connected with Tommy MacQuiggan's murder."

Russell lay back in the chair, saying nothing. He could see the old men sitting on the bench across the street, watching his hair cut.

"Where did you hear this?" Bobby said finally.

"From my wife. She heard it from Marie Barnes."

For a moment the only sound was the snip of the scissors. Finally, Jack rested his arms on the back of the chair and cleared his throat.

"I don't like this arresting of MacAllister. I hear Elmore Wayne don't like it either. It just proves what I've been thinking for some time now." He paused, looking down at Bobby expectantly.

"What's have you been thinking, Jack?"

"This town is going to the dogs. And the reason is, it's being taken over and run by the women."

"How do you figure that?"

"It's obvious. Communication and consumption."

"What d'you mean, communication and consumption?"

"Well, Sir, I'm reading this piece in the Reader's Digest, by some American professor who says that a society is defined by what it consumes and how it communicates. Interesting. So I got to thinking about this town, although of course he wasn't writing about St. Thomas in particular, seeing as how he's probably never heard of it, but still, the ideas apply. Look at us here. Only the women really know what's going on. They know it first and they know it before Al Parker or Grant MacKay or any of them that is supposed to run things. No question. Second, this whole town exists so that women can buy. The men work in the fields, or in the stores or wherever, do barbering or lawyering and such, set up this system, get wages, pay wages and what for? So the women can take the money and buy stuff."

"Is this new?"

"It's new compared with the old days, Bobby. You should read the professor. Back then men ruled, because their muscles were needed to clear the land and such. But now, we got tractors and all manner of machinery so muscles don't matter. Now it's communication and consumption, which is your female. Now it's their game. It'll happen right in front of your eyes."

"What d'you mean?"

"This arrest of MacAllister. They say he tampered with the mail. You never heard such nonsense. And then it's Tommy MacQuiggan's murder. Nobody in this town cares who killed Tommy, really. So it's as clear as the nose on your face, these ain't the real reasons for them arresting MacAllister. What I heard is really behind it is, he was foolin' with Millie Hall and he dumped her for this woman from Kitchener. The women in this town won't stand for that, they stuck together behind Millie, a St. Thomas girl. So they up and got this phoney baloney case against MacAllister that Elmore Wayne has to act on. Elmore don't know nothing about what's going on. None of us do. We're putty in their hands." Jack was glaring angrily into his mirror.

"Now, Jack, women can make things happen behind the scene sometimes, but it's going too far to say they're running the town."

"Don't you believe it." Jack put down his scissors and looked at his customer with scorn. "I got another example of what's going. Bill MacLean is going to switch the support of the Times Journal to the Conservatives." He waited for a reaction to his bombshell, but Russell just nodded. "For the first time ever, the St. Thomas paper will not be supporting a Liberal." He looked again but Russell didn't react. "You look at that and you think, what's going on, is he taking leave of his senses? But when you understand what's really going on, it all makes perfect, honest-to-God sense. Bill's supporting the Tories because he wants to sell the Times Journal to some rich businessmen in Toronto who are Tories, naturally. Him supporting the Tories and betraying everything he stands for is part of the deal they want. So why does he want to sell his paper? Does he need the money? Doesn't look like it. Nice house all paid for, trips abroad whenever he wants, daughter educated and on her way. It wouldn't look as if Bill MacLean needed money, but he does. And why? Because his wife wants to move to Toronto." Jack paused to let the full impact of his words sink in. "She wants to buy a big house in Toronto, hang out with all them rich bitches, go to concerts and I don't know what else." He shook his head in disbelief. "And if you don't think the women are running the show, buddy, you're dreaming. Communication and consumption. They got it all."

Russell looked at the frown on Jack Morris's image in the mirror. The man had been married for more than forty years; his four children were all girls. Life in the barber's family might give a man a certain point of view.

"I'm leaving for Toronto tomorrow, Jack."

"So I heard." He wiped his razor on a towel. "That'll be your land deal."

Russell smiled; there were no secrets in St. Thomas. "I also thought I might look around a bit."

Jack lowered his arms. "Bobby, that's a damn fine idea. You might find yourself a position there. Always lots happening in Toronto. Did you know I started barbering there?"

"No, I didn't."

"Sure. Went to barbering college in Toronto, then got a job in a barber shop down on King Street, then ended up barbering at the King Eddie Hotel. Met my wife there, she worked in the hotel kitchen." He smiled as he reminisced. "I liked it. Toronto always has lots going on. You don't want to stick around here, Bobby. Nothing happening. And women behind everything that matters." He took the white sheet from Bobby's neck and shook the hair from it. "That's the thing about Toronto, still run by men. Those big time politicians and businessmen, they know what's what. There ain't no

219

women runnin' that town, no siree Bob!"

Out on Talbot Street he stood on the sidewalk, wondering if he should go back home or walk up to the Grand Central Hotel and buy a Toronto paper. He turned to see constable Gus Campbell limping towards him, a bruise under his left eye.

"Jesus, Bobby, you've stirred up a hornet's nest," he muttered. "The son of a bitch is in jail, but it took three of us to put him there. I hope you got the real goods on him because if you ain't, we'll all be leavin' town for good."

Gus passed quickly and Bobby started to walk to the hotel, imagining George MacAllister in jail.

Staring at the sidewalk, he didn't see her, and her voice surprised him. "I hear you're leaving town."

He raised his eyes; it was Susan, smiling.

"Yes, I'm going to Toronto tomorrow."

"What a coincidence." She gave a nervous little laugh. "I'm also going to Toronto. To stay with friends."

He was wondering what to say next when he heard himself inviting her for tea.

"Sure," she said, suddenly tense. "I'd like to."

They entered the Malt Shoppe and took a table; neither of them spoke. She looked uncertainly at him. "You did want tea, Bobby?"

"Tea is fine."

"If you want coffee or a Coke...."

"Tea is okay."

He looked at her and saw the face he remembered. There was colour in her cheeks and her nose was starting to freckle. He remembered her freckled face on the beach at Port Stanley, seven, eight years ago. Now the sun was glinting off the faint red in her hair. He noticed the pink of her lips, the muscles at the side of her neck and her small ears. He held his breath for a moment, then looked for the waitress. Susan was examining him despite herself: the red face and the dark blue eyes, the hooked nose and the dark hair. *I know how that hair will look when he's old*, she thought. *It will turn grey one strand at a time, so for a while it will* be grey-black, and then suddenly it will be snow white. She could feel his presence. It's unfinished, she said to herself, and regretted the thought immediately. She forced herself to think of Toronto and her tall band leader and the week after next. Life was about to begin.

"So you're leaving for Toronto," she said finally. "For long?"

"I don't know. I have some business to attend to."

She frowned at the phrase. Her father had starting using it when she was ten. If he didn't have time for her he would say, "I have some business to attend to."

"You'll be relieved to get away from St. Thomas, I'm sure."

"I don't know what I'd do here," he said simply. "There's the dairy, but it's been doing pretty well without me."

"It seems there will be a vacancy for a lawyer in town," she said.

"You mean MacAllister."

She nodded. "I heard that you had to subdue him before he could be taken to jail."

"I had to subdue him? Where on earth did you hear that? From Marie Barnes?"

She smiled. "Actually I heard it from Mother who heard it from Wanda who works for us. She might have heard it from...."

"Marie Barnes." He raised his hand, laughing. "Maybe Jack Morris is right, and women do run this town. But I had nothing to do with the arrest itself, you know. It was Gus Campbell and the other boys."

She laughed uproariously. Too loud, he thought. Nervous. He said nothing, and this began the pattern of the next twenty minutes. One would speak, the other would answer eagerly, there would be an outburst of nervous conversation and laughter, and they would fall silent.

"I suppose Jean is unhappy you're leaving for Toronto," she said, trying to keep her tone casual.

"Jean?" Susan was watching him carefully. "I don't think she cares one way or another. I can't think why she would."

"Oh. I thought you two were...."

"No," he said and the silence returned again.

"That's right, you don't think much of women anymore."

He shrugged. "I wouldn't say that. It's just that things are different now. Susan, I probably said some things to you in your house that time…."

She held up her hand. "Not a word. You've been through a war and it's bound to have changed you. I didn't think anything of it. And as I recall, I said some things too."

"I don't remember."

She didn't reply. The teenage couple behind them got up and walked to the cash register. He watched them leave to avoid looking at her. When he turned his head back, she was watching him again. Immediately she lowered her eyes. He laughed.

"Everything's changing, Susie. I hear your father is coming out today with an editorial in support of the Tories. When the Times Journal supports the Conservative Party it's a new and different world."

"Mother won't speak to him."

"Jack Morris seemed to think that your mother was in favour of the switch."

"Jack Morris? What would he know about it?"

"Nothing at all. But this is St. Thomas."

They laughed with genuine, relaxed laughter. She set down her teacup and picked up her purse.

"I'm sorry, Bobby, but I have to go. I promised Mother I'd meet her in Robsons to look at a dress. I really enjoyed tea."

Her smile was brilliant. He smiled back, mumbling about the things he had to do. They walked out onto the sidewalk. She turned to him. "This is goodbye for a little while. Good luck in Toronto."

She held out her hand and he shook it. He watched her go, then turned and walked down Talbot Street to the courthouse to give his deposition regarding George MacAllister.

222

33.

A week later Robert Russell entered a door marked Corporate Records in the legislative office building at Queen's Park.

"May I help you?" An ageless woman, her grey hair piled in a severe bun, peered at him from behind her lorgnette.

"I have come to see the letters patent of Newcorp Investments, Limited, chartered, I believe, in the last year."

"You can't walk in here and look at corporate documents, Sir. They are confidential, and without the necessary authorization...."

He thrust a letter across the desk. She adjusted her lorgnette and read it.

"I see that Mr. MacKay has sent you. He is a Member, but he is supposed to route his request through the Provincial Secretary's office. This is most unusual, Mr....?"

"Russell. Captain Russell." He had twisted Grant MacKay's arm to get that letter.

"Well, I suppose it's all right."

She picked up her bell and rang it. A bent-over, elderly man shuffled to her desk. She wrote on a scrap of paper and handed it to him. He glided through a door to one side, his loose lips muttering. Within a minute he was gliding back, and handed his supervisor a rust-coloured docket tied with black ribbon. He disappeared into the back room as soundlessly as he had come.

She laid the file on a small desk in a corner.

Russell sat and began thumbing through the file, looking for the list of directors. He saw that the company had been incorporated on December 11, 1944, barely six months earlier and was empowered by its charter to develop real property in Ontario. When he came to the directors, he scanned the names quickly and was at first disappointed. But when he ran his eye over the names more slowly, he stopped at the company's secretary, Hugh R.W. Archer, barrister and solicitor, Eleanor's Uncle Hugh. He looked again. His address was given as 40 King Street West. That would be the offices of

Archer, Campbell and Torrington, the family firm. He shut the file.

"Thank you, Ma'm," he said. "You've been most helpful."

He caught the southbound street car at Bay and Wellesley, heading for the financial district downtown. He was going to the offices of Archer, Campbell and Torrington on instinct. It was a thrust into the enemy camp, a reconnaissance mission. He decided that connecting MacAllister and Matthews to the Archers was good for him. Since they did not know that he knew, it gave him a slight advantage. Did they know what had happened to MacAllister? Probably not; another advantage. He looked out the window. The street was suddenly full of men in suits and hats carrying brief cases. He got off at King Street.

He entered the lobby of Forty King Street West, the Empire Bank building. Carved stone pillars soared to a Venetian ceiling. Opposite the entrance doors, on the wall, a painting of three iconic figures representing industry, science and commerce gazed at a landscape that showed farmers in their fields, miners hacking at rock with picks and factory workers in a line before a machine. On the side walls were banks of elevators with gleaming brass doors. Uniformed women with white gloves stood in front of each one. He took an elevator, giving the name of the law firm to the attendant. At the fifth floor he stepped into a carpeted corridor and saw the name Archer, Campbell and Torrington on a brass plaque beside double oak doors. Inside, the reception area was walled in oak, with a deep blue carpet on the floor. On one wall was a portrait of King George, next to a smaller photograph of the Premier of Ontario. The Union Jack hung in one corner on a brass standard topped with an eagle.

There was no receptionist at the desk, so he walked quickly through the lobby and found himself in a corridor with office doors bearing names on brass plaques. He came to Hugh R.W. Archer at the far end of the corridor. Inside, the secretary, a woman with pale blond hair and an insolent smile looked up casually from the magazine she was reading.

"Yes?"

"Mr. Archer, please."

"He's in." She nodded her head towards the door. "Go right in. You won't disturb him. Don't worry."

He pushed through the inner door. Hugh Archer looked up from his mahogany desk, clear except for the hand of solitaire he had dealt himself. The blue eyes were annoyed, the red face flushed. Behind him was a window that looked south over Union Station and the railway yards to the blue of Lake Ontario. Archer began to gather up the cards, peering at him.

"I know you, don't I?" He gave a sheepish smile. "Sorry, old boy, just a bit of recreation, don't you know? Did we have an appointment?" He put the playing cards in his desk drawer. "All work and no play makes Jack a dull boy and all that. I find if I don't relax during the business day, the tension of my practice can get to me. What is your name, Sir?"

"My name is Robert Russell, and your company, Newcorp Investments, is trying to expropriate my land outside St. Thomas."

Hugh Archer stared at him again. "I was sure I knew you. You were with Eleanor a while back. Going to run for the Party down in Elgin County." Russell nodded. "I don't see that we have anything to discuss, Sir. Expropriation is clearly in the public interest. If you don't like it, appear before the hearing, coming up soon." He pulled out a diary calendar and leafed through it. "Yes, here it is, a few days from now, June 2. How time flies."

"How much did they pay you?"

"I don't understand you." Archer's face went expressionless. "If you are insinuating that I or anyone in this firm is susceptible to bribery, then you had better leave at once. No one has ever questioned my honesty in the twenty years since I was admitted to the bar."

"I'm not questioning your honesty, I'm asking how much Van Kleef, or maybe it was MacAllister or Matthews, donated to the Conservative campaign fund."

"Any citizen who supports democratic elections is obligated to support the political party of his choice."

"Of course."

Archer was beginning to recover his calm. "Why don't you wait here a moment, Mr. Russell. I want to check on something." He rose and left the office.

He's gone to check with his brother. Do they know about MacAllister? Who would tell them? MacKay? Van Kleef? But Van Kleef wouldn't know yet. Matthews can't have phoned them, he's in another world.

Through the window he watched an oil tanker, heavy-laden and low in the water, inch through the Eastern Gap of Toronto's island-sheltered harbour and plod towards the docks. The office door reopened and Hugh Archer was back.

"Edward would like to see you," he said. "But he's tied up now. Come to the house for a drink around six-thirty."

Russell rose to his feet. "I'll be there." He nodded to Archer and walked from the office. Outside the secretary didn't look up from her magazine. In the lobby the receptionist was back, a glamorous but well-dressed woman who smiled warmly.

"Mr. Archer sent me to make a private call," he said. You can charge it to the Newcorp account."

"Of course, Sir. Come this way."

She lead him to a private waiting room. He picked up the telephone and asked for the operator in St. Thomas.

"Put me through to Elmore Wayne," he said, as Marie Barne's chatty voice came on the line. She would listen, of course, as first Elmore's secretary and then the Chief came on the line.

"Where are you, Bobby? All hell is breaking loose back here."

"I'm in Toronto. I need to know the legal situation. Who's been charged?"

"So far only MacAllister. We can't stick it to Malone. He claims he only introduced the guy from Detroit to MacAllister and had no idea what the job was, and was shocked when he discovered there had been a killing. Claims he thought it was some kind of delivery job. Since neither MacAllister nor Matthews claims Malone knew what the goon was hired for, we don't see how we can charge him. By we, I mean the Crown Attorney's office."

"And Allan Matthews?"

"We're thinking that one over. No one wants to put Allan away, but I don't see how he isn't an accessory. I think they're going to do some deal if he co-operates with the investigation. Everyone is nervous because of the election. God forbid any of this should stick to Grant MacKay."

"Thanks, Elmore."

He decided not to go back to his hotel room. He walked over to King and Yonge Streets and bought a copy of the Globe and Mail, then boarded a street car headed north. 'Drew Says No Political Secret Police', read the headline. The Premier was denying his opponents' claims that he had formed a special branch of the Ontario Provincial Police to keep track of political subversives, which meant socialists and communists.

North of Bloor Street he saw a park on the east side, with men playing baseball. He left the street car and took a seat under a maple tree, from where he could watch the baseball as he read his paper. McMurtry's Furniture Company, in yellow jerseys, was playing the T. Eaton Company in red, white and blue. Just as he sat down he saw the yellow-shirted runner on first base break with the pitch and run to steal second base. He concentrated on his newspaper. He read the lists of men who continued to be reported killed, although the war had been mostly over for almost a month. There was an account of the shortage of food available to the German civilians who were emerging from the rubble of their cities. The Anglican bishop of Toronto was advising the faithful to consider well the implications of voting socialist CCF, for their freedom and for their prosperity. The Women's Christian Temperance Union was taking the Liberal leader, Mitchell Hepburn, to task for promising a group of farmers in Dunnville that, if elected, he would extend the opening hours for beer parlours.

There was yelling from the field and he looked over the top of his newspaper. One player was limping off the field, cursing, and the rest were milling around, pushing and shoving. The umpire, a short, barrel-chested man, rushed out from behind the plate and got between the most aggressive fighters. The turmoil paused, then subsided. The boys returned to their benches. The next pitch was decorous, the batter swung and missed. The game continued. In the next inning, the player who had limped off the field came to bat and hit the ball between first and second base into right field. He rounded first and sprinted for second, where he slid in with his spikes high, catching the second baseman on the thigh. Instantly the benches cleared and the punching erupted.

Russell watched with interest. This was rougher than the play in the southern Ontario league before the war. He had only seen a spiking once, although pitchers had thrown at his head more than once. Especially that last year, when he had been hitting well, and the word had spread. Suddenly he wanted to play baseball again; he wanted to swing the bat. It was then he realized that he hadn't brought a bottle with him and hadn't had a drink since the night at the Stork Club.

❀

The butler answered his ring at the door of the Archer house and ushered him in without a hint of recognition. He felt odd in the house again, like a spy behind enemy lines. The man sat him in the sitting room, with the view of the garden and the grand piano. The garden was flourishing with roses and daisies. The sitting room was empty.

"Mr. Archer is having a discussion with his son, Sir," said the butler. "I'll come and get you when they have finished."

As he waited, he began to hear one end of a heated discussion, the clipped, military tones of Edward Archer, interspersed with periods of silence when Owen was speaking in his quiet voice.

"I will not pay for it," Archer was bellowing. "Nor will the trust. It's time for you to get to work, Owen. Doing this pilgrimage to San Juan wherever with two old ladies and your parson friend is not getting down to it. Roman Catholic time-wasting, it you ask me. You must get something to do, my boy. Until you do, not a penny."

228

Another period of silence. Then the door opened and Owen walked down the hall and into the room without seeing Russell. He went to the piano, sighed and began to play. The music shimmered, with light-filled scales and soft, broken chords. Russell got to his feet.

"You play beautifully, Owen."

The playing stopped and Owen turned his dark, intense eyes to look at him. "Fauré, 'Impromptu Number 1'." A smile of recognition eased the tension in his face. "I know you, you're Eleanor's friend, the Captain. Sorry, I've forgotten your name."

"Russell, Robert Russell."

"That's right. Bobby." He rose and shook hands. "Eleanor isn't here right now. She may be in later on."

"I'm not here to see her, I'm here to see your father."

Owen rolled his eyes. "Good luck, then. Come and have a drink when you're finished." He returned to the keyboard and began the Impromptu again. The butler appeared in the doorway. Russell followed him down the hall and into the study. Edward Archer stared at him, with pain and confusion in his dark eyes.

"Sit down, Russell." The voice was not unfriendly. "I've just been talking to my son. As he looks at his future, he waivers between going on a four-month pilgrimage to some shrine in the Pyrenees with his mother and his aunt and his friend the parson, or going to Los Angeles and setting up as a hairdresser with another equally questionable friend." He stared at his desk. "Not your problem, eh, Russell? Back from the war, going into the law, good show. Now Hugh tells me you don't like this expropriation."

"It's our land," said Russell. "I don't like it being taken away under false pretences."

"False pretences." The man's voice deepened. "Don't be absurd. There's a good deal there, for all concerned. Van Kleef knows what he's doing, the leaders of St. Thomas think that it's good for the community, and it is. The plant will make that town. Grant MacKay, your own Member, supports it. The only opposition, it seems, Captain Russell, is you. And no one understands why, Sir. We have

229

not been able to find a solution to whatever your problem is, and fortunately we don't have to. The law provides a remedy in such circumstances, the remedy of expropriation. And we intend to use it, and we shall be successful. There is no question but that this project is in the public interest."

"And in some private interests as well."

"Yes, indeed, the investors will make money. No law against it, that's the way it works. Or have you succumbed to that socialist mumbo jumbo? All for one and one for all. Is that it?"

"There are private interests and private interests. This Newcorp Investments seems to be intimately associated with your family."

Archer rose to his feet. "Hugh is the secretary. We often serve as officers in our clients' corporations."

"And you have no interest in the company?"

Archer walked around his desk, clearly annoyed.

"Be that as it may, it's no concern of yours. What should concern you is that the expropriation will go through. The government of Ontario supports it. And that government will be re-elected next Monday, you can count on it. The citizens of St. Thomas want it. No judge is going to listen to the objections of a young man who doesn't understand his own interests."

"There's more to it than that."

"There is never more to it than that, Captain Russell." The man smiled at him. "There is always, ultimately, only the deal. Emotions, all the human frailties that come into play, are swept away by the deal. There is either a deal possible, in the mutual interests of those concerned, or there is not. We believe that in this instance the deal is there, and everyone else seems to agree. Now when this is over I hope you remember that you were given every chance to come in."

Russell realized that Archer had not heard of MacAllister's arrest. He rose to his feet, shook hands with Archer, who was still smiling at him in his confident, benevolent way, and left. In the sitting room, Owen had stopped playing and was talking with his mother, his aunt Hilda and his friend, the Reverend Peter Vincent.

"He absolutely won't pay a cent," Owen was saying. "Even when

I threatened to go off to Hollywood and go into the hairdressing business with Guy Brooks."

"Oh, Owen, you didn't." Peter Vincent had a look of disgust on his face.

Mildred Archer's face was lined with worry.

"What will we do? I've already subscribed for the tickets. We sail on the thirtieth. I have to pay the money by the tenth."

There was a gloomy pause. They were all unaware of Russell standing in the doorway.

"I have some money," said Hilda finally. "It was my share of what we got from Aunt Edith."

"Hilda, that was years ago and it was only fifty pounds."

"Three hundred and fifty dollars. But Hugh invested it well. It's over a thousand now. I can think of no better use for the money. Edward really is too much, Mildred, expecting Owen, with his talent and his sensitivity, to go into some horrid little position. It is our duty to prevent it."

"You'll pay my way, Hilda." Owen rose and kissed her on her cheek. "You are too sweet."

"The Lord proposes," intoned Peter Vincent. "And the Lord disposes."

Russell cleared his throat and they all turned their heads.

"Come and have a drink, Russell," said Owen. "You remember Peter Vincent? My mother and my Aunt Hilda."

"Will you join us for dinner, Captain Russell?" asked Mildred after the greetings.

"No, I really can't," he said. "I just came to have a word with Mr. Archer and I must be on my way. My mother is alone and she counts on me."

In the hallway came the sound of heals clicking on the tiles.

"God, I need a drink."

Eleanor's voice preceded her into the room. Without looking she walked to the sideboard and poured a whiskey. She was wearing a sleeveless green linen dress that emphasized her brown arms. She took a sip of her drink, sighed happily, and turned around. She saw

231

Russell and gave a little cry. Then she became completely silent, staring at him over the rim of her glass. Her beauty was still in her face, but it was hidden now, blurred by stress and anxiety, chipped away, under siege.

"Hello, Eleanor," he said.

"Hello." Her voice was hushed. "What brings you here?"

"I had some business with your father."

Her face fell. "I think I'll go upstairs. I'm exhausted."

"Eleanor, you must stay here and help entertain Captain Russell. He'll be gone soon."

Caught by her mother's voice, Eleanor turned and looked at him. He smiled. She shrugged and took the seat beside him on the sofa, the only one free.

"Eleanor is down," said Owen. "She has broken with her beau."

"He wasn't really a beau." Eleanor's voice was annoyed. "Timmy Riordan is just a … is just a…." Her voice faded.

"We remain unenlightened as to the exact nature of your relationship with Tim," said Owen, "which is just as well."

Eleanor turned to Russell. "Take me out for dinner. For old times' sake." She saw him hesitate. "Please. I shall go mad if I have to stay here tonight."

He nodded. "For old times' sake."

"Wait for me. I have to change."

She jumped up and ran from the room. Russell sat stunned at what he had agreed to, aware that everyone was looking at him.

"We're going out for dinner. For old times' sake."

"That's good." Owen went to the piano and began to play boogie woogie. "She really has been trashed by this Riordan. And Eleanor without a man…." He shook his head. "Is like me without music. Can one be addicted to sex?"

"Owen, please." His mother's tone was weary.

"Just asking. What do you think, Peter?"

The parson pressed the tips of his fingers together and set his face pompously. "Without a doubt. Passion without true love is a narcotic. Enslaves the soul."

"I'm not sure Eleanor is good for you, Captain Russell," said Owen.

Russell looked straight ahead. Owen was rocking to the beat of his barrel house rag. Hilda's eyes were still gleaming with intent. Peter Vincent smiled beatifically out the window. Mildred sipped her drink.

❀

"So, how has it been, back in St. Thomas?"

Eleanor was watching him from the other side of the table. He was annoyed with himself. She had carried him off, just like the first day in the bar. He tried to avoid her gaze by looking around the room. On this Tuesday evening the dining room of the hotel was half full.

"I've been away. I've changed, they've changed. It's a different world. It's hard to get used to a small town again. And there are business problems."

She pushed a strand of hair back from her face, watching him. "And your girl?"

She posed the question with the lift of her eye.

"As you say, she's a different person. I'm a different person. We move on."

He tried to remember the way Eleanor looked when they first met in the bar on that first day. She had been in her army uniform, khaki shirt and jacket, khaki skirt, nylons above her WAC shoes, a leather purse, and her lips a slash of red. She was still beautiful to him, but he could look at her calmly now. He could see, beneath her beauty, the hunger that devoured her, and something like fear in her eyes. She was smiling shyly; he couldn't remember shyness in her. Her hands were shaking.

She's a victim. She was part of the war, and now it's over. The war is gone and she has no life. *She's almost a corpse. Like me. With a shudder he thought of corpses, his mind back in battle, shrieking, splintering, wailing, shattering, wounding, killing, battle. That's where Eleanor belonged. He looked again and the skin of her face was skull-like taut; her smile was an obscene leer. He was afraid; he hated her.*

"How have you been, Eleanor?" She spread her hands and shrugged. "Breaking up with...."

"No, not that. There's lots more where he came from. It just that ... Christ, Russell, you're lucky you're a man."

"I'm lucky you're a woman." The gallantry was forced.

"You left me." She grimaced. "Look at me, Bobby."

He no longer saw the angel of death, just a lonely woman.

"My life has reached a sort of impasse; I'm stuck here right now. What to do is the question for Eleanor at the moment. I can't marry some stockbroker and raise happy, adorable children, like Janet. I can't be religious and love Jesus like mother or Hilda, forgetting sex, doing penance and arranging the flowers on the altar. Even if Daddy would let me, I can't work, I'm not trained for anything. What the hell am I going to do? The only thing I've done well was drive the general around London during the war. That was me. I was a good little soldier girl, no shooting, mind, but champagne and ... all that goes with it." Her eyes lit up momentarily. "But the war is over, they say. Good for the world, bad for me."

The waiter brought whiskey for him and red wine for her. He looked away again. She watched him scan the room.

He's different now, she thought. He was lost, angry, confused, away from his mommy and drunk. They were always drunk. That's where I came in. They got a mommy for a night or a weekend, and I got them. As soon as they were patched up they moved on. If only I hadn't loved them. But I did love them, I loved the way they were lost, the hunted look in their eyes; I couldn't resist it. I gave them love. Not the 'till-death-do-us-part' kind. It was the 'till-the-morning-do-us-part' kind. Bobby doesn't want to be here. He isn't lost anymore. He doesn't need me, I can see it in his eyes. So he's not for me. But maybe tonight, a guy who isn't lost, who knows what he's doing. I still like his hooked nose, the thin red lips. I still like the black hair, black eyes. I still like the fun behind the eyes.

The waiter set plates of soup in front of them.

"So what will you do now? Would you work in Father's firm?"

"Maybe."

She smiled. "You're so very cool. Young man considering his options. Planning his life. Very … judicious."

He laughed. "I still make mistakes."

"Like taking me to dinner?"

"This isn't a mistake. At least not yet."

The wine was soothing her and his laugh was warm. The conversation from the other tables, the rattle of crockery in the kitchen, and the waiters' smiles were suddenly part of a flow of food and wine and movement and voices. She loved the way he looked, sitting across from her.

"When do you go back to St. Thomas?"

"That depends."

He gave up trying to distance himself and gave in to the food and the whiskey, and the beauty of her face. He was startled to realize he wanted her. She bit into a piece of sausage and he saw a bit of the juice run down her mouth. She wiped it away with her napkin, leaving just a drop of grease that shone on her lip. The gleam of her mouth made him hungry; he cut into his steak. By the end of the meal, they were talking naturally, laughing, and looking without any pretence of modesty. He no longer worried.

"We could go dancing. I know a place where you can dance all night. Opens at eleven."

He looked at his watch. "It's ten. We can walk."

She took him to a blind pig, a speakeasy, a holdover from Prohibition days, not far from Union Station, popular with black railway porters and trainmen. She knocked twice at a basement door, and a grill opened. After a moment of scrutiny, the grill was closed, the door opened and they walked into an underworld of dim lights, cigarette smoke and dreamy, throbbing music. The doorman looked Russell over carefully.

"Evenin', Miss Archa'," he said. "Long time no see."

"I'm making up for it, Sammy. Can you find us a table?"

The place was plain; unvarnished wood floor, a bar at one end, and pictures of black jazz groups all over the walls. The bar was in the middle of the room, no mirror behind it, and a huge fat man with coal black skin and big eyes poured the liquor. Several young black girls in tight, brightly coloured dresses sat at the bar nursing their drinks. They looked up with interest when Russell entered, then went back to chatting when they saw Eleanor. Two white couples were dancing, arms tight around each other. The music came from a piano, a horn player and a bass – three black men on a dais to one side of the bar. At the back end of the room were tables with black men, drinking, talking and laughing. In the front of the house were the whites, all couples and all young. The doorman led them to one of the front tables. A thin black woman with a fierce glare and a blond wig came to them.

"Beer or whiskey?"

She stood with her hand on one hip, staring at the ceiling.

"What kind of whiskey," he asked.

She looked at him as if he were an idiot. "Chicago mash."

"He'll have whiskey," said Eleanor. "Bring me a beer."

The woman nodded and went to the bar. Soon she returned with a jug of beer, a glass jar of whiskey and a bowl of peanuts.

"Three dolluhs," she said.

Russell laid the money on the table. He raised his glass to Eleanor and sipped his whiskey. Then, he relaxed and began to take in the room: laughter, the tinkle of glasses, the sound of the horn, sailing into the night, the riff of the piano and the slow thudding of the bass.

"Let's dance," she said.

On the dance floor she nestled in, she cuddled, she whispered in his ear, she stroked his neck. The music and the bourbon came together and he could dance without thinking. The trumpet was muted now, and no longer sounded like a bold brass horn, but more like a steely hint, an insinuation, of the night to come, and the possibility of love. He had lost any sense of her apart from him. The music spoke, she spoke, and the language and the voice were the same, something that entered him not by the ear but through the body, through the veins. They danced clutched in each other's arms until the set ended. At the table she kissed him.

"I'll be right back," she said, and disappeared towards the rear of the bar.

The thin woman refilled their drinks. Another set began. He looked at his watch; it was midnight. People were drifting in the door, mostly couples now, black and white. The night was cool, happy and sexy and he felt at home. Music and whiskey. Passports to the world. The trio moved from a fast jive number to a slow, funky, thudding blues. Eleanor had not come back. He watched the fat bar man pouring drinks and joking with the men who sat on the stools. The dance floor was full and the room was heating up. Still no sign of Eleanor. He got to his feet and walked in the direction she had gone.

"You lookin' for your girl, mistah?" said the barman.

"Yes. She's been gone for ten minutes."

"Don't you worry 'bout her. She be back soon, real soon. She gettin' happy with her friend, Mary Jane."

He returned to his table. The door opened and a policeman in uniform entered. He walked to the bar and was greeted like a brother by the barman, who poured him a shot of whiskey. The policeman downed his whiskey in a gulp, received an envelope from the barman, and left. As he passed the table he looked at Russell and winked. Then he heard a rustle and Eleanor was sitting beside him.

"You've been gone for a while."

"Mary Jane," she said. "I had to find Mary Jane."

"So you found her. Friends in strange places."

"You have no idea. But let's get out of here. Let's go back to your room and fuck."

The invitation shook him. She looked at him as if he were not really just across the table, but across the room. There was an impersonal dreaminess in her smile.

"Don't think, baby. Let's dance. Then let's go."

They danced, and when the tune ended they left the bar. In the night streets a mist had fallen. They walked hand in hand past buildings

237

that were softened and hidden. The city was blurred into indistinct, romantic shapes. From the lake a fog horn sounded. Somewhere in his mind there was a caution, and a memory of a world of sharply defined objects, and everyday tension, but he wanted only her. She pulled him by the hand and he followed. He had walked down other streets, but they were far away and long ago, he couldn't remember. Tonight there were no ditches filled with flowers, no rolling fields. There was no town up ahead. There was only her. How did they get to his hotel and the room where, suddenly, she was lying naked on his bed? Not like last time, demanding her satisfaction. She lay smiling in a demure way, almost not present, as if there was still mist between them. Her eyes glowed with sleepy lust.

"It's all for you," she said, her voice husky and quiet.

He made love to her. She closed her eyes and sighed and smiled and gripped him in her arms and legs. She threw back her head and smiled and moaned, until finally he let himself go. Next they were beside each other, breathing hard, covered in sweat.

"I love that," she said. "It's what I live for. I'm never alive unless … unless…."She touched him. He seized her breasts and squeezed them. Her eyes went glassy, she shuddered and was still again. He stared at the ceiling as she snuggled into the nook of his arm.

"Can we go dancing Wednesday night? Real dancing? Here at the hotel?" Her voice was sleepy.

"Sure."

By Wednesday night the hearing would be over. His mind was clearer now as his breathing calmed. He wanted to wake in the morning without her, and start the day with no reverberations from this night.

"D'you want to go home now?"

There was no answer. He saw her closed eyes, then heard the soft snoring. "Damn," he muttered. Asleep, her face looked older. The lines around the mouth and eyes. He walked into the bathroom and turned on the tub faucet. In the mirror, a red, bleary face stared back at him. Charming, he thought. He lowered his body into the tub and let the hot water sooth his muscles and wash away his sweat.

34.

Robert Russell appeared at the Court of King's Bench at the provincial court house on Queen Street at nine-forty-five on the morning of June 2, 1945, in a daze. The night before, he had eaten by himself and had gone to see 'A Song to Remember' with Paul Muni and Merle Oberon at the Capitol. When he walked back to the hotel and entered his room he found Eleanor on his bed in her slip, a happy smile on her face.

"How did you get in here?" His first instinct was to toss her out into the hall.

"I bribed the bellhop." Her smile disappeared. "You're not happy to see me."

"I wanted to go to bed early. Tomorrow is a big day."

She sat up on the bed. Her hair hung over her shoulders and her slip revealed the tops of her breasts. "You can still get to bed early."

He smiled at her, and there was no more discussion.

❀

So here he was, outside the chambers, waiting for the clerk to open the doors. Edward and Hugh Archer appeared, walking briskly, carrying briefcases, wearing robes and white wigs, talking together. They nodded to him, each with his own expression of contempt, Edward smiling, Hugh scowling. He was beginning to regret his night with Eleanor. His head ached, his body was sore and the inside of his mouth tasted like sour wine. The doors to the chamber opened and the clerk ushered them in. The Archers took their seats at counsel's desk before the bench to the right. When Russell walked to the opposite desk to the left of the bench, the clerk whispered in his ear.

"Those desks are for properly attired counsel. You will have to sit in the public area. His Honour has agreed to let you present your case from there."

The door behind the bench opened and the judge entered the chambers. The clerk cleared his throat officiously.

"Oyez, Oyez, the Court of Kings Bench of the Province of Ontario is now in session, his Honour James Willoughby Barnett, KC, DSO, FRS presiding. All ye who have business with this honourable court draw near and be heard."

The judge was a skinny, red-faced man in flowing black robes tinged in red, his curled judge's wig slightly lop-sided on his head. He sat on his bench and glared at the court.

"What's up first, Wigley?" he said to the clerk. "Divorce, isn't it? But I don't see the woman. Can't have a divorce without a woman. I won't have it. Find the goddamn woman. And Archer, you seem to be the counsel. What are you doing here? You don't act in divorces."

The clerk came behind the bench and whispered in the judge's ear. The man listened, his thin cheeks drooping, his spectacles gleaming, then glared again.

"They told me the divorce was first. This place is a shambles. All right, it's an expropriation. An opposed expropriation. Let's get on with it and stop wasting the court's time. You are for or against the expropriation, Archer?"

"For, Your Honour."

"Then who's against." He scanned the court. "I see no opposing counsel."

Again Wigley whispered in his ear.

"And what is his name? Russell. Robert Russell. Is there a Robert Russell of St. Thomas in the court?"

Russell rose to his feet. The judge peered at him.

"Your opposing counsel, honourable men well known to this court, have requested that you be permitted to present your brief from the public seats as a non-accredited counsel, in the interests of the expropriation, which I understand is in the interests of the people of your town and has popular and political support from both the government and the Liberal opposition. Whom do you represent, Sir?"

"My family owns the land to be expropriated."

"I see. Under the circumstances I will accede to Mr. Archer's request and allow you to plead your case. Let me see your shoes."

"Sir?" Russell stared at the small, red-faced man.

"I said, let me see your shoes."

The voice rose and cracked. Russell shrugged and stepped down to the floor where the judge could see his shoes.

"They're brown," yelled the judge. "I won't have it. It is clearly understood that all counsel must be properly attired in my court. I will not hear you, Sir, until you are properly attired."

Russell looked at the Archers. Both wore black oxfords and blue suits under their robes.

"D'you mean I have to find a pair of black shoes?" Russell asked.

The judge began to shuffle papers on his desk and stare at his watch. Edward Archer beckoned to the clerk. Mr. Wigley approached and they whispered together. Then he mounted to the bench and whispered in the judge's ear.

"Absolutely not. I will not have it." He shook his head and hit his bench with his hand. Then he looked down at Edward Archer, and caught his breath. He waited thirty seconds, calming himself, and then looked at Russell.

"The court is going to suggest a compromise, Mr. Russell, only in the interests of justice in this most unusual situation. Your opponents want you to present your case, since they want the expropriation to proceed with all haste and are convinced that your arguments are without merit.

"Therefore, you may plead your case from the public benches, improperly attired as you are, but at no time shall your shoes become visible to the court. Should you fail to observe my rule and reveal your shoes, the court will adjourn immediately. Do you understand me?"

Russell gaped at the judge.

"Do you understand me?" he roared.

"Yes, Your Honour," said Russell.

"Very well, let us proceed. Mr. Clerk, read the particulars."

"In the matter of Expropriation number 45 slash 97, being a

parcel of land lot 12, concession four, township of Lyndhurst, county of Elgin…."

Mr. Wigley's voice droned over the court as he described the expropriation and the opinion of the attorney general of Ontario that it was in the public interest. Russell stared at the judge. The little man was impatient and kept staring at his watch; he seemed to want to finish as quickly as possible. Russell noticed that he wore a Freemason's ring on his left hand. Both the Archers were Masons and had rings on their left hands. Normally I wouldn't have a chance here, he thought. He's probably a member of the Conservative Party and has dinner with Archer once a month.

After the clerk had finished, the judge motioned to Archer. Archer rose and his brother handed him a file, which he rejected.

"This is a simple matter. The project is an outstanding one, and I shall be happy to describe it briefly and to demonstrate to the Court its overwhelming support in St. Thomas and in the government. I can only regret that the Court's time must be taken up with this hearing, caused by objections which, I am sure you will agree, Your Honour, can only be frivolous."

Archer was brief and appeared bored. He smiled confidently at the judge as he described the project, gave Van Kleef's credentials, named all the worthies of St. Thomas who supported it, and then mentioned that the only opposition came from the owners of the property, presumably for sentimental reasons.

The judge bristled at the phrase 'sentimental reasons'. Edward Archer bowed to the bench, and sat down with a smirk. The judge straightened his wig and turned his head to Russell.

"State your case, Sir."

Russell rose and walked from his seat to the floor of the court.

"Do not let me see your shoes," yelled the judge.

Russell hopped back into his seat.

"Forgive me, Your Honour. I have only one point to make. This expropriation by Newcorp Investments has been in the interests of Tyler Van Kleef, to aid him in building an automobile parts plant on my land."

"It's got to be on somebody's land," interrupted the judge. "All land is owned by somebody. Or are you one of these socialists who want to end private ownership of land? Hey? Is that it?"

"No, Your Honour."

"Well then, I wish you'd get to the point."

"I will try. Mr. Van Kleef is represented in St. Thomas by the legal firm of MacAllister and Matthews."

"And what of that? They have to be represented by someone. Why are you boring this court with such irrelevant detail?"

"I will try to be relevant. Perhaps you will agree with me that the fact that George MacAllister is now under arrest in St. Thomas, charged with being an accessory to a murder, is relevant. Even more relevant is the fact that the murdered man was a postman who delivered mail to our farm. The man was bribed by MacAllister to divert mail from my mother, while I was overseas. These were letters to her from me and from the military authorities which would have informed her as to my whereabouts. The lawyers in St. Thomas wanted her to think I might be dead. They thought they could convince her to sell the land that is now being expropriated if she thought I would not be coming home."

Russell paused. The judge stared at him, trying to assimilate what he had heard. Edward Archer was whispering furiously to his brother, who was shrugging and lifting his hands.

"Is this true? This murder business?" The judge glared now at the Archers as he spoke.

"Yes, Sir."

"You say accessory. Who committed the murder?"

Russell went through the connection with Vince Malone, and the hiring of the hit man from Detroit.

"A mobster from Detroit. This is scandalous. You'd better be certain that what you are telling me is factual. Are you sure?"

"It is all true, your Honour. If I may suggest, you could verify it by phoning the Crown Attorney in St. Thomas."

The judge stared, then turned to the clerk. "Wigley, phone the Crown in St. Thomas and see if they have MacAllister locked up as accessory to a murder. Find out the story." He turned to Archer as the clerk left the chambers. "What do you know about this, Archer?"

"Nothing, Your Honour. This comes as a complete surprise to us." Archer was stroking his moustache, his handsome brow furrowed. He looked angrily at Russell. "In fact, had we known of this problem earlier, we would not have come before Your Honour in this fashion. That having been said, your Honour, we submit that whatever has taken place in St. Thomas does not affect the merit of the expropriation. The project is sound and the expropriation has been arranged properly, as the law requires. I suggest to you that if MacAllister has committed some bizarre crime it has no more bearing on the matter before you than if he had been caught fishing out of season."

"Don't be ridiculous. This man is suggesting there's been a murder in order to suppress this diversion of the mails. If this is true, then all bets are off. Who knows what else has been happening? And, like it or not, you seem to be involved with criminal elements. Can't have that. Election time too, or have you forgotten. Use your head, Archer."

The clerk returned.

"The Crown Attorney in St. Thomas has told me that they are holding George MacAllister, barrister of that city, pending charges. The charges will be accessory after the fact to a murder, tampering with the mails and attempted fraud. They are in touch with the Federal Bureau of Investigation in Detroit, but do not expect to find the actual murderer soon."

"Well, that's it then. The objection is sustained. Mr. Archer, you are free to reapply when you get your mess cleaned up. Court's adjourned."

The judge swept from the courtroom. Archer slumped at his desk, staring at Russell.

"You son of a bitch," he said in a controlled voice. "You knew about this, yet you let us go ahead. You wanted us to appear here and be shot down. I congratulate you, Captain Russell. You have what it takes." He turned to his brother. "Why didn't you know this?

You were supposed to be keeping watch on St. Thomas while I was running the election campaign."

Hugh blushed bright red. "This just came up, Eddie. Last few days. And I was out of town. Had to be in Belleville."

"And why did you have to be in Belleville?"

Archer's cross-examiner's voice lashed at his brother, who stared at the floor.

"You had to be in Belleville for the opening of trout fishing with all those bums you hang around with down there." Archer threw up his hands. "Your little fishing trip will cost this project tens of thousands of dollars, when you figure out what this land will cost us now. Not to mention the delay."

Russell headed for the door.

"Russell, can we talk before you go back to St. Thomas?"

"I'm at the Royal York," he said over his shoulder.

He wanted to get on the train that afternoon and head back to St. Thomas, savouring his triumph, but he had done nothing about arranging his future. Grant MacKay had given him the names of two law partnerships which had been in favour under the Liberals; and he had agreed to take Eleanor dancing. He decided to phone his mother and stay over the weekend. He would visit the firms early next week and go home as soon as he was finished. The telephone beside his bed rang.

"Mr. Edward Archer to see you, Mr. Russell."

"Send him up."

He lay back on the bed and smiled. By the time the knock on the door came he was admiring the way Archer had accepted his defeat in court. He rose, straightened his tie, and opened the door. Edward Archer strode into the room followed by a tall man with a fringe of white hair, his glasses dangling on a black cord around his neck.

"Robert Russell, may I introduce Mr. Tyler Van Kleef."

"Captain Russell." The big man stood forward, his eyes

twinkling, and crushed Russell's hand in his grip. "Tyler Van Kleef. I understand that some of the approaches made to you have been ill-conceived. I apologize to you, Sir. Had you been dealing with me directly, none of this would have occurred. I deal straight and I deal square, Russell. I'm here to sit down with you and find some common ground."

"I hope that you won't take any risky action at this point, Gentlemen," said Archer soberly. "With this criminal situation in St. Thomas I would not like to see anything proceed before we know where we are. In the interests of all parties."

"Dammit, Archer, I haven't got that kind of time. This deal has been held up long enough already with lawyers dotting their 'i's' and crossing their 't's'. Time is money, man. I want to get a deal with this fine young man, just back, as I understand it, from serving his country against Herr Hitler."

"In defence of the legal profession, Mr. Van Kleef, I must assert that the dotting of legal 'i's' and the crossing of legal 't's' has saved many a party substantial dollars by avoiding the pitfalls that deals can engender. I must advise you…."

"If I want it, I'll ask for it, Archer. Until that time, perhaps you'd be good enough to leave me alone with Captain Russell."

Edward Archer withdrew with a smile and a bow, careful not to be flustered. "I'll be out of town for the next few days, working for the Premier. You can always contact me through the office if you need me."

Van Kleef went to the bed and stretched his six foot six on the coverlet.

"Forgive an old man for relaxing, Mr. Russell, but my feet are killing me." He sighed with contentment. "Can we do business?"

Russell did not like the direct question. He paced up and down the room.

"I was not looking to sell the land. We've owned it since my grandfather's time and we're using it."

"You don't need me, is what you're saying. But I need you, Captain. In my world, that means the price goes up."

"In your world you pay off the politicians and expropriate me. I've already seen what your world is."

Van Kleef shook his bald head. "That wasn't me, son, that was the lawyers. If you knew me you'd know that dealing with government is the last thing I like to do. I didn't know about the expropriation until it was underway. Now look." He sat up on the bed. "You've got the land I need. I've gone too far down this road to turn back and start somewhere else. Name your price."

Russell looked uneasily out the window.

"I've got people living on that land, a family that pays no rent to speak of. They do a little work for me in return."

"We'll hire 'em in the plant. Find a job for 'em. Pay more money in a year than they've seen in a lifetime. Give 'em company housing."

"Archie's illiterate."

"Not a problem. We'll make him flag man in the freight yard. Unless he's colour blind."

Russell shrugged and sat in the chair, looking at the American's face, an expression both open and cunning, a sharpness and tightness around the mouth but a gleam in the blue eyes.

"What will you pay?" he asked.

"Heh, heh," chuckled Van Kleef, rubbing his hands together. "Now we're getting some place. My boy, you've got me over a barrel so I'm prepared to be generous. The fact is, your land's not good for much; it's too wet to grow good corn, we both know that. Now it's eight and two thirds acres, and I figure the most you could get for it in your county is seven hundred and fifty dollars an acre. That would be sixty-five hundred dollars. Now wait." He held up one large hand. "That's what you'd get if you tried to sell it now, if you could find a buyer. I'm prepared to pay you double that, plus something for the inconvenience of this expropriation, which I sincerely regret. I'll pay you fifteen thousand dollars for that land. I'll find a house for your tenant family and a job for any able bodied men in it. Now that's a good offer."

"I'll take it," said Robert Russell instinctively.

"Captain Russell, you've made the right choice. I pride myself that no one who does business with Tyler Van Kleef lives to regret it. They're either dead or they're satisfied." His laughter filled the room. "There's another thing; Archer tells me you're a lawyer. I need a lawyer to do the work for me in St. Thomas. The land conveyancing, corporate work, employment contracts and so on. I can't use those two clowns MacAllister and Matthews any more. Why don't you do it, set yourself up as a lawyer?"

"You'd give me that work?"

"Why not? It's just paper pushing anyway, doesn't matter who does it as long as it isn't screwed up. I'll use Archer for the greasy political stuff in Toronto."

Russell walked to the bed and shook the big man's hand.

"You've bought the land, Sir. And you may have yourself a lawyer. I was planning to talk to some firms here next week."

"You don't want to be one of these city lawyers, Russell. They wear their undershorts so tight they can't fart without making a mess, and then they bill you for it. But you think it over. Right now, I think we should go and have a beer. Tie the knot on our deal."

When they reached the lobby, the sounds of bagpipes, drums and a brass band were resounding from the street. They walked out onto King Street. A parade was under way and a fife and drum corps in blue and orange were passing, 'Loyal Orange Order, Killmartin Lodge number 234', stencilled on the bass drum. At the front of the corps a pretty girl bore a sign, 'Orange Lodge Number 234 supports Premier Drew and the Conservative Party'. At the rear a young man bore another sign: 'Vote for Socialism This Time, Vote with a Gun at Your back Next Time'.

Next came ranks of men in dark suits wearing blue sashes proclaiming them to be members of a Masonic lodge. 'Vote Conservative, Defend Your Property Rights' said one of their signs. 'Vote CCF and Give Your House to the Government' said another. Next came pipers in plaid kilts, surrounded by signs supporting the Conservative Party and proclaiming the dangers of the socialist option.

"A political parade," said Van Kleef. "They sure seem worked up about these socialists."

"They won't get in. A few may get elected in Toronto and some of the industrial areas, but most people think that the government will be returned with a majority."

"Truth of the matter is, it doesn't matter. The same deals will get done no matter who's in power. If these socialists were elected, d'you think that means my auto parts plant wouldn't get built? Not on your life." He clapped his big arm around Russell's shoulder. "Let's have that beer."

35.

He thumped the brass knocker three times. No one came to the door. He walked back down the walk and surveyed the house from the street. There were lights on the second floor. There was a light somewhere at the rear of the first floor. He walked back onto the porch and tried the front door. It opened; he entered and stood in the front hall. He could hear voices from the sitting room.

"I'm sorry, Owen, but I can't give you any more money." Hugh's voice was nervous and uncertain. "Your father said no and I say no. You'll have to go with what you have."

"I have only two hundred dollars from Hilda to last four months." Owen's voice was sulky.

"How much do you need? Bread and water, sleeping in churches and all of that pilgrimage stuff. Shouldn't cost much. Not like golfing in Bermuda."

A chorus of outraged voices, including Mildred's and Hilda's, drowned out Hugh.

"How dreadful, Hugh, that you are so limited in your vision." Hilda's voice was high and angry. "The boy must have money for his journey. Would you have me sell my jewellery?"

"Depends on the price, Hilda. Get a good offer, flog 'em, would be my advice."

The angry chorus broke out again. Hugh emerged from the sitting room grinning from ear to ear and, not seeing Russell, ran up the stairs two steps at a time.

"Not to worry." Owen's voice was calm. "Peter and I will get by. I had hoped to spend some time in Paris before and after our trek, but it's clearly not to be." He sighed. "I've borrowed fifty from Mickey Masterson."

Owen left the sitting room and entered the hallway. He saw Russell standing by the staircase.

"Good God, it's the Captain." His smile was friendly. "Here for the fair Eleanor, no doubt. Does she know you're here?"

"No, she doesn't."

"I'll let her know. What is it tonight? The theatre? A concert?"

"Dancing. At the Royal York."

"How conventional; but Eleanor does love dancing. She thinks it's good for her hormones and body rhythms. Say, you wouldn't have an extra fifty bucks with you? Couldn't say you'd ever see it again, but it's in a good cause."

Russell shook his head.

"Haven't got much with me, I'm afraid."

"No matter, dear Captain, I shall get by. Now you want Eleanor. Let me see what I can do."

Owen walked quickly up the stairs, glancing back to see if Russell was watching him. Hugh passed him on the way down and stopped short when he saw Russell.

"What the hell are you doing here?"

"Picking up Eleanor. We're going dancing."

"You've got a hell of a lot of nerve, coming here after that ambush you staged in court. Not the way a gentleman behaves, that kind of trickery. If Edward were here he'd probably have you thrown out the door."

"I think he wants me to join your firm."

"What d'you mean?" Hugh's face fell. "He didn't say anything about that to me. Did he make you an offer? How could he have? Most irregular. Really most irregular." Hugh turned and scurried back up the stairs, muttering to himself.

Owen came back down. "Eleanor knows you're here. Quite an impression you seem to have made, Captain. She blushed when I told her and it takes a lot to make my sister blush. You must be quite something." He smiled and rolled his eyes. "But enough about you. The dear girl gave me her last thirty. I call that love and devotion. Be good to her, Captain, for my sake." With a wink, Owen walked into the sitting room.

"There you are, darling. Sorry to keep you waiting."

She was standing on the landing for effect, showing him her pink dancing frock, with half sleeves and a flared skirt. Her eyes were shining and her smile radiant. A date, he thought. Maybe I should have brought flowers.

"Eleanor, you're not going out tonight. The doctor says you need rest. I forbid it."

Mildred Archer stood looking from the door of the sitting room, concern in her face.

"Nonsense. I have been invited to go dancing. It will be good for me, Mother, you'll see."

"My dear girl, you have no idea what's good for you." Hilda's bird-like face appeared at her sister's shoulder in the doorway, her eyes round with shock. Mildred walked into the hall. Eleanor ran down the stairs and onto the porch.

"C'mon Russell, we're getting out of here. We'll find a cab on Yonge Street."

In the cab, she laid her head on the back of the seat and smiled at him dreamily.

"You know, Russell, I was thinking. We should get married." She saw the look on his face. "I know what you're thinking, but listen to me. I could live with you down there in St. Thomas. It would be good for me. I hate it here." Her face twisted with anger. "I could be your wife." She was smiling again. "I don't know how to be a wife, but I could learn. Most girls don't know those things when they start. I would change, Russell. No more parties, and … all of that stuff. I would make myself your wife. We could have babies if you

251

wanted them. I would learn to cook. And we could fuck whenever we wanted. It would be so perfect."

She wasn't looking at him, she was staring at the buildings as the cab moved through the city downtown.

"What an idea," he said gently. "I haven't been thinking about being married."

"Of course not. You're just back. But when you do think of it, think of me, darling. Promise?"

"I promise."

"Good. Oh, look at the bunting on the city hall." Her mind had moved on. "It looks so gay. Just right for a night of dancing with my Captain." Her eyes moved from him as if she were talking to the buildings outside.

"Eleanor, what did the doctor say to you?"

She did not turn her head.

"Nothing. He's an old quack. He prescribes pink pills for mummy and Hilda when they have nervous attacks. He doesn't like the way I live. Forget him."

The Imperial Room of the Royal York Hotel was full. Couples were already on the dance floor. Russell saw the tall, dark-haired figure of Gene Henderson on the podium, waving his baton.

"I know this band. They were at the Stork Club in St. Thomas."

"Oh, divine. Then you'll sweep me off my feet."

As they danced she seemed unfamiliar in his arms. She didn't move close, she danced away from him, as if she were following different music. He decided to take her home right after dinner. They sat down and the waiter brought their bottle of Sancerre. She had downed her first glass in a minute and was holding it out for a refill. She drank half of it in a gulp.

"I wasn't going to be here tonight," she said in a slurred voice. "Daddy wanted me to come with him campaigning, but I said no. He likes me too much." She was watching him with unhappy eyes. "He always wants me with him when Helen can't go. But it's boring, politics. I told him to find himself a wife. He got really angry, but it's a good idea. Poor Mummy." Her eyes were sad, her mouth drooping and pouty. Then she looked up and smiled. "But you'll marry me, won't you, Russell? Take me down to St. Thomas and keep me in your house. Babies. Anything."

He stared at the menu, avoiding any reply. She seemed so frail; he was concerned that his words might hurt her. He looked up and saw, over her shoulder, Susan MacLean dancing with the band leader, Henderson. She was folded in his arms, her head on his shoulder, her arm stroking his back. Russell's face flushed red.

"What is it, baby?" Eleanor noticed his expression. "We don't have to get married right away if you don't want to. Maybe you could just keep me as your girl. Just take me away from here. "

Russell said nothing. When Susan got up to dance with Henderson again, his eyes narrowed.

"Excuse me, I have to say hello to an old friend."

He walked across the floor, taking care that Susan couldn't see him approach.

"May I?" he said to Gene Henderson, and before she could react he had taken her, leaving the band leader standing alone.

"Bobby," was all she could say, staring at him.

"What are you doing here?"

"We're staying at Jean's aunt's house." She moved awkwardly in his arms. "I don't know where she's got to. We're down for the weekend."

"And Henderson?"

"He's playing here. Do you remember him from the Stork Club?" She was talking nervously, her words spilling out. "And what are you doing here, Bobby? Down for business, as I recall. Your expropriation. I hope it went well. Are you here with somebody?" Bobby glanced at his table. Eleanor was sitting quietly, sadness in her face, the way she sat. "Yes, I see. She's very lovely. A Toronto girl, no doubt." He noticed her emphasis on 'Toronto girl'. "How long have you two been going together?"

"We aren't. She's just the daughter of a lawyer I know."

"So you're not together. That's why she looks so unhappy."

They danced silently for a while.

"Where is Jean's aunt's house?" he asked.

She looked annoyed. "I'm not sure. I have the address somewhere, in my purse, I think. Jean knows."

"I thought I would drop over and say hello. Pay my respects, maybe tomorrow. I assume it's her Aunt Jennie."

"That won't be possible."

"Why not?"

"We're leaving tomorrow. Going back to St. Thomas."

"I'll see you in St. Thomas, then."

"Yes. When are you going back?"

The dance ended. Russell escorted her to her table, nodded to Gene Henderson, and rejoined Eleanor.

"That was your girl, wasn't it?" She was staring at Susan.

Russell shrugged. "Just a girl I knew in St. Thomas."

Eleanor's lips twisted into a pout. "She looks perfect for babies. Big hips, big tits. Why don't you marry her?"

"I'm not looking to get married."

"That's what they all say, until they do. At least that's what they say to me. No one wants to marry me. I wonder why that is, exactly. I've been a bad girl, it's true, but bad girls sometimes make good wives. I read that in the last issue of Liberty Magazine. Girls who've had experience know what to do in bed to keep hubby happy, and they are less likely to have affairs once they're married. They've researched it."

Russell could not hear her; he was staring at Susan. She got up to dance again and laid her head affectionately on Henderson's shoulder. She's sleeping with him, he thought. He raised his hand for the waiter and ordered a whiskey.

"You are a nice man, Bobby Russell. I love dancing with you." Eleanor's voice was faint. "I wonder if we will ever dance together again."

"Hard to say. You never know the future."

"That's so true." Her eyes were glassy and he could hardly hear her. "So let's dance. While the music is still playing."

She cuddled into him and sighed, but she couldn't move to the music; she leaned on him as if she were afraid of falling. When the tune ended, he took her back to their table. She sat down smiling, as if she were remembering a private joke. Russell ignored her. He saw the band leader get up from the table, leaving Susan sitting alone. He got up and walked across the floor.

"Dance with me, Susan." She rose, unsmiling. "I don't like watching you making a fool of yourself with the band leader."

She stepped away from him and glared. "Who do you think you are? Aren't you the man who no longer has any use for any women except his Toronto floozy? The man who has outgrown the entire town of St. Thomas. The man who grabs me from my table, forces me onto the dance floor and questions me about my private life." She paused as Gene Henderson returned to her table. "I'm going back to join my friend. Good bye, Bobby. I'm sure we'll run into each other in St. Thomas before I leave."

"Leave? Where are you going?"

"New York City." Her voice was aloof. "Jean and I are going to share an apartment in Manhattan."

She turned and walked away. Russell looked for Eleanor and saw that her chair was empty. He sat down and waited, forcing himself to keep his eyes away from Susan. Ten minutes went by. When he looked again, Susan was wrapped around her band leader. He motioned to the waiter and asked if he had seen Eleanor.

"She left, Sir. Told me she wasn't feeling well, and asked me to get her a taxi."

He ordered another whiskey and sat at their table.

What to do? At a dance without a girl. The war messes everything up. Or it's the whiskey. Or women. Eleanor. Susan. Something. Can't remember. She looks great out there dancing, even with the American. Full of life, strong. That's Susie. She doesn't belong here with that musician. He probably takes dope. I better get her out of here. He got to his feet, swayed and sat down. Not a good idea. Bobby, Bobby, Bobby.

He summoned the waiter, paid the bill, and got again to his feet, taking great care with his balance.

"Bobby."

He turned. Susan was smiling at him.

"You're drunk, Bobby, and your girl has left you. Can't say I blame her." She held up her hand as he tried to speak. "You can't talk any sense in the condition you're in. I just wanted to say that I'm sorry I was so hard on you. We'll have a cup of tea in St. Thomas when we both get back. Take good care of yourself."

As she walked back to her table, Bobby smiled, shrugged, and left the floor for his room. The next morning he telephoned the Archer house. The servant told him that Miss Archer had taken to her bed and was not answering the phone.

I just don't know. Eleanor's gone. And Susie's gone. Is anything wrong?

PART IV

Regeneration

36.

ON THURSDAY NIGHT before the provincial election of June 4, 1945, Elgin County paused, uncertain for once of the outcome. Ever since the settlement of the area Elgin County had voted for the Liberal Party. The Scots farmers despised the Conservative Party as the party of the English, which meant to them upper class Anglican privilege and exploitation by Toronto banks. Voting Liberal was as much a part of life as hard work, the Protestant religion, illegal liquor and the price of corn. But this night, uncertainty sounded in the flat, matter-of-fact voices of the sun-burned farmers and the merchants in town.

"I see where the Times Journal is supporting the Conservative Party," one would say, perhaps in a group in front of the post office in Union, or Iona Station, or New Glasgow.

"Yep," the other men would mutter, looking at one another, waiting for the expression of outrage at the betrayal by MacLean and his Times Journal of the good old Liberal cause. But the outrage never came.

"Seems hard on Grant," another would say.

"Yep." All would agree.

"What's MacLean up to, supportin' the Tories?"

"Seems like he thinks they'll have better policies for business. Go-ahead policies."

"Well, Grant ain't go-ahead. Not with the liquor he puts back."

The men would stroll to their trucks or wagons, thinking their previously unthinkable thoughts. There was change in the air. And, as if to intensify the unstable mood in the county, the moon rose in the late afternoon, before the sun had set in the west. The white orb hung pale and barely visible in a sky still azure blue.

Fishermen working on their boats on the pier at Port Stanley saw it first, rising out of the lake. They thought it meant good weather in the morning, smiled and kept chatting as they worked. Farmers in their fields noticed it and shook their heads. The early moon meant no rain in the morning.

Grant MacKay didn't see it when it first rose. He spent the day before the election on his farm, drinking on his front porch. By the time the moon was visible, he was not seeing much. Grant was confident of victory, but things weren't happening the way they usually did before an election. There was the betrayal of the Times Journal, unthinkable, and more than that, inexplicable. The editorial had talked about change, the end of the war, the men coming home, the expansion of business.

Well, the Member for Elgin was certainly for all those things. He had made a speech in the Legislature on exactly these points, one that his leader, Mitchell Hepburn, had bought a round for in the Members' Lounge. And how could Bill MacLean think that a rookie high school teacher like Ross Porter was better for the county than a man with years of experience, who knew every farm and every hamlet from Port Stanley to the Toronto highway? It made no sense. MacKay told himself that he was afraid for MacLean. The county would not soon forgive this kind of treachery. Vengeance was the rule; live by the sword, die by the sword. He took a large swig from his green bottle. There would have to be reckoning after the election. Yes siree.

But he was uneasy. In on evenings before elections past there would have been a stream of visitors to the farm, men to sit on the porch, drink whiskey with the Member, and pledge their support. Reeves and school board chairmen from all around the county. Prosperous farmers, or business owners from St. Thomas. People who owed him. But by evening there had been few visitors. His agent had come around. Several white-bearded farmers on the council in Iona Station, driving wagons, for heaven's sake, barely out of the stone age. And his brother-in-law from north of St. Thomas. A few others. But not in the numbers of years gone by.

He stared out at the horizon, where his neighbour's field met the sky. He saw the pale moon rising before there was a hint of twilight. Confused, he raised his arm to look at his watch. It wasn't on his wrist; he had left it somewhere. He took another pull at his bottle, smiled and abandoned himself to happy memories.

❀

Al Parker sat in his office late Sunday afternoon in the City Hall, talking over the election with Elmore Wayne. They often spent Sunday afternoons this way with the switchboard shut down and the building locked, discussing town business and politics.

"Al," said the Chief of Police, looking out the window. "The moon is rising."

"Ain't it supposed to?"

"Sure. But I don't ever recall seeing a moon rise this early."

The Mayor watched the pale silver circle in the blue sky for half a minute. "I got a feeling Grant's in trouble," he said finally, shaking his head. "The old magic ain't there. Nobody's saying much, but my gut tells me there's a lot of thinking going on. And when people start thinking, it ain't likely to end good. Especially if you're holdin' public office."

"People thinking is usually trouble," said Elmore Wayne, staring gloomily out the window. "Look at MacAllister. Smart as a whip, thinking and scheming since he was old enough to get laid. Now he's behind bars, and likely to remain there." The Police Chief shook his head. "Who you voting for?"

"I vote the Liberal Party ticket. Always have, always will. Don't mean it's gonna win, though." The Mayor's voice was flat, his expression pessimistic. "What with MacLean puttin' his newspaper behind the Tories and Grant seen as a drunk, especially by the women. It don't look good."

"What do we do if he loses?"

"We examine our consciences, check if the change in the direction of the wind is permanent, and if it is, we decide that our rightful home is the Conservative Party. Always has been."

"You'd join the Tories?"

"Sure I would. I've got no time for losers."

"But you don't have to do that to…?"

"To keep your job? Maybe not right away. But you want to be with the winning team. And everyone agrees that the winning team ain't Grant. He's drinking so much now he looks like a loser even when he's sober. Look at how he and MacAllister couldn't deliver that Russell land. And then the expropriation gets fouled up. Young Robert Russell stuck it to them in Toronto, I hear."

"You don't say. So the deal is off?"

"No, Sir. We got an American with cash, and we got some useless farmland with MacQuiggans squatting on it. It'll go through all right, but not because of Grant." The Mayor shook his head regretfully. "How is MacAllister?"

"He's still ranting and raving. Paces up and down his cell, talking to himself. Thinks the whole town is out to get him."

"He's right. Nobody likes a mean son of a bitch like that."

⚜

In the jail attached to the court house on Wellington Street, George MacAllister himself was screaming at Gus Campbell, who had just told him that he wouldn't be allowed out to vote.

"Of course I can vote," MacAllister was gripping the bars. "Every citizen has a right to vote. Being charged with a crime does not take that right away. Look it up in the statutes. You have no right to keep me from voting."

MacAllister was glaring through the bars.

"Geez, George, you think I'm gonna look up some statute? I

260

wouldn't know a statute from a statue. All I know is, when charges is laid, the only way out of here is on bail. And there ain't no bail for accessory to a murder, or so they say. So I can't see you votin', Mister. Unless you get yourself a good lawyer."

MacAllister winced. "I haven't seen my partner since I've been in here. Does he know I'm here? Did you tell him?"

"I told him." The constable's expression was uneasy. "George, he's in bad shape himself. Future don't look good for him. He may want to lay low awhile."

"Of course, coming to see me would not be good for him." MacAllister's words, terse and bitter, fell from his lips like stones. "The pariah. The untouchable. The people who run this town couldn't tolerate my success. A poor boy from the back concessions." MacAllister examined the constable's placid round face for a hint of sympathy. "So the first chance they get, they take me down. But not Allan Matthews. He keeps the widows happy with one hand on their backsides and the other in their pocket books." MacAllister spat on the floor of his cell. "He does nothing for his money, whereas I worked hard for every cent I got." MacAllister was almost screaming. "Well, you mark me, Mister Campbell. I will not go down. I will be back and I will not forget." His voice was now a theatrical hiss. "I will be revenged on the ones who did this to me."

Gus Campbell got up from his chair with a shake of his head, walked out of the cell corridor and slammed the door. He left the building to enjoy his favourite time of day, when the sun was just beginning to slant west. He noticed the early moon in the eastern sky, behind the trees on the court house lawn. Beautiful, he thought.

❀

The early moon was noticed all over the county. For some people the two orbs in the sky, one setting and one rising, were portents.

"I never heard of such foolishness in my life," said the barber, when his wife, Mabel, interpreted the moon and the sun in the sky together as signs of the election. "It's the goddamn sun and moon, Mabel. Got nothing to do with politics."

The couple was sitting on their back porch after dinner, drinking coffee.

"There is more goes on in the world than we know, Jack. There is significance in things we cannot read. "

Mabel spoke with the serenity of a higher vision.

"There's nothing to read, woman. The moon rises before the sun sets many times in a year. And most of the times, there ain't an election within a hundred miles."

"On those times, it has nothing to do with an election. That's as clear as the nose on your face. But you should pay attention to these things, Jack Morris. Change is in the air and in the arrangement of the planets. That could be the meaning of the early moon. Grant MacKay loses the election."

"You couldn't possibly know that, moon or no moon." Jack folded his paper and strode from the porch, looking for a sanctuary where common sense prevailed.

❀

Under the same moon, Margaret Ann Russell sat with Allan Matthews on her back porch, drinking sherry. As he admitted his part in the mail scheme, tears appeared in his eyes. She sat down beside him on the porch swing and stroked his hair.

"It's all right, Allan. I wouldn't have sold, I don't think, without knowing about Bobby. And as for what you did, I know George MacAllister and I know you. I can imagine what happened, and it doesn't mean we can't go dancing."

She said this with a broad smile that was slightly flirtatious. He smiled weakly, the first stirring of hope in his eyes. He brushed away his tears. Soon he was telling her gossip and stroking his moustache in the old way, and she was laughing. She went and fixed them tea and they sat admiring the moon.

"I think there's a chance that Grant will not be returned," he said.

"People are tired of him drunk all the time, and nobody's forgotten the escapade with the girl in the Toronto hotel." He rolled his eyes.

She shook her head. "I can't imagine this county electing a Tory. I shall vote for Grant no matter what others may do. Our family is Liberal."

"This time, Margaret Ann, I believe Porter will win."

"You mean they'll actually switch? Become Tories? And they say women are fickle." She laughed. "I don't really care who runs the government. But I've known Grant MacKay all my life, and I would never desert him."

The moon was higher in the sky now and the sun had set. The trees down by the creek and the furrows in the field were visible in the silver light. The hoot of an owl came from the dusk.

"Allan, you may be right. Poor Grant. I suppose life goes on if he's defeated. The beauty of this night is what's important, and the two of us sitting and talking together. What else is as important as dear friends? That's why I'm voting for Grant. And that's why you and I will go dancing."

"Even if they disbar me?"

"What's in a bar?" she said..

The echo of their laughter returned from the trees at the end of the field, silver now under the moon.

A short distance away on the Dorchester Road, just past the old school house, in his dilapidated, unpainted wooden house, Archie MacQuiggan lay on his cot, the moon shining in the window.

"Turn off that goddamn light," he roared. "It hurts my eyes woman. Turn the fucking thing off."

"It's the moon," said Leona sullenly. "Ain't nothin' I can do."

"You're useless, is the problem. Good for nothing." He rubbed his eyes. "My eyes hurt."

"Don't you rub 'em. It makes it worse. They'll be better in the morning."

"The morning. Shit on the morning. I won't wait for no morning. What's the morning gonna do for me?"

"Bring the sun. And it's the Election Day."

"Election Day." he sat up in his cot. "I ain't votin'. They won't do nothin for us no matter who gets in. They all forget the people on the bottom, soon as they get in."

"Are we on the bottom, Archie?"

"They're gonna sell this house right out from under us. They expect us to live under a tree or in the ditch. That sounds like the bottom to me."

They both were silent for a while, contemplating homelessness.

"Last poll, they give you some money and some liquor, fer pullin' out the vote," she said finally.

"They did?"

"Sure they did. Mr. Grant MacKay give you five dollars an' a bottle of rum."

Archie shook his head trying to remember.

"Well, maybe I'll work for him tomorrow. Wake me when the sun comes up. And get a goddam blanket across this window. A man who got to support his family can't have the sun interferin' with his sleep."

A child screamed in the next room. Leona turned her head.

"Never you mind that. Get me that blanket and get it now."

❀

In town, in their house on Walpole Street, the MacLeans watched the moon in the dark sky from their screened in porch.

"Everybody's talking about my recent editorial supporting the Conservatives and Ross Porter," said Bill MacLean, with a satisfied smile on his face. "Big change for a town like this."

"That's nice, dear," said Valerie, staring at the moon.

"You're not paying attention to a word I'm saying."

She looked at him and tried to focus. "I can't get my mind off Susan," she said finally. "Something happened in Toronto."

"What happened ? Is she in trouble?"

"Not yet. But she's been up to something, I can tell to look at her. For one thing, I'm sure she didn't stay with Jean's aunt, as she told us. I mentioned it to Ruth Robson, who knew nothing about it."

"Well, maybe she stayed with a school friend. Who was that Toronto girl she had down here last year?"

"She would have told me. The thing is, she's lied to us, and Susan's usually truthful. That means there's a man. She wouldn't lie about anything else."

"Well, she's old enough."

"They're never old enough."

They laughed together and took comfort from the moon, shining on their garden.

❀

In their apartment, Helen Partridge and Rose MacIlwain were serving tea to the two friends. Rose put a recording of Paderewski playing Chopin études and mazurkas on the gramophone.

Jean had seen the moon and the sun in the sky together, and was remarking on their meaning. "According to Marie Barnes, it means that the Liberals are going to lose tomorrow."

"I've never heard such nonsense," snapped Rose. "We educate these girls, Helen, and they end up listening to Marie Barnes and her astrology! Really!"

Helen smiled. "I think there's something in it. People do seem to be fed up with Grant MacKay. I may vote for Ross Porter myself. He says that if he were elected he'd support more money for books for the library."

"I shall vote Liberal. My family is Liberal, my uncle was a Liberal senator, and Grant MacKay has served us well."

"He looks like a little red-faced penguin to me," said Jean. "I couldn't vote for a man who looks like that."

"Voting for a man's looks?" said Rose. "Jean, you shouldn't be allowed to vote."

"Doesn't matter to me. You can't go by what they say because they never do what they say. How about Susan?"

They all looked at Susan.

"I don't think I'll vote." She got up from the table. "I have to go now."

"Wait, Susan," said Helen. "Look at the moon now."

The moon was visible through a maple tree, high in the sky now, and more golden. It shone on the town, it shone on the fields, it shone on the lake. And it shone through the apartment window as Susan left.

37.

The Russells always voted in a one room school house several concession roads to the west of their farm. He drove the Buick to the polling station, the car swerving from time to time as he kept looking uneasily at her.

"Mother, I've decided to vote Conservative."

"Not you too." She turned to face him. "There's no loyalty. You'd vote for this Ross Porter, a high school teacher?"

"There are sound men in Toronto running the party."

"Toronto," she said. "As if anything good has ever come out of Toronto. Just an overgrown small town with pretensions and bad manners is all Toronto is, if you ask me."

Russell continued his attempt to re-educate his mother politically. Her life-long commitment to the Liberal Party was no longer acceptable in the climate of change and expansion that was sweeping not only over Elgin County, but the entire province of Ontario, he told her. New ideas and energy were needed. George Drew was an intelligent, forceful man, well connected with business and in touch with the wave of economic expansion that was due the country after the war. Of course it would be difficult to abandon Grant MacKay, but the prosperity of Elgin County was more important than Grant's career.

She listened to him, nodding her head with affection. By the time they reached the school house, he was sure that he had convinced her to vote Conservative.

The school was a wooden structure with a slanted roof and a bell tower at the rear. The boards were weathered, with faint traces of red paint. A man dressed in a shiny black suit cut in the style of thirty years before, with big black laced boots on his feet and a white beard under a black hat, sat at the door.

"Afternoon, Mrs. Russell, Captain Russell. Good to see you here this fine day."

"Good afternoon, Jed," said Margaret Ann, smiling sweetly as they entered the school.

"That's Jed Stuart, scrutineering for the Liberals," she whispered.

"Where's the Conservative?"

"There's never been a Conservative vote at this poll. They never send anyone."

"We'll change all that today."

The poll clerk was Leona MacQuiggan. She was sitting at the teacher's desk with a supply of ballots and a list of eligible voters in the poll. She wore a white satin dress that could have been her wedding dress but was now too tight for her. She bulged out of it at the arms and bosom, and her red hair poured down its back.

"Why, Leona, I didn't know you had taken to poll-clerking," said Margaret Ann.

Leona smiled shyly and looked away.

"'Twas Archie's doin'. He went to Mr. MacKay and got me this job. Pay is two dollars. Pretty good, I guess."

She handed them in turn a ballot and ticked off their names on her list. They went behind the screen, marked their ballots, came out and deposited them in the ballot box.

"I hope you buy yourself something nice with your pay," said Margaret Ann as they were leaving.

Leona smiled and said nothing.

"Thanks for coming, Mrs. Russell, Captain Russell." The Liberal Party worker tipped his hat.

"He thinks he's got us," said Bobby. "Look at him, Liberal since the day he could vote, without a thought in his head. And a five dollar bill every election. That's what has to change."

"I know what you mean. Now let's go home and have a cup of tea."

❀

The ballot boxes were brought to the Court house on Wellington Street after the polls closed at seven o'clock. The city polls arrived first; the country polls straggled in for hours, brought by the poll clerk by car and in a few instances, by wagon. The ballots were counted in the Court House and the results, poll by poll, were sent to the offices of the Times Journal on Talbot Street by a fourteen-year-old runner. A crowd gathered on the sidewalk in front of the newspaper office. As the poll results came in they would be posted on a huge blackboard that had been rigged on the sidewalk.

Election night had always been a celebration in St. Thomas. A number of men would be staggering drunk even though the taverns were closed on Election Day. Young people took advantage of the night as one of the few occasions they were allowed out after supper unsupervised. Children were scurrying among the crowd playing tag, ignored by their parents as the vote came in. Above all there would be laughing and cheering in celebration of the inevitable Liberal victory.

But this night was different. For one thing, Grant MacKay, who in times past would have arrived from his farm and established himself in the Party headquarters on Talbot Street, had not appeared. Nor had the usual flock of Party workers arrived. They had always assembled in front of the Liberal offices, boisterous and triumphant, preparing to haul Grant out, put him on a wagon and cart him down the street in a torch-light victory parade as soon as the sun went down. But this time there were only a few people. Party functionaries in the town and some of the aldermen and school trustees were standing on the sidewalk and staring down at the crowd in front of the newspaper offices with worried looks on their faces. When the results of the first polls were posted, polls from the city of St. Thomas, there was silence, punctuated by the occasional low whistle of surprise. Ross Porter was outpolling Grant MacKay by roughly two to one. The socialist candidate, Ray Murphy, was receiving only a scattering of votes here and there. In past elections, MacKay would establish a modest lead in the St. Thomas town polls which would be projected into a landslide as the overwhelmingly Liberal country polls arrived.

"If this keeps up, I don't think there are enough votes in the country to save Grant," said Russell. "Porter's going to win."

His mother said nothing. He looked and saw darkness around her eyes. Immediately he understood.

"You voted Liberal, didn't you?"

"Of course. We've always voted Liberal."

He started to chuckle.

"What's so funny?"

"You and me," he said, and continued to laugh.

Gus Campbell walked up to them on the sidewalk. He stared at the blackboard where the tally was being reported, tension in his eyes.

"Ain't that something," he said. "Ross Porter ahead in St. Thomas. I wish I could hang around and see what the country polls come in like."

"Why can't you?" said Margaret Ann. "The whole town is here."

"I got George MacAllister back in his cell goin' looney on me. I'm afraid for him. Right off his rocker. Yellin' and screamin' cuz I didn't let him out to vote."

"Is he entitled to vote, being under charges?"

"That's the question, right there, and nobody knows the answer. I asked Elmore and he don't know. He asked the Crown Attorney and he don't know."

"I'll come down and have a talk with him," said Bobby. "A little company might calm him down."

"Captain Russell, that'd be fine. He scares me."

At the station house. Gus opened the door to the corridor of four cells. It was in darkness.

"He wanted the lights out," whispered Gus. "It was the only way I could get him to stop yelling. First cell on the right is his."

Russell stood in front of the cell. As his eyes became accustomed to the faint light he saw the outline of the bunk.

"MacAllister," he said.

The figure raised its head.

"Who is it?" The voice was a hoarse whisper.

"Robert Russell."

The figure rose from the bunk and came to the bars of the cell; Russell could barely see the face. The blue eyes were looking for him, but not focusing. There was a gleam of saliva on the lips. The other features were in shadow.

"They won't let me vote."

"So I hear. If it's any consolation to you, your vote won't matter."

"It matters." The voice was tense with anger. "I have as much right to vote as any man in this town and they denied it to me. As if I were a foreigner or a crazy man."

"I was going to say that it looks like the Conservatives are going to win. Porter is leading in the town by enough that I don't think the country polls can save it for Grant."

"So Grant MacKay will finally be out of a job." There was a rasping sound that could have been chuckling. "He'll have to stay sober now if he wants to farm. A drunken politician is natural but a drunken farmer hasn't got a hope in hell." He fell silent.

"The people seemed to think it was time to move on."

"But not me. I'm not moving anywhere. I guess it was you that put me in here."

"It was the mail fraud and Tommy's murder that put you in here. I happened to find out about them, is all."

"What is wrong with the world, when I, who wanted only to make something happen in this God-forsaken town, get locked up and you, a tender, drunken young fool, roam the streets a free man?" His voice was calm and flat. "When you come from where I've come, you can't get ahead without ruffling feathers. The people who run things like it better if you stay where you are and don't disturb things. They made Father fail in order to keep us poor. If there are no poor, how can they be rich?"

He began to pace in his cell."When I was on the verge of making the deal that would have made me rich, you found a way to put me here. You don't want me with money in the bank and a house on the hill, because you are afraid of me and what I can do." MacAllister came to the bars. His face was contorted, his jaw clenched and his eyes burning with unfocused hate. "You will not hold me here, Master Russell. They call you Captain, you whose stomach turns and who reaches for the bottle whenever the going gets nasty. You will not keep me here."

Russell turned to go. MacAllister grabbed the bars.

"Sissy. Drunken fool." He yelled, spittle spraying from his lips.

Russell walked back to Talbot Street and looked at the tally board. With all but ten of the country polls reporting, Porter had four thousand and fifty votes to Grant MacKay's three thousand, one hundred and ninety-five. The ten polls, even if they were all Liberal votes, couldn't reverse the margin. Porter had won. There was no evidence of the whooping and hollering of times past, or the torch-light victory parade. The Conservatives, it seemed, were as unprepared for their victory as the rest of the citizens. He entered the newspaper office and went to the large sheets of newsprint taped to the wall where the results for each poll were listed. He found the poll where he and his mother had voted, Lyndhurst Poll Nine; the results showed thirty Liberal votes, with no Conservative or CCF votes.

He found his mother standing with Allan Matthews. Allan flashed a hint of the old smile, but was keeping his eyes on the vote total; he looked quietly pleased.

"It seems I voted Liberal after all." Bobby threw one hand in the air. "I put my X beside Ross Porter but believe it or not, to someone that was a Liberal vote. Our Leona earned her pay tonight."

"Grant will be pleased to know that despite his defeat, some of his old friends stuck with him." Margaret Ann had a twinkle in her eye.

The tally on the board was now marked final in big black letters. Porter had won by over a thousand votes. All over the street people were gesturing at the board with excitement; some were clapping cautiously, looking around to see how their neighbours were reacting.

"Look at them. They can't believe that the Liberals are finally out." Allan's eyes were sparkling. "And even though they voted for Porter, they feel guilty."

"As well they should." Margaret Ann shook her head in mock anger. "Poor Grant."

Al Parker and Elmore Wayne had just received news of Ross Porter's win. They were sitting on opposite sides of the Mayor's desk listening to the election coverage from Toronto. The Conservative win in Elgin County reflected what was happening across the province of Ontario as the government of George Drew won a solid re-election.

"It's just as well," said the Mayor. "We been on the outs with the government in Toronto. Now we'll have a government Member, and one who's sober at that. See what this Porter can do for us."

"So now we become Tories, Al? Just switch, after a lifetime?"

"Of course we switch. Everyone here was a Liberal, so there won't be enough old Tories to go around. That's where we come in; they'll need us. And naturally we don't switch right away, which would have a smell to it. We make it gradual. I think the first thing we do is send a police escort around to Mr. Ross Porter's house tomorrow. When he leaves to teach at the Collegiate, he is shown the way by two of St. Thomas's finest."

"What for? He's in no danger."

"It's not the danger. The constables tell Mr. Porter that the Mayor and the Chief of Police have ordered the escort for his protection and to mark his outstanding victory at the polls."

"Ah, go on. He'll know we're just trying to butter him up."

"You ever seen a politician you could flatter too much? He'll love it and he'll remember."

❀

Archie MacQuiggan heard of the historical defeat of the Liberal party in Elgin County over CVSM, crackling over an old wireless set he had set up on his porch. Throughout the evening, as Liberal prospects sank, his face grew redder and his brow more furrowed. He was drinking steadily from a bottle containing a white fluid the odour of which blended with the other smells in the house.

"Well, that's it then. We're fucked."

He turned to Leona when the final count was reported. She was knitting a child's sweater, sitting in a rocking chair humming to herself. Leona was tired, having walked the two miles from her poll, but she was also content, knowing that she had two dollars coming to her from Liberal headquarters.

"We'll be out on our asses in a week. Grant MacKay was our last chance. Now he's gone, no one can save us. Homeless. The goddamn bastards. Well. They ain't gonna put Archie MacQuiggan out. Nobody tells me where and when to go, or what to do. Leona, we're leavin'."

Leona paid him no attention, thinking her own thoughts, knitting and humming.

"Leona." Archie roared, slamming his glass on the table. She looked up cautiously. "I said we're leavin'."

"What d'you mean, we're leavin'?"

"We're pulling out of this damn house now. Nobody's gonna throw Archie MacQuiggan and his family out on their asses. We're leavin' here and we're leavin' tonight."

"We can't leave here tonight, Archie. We got all them kids." Her eyes were terrified as she began to count them on her fingers. "An' we got no place to go. An' nobody is tellin' us we got to go. I know Captain Russell and Mrs. Margaret Ann Russell; they ain't gonna turn us out."

"What do you know, you goddamn fool? They'll sell this land, with this house that we lived in, forgetting the work we done for them. They'll try to make me work in their factory. Well, I'm a free man, who fought for his country. Ain't nobody gonna make me work in some factory. And there ain't nobody gonna order me out of my house. On your feet woman and get packin'. We're leavin' tonight."

As she looked into her Archie's red-rimmed eyes, a sense of hopelessness sank from the pain behind her forehead to the pit at the bottom of her stomach. His veined nose and fleshy cheeks were fiery red. The blue eyes had shrunk to fearful, darting orbs of anger, almost hidden by pouches of flesh. His thick lips drooled spittle. He sat staring at her, slouched in his chair, his huge fist grasping his glass, his belly spilling out of his shirt over his pants. The hopeless stupidity wore her down, numbed her with apathy. With a sigh she got to her feet.

"Good," said Archie. "I'll go out and hitch up the wagon."

38.

The sun rose hot and orange the morning after the election. The political revolution had settled over Elgin County like a change in the weather. It was more apparent to some than to others. It depended on who you were and where you were placed in the social and economic structure of the county.

Joe Walker brought his forty-foot, snub-nosed, motor-powered fishing boat the *Mary Kay* to the fish dock at Port Stanley at about nine-thirty in the morning. He had been out since before sunrise with his nets down and had a catch of perch, lake trout and whitefish, ready for the women who would sort, gut and fillet them in the fish plant at the end of the dock. Joe was a silent man with a big smile, who had never voted in his life. He paid more attention to the condition of the lake than he did to politics, and what happened in St. Thomas or Toronto was of little interest to him unless it affected the price of fish. He also thought about the state of repair of the dock (never good enough) and the condition of his engine. He was constantly listening to his engine, even when he was thinking about something else, listening for any interruption, any hiccup or sputter, in the low steady hum on which his livelihood depended. Sometime between eight and nine o'clock he would decide that he had a big enough catch, or there were no more fish to be had, and he would head back to port and the fish plant. So when he came in from the lake that morning Joe had no idea of the change that had come to the county the night before.

"So Grant MacKay was defeated last night," Sadie MacLachlin said to him. Sadie ran the fish plant, a stout woman in an oilskin apron.

"No shit," said Joe and started to tell her about the high winds on the lake.

On the farm outside Union that he ran with Reg, his younger brother, Lorne Luscombe had been working since the sun rose at five o'clock. One of the cows had been sick with fever and diarrhoea, and he and his brother had been moving the other cows out of the barn and milking them outside, quarantining the sick one. After the milking, Reg had gone up to the house, leaving Lorne alone to work on the tractor engine. The tractor had started smoking yesterday so Lorne was tinkering with the carburetor, trying to adjust the fuel intake. Finally the tractor engine began to turn over with no sign of smoke. Lorne put his tools down with a grunt of satisfaction and headed for the house.

Although he was aware of the election, he had not voted. Lorne Luscombe despised politicians as a cabal of parasites and idlers whose purpose was to skin the honest farmers. When he entered the kitchen, Reg was sitting at the table listening to the radio and drinking coffee. His wife, Ellen, was at the stove.

"The Liberals are out and the Conservative are in," said Reg. "Grant MacKay's out of a job."

"Won't affect me none."

Ellen put out platters of scrambled eggs, fried tomatoes and sausages. He smiled at the food, his first grin of the day. Lorne liked to eat.

❀

The School Board in Dutton, a village of several hundred people west of St. Thomas, was Liberal to a man, as was everyone in the village except the veterinarian (who had the alien English name Smithers). "Check it with Grant" was a phrase heard in the town before any action was taken which had political implications. Two months ago he had promised them a new brick school nearer town. He had also arranged for the daughter of the chairman of the School Board, Doug Stewart, to get a job as secretary in Toronto, working for the government. The morning after the election the Board met in the room behind Doug Stewart's Dutton General Store.

"If this isn't a fine mess," said Charlie Thomson, who farmed north of the town. "No new school with Grant gone."

"Not to mention Ailine's job," said Angus Finlay, an older farmer with a long white beard.

"Boys, don't panic," said Stewart. "This is a bad result but it isn't the end of the world. This new man, Ross Porter, he's the Member, but he's going to need friends in the county just the way Grant did. Am I right?"

They looked at one another, trying to figure out where the chairman was heading. "Sure, Doug, but he's a Conservative," said Charlie Thomson." We're Liberal."

"I know that." Stewart looked at the speaker with a smile. "But who isn't a Liberal in Dutton? Who's Porter going to work with who isn't Liberal? Smithers? He's the only Tory around here, and if he isn't up to his ass in cow shit, he isn't happy. So who's Porter going to have to deal with here?"

The men smiled. "Us," said Charlie Thomson.

"Right as rain."

"But Doug, we are different parties, him and us. How can he give us a school, or anything? His party won't stand for it."

"You're right, that is a problem. So we have to solve the problem and make it easy for Porter. "

"And how do we do that?"

Stewart looked at each member of the Dutton School Board in turn.

"We join the Conservative Party."

There was a stunned silence in the room. Finally Angus Finlay spoke, stroking his beard.

"But Doug, we're Liberals."

Stewart's smile was patient.

"Never mind that. We got Ross Porter to deal with, and if we promise to deliver the votes in Dutton next time and kick in a few bucks for his campaign costs, you think he won't talk to us? If we take out memberships in the Conservative Party, having come to our senses after all these years, you think they'll turn us down because we were Liberals for Grant MacKay?"

The men nodded. It made sense. They looked at Doug Stewart with admiration.

And so the change spread throughout the county, affecting people more or less, depending on their relationship to the political system. In town, Al Parker was working furiously to establish contact with Ross Porter. Two police constables did show up at Porter's modest house on Elm Street to escort him to the Collegiate for his day of teaching. The newly elected Member had to refuse the Mayor's invitation, relayed by Gus Campbell, to join him and the Chief of Police for lunch at the Grand Central Hotel. He was still a high school teacher until the end of term and had his classes. But he liked the police escort.

"We'll get him, Elmore," said the Mayor. "It may take some time, but we'll get him."

In Toronto, the big Conservative win in Elgin was noticed with satisfaction. On the afternoon after the election Edward Archer was in his office with the regional campaign directors, reviewing the results.

"So we beat Grant MacKay in Elgin County, Tom," he said. "If we can win there, we can win anywhere."

"Yes," said Tom Brennan. "But I have to tell you, Eddie, Grant did it for us. He drank himself out the door."

"What's our man like, this Ross Porter?"

Brennan shook his head. "Not strong. A high-school teacher with no experience."

Archer stared. "We need somebody to tidy up the expropriation mess. Van Kleef's in town, roaring and ranting about the delay. He wants to do the deal without us. If Porter isn't the man, what about Russell? We have to get him with us fast."

"Is Russell up to it? Will he play?"

"He's up to it. Look how he sank our expropriation deal. And I think he'll play. Just back from the war and making up his mind. A little opening from us may be what he wants."

Archer reached for his telephone.

❀

Russell spent the early part of the next day on the farm, painting the wood trim on the front porch. Lulled by the music of the birdsong and the soft slopping of the paint brush, he was wondering what the political change meant to him. His father would have known; he would be deciding what he wanted, who to talk to, what to say. Perhaps he would go to Toronto after all. But there was Susan. He had felt her there at the edge of the crowd even when he wasn't looking at her, and remembered how she looked away when he caught her eye. He smiled, adrift with his thoughts, and put too much paint on his brush; a drop fell on his foot. He stooped with his rag to wipe it clean. His mother opened the screen door.

"Telephone call for you. From Toronto."

He laid down his paintbrush and went to the telephone.

"Captain Russell. This is Edward Archer in Toronto."

The sound of Archer's voice took him back to the house in Toronto and Eleanor.

"Hello," he said. "Congratulations."

"The people spoke, Russell, or the Good Lord. But thank you. I wish you had been our man."

"The timing wasn't right," said Russell.

"Perhaps, but I still want to do business with you. I don't like losing in court, but I can take it when it's well done. I realize you've sold Van Kleef the land, but there are other arrangements to be made. We're meeting down there on Thursday, lunch at the Grand Central Hotel, and I'd like you to be there."

"I'll come." He spoke without thinking.

"Good. I'll see you there."

He hung up the phone, shaking his head.

"What was that?"

"The lawyer behind the expropriation. A big Tory. He wants me to join a meeting in a few days with the American who's behind the factory project and I don't know who else."

His mother smiled mischievously.

"So you're really in with the Tories." He shrugged and her smile softened. "Well, they've just risen in my estimation; they know a bright young man when they see one."

The screen door opened before he could answer. Calvin entered the kitchen and stood staring at him.

"They've gone," he said.

"Who's gone?"

"Them in the other house. Pa an' them."

"They've gone to town. They'll be back."

"No. Mam's gone and them kids, all of 'em. Clothes is gone,

279

food is gone, wagon is gone. Everything's gone."

Russell frowned.

"We'll go and have a look."

Five minutes later the Buick pulled into Archie's lane. They sat in the car for a moment staring at the house. The screen door on the front porch was open, swinging and creaking in the wind. There was no sound from the house; the MacQuiggan family had left. In the front room of the house were children's toys and rattles lying in the corner, food-stained plates on the table and piles of clothes in the door to the large children's bedroom. He looked in another bedroom and saw a mattress on the floor with Leona's dresses lying across it, and a crib in one corner. The cupboard in the corner had been emptied, only a few wire coat hangers left on the rod. They had taken only what they could carry.

"They sure are gone, Calvin. Well." He smiled at the boy. "It just you and us now. We're on our own."

"That's fine." Calvin was smiling happily. "I be all right."

However, Archie hadn't disappeared completely. A week later he showed up at the Russell house, neatly dressed, hat in hand, explaining that he thought they owed him some money from the last ploughing. Russell stood in the doorway, evaluating the tentative, calculating look in the man's blue eyes. He knows I don't usually pay him as he works for his rent. But now he's made his move he wants to see if he can get me to pay him good-riddance money. He nodded agreement and went in to get the five dollars. When he came back Archie was tapping his foot impatiently and licking his lips.

"Where are you now, Archie? I hope the family is well."

"We're where we want to be and we're fine, Sir." Archie pulled himself to full height and looked as dignified as he was able while pocketing the money. "Making our way, beholden to none. It's the MacQuiggan way. I'll say good day to ye'."

He watched Archie walk clumsily away. He remembered playing with him as a boy, in the fields, by the creek or around the tiny, dilapidated house resounding from the screaming of many dirty children, Archie's brothers and sisters. He returned to his chore, finished painting the porch and joined his mother for tea.

"I suppose they'll all be back in a few days," said Margaret Ann. "They'll run out of money."

He began to recount the stages of Archie's descent into alcoholic chaos over many years when the telephone rang. He picked it up to hear Gus Campbell's voice. He listened, stunned, and set down the receiver.

"What is it?"

"George MacAllister tried to hang himself in his cell."

"Great God Almighty," said his mother.

She looked more bemused than shocked. Calvin stood without expression, looking from face to face.

"I had better go up." Bobby rose wearily to his feet. When he got to the police station, Al Parker and Elmore Wayne were sitting at the sergeant's desk whispering together. Gus Campbell was standing by the doorway watching Doctor Stuart pack his black medical bag.

"You come to my office in the morning and we'll figure out what to do," the doctor was saying. "I haven't got time for this damn suicide foolishness. I've got a woman who was due yesterday in labour at the hospital." He shook his head. "He thought he could hang himself with his underpants, which shows a lack of understanding of basic physics. MacAllister's irrational, possibly insane, possibly permanently."

The doctor nodded to Russell and hurried out the door, muttering to himself. The Mayor smiled at him.

"Insane, is he? Probably always was, a mean bastard like that," said Parker jovially. "If he's nuts we can't try him, which saves the good citizens of the county the expense of a trial. MacAllister was always an economical man."

"I don't like it," growled the Chief of Police. "He shouldn't have been able to go that far. Standard procedures were violated." He glared at Gus Campbell.

"It was a madhouse in here that night, Elmore," said Campbell. "The election was goin' on outside. He was rantin' and ravin'."

"Let me have a look at MacAllister," said Russell.

"Why would you have anything to do with it?" said the Chief. "We've had the doctor, we have the appropriate police and elected officials, and the Crown Attorney will be here any minute. I don't see how you're involved."

"Come on, Elmore," said the Mayor. 'Forget the procedural stuff. You may remember that Captain Russell brought MacAllister's crimes to our attention. Let him in."

The Chief threw up his hands and Campbell led Russell to MacAllister's cell. The man was laid out on his cot wearing only his pants and a cotton shirt. There were red marks on his neck and the blue eyes were staring at the ceiling, now without anger. The lips were blue.

A loner. And being too much alone makes you stupid. Like me. I have to be less alone. He steals the mail, hires the Detroit goon, and thinks it will all work out. Stupid.

In the station house, Elmore Wayne had begun to relax and was laughing at something the Mayor had said.

"So what d'you think, Captain?" said the Mayor with a wink when Russell returned. "Is he nuts?" Russell shrugged. "And isn't it the best thing for everyone? Sure it is. Put him in the nut house down at Union for the rest of his life. No problem for anyone."

Russell walked out of the station house relieved, feeling light on his feet. The sky above the green maples on Wellington Street was the only substantial thing he could see. His own sense of lightness seemed to infuse the town itself. The solid houses, the clipped lawns, even the townspeople going about their business up on Talbot Street, seemed light as air, almost floating.

This town he had returned to seemed, after looking at MacAllister in his cell, entirely changed. Nothing was substantial, nothing would endure. Now you're here, now you're gone, poof, just like that. MacAllister, who had been so obscenely alive, gone. The MacQuiggans, gone. Everything changing. The people around him were unknowable. He could not say what people wanted or why they acted as they did. He could not imagine the life and the hunger of George MacAllister, and Archie MacQuiggan's rage was beyond madness. His mother and Susan. Unknowable landscapes, places to get lost. And being lost, he was alone.

39.

Russell continued to repair the house, painting, hammering and replacing loose shingles. Calvin continued to followed him with devotion, holding his hammer, running to get him a glass of water. On Wednesday afternoon he drove to the dairy to see the first of the new pasteurizers Tom Allan had ordered from Cleveland. He stood gazing at the gleaming steel tank, with its thermometer and gauges, listening to Tom explain how much greater the capacity was, and how much subtler the measuring devices were. He feigned enthusiasm but returned home as soon as he could. Calvin entered with a jar of minnows he had caught in the creek. Russell patted his head, then sat with his mind absent as his mother chatted. He wondered if he should telephone Susan, but did not. Occasionally he dreamed of her.

On Thursday morning he picked up a post card his mother had put on the table. It showed a domed white palace surrounded by palm trees and the sands of a desert. In the background a train of camels, laden with packs and men in turbans, moved towards the setting sun. The sprawling writing was in violet ink.

"I am here now. It is hot. There is light everywhere. Even at night. Can't tell night from day. He is nice, but…. What shall I do, Bobby? Light everywhere. Light, light light. Miss you. Love, Eleanor."

His mother glanced at him. "What is that?"

"A card from a friend I made in Toronto. She's somewhere in Morocco. Wadi Riff, it says."

❁

Archer's lunch at the Grand Central Hotel was at noon. By this time in the middle of June the bustle and commotion of early spring

283

had subsided and there was a pleasant lull in town. The heavy work on the farms was done and the farmers were on the streets more during the day, with more time to talk at the post office or sitting over coffee at the Malt Shoppe. Russell walked to town seeing nothing of the day around him, lost in his memories of a woman whose voice he could still hear, whose scent he could still smell, but whose personality was barely an impression, a wisp of an outline in violet ink. He walked past Jack Morris's, stopped, and remembered he had come for a haircut. Jack had no customer and was sitting in his chair reading the Times Journal, his glasses perched on his nose.

"I see in the paper that Ross Porter wants open immigration from Europe." Jack shook his head. "The Liberals were right about that. Not a single immigrant until the army boys all get jobs again. That Porter has no sense."

"I don't know, Jack. There'll be jobs for everybody when the economy starts to boom. And think of the haircuts, if you get several hundred new families in the county."

Jack motioned him into the chair. "Won't matter to me. I'm thinking of retiring."

"Retiring? You? How old are you?"

"Seventy years. It ain't that. I'm feelin' fit as a fiddle. But I just don't want to do it any more. Don't enjoy it. Everything's changing. Used to be, I'd have the whole town council in here at least twice a month, Grant MacKay and everyone. I knew the score. But now." He shook his head. "Conservatives and women running things. It ain't the same."

"The town can take a new Member of the Legislature, but a new barber, Jack, that would be a disaster."

Jack smiled and rested his arms on the back of the chair.

"This man Porter." Jack shook his head. "Why a man with no hair to speak of would go all the way to London for his haircut makes no sense at all. Don't talk to me about Porter."

He fell silent as Jean Robson and her mother walked by on the sidewalk. Jack rested his arms again and smiled in appreciation.

"Now there's a girl with all her parts in the right places, eh,

Bobby?" Russell smiled and nodded. "I hear her and the MacLean girl, Susan, are leavin' for New York."

"Who told you that?" Russell raised his head.

"The wife. She heard it from Marie Barnes. It seems that old man Robson is gonna rent them an apartment."

He had forgotten about Susan in New York.

"Oh God, will you look at this now." Jack stepped back from the chair and gestured out the window. The feed store oldsters, accompanied by two of the returned soldiers, were approaching the barber shop. "I told those old farts a hundred times I don't want 'em hanging out in here."

The men trooped into the shop and sat in the waiting chairs.

"Captain," said Fred Chisolm with a worshipful grin. "Archie MacQuiggan been tellin' us about the time you led our boys through some church in the middle of the night, and then through a whore house, to get behind them Germans in that little wop town. Is that true, Captain, or just Archie's bull?"

The old men watched Russell with eager eyes.

"Castelvecchio was the name of the town," said Russell. Chisolm turned to the men with a triumphant smile. "And Archie was telling you the truth, more or less. Although we didn't know it was a whore house until we got inside." He paused to let the old men chuckle and leer. "In those days we made everything up as we went along." The old men laughed and slapped their thighs.

"Now you fellahs get out of here." Jack snapped the towel as he took it from Russell's neck. "I got a business to run."

They rose to their feet.

"Hold your horses, Jack, we're leavin now," said Fred Chisholm. "Captain Russell, they say you're meetin' with Ross Porter and some big shots in the Grand Central today to figure out this new parts plant they're buildin'."

Before he could answer, Jack exploded.

"Get out of here, the lot of you. And you stop questioning my customer. It ain't none of your business. Go on, git."

The men rose and shuffled out of the shop.

Bobby looked at Jack. "This town is amazing. How did they know about the meeting?"

"Marie Barnes. She listened in on the phone call that Toronto lawyer made to you. My wife told me. Everybody knows."

⚜

Mr. Dooley sat at his desk outside the kitchen of the Grand Central Hotel, a triumphant smile on his face.

"It is gratifying to have one's talents recognized, Mrs. MacLellan. Much as I have enjoyed working in this establishment." Here Mr. Dooley raised his left eyebrow and sniffed. "I have, as you know, worked in much finer, much more elegant hotels. To be accepted by the Stodlemeyer House in Kitchener is most gratifying. Forty rooms, done in the most exquisite taste and a dining room that has fed the British aristocracy. The Duke of York, can you imagine, before he became King."

A faraway look entered Mr. Dooley's eyes. Audrey MacLellan shifted impatiently in her chair.

"It's a happy development, Mr. Dooley. But until you arrive in Kitchener and start entertaining the crowned heads of Europe, we have this private dinner to provide. The cook needs a menu."

Mr. Dooley looked at Mrs. MacLellan with a languid look and dismissed the dinner with a wave of his thin hand. "There are only four or five of them, Mr. Porter and his guests. What do high school teachers eat? How could I be expected to know? Feed them anything, what do you think?"

"The choices are steak and onions, roast pork or pan-fried perch, Mr. Dooley."

"Roast pork, I suppose. Impossible to ruin it and if you do, ladle on the apple sauce and gravy."

"Mr. Dooley." Audrey MacLellan's face was red. "Our patrons are not yokels. We are not Toronto people here, and we do not eat food smothered in French glop in the Toronto style. But this hotel was good enough for you when no one else would hire you. I'm not

286

sure your fancy Kitchener hotel would take you if they knew your fondness for liquor, morning, noon and night."

Mr. Dooley looked at her with concern, and immediately changed his expression.

"Dear Mrs. MacLellan, Audrey, I meant no disrespect. I have enjoyed my time here with you immensely. In fact I was saying just that to the hotel manager yesterday, when I told him I would be leaving. I recommended you particularly as my replacement."

Her face softened.

"Thank you for that, Mr. Dooley." She smiled fondly at him. "Your recommendation is much appreciated I'm sure, but we still have a menu to arrange. And I have it on the very best authority that one of the guests is to be Mr. Edward Archer, a lawyer from Toronto, who is chairman of the Conservative party."

Mr. Dooley sprang to his feet.

"Edward Archer." His eyes were sparkling. "Why wasn't I told of this? How do you know?"

"I heard it last night from Marie Barnes."

"He is a most important man. This dinner must be magnificent." He rushed into the kitchen with Audrey at his heels, clapping his hands. "Everybody, to me. Quickly. We have work to do."

Russell wandered into the lobby of the Grand Central, not sure where he should go. A huge, red Persian carpet covered the lobby floor, and stuffed horsehair furniture, potted plants and ornate floor lamps filled the space under a crystal chandelier with bulbs in the shape of flames, linked by chains of crystal beads. Behind the dark wooden desk was a picture of King George VI of England in military uniform, his hand on his sword. Russell approached the woman at the reception desk who directed him to a room down the hall to the left of the desk.

He entered and found a table set for five and shook hands with Archer, Tom Brennan and the ever-smiling Tyler Van Kleef. Ross

Porter, a short, stubby man in a tweed jacket and grey flannels, beamed and shook his hand vigorously.

"Captain Russell, delighted. Heard about you for years. Fine old family in town. Delighted."

The man spoke with the soft vowels and languid drawl of a wellborn Englishman. He wore a blue and yellow polka-dot bow tie and an olive-green waistcoat with the air of the dandy. His moustache drooped and was twirled at the ends, and he liked to open his jacket and project the olive-green waistcoat over his modest paunch. When Russell complimented Porter on his election victory, the man shook his head in theatrical modesty.

"It's not just my triumph, or the triumph of the Conservative Party. I see my win as a vindication of those principles of freedom under the law and respect for the Crown which have been the foundations of Anglo-Saxon society since Magna Carta. I see it as the extension of the battle against tyranny which we have so recently won in Europe. Freedom has come to Elgin County."

The teacher was boring Van Kleef, whose eyes began to blink rapidly. As Porter launched into an explanation of the importance of his election victory to the British Empire in the post-war period, Archer interrupted. "Fine, Porter. Glad to see you take an interest in the history side. But these men have come here to decide how Mr. Van Kleef's project will go ahead, now that all the land has been assembled."

"Project? How do they usually go ahead? What's stopping it?"

Archer looked at Russell and rolled his eyes. Van Kleef was grinning at Porter as if he were a mischievous boy.

"There are arrangements to be made, Mr. Porter, that have political ramifications. Letting of contracts, employment on the project, and so on. Since you are newly elected, we are meeting to discuss these issues. The general contractor, for example. This is not a simple barn-raising. The project requires experience and substance in its contractor. There is a Toronto firm, J.P. Martineau, that has experience of the appropriate kind all over the province and is a strong supporter of the Party."

Porter frowned. "We have a perfectly good local contracting firm, Harris and Brown. They rebuilt the pier at Port Stanley last year. They are capable and I see no reason why they shouldn't be given the work."

"They're Liberal, Ross," said Tom Brennan, cracking his knuckles. "They got the Port Stanley job through Grant MacKay."

"You mean to tell me that these jobs are for sale to the highest bidder? That is unconscionable, Sir. That is corruption of the rule of law, it is patronage of the worst kind. I will not tolerate it."

Archer exploded, his lips quivering. "Who the hell are you not to tolerate anything? You're a goddam teacher who got lucky. You're a new man in the Legislature, a back bencher without power and influence, and likely to remain so, if what I see today is any evidence."

Porter was taken aback but not intimidated. He caught his breath, swelled his olive-clad pigeon's breast out to its full expansion, and rose to his feet.

"I, Sir, am the Member of the Legislature for Elgin County. I am the duly elected representative of the people. I take my duties very seriously and I intend to carry them out to the best of my ability. One of my responsibilities is to see that justice is done. And the buying and selling of construction contracts is not justice. And who is it that proposes these squalid arrangements? A private citizen, without any constitutional responsibilities. Who, exactly, do you think you are, Sir, if I may ask?"

Archer was unable to speak, and sat glaring in his chair, his hands trembling. Van Kleef, however, was smiling. He moved his body forward in his chair and laid his large hands on the table with a thump.

"Mr. Porter. You are a man of democratic principles, and as a citizen of the world's first true democracy, I respect that. But I want to tell you, as someone who has dealt with governments all over the world in construction and commercial projects of various kinds, that life outside the legislature, or the parliament, is complex. And arrangements that might look correct to you on paper, often need some modification, some political input, before they hit the street."

"But surely these jobs should go to the best qualified, not just to loyal supporters of the Party?"

Van Kleef chuckled. "That's exactly what I used to think, Porter. If I'm going to build a bridge, why can't I just get the folks who have built the best bridges, strike a mutually acceptable price and get to it. But we have government that has to be involved, protecting the interests of the people. We have folks who have to be taken care of, one way and another, for all manner of reasons you wouldn't even dream of. The hogs got to be fed, or there won't be no bacon."

At this reference to hogs Archer throw up his hands. Porter was responding somewhat to Van Kleef's salesman's good humour, but he was still not satisfied. He smiled sheepishly at the big American, but began frowning and sticking his paunch aggressively even further forward. Archer's eyes were shooting daggers. Tom Brennan cleared his throat.

"Thing is, Ross, there'll be lots of work for Harris and Brown on this deal. You have my word. But politics is politics. You got four years to build a system down here and get re-elected. So you get work for your friends, the people who supported you. We're here to help you do that, so that in four years' time your friends will be able to say that Ross Porter came through for them. But we need you to help us. We owe J.P. Martineau, and we need to take care of them. They are highly competent."

"But why are you involved at all?" Porter's voice rose even higher. "Mr. Van Kleef is the man who's building the factory. Why doesn't he just hire whomever he wants?"

Archer rose. "He still doesn't get it. I'm going for a walk."

But at that moment Audrey MacLellan wheeled in the lunch trolley. Immediately behind her, his hands pressed together and his eyes darting from person to person, was Mr. Dooley.

"Sit down, Archer, and let's stop talking." Van Kleef laid a hand on the lawyer's shoulder and thrust him back into his chair. "Time for some grub."

"Mr. Archer," said Dooley with great excitement. "Alphonse

Dooley, Sir, at your service. I used to serve you in the dining room of the King Edward Hotel in Toronto, many years ago."

The lawyer gave Mr. Dooley a brief smile, then turned away. Dooley lingered beside his chair.

"The freshest perch, caught today just south of here, cooked à la bonne femme, Sir. I do hope it is to your liking."

"Good. I'm sure it will be."

Archer turned to Van Kleef but still Dooley lingered. The lawyer turned back to him.

"That will be all, thank you."

Archer's voice was barely more than a growl. Dooley's smile shattered. He scurried for the door, where he paused and turned.

"Do summon me, gentlemen, if there is anything you require."

No one looked at Mr. Dooley, who summoned up his brightest smile and left with his head high and his gaze fixed on the future.

As they ate, Brennan began to introduce the business at hand in a calm, matter-of-fact way, mentioning firms and people who would be useful, never referring to the need for favours. Russell could see the tension in Porter as he listened, not understanding the politics of what was being said. He began to think of Susan dancing in Toronto with her band leader when he felt someone shaking him. Van Kleef was smiling down at him.

"C'mon and take a walk with me, Captain, while the politicians do the dirty work."

They walked out onto the sidewalk in front of the hotel. A grey-bearded farmer was clucking to his horses, pulling a wagon of feed down the main street of St. Thomas, headed for his farm.

"Look at that old fellah," said Van Kleef. "Years behind the time, but doin' it. Doesn't he look grand up there on his rig, master of his team and his forty acres. I'm sure he's got more to tell us than all these political operators. Look at me, Russell." The blue eyes were fierce. "I don't mind talking up to a point, but there comes a time when the chatter has to stop and the production has to start and we're at that point with this project. Now I hope you understand me when I say that your Mr. Porter, surely a fine history teacher, is not a production man. He's a talker." Russell nodded.

"Now, Archer and Brennan are talkers too, but they don't know it. They operate only in the world of words, my friend. I got my land, I got my permits, and I'm ready to build. We have to get down to doing it and Captain Russell, I want you with me." The big man beamed at him.

"You know this town and the people, and they know and admire you, from what I hear. And you're a military man, which means you know how to do things."

When Van Kleef finally finished his sales pitch, they agreed that Russell would act as legal counsel for the company that would build and operate the plant.

"I've got things to do." Van Kleef turned to go. "All they're doing in there is setting that rooky politician straight with a lot of chatting."

❀

Russell walked to the MacLean house on Walpole Street, feeling giddy. He had just committed himself to Van Kleef for the next few years, but wasn't sure what that meant. He rang the bell and after several seconds Valerie MacLean opened the door and looked at him with a smile.

"She's not here, Bobby. I think she went to the beach at Port Stanley with Jean and Will Matthews. "

He nodded. "I hear she's leaving for New York."

The mother's face turned sour.

"Without our permission. Bud Robson is getting her and Jean an apartment. I can't imagine what he's thinking."

She looked closely at Russell. "She's only doing it because," she smiled affectionately at him, "she has nothing better to do."

40.

Russell drove in the Buick to Port Stanley. It was early in the summer and the rides, the ferris wheel, the roller coaster, had been assembled and painted but were standing still. The hotdog stands and fudge shops looked clean and ready, but were all shuttered up. The beach was empty, but the blue lake sparkled with whitecaps under a warm sun and a westerly breeze. Down by the pier the fishing boats bobbed at anchor, their day's work done. He saw Jean and Will sitting on a blanket and walked over to them. Jean gave him a friendly but distant smile. Will scowled.

"Is Susan with you?"

"She's swimming."

Jean waved towards the lake. Susan was doing a steady crawl parallel to the beach.

"Mind if I sit down?"

"There's always room for a handsome soldier."

She smiled provocatively. Will turned and stared at the lake.

"I hear you and Susan are moving to New York."

"Isn't it fabulous? There's nothing in this town for either of us." Russell saw Will wince. "Daddy's getting us an apartment. Just wait until they turn us loose on that town. Broadway, Haarlem, Central Park, the Village. We'll take it apart."

"I don't see the big deal about New York," said Will. "You can do anything here you can do there and they haven't got a beach as nice as this one, let me tell you."

"Yes, you can eat here, but it's not really eating. And you can drive to Toronto and see a show, but it's not Forty-Second Street. Best of all are the guys who know their way around Manhattan." She turned to Russell. "Now, the rumour is that you are in with the new Tory government." He said nothing. "And they say that you and some Toronto lawyer and the American who's running everything are behind this new plant they're building."

He watched Susan swimming; her stroke strong and steady.

"At least we'll be doing something."

Jean rolled her eyes. Will whirled. "I'm going to law school in Toronto next year. I got my acceptance yesterday."

"That's fine, Will," said Russell. "The law can lead to many good things."

Will was looking at Jean who continued to ignore him.

"Soon you'll be running this town, Bobby," said Jean. "You'll be the Mayor or the Member some day."

He shook his head.

"Not me. Too much talking."

Susan was walking out of the waves. Russell watched every step she took. The water dripped from her body, not yet browned by the sun. She squeezed the water out of her hair; she had worn no cap. The sun shone on her, making the water sparkle, making her wet hair shine, highlighting the strong woman's body, the shoulders, the full breasts, the round hips and long, strong legs. For a moment the beach seemed completely silent, and everything was motionless except her figure, walking towards him. She was looking at the sand and had not yet seen him. He tensed. She saw him and stopped, six feet from the blanket.

"What are you doing here?"

"The same as you. Enjoying the beach."

She walked to the blanket and began to dry herself. She didn't look at him but busied herself drying with her towel.

"They say you're going to New York," he said.

"Yes," she said, furiously rubbing her hair. "We'll have an apartment, maybe in Greenwich Village. It will be too perfect."

He didn't speak. She looked quickly at him and continued drying her hair.

"Bobby's going to be a big man in town," said Jean. "He's in with Ross Porter and the Tories and he's going to be running things. But he'll be the man behind the scenes, not the Mayor. Bobby's a man of action."

"How wonderful. We'll all get what we want, it seems. Hold my towel, Jean, I'm going to get some soda."

With a toss of her head she started to walk towards the stalls. He ran after her. She saw that he was following and increased her pace. He caught her just as she reached the boardwalk.

"May I buy you a soda?"

"I have money."

She bought the soda and walked to a bench. She sat down, sipping the soda, gazing over the water. He sat beside her. She kept watching the water. He was aware of the freckles on her arm, her wet hair and the sand between her toes. The sun beat down on them. He could smell it drying her skin.

"I don't think you should go to New York."

For several seconds she kept her eyes on the water, as if he hadn't spoken, then turned her head and looked right at him. The sun on her hair, the darkness of her eyes, shook him.

"Interesting. Should your view on the subject matter to me?"

"Yes."

He saw a hint of a smile on her lips.

"Oh, I see. You have so many opinions these days that I can hardly keep up with them. You did say you find the women of St. Thomas cloistered and arrogant, as I recall. And the town is boring."

"That's true."

"What?" Her eyes were flashing.

"St.Thomas is nothing like Europe now and that's good. But … when I first got back … I couldn't calm down." He saw a flicker in her eyes. "It's over now. And I am slowing down. Getting used to ordinary life again. It feels great, just to be ordinary."

"Even surrounded by arrogant women?"

"Even surrounded by arrogant women."

Down by the pier the engine of one of the fishing boats sputtered and then roared as it began to move out into the lake. They both watched it as if by agreement, avoiding their conversation. White clouds scudded by, gulls soared and the lake was sparkling with sun glistening on the whitecaps.

She reached into her beach bag and brought out a striped jersey, which she pulled over her head. She patted her hair in place and reaching in again, brought out sunglasses. She smiled. Her teeth were white, her lips gleaming red beneath the dark glasses.

"I don't see what business it is of yours if I go to New York."

"That depends."

"Jean and I have been planning this for some time."

"And you're not afraid of the big city."

"I'm not afraid of anything." Her smile vanished.

"You're going with the band leader?"

"Gene Henderson? Oh, that." Her laughter was nervous.

He looked down the beach; Jean and Will Matthews had gone.

"Is this musician going to be in New York?"

Her stare was softened by a light in her eyes.

"'This musician'. Why do you ask?"

He had nothing to say. She looked at the veins on the backs of his hands, and his neck and ears. It occurred to her once again how lucky he was to be sitting beside her, alive and not a mark on him. She had a sudden sense of his frailty, how he must have had to struggle to survive and come home. She caught herself. No, not now, she thought. He's nice, but I'm going to New York.

"I think I'd better get home now," she said.

They walked back down the boardwalk, her hand next to his. He didn't take it. She knew he wanted to and she was disappointed, despite herself. The sun was paler now, beginning to slant along the beach, leaving the sand, the driftwood and the stalks of grass washed with late afternoon gold. The wind was cooler. She put on her sandals and gathered up the blanket. He watched each move she made, spellbound.

"Will you drive me back to town?"

"Why don't we have dinner somewhere?"

Her expression became cautious, almost cunning.

"I can't. I promised Jean I'd go over to her house and…."

"Oh, for Christ sake, Susan."

He glared are her. She smiled.

"Well, I could call Jean. Since you and I won't be seeing each other for a while."

He sat in the living room of the house on Walpole Street while she went upstairs and changed. Valerie and Jim MacLean entered the room, smiling at him.

"I hear you two are going out for supper," Valerie said.

"That's right." He was at a loss for anything more to say.

"Wasn't that an election!" Jim was sitting on the sofa. "A Tory Member from Elgin County."

"A real change. Should shake the place up some."

"Jim." Valerie's voice was controlled, firm. "Bobby didn't come here to talk politics."

"Right, right."

There was an awkward silence until Susan entered and the two left together.

"Where shall we go?" he asked in the car.

"Back to Port Stanley. Have some fish and watch the lake."

He drove to a fish restaurant on the edge of the beach in Port Stanley, a small white clapboard building with lobster pots and fish nets around the entrance. There was no one else in the dining room. The waitress handed them their menus and returned to the kitchen. They were sitting by the window, facing the sand and the lake. The beach was in shadow. The end of the pier was still in sun, and the lake itself was bright blue.

"It's beautiful," she said.

"Yes, it is. Thank God we're here."

"What do you mean by that?"

"Nothing. We could not be here, that's all."

"Of course we could not be here. We could be in the Grand Central. Or I could be at Jean's as I promised." Then she looked at him, and raised her hand to her mouth. "Or you could be dead. Or still in Europe."

Her reference to his death shook Susan; she blushed and began to read her menu. Russell felt lost; he opened his mouth to speak, then closed it. The waitress came bustling in from the kitchen and stood with her pad at the ready. They ordered and fell silent.

"You were just about to say something when the waitress came in," said Susan.

"Was I?"

"Yes."

"Are you through with Henderson?"

"That has nothing to do with you." She tossed her head.

He grew red in the face. "Of course it does. It has everything to do with me." He stopped; she smiled shyly.

"I'm not seeing him anymore."

She turned away and concentrated on the sunset, just a band of brilliant colour, from fiery orange to vermillion, at the western end of the lake. The pier was in darkness. The water and sky met in the blue-black of night, dotted with whitecaps.

"Then see me."

"I can't. I'm going to New York."

"Don't go. Stay here."

"Why?"

"Because I want you to."

"'Because you want me to'."

She looked him fully in the eyes for the first time since they had arrived. Her face was now very serious and he could see the tension in her body. He wanted to put his arm around her, was longing to touch her, but there was the table between them, and the waitress rattling around in the kitchen. Another couple entered the restaurant, a white-haired farmer and his wife, who recognized him and waved. They sat back silently. Frustrated and angry, he decided it had been a mistake to bring her here.

"Yes, I want you to." His voice was soft now, urgent.

"We all want things, Bobby. I want to go to New York."

He thought she was unsure of her words. The tips of her ears were red and he could hear her breathing.

"I love you. I want you to stay with me."

She became very quiet.

"We were always together, Susan. When I left, I didn't leave you, or at least, that's not what I meant. I thought you would understand. Nothing could come between us, I thought."

"You didn't even speak to me."

"I wouldn't have known what to say."

"And when you came back, you were horrid."

"I know. I'm sorry. Those were tough times."

"I know that."

She couldn't look at him. She had to go to New York.

"You are very sweet." She said this still not looking at him, still staring at the lake, now mostly dark.

"I'm not so sweet anymore. But I do love you."

She was clenching her napkin in her hand, twisting it back and forth. Before she could speak the waitress barged through the swinging doors with a plate in each hand.

"The plates is hot, folks."

They let the plates sit on the cloth, steam rising. Susan looked for a moment as if there were tears in her eyes. "Damn," he heard her mutter.

"Things never work out the way you plan, do they?" Her voice was so low he could hardly hear her. "I thought we were finished. The war had changed everything and we were different people. Yet here you are, sitting there, telling me you love me. Telling me not to go to New York." She raised her napkin and wiped her eyes. "I probably love you, Bobby. I always have. Even when I hated you, a month ago, even when you were being so awful."

She smiled tenderly at him, and shook her head. I'm in, he thought. She's going to stay. I knew it.

"But I'm going to New York."

"What d'you mean? We love each other."

"Love?" she paused. "I don't understand the word anymore. Is it enough to build a life on? I don't know, but I have to go. You want me to stay. My parents want me to stay. It seems like the whole town is just set up to keep me here." Outrage sparkled in her eyes. "There's more to life than … than…." She kept looking at him, unable to complete the sentence. "So I am going. And that's it."

She turned sideways and folded her arms across her chest.

He sat rigid in his chair. "I'll take you home." She nodded. He waved to the waitress.

"You haven't touched your food, folks," she said. "I hope nothing was wrong?"

"Not with the food," he snapped.

41.

Russell slept little that night. He lay awake the next morning, obsessed with Susan. By the time the sun shone in his window he was debating with himself. He could start planning his move to Toronto or he could stay and talk to her, find out what she really wanted. The turmoil continued until his mother knocked rapidly at his door. "Bobby, get up! You have to see this." He opened the door and she thrust her copy of the Times Journal at him.

The headline read, "Our Boys Home Tomorrow", and beneath was a report of the scheduled arrival of the St. Thomas and Elgin Highlanders at the Exhibition Grounds in Toronto the next morning. He stood stunned, staring at his mother, speechless. He went to his cupboard and got dressed. Within an hour he was at the station, waiting for the London train, then on to Toronto.

Russell arrived at the Canadian National Exhibition Grounds at two o'clock the next afternoon. A demobilization centre had been set up, a series of tents where the paper work would be done to process the men out of the army and into the future. At first the sight of so many men in khaki unnerved him. He had not been with soldiers since he left Europe. Men with brief cases were marching to and fro, trying to look busy. Officers were standing in front of the tents, chatting and smoking. He went to a tent with an 'Information' sign over it.

"The new batch will be arriving on the train from Montreal any time now. Give 'em half an hour to get trucked over, and we're off to the races. You a relative, Sir?"

"In a way."

"Well, you have to be a little slow with the boys at first. They been through a hell of a lot, and they tend to be changed."

He was tense. Perhaps he should have brought his uniform, but he had left in a rush, without thinking. And he probably shouldn't be in uniform. Would it matter to them that he had left early? He suddenly wanted to leave, but he could not. All at once the men around him were looking east, and waving their arms. He looked and saw a convoy of army trucks rolling in the gates.

"Here they are," someone shouted.

There were at least twenty trucks. They pulled up in a line across the road two hundred yards away. Men in battle dress began to leap from the rear of the trucks; their kit bags were thrown out onto a pile. They picked up their bags and formed into ranks. An officer barked out the orders and they began to march up the road towards the tents. There were people lined up three and four thick along the road, clapping and cheering. A woman rushed from the crowd and threw her arms around a soldier, who beamed, kissed her and thrust her away as he kept marching. They seemed to be marching in regiments, each one behind an officer. He stared at the men as they drew near, looking for a familiar face.

Suddenly he stared at one lieutenant, ahead of his men. It was Alton Johnston, his lieutenant. There they were. He saw the Graham brothers, Leonard and Alec, and Murray Pierce, who had worked on the railway, and Joe Mullens and Tom MacInnis who had been warehouse men for the feed store on Talbot Steet, and Sinclair Hemmingway and Ike Wilson, and that rat-faced sergeant, Jim Botts, who had been stealing rations and selling them for cigarettes, and Sam Ross, who, Russell thought, had been killed in Italy, but obviously had not, since here he was, not a mark on him. He stared at the faces. Some were red-eyed from drink. None were smiling. All looked tired. But then, the faces he knew stopped. A new officer marched by, another regiment. There had only been ten rows of five, about fifty of his soldiers.

The men came to a halt in front of the tents. A major came forward and made a short welcoming speech, followed by instructions. They were to go to this tent for discharge papers, another one for pay, that one for travel vouchers, and accommodation for two nights in Toronto was available.

"Dismissed."

The ranks dissolved. Friends and relatives rushed forward. There were tears, hugs and kisses. The men who were not being met walked to the tents. Many of them were confused, unsure as to what they were doing. The St. Thomas and Elgin Highlanders were moving in a group to the discharge tent. Alton Johnston was lingering behind, explaining something to a woman who was looking for her man. Russell walked up behind him.

"Hello, Alton."

The lieutenant turned his head casually, and then whirled around, his mouth gaping.

"Jesus Christ, Bobby. Captain Russell! What on earth are you doing here?"

"I came to meet you. Where are the other men? There are only fifty here."

"That's all that's left." Alton's dark, quiet face clouded over. "There's a few in hospital still in England and France, but other than that...." He shook his head. Immediately a warm smile broke out and he looked Russell up and down.

"Captain, we heard you were invalided out, but you look fine now. Hey, let's go and find the guys. They have to see you."

Alton Johnston drew him by the arm over to the discharge tent. "Wait here," he said. He went into the tent. Russell heard the familiar voice give one more command. "St. Thomas and Elgin, form up outside the tent on the double."

"Shit, Alton, what's this nonsense? Time to go home."

Grumbling, they strolled out of the tent and stood in a group, waiting for the lieutenant with defiant stares, not noticing the young man in civilian clothes behind them. Alton Johnston came out of the tent.

"Don't look at me with your little pouts. Turn around and see if there is someone you recognize."

Russell froze as they turned. They looked at him, and then smiles broke out on the angry faces. Nobody moved. They began to cheer. Then Leonard and Alec Graham walked forward, grabbed him, and hoisted him onto their shoulders. The men crowded around and cheered and cheered and cheered. Then they began to touch him, patting his leg or his arm. Then someone pulled him off the shoulders of the Graham boys, and they pressed around, delight in their eyes, shaking his hand, some even embracing him. An officer emerged from the discharge tent.

"Hop to it, you men." His tone was officious. "We haven't got all day to wait. Let's get this show on the road."

"Aw, fuck off," came a belligerent voice. "This is our Captain."

The cheering continued; the officer shrugged, turned and went back into the tent. Eventually, when Russell had shaken hands with or embraced every one of the fifty men, the noise decreased.

"You men go back in and get processed," Russell shouted. "We'll have some beer in town when you're all done."

They turned to the tent, talking happily, looking back at him.

"They missed you," said Alton Johnston. "You should have seen the reaction when you were captured. Some of them were crying. They wanted to organize an assault squad to go and get you back. They were ready to go right to Berlin."

Russell shook his head, stunned. In that brief five minutes a great burden had been taken from him. The touch of those hard, weary hands, gripping his hand or pounding his back had restored to him his place in the world. In their smiling eyes, he saw who and where he was. The men began to drift out of the tent, looking for their bags.

"Where are the other officers?" Russell asked.

"The colonel is still in England. He faked some business with the Canadian High Commission, but really he has a girl there.

Some went right home, got demobbed in England. And some...."
He shrugged. "I was told to lead these guys back. I'd better go in myself and get processed."

Russell noticed civilians circling among the soldiers. There were women from the churches and the Salvation Army, offering food and lodging. There was a young man with pad and pencil, a newspaper reporter, talking to the men; a photographer was taking pictures. Most of the men stayed away from Russell. After the first outburst of affection, respect for rank reasserted itself. By the time Alton re-emerged from the tent, he was standing alone; the men were clutching their bags, looking occasionally at him and talking quietly.

"Welcome home, Alton."

Alton Johnston smiled shyly and looked at the ground. "I guess," he said. "You going to buy them beer?"

"I guess."

They drank in the men's room of the Sherbourne Hotel, to the east of downtown, a popular spot with some of the men from before the war. The room was dark, and the waiter brought trays of draught beer around to the tables.

"Where are they all?" said Russell when they were seated. "There are only about half of them here."

"Some have taken the pledge. No drinks. Sam Ross is one of those. We had trouble with him trying to preach to the boys who didn't want to be preached to. His father, Malcolm Ross, has that little shack of a church near Iona Station; the Free Independent Presbyterian Church of God, they call themselves."

"I didn't realize we had so many clean-livers."

"Not that many. Some of them are out looking for women."

Russell shook his head. "God help them when they hit St. Thomas. It's not ready for them."

"I'm sure of that. Have you seen my parents?"

"I see your father on Talbot Street. He's well."

Alton smiled. "So we had an election in June. And St. Thomas went Conservative. I couldn't believe it."

"Big change, things were different this time. The Times Journal supported the Tories."

"No!" Shock registered on Alton Johnston's face.

"Jim MacLean has decided that the Liberals were going nowhere. Grant MacKay, who was still our Member, didn't help. He was drunk as a skunk just about any time you ran into him."

Alton shrugged. "So when do we go back?"

"Tomorrow!" Ike Wilson, a tall, red-haired man with a good-natured smile, rose with a glass of beer in his hand. "We go home when we want, right boys?"

There was a roar of approval from the Elgin and St. Thomas Highlanders. Russell raised his hand.

"Well, I was talking to Al Parker on the phone and he says we need the okay of the Chief of Police to parade. A permit."

"Al Parker." Ike Wilson was laughing. "Is that mealy-mouthed ass-kisser still mayor? Boys, we got to do something about that. We'll put the Captain up for mayor."

The men cheered.

"Captain, you'd be some mayor. I remember that little cattle raid you took us on. Remember boys, when we reached the Dutch border with Krautland. Them Germans had driven all the local beefs back into Germany as they retreated. All the Dutchmen is starving, men, women and children. 'We'll see about that,' says the Captain. He gets all the farm boys together one night, I think it was in March, still colder than a witch's tit, and says, Boys, we're gonna go get them cattle. So off we go after dark. Finding them was no problem. Our boys could smell cows a half mile away. It might be a German unit, they would be asleep, without proper pickets at that time, cuz they had pretty well given up on serious fighting. We would march right in, cut the tethers and march out without a sound, driving a couple of head back with us. Or one time I remember it was a farm, rich farm, big house with a thatched straw roof. That old farmer heard us, and he comes out with a gun. He did not want to give up them beefs. Captain Russell pulls out his pistol and says, your cattle or your life or something like in the Kraut language, and the guy gives up and goes back to bed. Heh, heh, heh." The men were listening, staring first at Ike and then at Russell with wonder and affection. "By the time the sun was up, we were heading back into Holland with over a hundred head. Boys, oh boys, was them Dutchmen glad to see us. And the girls. My, my, even Joe Mullens got his little blond sweetheart that day."

There were whoops and cheers. Joe Mullens, a huge homely man, smiled shyly.

"So that's why we need to put Captain Russell in as mayor. Al Parker." Ike Wilson looked around the room with disgust on his face. "Jesus H. Christ."

The cheering broke out again. Russell held up his hand.

"Thank you, boys, but I don't fancy the political life. Cattle rustling with Elgin County boys is one thing, but having to choose who gets the contract to fix the roads is another. I'd just as soon leave that to Parker."

Boos rang out in the tavern.

"Tell me, Captain." The speaker was Sinclair Hemmingway, a lean, serious man already going bald. "Will there be work for us when we get back? Those who won't be farming."

Russell glanced at Alton Johnston, then cleared his throat.

"I can't answer that for certain, but I can tell you that times are good right now, and people who know say they are going to get better. People do without during the war, then when peace comes they buy everything in sight. Makes lots of jobs. Why, there is going to be an auto parts plant built near St. Thomas. There will be jobs there for over two hundred men when it's finished."

There was silence while the men digested this information.

"Factory," said one of them finally. "I ain't gonna work in no factory. That's what they do in Toronto, Hamilton and them places. Join the union, work nine to five, kiss the foreman's ass everyday? No siree Bob."

There were murmurs of agreement from many in the room. Before anyone else could speak there was a loud retching sound from a table near the wall. Everyone turned to look. Leonard Graham had vomited on the table and crashed to the floor.

"Sargent Botts," said Johnston. "Deal with him."

Botts and another soldier dragged the man by the neck of his collar into the toilets.

"It's time for us to leave," said Johnston. "It won't be getting any better from here on in." He rose to his feet. "Attention." The conversation stopped. "Captain Russell and I are leaving. I want you to stay together and take care of one another. This isn't Naples, but even in Toronto a fellah can get in trouble on a Saturday night. Your beer is paid for. Report at eight-thirty hours, Union Station, tomorrow. We're taking the nine-thirty train to London. Any man drunk when we get to town will not parade. We're going to get us a piper and we're marching down Talbot Street tomorrow afternoon, permit or no permit."

The announcement was greeted by a loud cheer. Russell and Johnston left the room. When they reached the street, Johnston stopped and stared across the street. A tall, thin soldier with the patch of the Elgin and St. Thomas Highlanders was talking to a short, squat woman about half his height. She had dark, stringy hair, wore a brightly flowered dress that revealed the tops of her breasts, and appeared to have her front teeth missing. She was stroking his arm. He had a dazed, foolish grin on his face.

"That is private Jack Sharp, from London," said Johnston. "He survived the fighting. We'll see if he survives his new friend."

They walked away. "Let's go to my hotel and get some supper."

Johnston nodded. "I've been minding the boys all the way from Holland and I'm sick of them."

In the hotel dining room, Russell saw how Alton had aged. The lieutenant kept looking around the dining room, the ornate columns and the painted ceiling, as if he couldn't quite locate himself. He would forget that he had food on his plate as he talked non-stop, punctuating his sentences with hand gestures.

"You look all in, Alton."

"Yeah. It's been so long since I … since I … could just relax. Or talk to someone who wasn't crazy. Everyone was crazy over there, Bobby. You had to be."

"I know. There was no other way." He lowered his voice. "Was it worth it?"

The lieutenant looked at him nervously. "It doesn't matter. It happened. You did it. Forget it." Neither spoke as the waiter served their drinks. "How did you find it, coming back?"

Russell thought. "Difficult."

"Susan?"

He shrugged. "Not the same."

"Too bad. What d'you plan to do, then?"

"Probably practice law. The dairy runs itself pretty well. I thought I might try to work for a Toronto firm."

"Life in the big city?"

"Why not? I can't imagine doing real estate deals and wills in St. Thomas for the rest of my life. Although, there may be some work for me from this new auto parts plant." He outlined the proposal Van Kleef had made to him.

"Well, that's great. What a start. Why wouldn't you grab it?"

"Pushing paper for the rest of your life? I don't know."

"You'd need a girl. That sort of life only makes sense if there's a woman in it."

"Women!" He thought of Eleanor. "Remember the women lining the roads watching us march into those Italian towns?

"Not really. What of them?"

"I hated looking at them. I don't know if I'm up to women right now."

Alton Johnston stared at him. "I never thought of the women, or the men, or the children," he said. "Even the killing didn't bother me. It's supposed to, but it didn't."

"It did me."

"There you go. Different guys."

308

42.

There were few other passengers in the swaying coaches of the London and Port Stanley Railway's morning run. The men in of the St. Thomas & Elgin regiment sat staring at the familiar landscape. Four were playing cards at the rear of the coach, their eyes red-rimmed, stubble on their faces. Three were missing; they had not been at the station in Toronto when the train left. But the rest were whispering together, pointing out a familiar crossroad or farm, their eyes shining

"It's the same," muttered Alton Johnston. "I can't get over it. Look there, that's Glen Murray's farm. And that's Glen, backing his wagon into the barn."

Russell looked, but the barn, the gabled house, the arching elms were disappearing behind them.

"It isn't the same," he said. "It looks the same but it isn't."

Someone had stitched the St. Thomas and Elgin shoulder patch and captain's insignia, cut out from canvas, on his jacket. He was back in uniform.

"Don't it look great, Captain," said Ike Wilson, a huge grin on his face. "All the farms. All the green."

"Ike, the sun is shining for us."

"They gonna let us parade, Parker and them?"

"They have no say in the matter," said Russell. "We're here and we're marching down Talbot Street."

The men cheered and went back to watching the landscape slip by. Even the gamblers put their cards away. With each mile the excitement in the coach rose.

"I hope it's as good as they think it will be," said Alton.

"It can never be that good," said Russell. "But by the time they figure that out, they'll be working again, grinding it out. Then one day, they'll wake up and it will all be past, a memory."

"Already, sometimes I think I dreamt it."

Susan and Jean were sitting in the Malt Shoppe drinking tea. Susan was shaking her head, inhaling the fragrance from her cup.

"I like his music, but he's not for me. He's skinny and bony and covered in black hair. I don't ever want him to touch me again." Susan's face conveyed her revulsion.

"Well, I can see Gene didn't work out. But no harm done. On to the next."

"There isn't going to be a next one. I'll never have another man. I'll turn Catholic and join a convent. Or I'll move in with Rose and Helen."

Jean burst out laughing; Susan tried to maintain a straight face, then began to giggle.

"Darling, you're not made to be a nun. You have a body like a Venus. I bet Gene Henderson is dreaming about it right this instant. Give yourself some time, and try again."

"My mother's on to me."

"My God." Jean looked worried. "If my mother finds out I lied for you, she'll kill me."

"Mine doesn't know exactly, but I can see by the way she looks at me that she's suspicious. I'm sure she doesn't think that I stayed at your Aunt Jennie's."

"You didn't say a word at Rose and Helen's last night. Anyone could figure out that something's wrong just by looking at you."

Susan stared at her teacup.

"I don't want anything to do with him again. But I can't stay here anymore. I don't feel the same. Let's go to New York and get that apartment."

"Now you're talking." Jean smiled. "I'll get Daddy to find us a place. Just the two of us." Her face turned serious. "What will your parents say?"

"What can they say? I'm over twenty-one."

Suddenly from the street came the sound of bagpipes and the beating of a bass drum. They noticed people rushing to the sidewalk outside the Malt Shoppe window.

"It can't be the high school band. It's still summer," said Susan.

"Can't be. They don't have bagpipes." They got up and walked to the window.

❀

Down the street, Jack Morris was just finishing cutting the hair of a farmer when he heard the skreel of the pipes. He walked out onto the sidewalk and saw the men of the St. Thomas and Elgin Highlanders marching down Talbot Street behind a solitary piper. Behind the piper marched Ike Wilson carrying the regimental flag, then Captain Robert Russell and then the men, in four rows, marching with no expression on their faces, looking straight ahead. Behind the ranks of men Alec Graham was beating a huge bass drum tied to his chest. And behind him, marching in step, his wounds still visible on his legs, was Calvin MacQuiggan.

People were rushing from the stores and apartments to stand on the curbs and clap and cheer. The town was exploding. Jack stood still, scratching his head and thinking. At first he calculated the rise in monthly business all these new male heads would amount to. He figured five extra dollars a month, and he broke into a smile. And then it occurred to him that the return of the soldiers might reverse the trend to female domination in St. Thomas. This thought filled him with joy, and he began to clap and cheer with everyone else.

"Hey, you gonna take off this sheet?"

The farmer was standing in the door, staring at the march past, a hair-covered white cloth hanging around his neck.

"Aw, hold your horses," said Jack. "The boys is back. I'll get to you in a minute."

❀

"It's Bobby," Susan was saying, just a few doors down the street. "Look at him."

"It's not just Bobby. It's the regiment. Shouldn't there be more of them though? I thought there was a lot more. But they look gorgeous. Who's the cute lieutenant, marching beside Bobby?"

"Alton Johnston. A farmer's son from south of here."

"That's Alton Johnston? Wow."

"Look at Bobby." Susan was shaking her head. "I saw him just recently. He didn't look like that."

"You saw him? You didn't tell me."

"I'll tell you later. But he looks so much … better."

Jean noticed the smile on Susan's face as she watched Bobby Russell march past.

"Where do you think they're going?" Susan was excited.

They left the Malt Shoppe to follow the parade.

❀

Al Parker and Elmore Wayne were in the Chief's office, planning once again their fishing trip on the French River. When they heard the pipes and drum coming nearer they went to the window to look. On the street below, they saw the returning regiment march to the war memorial and come to a halt.

"God damn it to hell, I told them you needed to give them a permit. Did they get one?"

"Nah." The Chief was smiling. "What you want to do about it? Arrest them?"

"Don't be ridiculous, Elmore. You can't arrest an army, for Christ's sake. But that goddamn Alton Johnston. There's got to be something we could charge him with."

"Look at them. They've been fighting for three years and they're still on their feet. Don't they look wonderful, though."

"Yeah, they do. You wouldn't catch me over there…." He paused and looked at the Chief, whose eyes were fixed on the marching men. "So we do nothing?"

"Never do nothing, Al. What we do is, you go down and make a speech."

Marching down Talbot Street, Russell smiled at the good feeling of marching with the men again, the swing of the arms, the sound of the boots on pavement, the muscles in the legs. Not like the other marches into other towns, with splintered buildings and cratered roads and the women, watching without hope. This was a march into the delight of being and belonging. He saw people running towards them. He saw the old men on the bench outside the feed store rise to their feet, years tumbling from them. There was Jack in his white smock and there was his customer with lather on his face, smiling and waving. A group of young men in blue coveralls were running up from the roundhouse where they had been working on the railway engines. Girls poured from the shops.

They marched past an alley between two stores and he remembered an old wooden outhouse, overgrown with weeds, where the boys in the upper grades used to come and drink beer at night. Further down, behind the shops, there was a dump where Wilson's Garage and Automotive threw their old oil cans and grease pots. The town was standing as it always had, red brick buildings, the occasional grey limestone, two and three stories high, under maples, oaks and elms, baked by the sun.

I belong here. Down that alley, around that corner, this small, modest place. Just smiling faces and the normal walking, the normal feeling, of an ordinary man. That's what I am.

They reached the old war memorial in front of the City Hall and halted. He faced his men and saw Calvin, who alone of all the crowd was not smiling. He was staring at Russell with an expression of wonder. He winked at Calvin, and drew the briefest smile. Then he saw Susan and Jean arriving from Talbot Street, clapping and cheering. He saw Susan's laughing eyes and her hair, red in the sun. As soon as she saw him looking at her she stopped clapping and turned her face away.

In the town, word of the arrival of the regiment spread quickly. It took Marie Barnes ten minutes from the time the men started marching down Talbot Street to hear of it. She quickly relayed the news to six or seven of her best correspondents and the story was out. Valerie MacLean heard it and telephoned her husband, who ordered a Times Journal reporter and photographer to the war memorial. Margaret Ann Russell heard it, put on some lipstick, got in the Buick and drove to town.

❁

The Mayor stepped forward to the microphone and was greeted with apathetic applause. He looked confused, uncertain as to what he should do. Elmore Wayne put his arm on the Mayor's shoulder and whispered in his ear. Realizing that this was not his moment he paused briefly, then stepped down. Russell approached the mic and the applause boomed. The Mayor walked away with the Chief of Police.

"These are your men," said Robert Russell quietly. "The men of the St. Thomas and Elgin Highlanders, who have done what you asked them to do." The cheering lasted for several minutes. The men in their ranks broke into broad smiles. "Coming home after years of fighting will not be easy. Please take care of them."

More cheering. Russell spoke for another minute or two and dismissed the men. They started to mill around, talking to their friends, being clapped on the back. Joe Hunter moved in with the CVSM mic and began to interview the regiment's Captain. Calvin MacQuiggan stood to one side, watching Russell with the glow of love in his eye.

As she watched, Susan was shocked by the fragility of the men, the delicacy of their skin, the weakness of their bones, the simple humanity in their eyes. She looked at Bobby, standing at the mic, his face shaded by his cap, his jacket hanging loose. With a jolt she realized he would always be part of the world she lived in. Immediately she caught herself.

"Jean, let's get out of here."

The Mayor and the Chief of Police walked back into City Hall shaking their heads. They had been cast aside.

"There's no gratitude for what you do, Elmore," he complained. "There's no goddamn justice."

The Chief of Police nodded sadly, then shrugged. "But the boys are back. You know, Al, that's what matters."

❁

Russell saw the men breaking their ranks and mingling with the crowd, hugging and laughing. He grew tired of answering Joe Hunter's questions and gave him a cut signal. Joe nodded. Then his mother was by his side, hugging him. Men were coming up and slapping him on the back. He looked for Susan out of the corner of his eye, but she and Jean had gone.

"Susan and Jean have just gone back to Talbot Street," said his mother, reading his mind.

She was here, he thought, she said she loved me; and she left. He shrugged and turned to Calvin MacQuiggan who was standing on the sidewalk, watching him.

"Hi Calvin," he said.

Calvin nodded. "That there is soldier's clothes," he said, pointing at the men. "Like my pa has. He got soldier's clothes too."

"We were soldiers together, your father and I."

Calvin began to scratch a sore on his bare leg.

"Don't pick your scab, Calvin," said Margaret Ann. "It will fester."

He left his scab alone and began to walk beside them.

"I guess there's good soldiers," he said.

43.

Overnight the weather turned. Russell woke the next morning to rain streaking down his window, grey clouds and water running in the gutters. His feet were cold when they touched the floor. He put on a wool sweater and went to the kitchen. His mother was there, sitting at the table drinking coffee. He poured himself a cup and sat down.

"Allan and I are getting married."

Allan Matthews. The handsome face, the blue eyes, the white moustache. An old woman's folly.

"Good," he said, without looking at her. He stared at the rain.

"I think it's good," she said, watching him carefully. "Bobby, I hope you aren't going to be difficult about this. We're not kids." He nodded. "It's not going to be a big wedding or anything. But we like each other and we're both tired of being alone.

"You're not bothered by his legal problems?"

"No, I am not. Listen, I know Allan, and while he may not be the strongest man, even foolish on occasion, he is not malicious. He did not mean to hurt me."

"But if he's disbarred…"

"He won't be disbarred."

"How can you know that?"

"He's already been told. The secretary of the Law Society was a classmate of his. They say that since MacAllister will not be tried in court, and since no one actually lost money and since he had no direct knowledge of the arrangement until after the fact, they are letting him off with a reprimand."

"I see." He stared gloomily out the kitchen window. "I know you hate being alone."

Without waiting for her reply he took his coffee and went into the sunroom where he could sit and watch the rain fall. Yet another change, without warning. He tried to picture living in his house with Allan Matthews. He would have to move out. After several seconds

Calvin entered and sat beside him.

"What we going to do today?" asked Calvin.

"Nothing. It's raining."

"Doesn't mean we can't do nothing. We could...."

"I said 'nothing'."

His tone was angry. Calvin looked at him seriously, then scurried away to the kitchen. Russell rose to his feet, grabbed an umbrella from the coat rack in the hall and headed out to the Buick. He would go to the library and read a Toronto paper. The tires spun on the gravel. He'd make arrangements for interviews in Toronto. He couldn't stay in St. Thomas. Van Kleef could get another boy to do his running and fetching. By the time he reached the library, he was in a fury. He walked into the reading room, found a day-old copy of the Toronto Globe and Mail, and spread it out on the table. He couldn't concentrate. The only stories he could follow were on the sports pages.

"Hello." Helen Partridge stood across the table from him. "I want to talk to you; come and have tea."

Before he could answer, she grabbed him by the hand and led him out of the reading room, across the main hall of the library to her office.

"Sit down," she said, as she prepared a pot of tea for the electric ring. "So she turned you down and she's going to New York."

He sat up sharply in his chair.

"This prying, miserable little town," he muttered. "How in the name of Christ...?"

But he knew. The waitress in the restaurant had listened to them and reported to Marie Barnes, as soon as she could find a telephone.

"It's life in a small town," she said, turning to him. "Everyone knows about the problems you and Susan are having. It's annoying, but keep yourself focussed on the real issue."

"Which is?"

"Susan."

"She's not an issue any more. She's gone."

"Do you love her?"

"What's that got to do with it?"

"Everything. When you hurt, and she won't make any sense, love is the only possible way."

"I have no idea what you're talking about."

"Yes, you do." She set down his tea in front of him. "What you are facing is something like the war you have been through. If you love, you set off on a journey with no destination. There is no map. Love isn't reasonable, and if it isn't reasonable, you can keep going forward when there is no hope." Helen took a sip of her tea. "Susan is everything you don't know, everything you need to find out. So find out or you will live the rest of your life not knowing. Don't be angry. If you are angry, you won't escape your solitude. Gamble and take what comes. If she rejects you, you'll be alone for a while, but not as alone as you would be if you never tried."

He saw the loneliness in her eyes. She envied him. Just another old woman, he thought.

"Helen, I have to go," he said. She was looking at the table, avoiding his eyes. "Thanks."

Her voice was just one more in the babble he was hearing, including his own. Her sad eyes weighed him down. He walked half a block down Talbot Street, staring at the sidewalk, talking to himself. Then he heard someone calling his name He looked to see Alton Johnston, out of uniform, walking toward him. They decided to go to the Malt Shoppe for coffee.

"I've noticed the boys on the street," Alton said when the waitress had brought their cups. "Lounging around in uniform. We should do something about it."

"As long as they don't bring disrepute, blah, blah, blah. Let them have their slack time, Alton. They've earned it."

"You're right. They're not my problem anymore." He shook his head. "I'm only home a day or so, and I have to get going again. I can't stand it here. Everything moves so slowly."

"Be patient. It took me a month before I could talk to anybody. So when do you leave?"

"Next month. But my father doesn't know I'm going. He thinks

I'll take over the farm. All through the war I was getting letters from him telling me what we would do together when I came home." He scowled again. "He isn't going to like it."

"You have to tell him."

"I know." Alton sighed. "What about you?"

"My mother is getting married, to Allan Matthews."

"The lawyer? The one whose partner tried to kill himself?" Russell nodded. "Hell, Bobby. What d'you think of it? I don't suppose she asked your permission?"

Alton winked and Russell laughed.

❀

Susan arrived at the apartment that evening, sad that this could be her last evening in this sanctuary of music, art and coming of age. Jean was reviewing for Rose and Helen possible locations for their apartment in New York.

"Here's our girl," said Rose. "You didn't give in. You remained true to yourself. I am so proud of you, Susan."

"Rose." Helen attempted to break in.

"Never you mind, Hellie. Some things have to be said. Susan has created a future and a life for herself. She has said, I am a free woman, with a mind, a heart and a soul, and I intend to develop my mind, explore my heart and free my soul. Bravo, my dear."

"How do you know about Bobby and me?" If Rose knew, the entire town must know.

"Marie Barnes told Joanne Robb, who works in the library, who told Hellie, who told me."

"I wish people would mind their own business."

She wanted to leave. She did not want to discuss the decision she had made. It had seemed right, despite Bobby's declaration. But now, as she looked around at the familiar faces, she was lost.

"Rose, Susan doesn't need our advice." Helen's voice was calm, affectionate.

"Maybe not. Well, anything that gets her out of this town and away from the pathetic old men who run it has to be good, if you ask me. You know what I mean, Helen." Helen shrugged. "This Porter who's got himself elected is going to be on the library board. He was talking to Helen and he isn't sure the budget can be increased for new book purchases. And him a teacher. That's what this place is like. You're well out of all this, Susan."

"This has nothing to do with the library budget. It's about me and Bobby." Susan began to sob. Helen put an arm around her.

"If you ask me, she's stuck on him," said Jean.

"You can't build a life on good looks." Rose was frowning. "How many girls have fallen for a smooth-talking, handsome good-for-nothing, and regretted it for the rest of their lives, raising children and growing old."

Susan began to cry into a handkerchief. "Leave me alone." Rose fingered the amber beads at her neck."I'm sick of all this gossip about Bobby and me. You don't know anything except what Marie Barnes passes on from her spy system." Susan was standing by the door with her fists clenched at her sides, glaring around the room. "I probably will go to New York, but I don't know what I really want, and neither do you."

Grabbing her umbrella she let herself out. She walked quickly through the rain to her house on Walpole, crying.

44.

Russell arrived at the jail behind the courthouse to see Private Jim Murray of the St. Thomas & Elgin Highlanders standing handcuffed in front of Gus Campbell, who was sitting at the desk. Murray's face was flushed, his eyes glazed and blood ran from a cut on his cheek. Three other soldiers stood around the desk. Neither Gus nor the men noticed Russell, watching from the doorway.

"Gus," said Private Sam Ross. "Jimmy's a good guy, you know that, just a little too much booze. Let us take him and you won't hear another peep out of him."

Gus shook his head. "Ordinarily I might agree with you, but this here assaulting of a female is a serious matter."

"'Assaulting of a female'." One of the men spat on the floor. "She weren't no ordinary female, she was a hooker working in the Confederation House sellin' beer. She was going to go with Jimmy, then she changed her mind. Jimmy grabbed her and she scratched his face. Then he hit her. Now how in hell is that assaulting of a female?"

"I got to think on it." Gus scratched his head. "You fellahs got to realize that you can't behave like you was still at war here. We got laws here."

"Fuck you and your laws."

It wasn't clear which one of the three had spoken. Each one was looking grim-faced at Gus, close to grabbing their pal and running. Gus was tense. Russell stepped forward into the light and the soldiers did a double take; then came to attention.

Gus smiled. "Captain Russell, thanks for comin' so fast."

Russell glared at the offender. "What if we put Private Murray under military arrest, Gus, and I ask you to keep him overnight in a cell for me until we can deal with him in the morning? That way justice will be done, the Private will be dealt with, but you won't have to go through pressing charges."

The three soldiers smiled. Gus Campbell continued to scratch his head, but was looking relieved.

"I guess we can do that. I know you'll deal with these men, Captain Russell. We can't have them drunk, disorderly and offending the women. This here's a law-abiding town."

The soldiers sneered but kept quiet. Bobby looked them over carefully. The four of them, Privates Murray, Burns, Mills and MacInnis had been obstreperous but not malicious soldiers.

"The rest of the regiment has gone home by now. But you idiots prefer to drink and wander the streets molesting the citizens." The men began to protest but he held up his hand for silence. "I want you to go home now. If the constables find you on the streets tonight they are to hold you in cells for court martial. Now get out of here, immediately."

The men stared, turned, saluted, and left the station without a word. Gus turned to Russell, a broad grin on his face.

"You moved 'em, Captain. They didn't like the mention of court martial."

Russell laughed. "They don't realize it, but they can't be court martialled. They were discharged in Toronto on Saturday."

"And what do we do with Private Murray here?"

"Hold him. Find out about the woman. If there was a crime committed, charge him. If there wasn't, let him go."

On Saturday afternoon Privates James Murray, Ike Wilson, Tom MacInnis, Athol Burns and Sam Ross were drinking beer in the men's room of the Confederation House, celebrating Murray's release from jail that morning. They had come in from the sunshine about two o'clock and by two-thirty they were drunk. They had been telling tales of the regiment's campaign through Holland to the others in the men's room; the tales becoming more bloody and scatological as the afternoon wore on. Archie MacQuiggan entered in the middle of the history of the Dutch campaign and took a table just to one side. The faces were red and the voices raucous. The smell of the beer was overpowering; the room had been full since noon. James Murray launched into a description of a raid that their Captain had lead on a warehouse that housed the local German command in the Dutch town of Appledorn. At the mention of Russell's name, Archie turned his face away.

"Say, Jimmy," said Ike Wilson. "I heard today that the Captain's girl has turned him down. Leaving him to live in New York City."

"No." Private Murray's bleary eyes widened. "How could she do that? Who is she?"

"Susan MacLean. Daughter of him that runs the newspaper."

"The little bitch. Does she know what she's doing? Turning down the best goddamn captain the Canadian army ever had?"

Murmurs of disbelief were heard in the room. The waiter laid another round of golden glasses on the table.

"Now, Ike, how do you know what's going on between the Captain and his girl?" Tom MacInnis was squinting through the stale air and smoke.

"Cuz my mother got it from Marie Barnes. Seems they had a big fight in a restaurant down at Port the other night."

There were more grumblings. They all knew Susan. Some had been in high school with her.

"There's no way this should happen," bellowed James Murray. "She doesn't know what she's doing. Probably of unsound mind. We got to do something."

"What are we going to do?" Sam Ross, always cautious, was shaking his head. "It's a free country, boys. She don't want the Captain, she don't have to have him. She wants to go to New York City, she can go. Ain't no business of ours."

Then nothing was to be done? The table turned to look at Murray.

"Jesus, Sam," he yelled. "We're talking about our Captain and his happiness. This is the girl he wants, and she won't have him. She wants to go to New York. And we just sit back and do nothing? The boys who waltzed through Europe, outfighting and outsmarting the Wehrmacht at every turn? And our Captain, who led us in and out, up and down and saved our bacon when we thought it was cooked, time and again, needs us? And we do nothing?"

Cries of outrage. Sam Ross shrugged and was quiet.

"So what do we do?"

Murray thought for a moment and then turned to Ike Wilson.

"Ikey, have you got your truck outside?" Ike nodded. "Beautiful. Now here's what we do. We go get that girl, take her in the truck, and deliver her to the Captain at his place. When she gets there, she'll probably come to her senses. You know how women can be. They need firm action sometimes."

The bleary red faces around the table nodded.

"I don't know." Sam Ross was shaking his head. "It sounds an awful lot like kidnapping. And how do you know it will work? It may just piss her off the Captain, and get her to New York even faster."

The men turned back to Murray. "Sam, you're talkin' too much an' talkin' never solved nothin'. Maybe it works, maybe it don't, so what? We ain't gonna know unless we tries it. So boys, are we gonna do it or not? Who's with me?"

There were enthusiastic cries from around the table, except from Sam Ross. He turned to Archie MacQuiggan across the aisle.

"What do you think, Arch? Is this a good idea?"

The big man turned red. "Don't ask me. I got nothin' to do with your Captain Russell."

"Then lets' do it."

James Murray led the men up from their table and through the door to the parking lot and Ike Wilson's battered old pick-up truck. Behind them the waiter was standing in the doorway yelling that they had not paid for their beer, but his words were lost in the laughter and yelling. Wilson drove the truck onto Talbot Street, with Murray and MacInnis beside him in the cab and the uncertain Sam Ross with Athol Burns in the back.

"Where's she at, Susan?"

"Lives in a big house on Walpole Street."

"Let's go see."

Wilson accelerated to a speed seldom seen on Talbot Street and attracted the attention of Constables Gus Campbell and Glen Morrison, standing on the sidewalk outside the Malt Shoppe, where they had just finished a cup of coffee and a chat with Adele, their favourite waitress.

"Shit," Gus Campbell muttered as he saw the truck careen around the corner at Walpole Street. "That's Ike Wilson, drunk as a skunk. Let's get the car."

Ike drove down Walpole, pulled up in front of the MacLean house and parked his truck, the engine running. Murray went to the door. Wanda, the cleaning woman, told him that Susan was up town shopping in Robsons. He returned to the truck.

"Back up town. She's at Robsons."

The truck drove around the block, back to Talbot Street, missing the two policemen coming down Walpole looking for them. They parked on the sidewalk in front of Robson's department store. James Murray took a flask from his hip pocket and put it to his lips.

"Best stuff, boys," he said, passing it around. With redder faces and bloodshot eyes, they watched the front of the store. Finally Susan emerged, carrying a shopping bag.

"There she is," whispered Murray. "Probably buyin' clothes to run away to New York in. Listen, I get her over here, talk to her, and when there's nobody around I give the signal and we whip her into the cab of the truck and get out of here. Got it?"

The men nodded. Murray opened the door and got out of the cab.

"Susan, come here for a minute," yelled James Murray.

Susan recognized the men, waved, and walked over to the truck with a question on her face.

"Well hi, Susan," said Murray with a broad grin on his face. "You been shoppin' for New York City, I expect."

Susan nodded, uncertain, smelling the liquor on his breath and noticing the bloodshot eyes. At that moment the police car pulled into a parking spot across the street. Murray waved his arm, and grabbed Susan under the arms. MacInnis grabbed her by the ankles and they swung her into the cab of the truck. Murray and MacInnis jumped in after her and slammed the door. She started to yell, glancing from face to bleary face. Gus Campbell and Glen Morrison jumped out of the car and came running across the street. Morrison walked around to the sidewalk while Campbell came up beside the car on the driver's side and leaned in the open window. He saw Susan between Murray and MacInnis. The men had their khaki shirts rolled to the elbows. Murray wore his battle jacket with the Canada patch and the patch of the St. Thomas and Elgin Highlanders.

Campbell frowned. "All right, boys, the party's over. Ike, you've been speeding. And now you're abducting a female off the street. And you're drunk. Give me the keys, you're under arrest."

The men looked at one another.

"Gus, we can't," said Murray. "We're doing something really important, which I can't explain to you right now. But you would understand if I did. We got to keep going."

"I understand that you idiots are drunk, and if you don't give me those keys now, you're heading for trouble. You've got Susan jammed in there, looking like she'd rather be somewhere else."

"They're crazy, Gus." Susan's voice was quavering. "They just grabbed me and pulled me in here."

Murray's eyes clouded with confusion, looking first at Susan, red with indignation, and then at the scowling, solid Gus Campbell. His clouded eyes blazed suddenly. "Hit it, Ikey," he yelled. Murray pounded Ike Wilson's shoulder and the truck leaped away, brushing Campbell to the ground. "You'll understand, Gus, later," Murray yelled from the window. Gus Campbell picked himself up and watched the truck weave its way down the street. He and Morrison ran back to their car, and were soon pursuing the pick-up out of the town and along the Lyndhurst Road, following its plume of dust.

"This can't be a rape, Gus. It's broad daylight and they know we're after them."

"I don't care what it is. Those boys are going to jail. Since they've been back I ain't had a moment's peace."

In the truck Susan started to struggle but she was wedged in so tight between Murray and MacInnis that she could barely move.

"Where are you taking me?" Her voice was furious.

"Now Susan, don't get this thing wrong." Murray spoke slowly and earnestly. "This is gonna be all right. When you see what's happening, you won't be mad none. You got to relax."

"You tell me where we're going. My mother is expecting me at home."

"We're taking you to Captain Russell's farm. We...."

"Captain Russell? So that's what this is all about?"

She grew silent, dumb with fury.

"You don't want to go to New York, Susan." Sam Ross pitched in with sincere tones and earnest eyes. "The Captain's the finest man I've ever known. You don't want...."

"You're telling me I don't want to go to New York? Even you total morons know what I should do. You and your Captain. When I get out of here, you're going to wish you hadn't been born."

They looked concerned. Murray turned to her, but her face kept him silent.

"You're all drunk. Look at you, James Murray, your fly's undone and your shirt is ripped. You're a mess." Murray hastily buttoned his fly. "If he's going to kidnap me, you'd at least think he could send kidnappers who are clean and sober."

"Aw, shit, Susan, we aren't kidnappers." Murray's voice was full of hurt. "You got it all wrong, girl."

Susan turned away from him, which meant sitting face to face with Tom MacInnis. She looked into his stupid, mean little eyes, turned away in disgust and sat with her eyes fixed on the road. No one else spoke. In the back of the truck, Sam Ross and Athol Burns watched the cloud of dust from the pursuing police car, half a mile back on the gravel road. Sam was shaking his head.

"Athol, I told them they got no right to grab her off the street like that. Her family's prominent. No good will come of it."

Athol Burns looked at him with scorn. "We didn't have to be here Sam. We could have stayed drinkin' beer. Now we're here, best to shut up."

Before Sam could answer the truck swerved into the Russell laneway without slowing down, sending him over on his side. Behind them, the two policemen saw the dust cloud swerve left.

"They're turning into Russells'," said Morrison. "Could Bobby be behind this?"

Campbell shook his head. "Nah, it makes no sense. Pull into the head of the drive and stop. I want to see what's going on before we nab them."

They turned off the road. The truck was standing by the house and the five men were standing beside it. Margaret Ann Russell was in front of them, shouting and waving her arms.

"Look there," said Gus, beginning to smile. "Mrs. Russell's giving 'em what for."

Susan stepped out of the truck, her fists clenched. Murray and MacInnis began to argue with her. Burns and Campbell got down from the back of the truck and Ike Wilson got out of the cab.

Margaret Ann dismissed the men with a wave of disgust, walked over to Susan and embraced her, patting her shoulder.

"Let's go," said Gus. "Looks like the main event is over."

The two started walking up the drive. As they approached Russell came out the front door and stood on the porch with his hands on his hips.

"What's going on?"

A torrent of voices answered.

"As if you didn't know," yelled Susan. "You've gone too far, Bobby. If this was a joke, it wasn't funny. And if it wasn't a joke, you ought to be locked up."

"What are you talking about?"

"Your goons grabbed me on Talbot Street as I was coming out of Robsons and put me in this truck and brought me here. It seems they think I shouldn't go to New York."

"She was your girl, Captain," said James Murray, crestfallen, starting to have doubts about the wisdom of their mission. "We just thought that she was making a mistake, that if she really understood, she would make her mind up different. So we brought her here."

Russell sighed and threw his arms in the air. "Boys, Susan makes up her own mind. I appreciate … I appreciate…." His face started to crack and giggles bubbled up from his chest. He tried to keep control, but the laughing would not stop. He looked at the four men, downcast and sheepish, glancing nervously at one another, and burst out with a roar.

"What is so funny?" yelled Susan.

Margaret Ann glared at her son. "Bobby, this is no laughing matter. This is close to rape. No matter what they thought they were doing."

Gus Campbell moved forward.

"Thinking is beyond these boys, Mrs. Russell." He glared at the men. "This was the stupidest idea I ever heard, and you boys will be charged. Susan is the daughter of the publisher of our newspaper, not a Nazi spy. Captain Russell, do I understand that you didn't know this was going to happen?"

Russell shook his head, trying to keep a straight face.

"He didn't know nothin," said Murray. "It was our idea. And Sam here didn't agree. But he went along."

"Agree, disagree, don't matter. He went along and he's an accessory. Now, do Glen and I have to put the handcuffs on you, or are you fellahs going to behave?" The men nodded sullenly. "I want you, Murray and MacInnis, with me in the car. Glen will go with Ike Sam and Athol in the truck." He turned to Susan. "Would you like to be driven home, Miss Robson?"

Margaret Ann stepped forward. "We'll take care of her, Gus. She needs to sit and have a cup of tea. Then we'll take her home."

The two constables and their prisoners went to the vehicles. Margaret Ann led Susan by the arm into the house. They passed Russell without looking at him. He followed into the house.

"Go out on the back porch, Bobby," said Margaret Ann from the kitchen. "We'll be out with the tea in five minutes or so." He sat on the porch, watching Calvin chase a grasshopper around the lawn. She's furious, he thought. The boys messed everything up. She'll be going soon and she won't want to meet after this. The thought depressed him, but when he pictured the five men, standing by their truck, their plan in shambles and Gus glaring at them, he began to chuckle. By the time his mother and Susan returned with the tea, his spirits had recovered. Susan sat on the couch opposite without looking at him. Her eyes were dark and her cheeks still flushed red.

"Susan, that had nothing to do with me." She kept her eyes on the lawn. "They're not bad guys, but when they drink…." He shrugged. "It was a mess."

She said nothing.

"Those men will be some poor women's husbands some day," muttered Margaret Ann. "There ought to be a law."

"Speaking of husbands, I have heard that you are marrying Allan Matthews, Margaret Ann." Susan spoke in a brittle voice. Margaret Ann smiled and nodded. "I think that's wonderful. And what are your plans, Robert?"

When he looked he saw that she wasn't waiting for an answer.

She was trembling and tears welled in her eyes.

"Susan, what is it?" He sat beside her and took her hand.

Margaret Ann put her hand on Susan's forehead. "She's hot. It's shock. You don't get seized on the street and carried off by drunken maniacs without some after-effect."

"Oh Susie, I'm sorry." His voice was tender and serious. "They had no idea what this would do to you. What can I get? Cold water?"

She turned and looked at him for the first time. "I'm all right now." She smiled gratefully at him. "Bobby, I know you had nothing to do with it."

"He could at least have kept from laughing." Margaret Ann's tone was severe.

"I can see the humour in it. Although I'm not ready to laugh yet." Susan smiled again at him. "Those poor guys worship you."

Bobby laughed. "That seems to be the best I can do right now."

Margaret Ann began to talk about the five men, wondering what they would be charged with. Susan shook her head.

"There is a part of me that doesn't ever want to see them again. They could lock them up and throw away the key. But they are so stupid. To think that they could...." She started to chuckle.

"Don't laugh, Susan." Margaret Ann grimaced. "No man should ever treat a woman that way. Think what the poor women of Europe had to put up with during this war. Men like that from one nation after another, marching through your streets. Lord God Almighty."

The afternoon sun was past its height, the light was softening. The first shadows were appearing on the lawn, from the apple tree, from the barn and from the row of blackberry bushes behind the fish pond. Susan relaxed. They talked about the election and Grant MacKay, who had not been seen in town since his defeat. They talked about the Russian army abandoning the search for Hitler, as reported in the St. Thomas Times Journal. A rabbit appeared from behind the blackberry bushes and scampered across the lawn, pausing to look at the porch before he disappeared over the side hill. Time went by, and sounds of conversation and laughter floated from the porch across the lawn into the late afternoon.

"I'm going to fix us some food, Susan, if you'll stay for supper. Bobby will drive you home."

Margaret Ann left the porch. Susan continued to stare into the distance, at the fields and the trees down by the creek. Bobby was watching her face.

"I guess you'll be leaving for New York soon," he said.

"Maybe." She kept looking away.

He frowned. "I understood you would leave next week."

"That was a possibility."

"Have you changed your plans? Going later in the summer?"

"I may not go at all."

His frown turned to a scowl.

"Susan, I hope those men haven't … intimidated you. You wanted to go to New York. I don't think you should let a crazy thing like this put you off."

"Thank you. But I may not go."

"They've made you fearful. You should go."

She turned on him in a flash.

"Everyone has an opinion about me and New York." Her voice was trembling again. "Jimmy Murray thinks I should not go. Rose MacIlwain thinks I should. My mother thinks I shouldn't. Now you think I should." She sat straight in her chair. "But I don't want to go. And I wish everyone would keep their opinions to themselves."

"I don't get it. What made you change your mind?"

Susan took a huge breath, then threw up a hand in resignation.

"You," she said in a low voice that he could barely hear.

"Oh," he said after several seconds.

"It was after those idiots brought me here. I was furious, I wanted to kill the five of them, but I saw you standing there laughing and I knew laughing was right. And I knew I didn't want to go to New York. I hadn't wanted to go for days, but at the same time I did. Then today, everything changed. I'm staying."

"You're staying. That's so good. Will you…?"

"Be your girl?"

"Yes."

"That has got to be the stupidest question. Maybe I should go to New York after all."

He gestured with both hands. "This is so fast. Aren't I entitled to one stupid question before I get it right?"

When Margaret Ann brought the plates of cold chicken, potato salad and pickled beets and glasses of lemonade, they were holding hands. She pretended not to notice.

Margaret Ann chatted about their chicken, which Calvin had killed that morning, and about the need for rain on the fields. When they had finished eating she picked up the plates and went back inside. They watched the shadows lengthen on the green grass. They watched a hawk spiralling over the darkened fields up high where the sky was still sunny. The fireflies came out, sparking the dark lawn with silver. The moon rose over the trees. The night got cooler and they huddled together. They talked, but said nothing out of the ordinary for the situation they were in. Susan did not go home that night. When Margaret Ann came down the next morning to make coffee, they were still there, asleep in each other's arms.

45.

It took time for news of the romance, born from its ashes, to get around town. The news of the kidnapping, however, spread immediately, from Gus Campbell through the Marie Barnes network on the day it happened. The women of St. Thomas were outraged. What had happened, they agreed, was all you could expect from men of that kind, wild and rough farm boys.

In the early afternoon of the next day, Susan returned home. She walked into the kitchen with a grin on her face, and blurted to her mother that she and Bobby wanted to marry. Valerie gaped.

"So you're not going to New York?"

Susan shook her head. Valerie was caught off guard. It was so like Susan to leap into things, without thinking of planning. Then, she saw the blush on her daughter's face.

"Well, thank God." She put down the rolling pin and took off her apron. "Bill, come in here."

⚘

Wanda, the MacLeans' cleaning lady, working late one night, saw the two of them holding hands in the back yard of the house on Walpole Street. She told Adele at the Malt Shoppe, stopping for coffee on the way home, who told Marie Barnes, and the news was out. Still, certain observers couldn't believe that the renewal was permanent. However, when the church secretary at First United revealed that the couple had made an appointment with the Reverend Fitch, the situation was clarified for the many interested parties.

Two days after the night on the Russells' porch, Susan met Jean in the Malt Shoppe. After some nervous hesitation she told Jean about her wedding. Jean's face fell.

"So, no New York." Susan shrugged, her cheeks red. 'Hell, Susan, what do I do now? There's no man left but Will. You've got the only decent guy in town."

"What about Alton?"

"Alton Johnston? I couldn't marry a farm boy."

"Then there's only Will. Or, I know a band leader I could refer you to."

They roared with laughter.

There began a period of intense activity in the MacLean household. Susan had simply found love again, and was in ecstasy; but for her mother, the wedding was a series of problems and chores. She decided that it was her duty to make Susan face reality, and so tension mounted between mother and daughter.

The first showdown was over the wedding dinner and reception. Valerie wanted an elegant wedding that would be covered in the London papers. There would be a wedding dinner at the Grand Central Hotel, bridal fittings at Robsons and all the other wedding etiquette that the family's station required. She bristled, however, when she learned that the Russells wanted to invite to the reception

333

farm families who had sold their milk to the dairy over the years, as well as the dairy employees, and the men of the St. Thomas and Elgin who had served with Russell.

"We can't fit the entire county into the hotel dining room," said Valerie firmly to her daughter. "And anyway, most of those people would not feel comfortable sitting down to a formal dinner. I'll speak to Margaret Ann."

But Russell was adamant; his people were not to be excluded. Valerie would not hear of it. Since all communication on the subject went through Susan, she became more and more upset. Late one night, after a particularly nasty exchange with Valerie, Susan declared that she and Bobby would elope and get married before a judge in Toronto. Her mother was horrified; the prospect of no wedding was unbearable. At that moment the compromise was born. Valerie inhaled deeply and forced a smile; Susan dried her eyes and stared at the table cloth. There would be two events; an exclusive reception at the Grand Central Hotel, and a second one on the lawn of the Russell farm, later in the afternoon.

"Yes, I will come to Russells'," said Valerie angrily. "But I don't know why – hobnobbing with farmers and the soldiers who kidnapped you. It doesn't get your married life off to the right start."

Helen Partridge invited the girls to tea to celebrate the engagement. She served egg salad and salmon sandwiches, chocolate biscuits and English tea, served on a silver tea service with thin china cups. Rose sat at the table looking uneasily at Susan.

"I have something to say," she said finally.

Helen tensed and stared at the floor.

"As you know, I cannot pretend to be an expert on men or marriage. Neither has attracted me." Her elegant face was stiff with intention. "I have encouraged you girls not to surrender too easily to men, to be yourselves, to find what you want in life and pursue it. And now Susan tells us she is marrying Bobby Russell." She relaxed into a smile. "He is a fine young man. I might say the only man in this town worthy of Susan. So, my dear, if you are doing what life and your heart call you to do, then blessings on you."

※

Russell spent most of the next week at the dairy. More new equipment was arriving from the States, and Tom Allen needed him. He didn't go to town, to avoid the jokes and the slaps on the back. He spent some time explaining the wedding to Calvin, who understood little. At first the boy was upset, thinking of Archie and Leona, but he calmed down when Russell began to describe the celebration, the people who would be there, and the food. Two days after the night on the porch Russell went in to the jail to see about his men.

"We're going to let Sam and Athol Burns go," said Gus, sitting behind his desk with his feet up. "They're both good boys and they wasn't in it that much. But the other three get charged. Jimmy Murray is wild; he has to be toned down. Ikey was driving the truck drunk, so I got no choice with him. And MacInnis is a mean little bastard. He beat up old man Taylor before the war, cut his face over an argument in the Confederation House. It was his word against Taylor's so we couldn't charge him, but now we got him."

Russell nodded. "How much time will they get?"

"A month. They can serve it here. All the comforts of home."

"Can I see them?"

Gus nodded and opened the door to the cell corridor. The reek hit Bobby as soon as he walked through the door. Stale liquor and unwashed bodies. In the first cell, James Murray and Ike Wilson were asleep on their cots, lying in their uniforms. Wilson was snoring loudly. In the second cell, Tom MacInnis was still asleep, but Sam Campbell and Athol Burns were awake and talking quietly.

"Ross, Burns, get out of here. We're lettin' you go."

Tom MacInnis woke up as the cell door shut.

"Hey!" he yelled. "Ain't you gonna let me go?"

"No, MacInnis," said Gus Campbell. "We got plans for you."

335

MacInnis grabbed the bars and shook them. "This ain't fair. I didn't do much. It was Jimmy and Ikey."

Campbell laughed. "So there it is, Captain. Two free and three on charges. Good day to you."

❁

The days and weeks before their wedding passed in slow time. They lay on the beach at Port Stanley, went to parties in the town in their honour and drove to London for a movie. They resurrected jokes from years before. They spent hours talking about things they had done together, midnight swims, and picnics and parties. Bobby began to joke and cut up again, trying to make her laugh. She enjoyed this rebirth of joy in him, but reacted differently now. Sometimes his high spirits were excessive; she had grown more sedate, more cautious.

They would have avoided their interview with the Reverend Fitch, but the interview was a condition of being married in his church. Susan thought they could avoid it by having a civil ceremony in the hotel. Her mother would not hear of it.

"I am not marrying my daughter in some room that the Rotary uses for its meetings, Susan. I was married in a church, Margaret Ann was married in a church, and you will be married in a church. It's out of the question."

Susan surrendered. All that was involved was an hour or so with the Reverend Fitch.

Russell went to get his hair cut on the morning of the interview. Jack was alone in his shop, and beamed when he walked in.

"Is this the wedding haircut? I do them fer nothing, you know."

"The wedding's two and a half weeks away. I expect I'll be in before then."

"Okay then. This one will cost ya'. Geez, here they come. I'll get rid of 'em Bobby. Don't you worry none."

"Let them come, Jack. I don't mind."

The men from across the street filed into the barber shop.

"Captain Russell," said Fred Chisholm, with a twinkle in his watery blue eyes. "We heard you was gettin' married. Me and the boys wanted to wish you the very best." The others mumbled congratulations, broad grins on the wrinkled faces.

"This is a good match," said Jack as he snipped away. "Susan is a fine woman, but a strong one, so she needs a strong husband. She marries some weak little fellah, then we got one more situation where the woman is ruling, and we got too much of that in this town already." The old men nodded. "But Bobby ain't no little bunny rabbit. He whipped them Germans, and he can handle Susan. Three cheers for the two of them, is what I say."

The men cheered.

"Thanks, boys," Russell said with a grin. "I'll do my best."

⚘

They met at the church office. Susan winked at Bobby as the secretary ushered them in to Reverend Fitch's office. The man of God was writing at his desk. They stood waiting for half a minute until he finally looked up. Usually his practice of making the young couple wait was his way of imposing his authority over the interview, but this time the tactic hadn't worked. She was staring at him with a hint of annoyance in her eyes. Russell's expression was one of amused patience, tolerance even.

"My goodness," he said. "I was writing my sermon and got carried away. Sit down, please, won't you."

He was struck by their physical beauty. Her copper hair, dark eyes, the hint of freckles around the nose, full lips an elegant neck and a full woman's body. The Reverend Fitch had had six children with his stout and robust wife and understood the physical side of marriage. It was his custom to make it a central part of his marriage talk. But Susan took his breath away. And her young man, relaxed, dark eyes, curly dark hair, young and bonny. A soldier.

He wondered if he had anything to say to them. As he chatted he went through his mental list. Work hard and earn a good living, addressing the man. In this case, there would be plenty of money. Even if he hadn't known the families he could see money in their clothes, in the relaxed, confident way they moved. He would stress the importance of a healthy physical relationship, enjoyment without excess. He watched them smiling at one another and passed on. They were both attractive. He wondered if they were already having intercourse, then drove the thought from his mind as prurient. He would concentrate on the raising of children. Being firm but loving. Teaching them how to work and how to play, how to be loving human beings. And finally, he would talk about Christian marriage and the necessity of being constant in the faith.

He sighed. They would be married in the church, would be in the congregation from time to time, especially at Christmas and Easter for the big celebrations, would have their children baptized, would support the church with money, but otherwise wouldn't give him or his faith another thought. And that was all right with the Reverend Fitch. He was the son of a farming family, and liked solid, hardworking and prosperous Christians who didn't analyse religion or get in his way. These two, indifferent to the point of arrogance, would be fine over the long run, but he had to talk to them now.

"How long have you been back, Bobby?" he asked.

"Over two months."

"It must have been quite an adjustment, getting to know each other again after such a long absence."

They looked at one another, smiled, and said nothing.

"So you have come to this decision willingly, with love and respect for one another, planning to enter the sacred institution of Christian matrimony with knowledge and understanding of the obligations such a contract involves. For you are undertaking a contract. With one another and with Jesus Christ."

He watched their faces. She was clearly bored. He decided to get through his talk quickly. He skirted the money question with a brief reference. He spent a little more time on the role of sex in marriage. He ended talking about the duties and responsibilities of raising children in the faith. When he looked up, Russell was looking at his watch and Susan was staring out the window. He was relieved to be finished, but touched by their arrogance. It was not a bad thing to start off with your head high, even cocky. Life would humble them. They rose, thanked him and left. He watched them go, smiling despite himself. They were beautiful.

The time that followed was the happiest they would ever experience. For Susan, the doubts that had been plaguing her fell away. Bobby was beautiful to her. She walked with him everywhere, holding his hand, her head on his shoulder. They went around together, in the heart of the summer, when the shirts on the backs of the farmers in town were dark with sweat under the afternoon sun, and when people sat at night on their porches sipping lemonade and fanning themselves. Susan became completely herself, powerful, full of life and passionate. He set her free and made her confident. His arms, his smile were her freedom. She tolerated her mother. She beamed at everyone she met, and people stopped in the street to stare at her. No summer had ever been more beautiful, more green, more luxuriant. The world was open before her, the sky was smiling.

Russell no longer thought as much about the war. St. Thomas was his town now, full of old friends. He loved walking down Talbot Street with Susan, seeing the smiles on the faces of everyone they met. The crustiest old farmer would doff his hat and beam as they passed on the street. He no longer worried about whether he would stay in town and work for Van Kleef or move to Toronto; he could see it working either way. Right now, something else was happening. It felt as if they were dancing and every step, every turn they made, was graceful and right. Susan was with him and he was no longer alone. He felt that he could do anything: hit a baseball, write a poem, make money, win a war. He was free from pain and full of laughter.

Susan and Bobby were open to this brief, blissful moment in their love for one another. This ecstasy cannot last, but it is necessary to create what might last. It is a glimpse, for a short time, through imperfect eyes, of what life without suffering would be. For those who have experienced it, the memory of this early, unqualified and, as far as we can tell, unselfish love will sustain them through the inevitable suffering that comes from human pettiness and the fading of the body. It is a hint of what is sometimes possible.

This was the love that Bobby Russell and Susan MacLean found through the summer of 1945.

PART V

Finale

46.

THEY WERE MARRIED on the first Saturday of September, 1945. The summer was still warm; a fiery sun baked the fields where the corn was high, and the gravel concession roads were parched. By one in the afternoon the church was sweltering, men in tight collars and suits were sweating and the women in summer dresses and girdles were fanning themselves. When the Reverend Fitch, in his robes and preaching tabs, entered from the side to stand at the front of the church, the whispering stopped. And when, a moment later, Bobby Russell, accompanied by Alton Johnston, his best man, entered and stood to the preacher's right, both in their black, silver and blue dress uniforms, the women stopped fanning themselves and smiled. The parson stood authoritatively in front of the people, his face kindly but firm, as if to say that although a wedding was a happy event it was not to be taken lightly, and it was time to get on with it. Then the organ began the processional music and everyone in the pews turned to watch.

Susan entered on her father's arm. She walked down the aisle in a beautiful white silk gown from Robsons. Jean, dressed in a violet gown of the same cut, followed in her train. Susan had had a quarrel with her mother about the gown; Valerie had wanted something more formal, with more lace. But the church, the music, the smiles and the flowers washed the bickering away; Valerie watched her daughter enter and smiled. Susan looked from side to side as she walked, nodding and rolling her eyes to her friends; at the front of the church she smiled at Bobby. He grinned.

The words that were said in the next half hour are familiar and not remarkable. The vows were exchanged, the rings were given. The Reverend Fitch preached a homily based on St. Paul's Epistle to the Corinthians, invoking faith, hope and love, as he had done at every wedding he had celebrated. The couple embraced at the end of the service and went to sign the register and the documents by which the province of Ontario recognized their marriage.

The worthies of the town waited for the signing to be finished, looking even hotter at the end of the service. Mayor Parker and his wife sat beside the Chief of Police and his wife. Ross Porter, unmarried, sat not far away in a wrinkled grey suit. Dr. Stuart and his wife, the Crown Attorney Mason and his wife, the aldermen and their wives, many of the merchants from Talbot Street and their wives were present. There were also friends of the MacLeans from out of town, couples from London, Stratford and Chatham, bankers, lawyers and merchants and their wives, in good summer suits and beautiful summer dresses. Edward Archer had come from Toronto, with Helen Clarkson and Hugh. Helen wore a grey, summer silk suit and a string of pearls, and looked relaxed and cool throughout the service. Both men both wore grey linen suits, Archer looking sleek and impatient, his brother confused. Beside them sat Tyler Van Kleef and his son, both in light brown suits, the father smiling genially, wiping the sweat off his bald head with a large handkerchief, the son staring at Jean.

The couple returned from signing, now man and wife, and walked out of the church to the sound of the organ. On the lawn they accepted congratulations from their friends. The ritual was over. Margaret Ann hugged her son, tears in her eyes. Valerie stood by Susan trying to rearrange her hair at the rear, to her daughter's impatience. After the hand shaking and the back slapping, those who were invited began to wander towards Talbot Street and the Grand Central Hotel for the wedding meal.

Valerie considered that this meal was her stamp on the wedding, something that Susan, in her infatuation, could never have managed. She had laboured over the menu and the guest list for weeks. She had convinced Mr. Dooley to come back from his new position with the Stodlemeyer House in Kitchener to oversee proceedings, to Audrey MacLellan's great displeasure. The table linen was spotless, the silver gleamed. There were bowls of roses at every table and at the head table, a beautiful array of gladioli and lilies in front of the bride and groom. Mr. Dooley, in his cut-away morning coat, was at his imperial best, standing at the door to the kitchen with his hands in white gloves, raised to shoulder height like the conductor of an orchestra about to give the downbeat, his eyes darting over the room, motioning to a waitress if a glass was empty, or a table setting incomplete.

There was one glass of red wine set at each table; the glasses were not refilled. This was a compromise between the forces of temperance led by the mother of the bride, not a teetotaller herself but aware of the sentiments of many in the community, and Russell who wanted wine for his friends.

Edward Archer, sitting at a table with Helen Clarkson and his brother Hugh, sipped the wine and set it down with a grimace.

"Can't drink this, Hughie. I'll bet they make it locally out of corn and turnips."

"Right, Eddie. And there isn't a bar. What are we going to do?"

"You're going to eat the food that's put in front of you and stop complaining," said Helen. "This is a celebration for these beautiful young people. You can get drunk back in Toronto."

Archer smiled fondly at her; his brother shrugged; they sipped their wine.

The women in the room were looking at Susan, commenting on her dress and her bearing, evaluating her ability to handle her man and bear up under the married decades ahead. The men looked at Bobby less critically. They had all known his father and had watched his own progress through the early years of his life. They had admired him as one of the best athletes St. Thomas had produced. They knew all about his exploits overseas, including his capture and subsequent depression. They thought he was the right sort of boy to be married to Susan MacLean.

There were the customary speeches. The Reverend Fitch asked the blessing before the meal. The father of the bride, the best man and the bridegroom uttered familiar words of congratulations, best wishes, and gratitude.

By the time the speeches were over, the women were fanning themselves again with the wedding menus and the men were staring at their watches. The bride and groom rose from the table and the room rose with them. They walked out to Talbot Street, where an old carriage, a landau drawn by four white plough horses, stood waiting. Bobby and Susan, Jean and Alton Johnston entered the coach. The driver clucked and the horses pulled forward. A piper, the same man who had piped the regiment down Talbot Street, lead the coach away from the hotel playing 'The Road to the Isles'. They went down Talbot Street to the Lyndhurst Road, down into the valley and the Russells' farm.

⚘

The lawn in front of the house was lined with trestle tables. The reception was due to begin at four o'clock, but people began arriving from the outlying farms as early as two. They brought jars of preserves and bottles of whiskey. They brought cauldrons of thick soup, tomato, leek and potato and chicken. They brought green salads, vegetable salads, potato salads, chicken salads, macaroni and egg salads. They brought breads and buns and dark rolls and Parker House rolls. They brought baked fish. They brought hams and roasted chickens and meatballs and platters of ribs and pork chops and pots of lamb and beef stew. There were cakes, chocolate, orange, lemon, marble, angel food, and pound cake. There was every kind of pie, apple, cherry, rhubarb, raisin, blueberry, blackberry, raspberry, peach, lemon and banana cream. There were butter tarts and custard tarts and cream tarts and turnovers and brown betties and upside-down cakes and meringues and trifles and puddings. By mid-afternoon the tables were laden with platters of all manner of cooking and baking from the kitchens for miles around. The men lifted the containers in from the cars, trucks and buggies that lined the Lyndhurst Road, and the women arranged them on the tables, complimenting each other on their cooking and baking.

Down the side hill two farmers were roasting a pig on a spit. Beside the garage, cobs of corn were boiling in a pot over a maple fire.

The people had come early to help set up and to talk. Farmers in hot heavy suits and their wives in flowered dresses stood on the lawn and gabbed and joked and laughed. The sun beat down from a cloudless sky, and the cicadas droned away the hours. Butterflies, black and orange or yellow or white, flitted among the flowers. The perfume of the flowers and the hot grass, the sweet, ripe fragrance of late summer, blended with the smell of the food on the tables.

The house and the garage were gleaming with fresh white paint. There was a blue and white shade, under which drinks had been set out: lemonade, orangeade, sweet cider, ginger ale and Coca Cola. There was officially no alcohol at this reception to avoid upsetting the teetotallers, but Bobby had beer in the house, as well as bottles of rye whiskey, rum and gin, for those who found their way. It was understood that many of the farmers and certainly the men from the St. Thomas and Elgin would bring their own bottles.

Before the coach was visible, the strains of the pipes echoed over the valley. The piper appeared at the head of the drive and led the coach in just after four o'clock. Bobby and Susan stepped down and walked to the house, waving and shaking hands. They sat in the sunroom, smiling at each other, relieved and happy. Valerie kept fluttering around her daughter, fixing the hem of her dress, combing her hair.

Calvin kept running around with a pitcher of lemonade trying to pour for everyone. Margaret Ann made tea. Outside they could hear the laughter and the shouts of welcome as more guests arrived. Soon the sound of rhythmic clapping came from the lawn.

"They want us," Bobby said to Susan.

Holding hands, they walked out on the porch. Bobby kissed her and the crowd cheered. Then they walked down onto the lawn and went among the people. There were men from the regiment there, including James Murray, Ike Wilson and Tom MacInnis whose jail sentences had been cut short for the wedding. Many of these men took their plates of food and drink and found their way under the trees beside the lawn, where they opened their shirt collars and took out their flasks of whiskey. Girls found their way to them, girls who worked in the dairy, girls who worked in the shops in town and some girls from the farms, unmarried girls with wide smiles.

Ike Wilson found a dead willow branch lying in the grass and breaking it up into twigs and pieces of wood, built a fire. The men and girls cheered and settled in to a warm afternoon, looking at one another at first shyly and then pairing up as the evening approached.

The air was fragrant with summer's sensuality, under the green-leaved trees, in the smell of the willow smoke, in the happy laughter from the lawn and in the sound of tinkling glasses.

The Archer brothers and Helen found their way to the porch where the MacLeans, Margaret Ann, Allan Matthews, Ross Porter and the Mayor and his wife were sitting, drinking and watching the crowd.

The Van Kleefs arrived, father and son, and sat with Edward Archer, who had chosen a table as far away from Ross Porter as he could find. He was stiff for the first few minutes but Helen made up for him, talking easily and openly with Margaret Ann and Valerie. Archer, under the influence of whiskey and the warmth of the day and Tyler Van Kleef's genial, booming voice, took his tie off and began to tell jokes. Helen smiled and took his hand.

Hugh Archer was sitting at a table with Jean and Will Matthews. He had been attracted by Jean in the church and began to tell her jokes. He filled her glass at every opportunity. He told her of his trips to Palm Springs, Bermuda and Europe before the war. Will listened to these tales of world travel and his eyes clouded over. He tried to talk of being accepted in law school, and about how his father might buy him a car next year, but the older man held the floor. Jean, attracted to neither of them, batted her eyes at Hugh Archer. Will retreated in despair.

A dusty black Ford pulled into the driveway. The doors opened and a white-haired figure in a good blue suit, his eyes behind sunglasses, his hands shaking, got out on the passenger side. His wife, who had been driving, took his arm and led him across the lawn, to good-natured applause. Bobby and Susan shook the man's hand and escorted him to the porch .

"Jesus Christ, it's Grant MacKay," muttered Edward Archer.

He, Allan Matthews and Ross Porter rose and brought the old campaigner to their table, while Bobby went into the house and fetched him a glass of straight rye whiskey. MacKay had not been seen in town since the election, and everyone noticed that he had aged. His hands shook, his lips were blue and his speech was slurred.

"Haven't seen you around, Grant," said Allan Matthews. "We're all delighted that you're here."

"Yes, indeed," said Ross Porter enthusiastically. He had been looking at MacKay with horror, for the first time considering that those who live by the polls can also die by the polls, and that such a death is not easy.

"Well, I've been keeping a low profile," said MacKay in a hoarse voice so low that people had to strain to hear. "I was afraid that if I appeared in town I might get shot, with all these Tories around now. And the first time I come out, who do I see but the biggest Tory of them all. Your good health, Sir." He raised his glass to Archer who nodded with a smile. "The truth is folks, when the son of one of the good old Liberal families in this county gets married, I want to be there. Here's to you, Bobby Russell, and your fair bride, and to your mother as well." He raised his glass again.

Out on the lawn, Gus Campbell and Jack Morris were standing with their wives, watching the group on the porch.

"There, before your very eyes, is a tragedy," Jack was saying. "Grant MacKay, our unemployed politician. How many of them, shaking his hand today, must have double-crossed him. And look who they turn to. Ross Porter." Jack spat on the grass. "Look at his hair. The fool goes all the way to London for his haircut, and he looks like an eight ball with peach fuzz glued on. He looks like he's wearing a wig."

"Jack," said his wife. "You cut the hair of every other St. Thomas man on this porch. Ross Porter doesn't have enough hair for a man of your skill and experience to bother about."

Jack broke into a smile. "You're right, my dear. This is a wedding, not a barber's convention. And what a glorious wedding it is, a beautiful woman and her handsome young man. Don't it make the world go round, though." His wife smiled at him and took his hand.

"It is a fine day," agreed Gus Campbell. "If only those fools getting drunk under the trees don't ruin it. When I was a kid, a wedding like this would be teetotal. Everyone had a good time, and you didn't have to worry about the effects of cheap liquor on the likes of them." He nodded toward the trees, where wood smoke and boisterous laughter rose through the leaves.

"Those boys are harmless, Gus," said the barber.

"Mostly. But Tom MacInnis is ugly. I hear that he has it in for me for arresting him, and he's carrying a knife. Elmore," he called.

The Chief of Police was crossing the lawn trying to balance a glass of beer and a plate filled with food. He heard his name and stopped.

"Elmore, I'm worried about MacInnis. He's over there under the trees getting drunk and he's supposed to be carrying a knife."

"I'll go down and talk to him. If I don't like the sound of it, you and Glen can put him back in a cell for the night."

There was burst of cheering from the front of the lawn. They turned to look and there was Archie MacQuiggan who had obviously just arrived and was standing by himself, in his army uniform, much too small for his huge stomach, weaving on his feet, staring uncertainly around the lawn.

"Here's Archie,' cried someone.

Bobby came across the lawn to Archie, his hand extended. A crowd formed around the two.

"Well, Captain," mumbled Archie. "I heard about your gettin' married...." He looked at the grass. "I thought I would...."

Archie started to weep, great sobs wrenching his chest and tears streaming from his eyes. Bobby stepped forward and embraced him.

"Arch, it's so good to see you. Where are you living?"

"We was livin' in a place out by Dutton, but we can't stay. They need it for a storage shed. So we'll...." He was overcome by tears. "So we'll be ... movin' on."

"Come back to your old house, Archie. It's still there, just as you left it. And when the factory goes in, we'll get a new place."

"Captain, I would be most grateful." He was shaking his head. "Fact is, I been in some tough spots, but this one, I didn't know what to do. All them kids, and Leona, just lookin' at me, waitin' for me to...."

"It's settled." Bobby smiled, and the affection in his voice reduced Archie to tears again. "You'll move back tomorrow. And now, come and have some food. And some drink. Unless you've stopped drinking, Arch? With all your problems?"

"No, Captain." Archie smiled for the first time. "I ain't stopped drinkin'. You know me."

Calvin watched the exchange with intense interest. At first he had stood frightened at the edge of the crowd, but when Bobby embraced the bedraggled man, Calvin's face lit up. He scampered off and joined a game of hide and seek on the lawn behind the house.

Helen Partridge and Rose MacIlwain, dressed in smart summer suits, walked gingerly around the lawn, avoiding children chasing each other among the tables, and the farmers, soldiers, men and women, streaming to the tables and piling the food on their plates. They were looking for some place quiet to sit. They had been up on the veranda for a while, but left when Rose became offended by Hugh Archer's lecherous pursuit of Jean.

"Rose, you mustn't worry. Jean can take care of herself."

"I know that. But he's such a flabby old fool. Revolting."

They peered down the hill and understood that there was no place for them among the boys and girls around the fire. They wandered a bit, talking to people Rose had taught in the Collegiate, most of whom, farming or running a store on Talbot Street now, looked at her with a mixture of respect and tolerance. Finally, they settled with a group of unattached women, a nurse from the hospital, Eileen, the saleswoman from Robson's Department Store and Marie Barnes herself, a woman of fifty or so years with oddly coloured red hair, strangely silent without a telephone line connecting her to the world.

"How long do you want to stay," Rose whispered to Helen.

"For a while." Helen looked at the boys and girls, coming up hand in hand from the side hill, with interest. "I like weddings, and the afternoon is gorgeous. There is something in the air."

Hours passed. Bobby and Susan moved among the tables, talked to the standing groups, and went down the side hill to stand by the fire, holding hands together, talking and laughing with their friends. Susan was still in her white dress, but she had taken off her shoes and stockings and walked barefoot. Bobby had taken off his jacket and went around in his shirt, the sleeves rolled up and the black suspenders crossing in the back. Wherever they went, the conversation stopped.

The older folks beamed at them. They were reassured by the wedding; proof to them that the future would be good in Elgin County. The younger people were dazzled. Some of the girls looked at the ground when they approached, while the boys smiled awkwardly. The beauty of this man and this woman and the fruitfulness of the sultry, sunny September afternoon, evoked in them things that they were not ready to think about. They looked at one another shyly, and were relieved when Bobby and Susan walked on. The soldiers raised their glasses. The farmers shook their hands and their wives kissed both of them with loud smacks.

The MacLeans and Margaret Ann on the porch watched their children's procession, with pleasure. Helen Clarkson followed them with fond eyes. She stroked Edward's hand.

"Too bad for Eleanor," he said. "I would have liked her to be here."

"Not here," Helen said. "Not today."

Susan and Bobby moved under the trees, into the sun, under

the trees and back. The sun began to slant towards the west, the shadows lengthened on the lawn. People began to leave, saying their farewells and heading for their cars or trucks on the road.

The noise on the lawn lessened. Bowls disappeared from the tables and several dogs scavenged underneath. Helen Partridge and Rose MacIlwain left. Edward and Helen said their farewells and went to drive back to Toronto. Hugh decided to stay; he sat by himself on the porch, whistling softly, his eyes on Jean, who was walking on the lawn, talking to people she knew. Van Kleef left, pounding Bobby on the back and kissing Susan fondly. His son did not leave. He had discovered Jean also, and was beginning to follow her around the lawn. She responded gaily, glancing occasionally at Hugh Archer who was scowling from the porch.

The bride and groom retired to the house. The entire lawn was in shadow. After a quarter of an hour they emerged again, Calvin and Alton following with the suitcases, ready for the car that would take them to London. The sky was black, the moon just beginning its ascent.

They were going to New York. They would spend their first night in the Empire Hotel in London, and then go on by train the next day to Toronto and by air to New York City. They set out in the green Buick, down the Dorchester Road to the London highway, on to the future. They left the dark lawn in front of the white house for a honeymoon, for a life, for whatever fate would bring. Never as happy again, perhaps, which is sad if happiness is what matters, but together, in all that they did.

Back on the porch, the MacLeans, Margaret Ann and Allan Matthews, Jean, Tyler Van Kleef Junior and Hugh Archer sat with their feet up, sipping lemonade and watching the fireflies. Calvin and a few of the children were playing tag, laughing and bumping into the tables. Down the side hill, the willowwood fires burned downed to embers, as young men and women huddled under the trees, under the leaves, whispering. The subtle, rustling life continued behind the shadows, beneath the silence. A warm breeze blew. At the foot of the fields the creek gurgled to the south. At its mouth, fifteen miles away, the lake was silvery and calm. In the town and in the county's farm houses the lights went out one by one. Husbands and wives lay in their beds smiling, thinking of the slender, dark-haired young Bobby Russell and Susan, his beautiful bride.

The day was done, the wedding was complete, and the moon rose over Elgin County.

Made in the USA
Charleston, SC
12 February 2017